STAR MARQUE VENDETTA

SHAMI STOVALL

Published by
CS BOOKS, LLC

This is a work of fiction. Names, characters, places, and incidents either are the product of author imagination or are used fictitiously, and any resemblance to actual persons, living or dead, business establishments, events, or locales, is entirely fictional.

Star Marque Vendetta
Copyright © 2021 Shami Stovall
All rights reserved.
https://sastovallauthor.com/

Cover Design: Darko Paganus
Editor: Amy McNulty, Nia Quinn

IF YOU WANT TO BE NOTIFIED WHEN SHAMI STOVALL'S NEXT BOOK RELEASES, PLEASE CONTACT HER DIRECTLY AT
s.adelle.s@gmail.com

ISBN: 978-0-9980452-4-5

To John, who never stopped believing.
To Gail and Big John, my family.
To Beka, forever.
To Brian Wiggins, for giving a voice to the characters (again).
To Emily, James, Mary, & Dana, for all the jokes and input.
To my Facebook group, for all the memes.
To my Patreons, for all the support.
And finally, to everyone unnamed, thank you for everything.

ONE

Vendetta

Enforcer captains gathered in the mines of Vectin-10 to bid on the latest assignments, and I planned on winning at least one.

They crammed together in the underground administration office, waiting by the foreman's station. The terrible ventilation, coupled with the stink of unwashed men, reminded me of home. I crossed my arms and glanced around—I was taller than the rest of these sad sacks, and in better shape, too. If it came to a fight, even if it was me versus the other ten here, I could take them. They carried plasma pistols and rifles, sure, but they all had the wary look of men who should've retired or died five years ago.

"Listen up," the mining foreman called out. "We have two assignments. First, we need a team of enforcers stationed at all of the mine's exits. Too many of our supplies and too much of our equipment has gone missing lately. Our workers, or some sneaks, are hustling our shit, and I want them caught."

The foreman, a muscular guy with a gut large enough to carry twins, held up a small tablet with the information scrolling across the screen. He tapped the side, sending the info to all nearby Personal Assistance Devices—the PADs hooked on most people's left forearm. My PAD vibrated, but I ignored it. I didn't have enough crew for that assignment. I had half the complement of a starship, if that. I still needed to fill a hundred empty seats. And it was a shame. Guarding mining tunnels and shaking down thugs would've been easy work.

"The *Ring Chaser* can handle this," an enforcer captain shouted. "10,000 credits a day." He stood near the front of the group, his bald head reflecting the lights mounted in the walls. It wasn't baldness from hair loss, either—he had the waxy sheen of someone who had been burned.

Another captain, some woman with broad shoulders and a chin the size of a fist, raised her hand. "The crew of the *Sidewinder* can get it done for 9,000 credits a day."

"8,900," the first captain barked. "And that's me breakin' even."

The woman closed her mouth, her lips turning an odd shade of white. No one liked getting underbid, and she shot that bald asshole a look that could wound.

"Deal," the foreman said. He wheezed as he plugged in the information on his tablet. "The *Ring Chaser* will handle the assignment. Contract is on a month-to-month basis. 8,900 credits a day."

My vice-captain, Lysander, gave me a quick glance before returning his attention to the front. We had gotten good at nonverbal communication. He thought the next assignment would be something for us, so I straightened my posture.

Not as straight as Lysander's, though. He stood out like a gun in a nursery. Everyone else in the room hunched or leaned against the wall, but Lysander kept himself stiff and upright. Tense. Crew-cut blond hair. His hands held together behind his back. The guy screamed military, and I'd have bet good money none of the idiots around us knew what the inside of a barracks looked like.

The foreman tapped his tablet again, sending out another wave of information. "We've got a bigger problem. My men found a nest of wraith bugs a few days back, and I need a crew that can handle the extermination."

I elbowed Lysander. "What're wraith bugs?"

With his eyes half-lidded in a semi-sarcastic glare, Lysander said, "They're commonplace to Vectin-10. Big. Most weigh thirty-six kilograms. Their exoskeleton is translucent. They infest mines and damage the equipment with their wax and mucus hives."

Damn bugs. I had dealt with a ton on Capital Station. Not wraith bugs, but I had seen roaches the size of children, and some with the temperaments of drunken schizophrenics hopped up on chems.

That same bald captain smiled. "The *Ring Chaser* can handle that assignment as well. 700,000 credits for the extermination."

And then the broad-shouldered woman said, "My crew will have it cleared out in seven days. All for 630,000 credits."

Grumbling spread among the other captains. *Too low*, this and, *not worth it*, that. Sweat dripped from everyone, adding to the stickiness of the floor. Most wore jumpsuits, and they, at least, absorbed the stink. My enviro-suit—more high-tech than half the stuff in the room—kept my temperature regulated.

"The *Scorpio* will exterminate those little bastards for 600,000," some guy leaning on the wall shouted. "And we'll have it done in *six* days."

The other captains and vice-captains exchanged odd glances. The captain of the *Scorpio* had enough cybernetic tubes in his neck and shoulders to build a pipeline. The cyborg punk sauntered through the crowd, pushing his way toward the front, his plasma rifle hanging off his shoulder on a well-worn strap. The guy liked to strut, but that didn't impress me.

His vice-captain strolled up with him. The man didn't have ears, just machine bits, no doubt so he could hear.

For a few moments, no one else offered any bids. A couple of people murmured, and one lady half-lifted her hand, but her vice-captain stopped her. They all pointed to the *Scorpio* captain with knit eyebrows and slumped shoulders. He and his vice-captain were the only ones with blatant cyborg enhancements. Those machines were expensive, and humans rarely had the cash to get them implanted.

The *Scorpio* captain must've been top dog—the alpha nitwit for this tiny outpost.

Pathetic.

"The *Star Marque* will handle this for 500,000 credits," I said. "And we'll do it in five days."

That got everyone's attention.

Hell, even Lysander glanced over like I had punched an old lady in the face.

"Are you insane?" Lysander growled under his breath. "We're understaffed and we've never handled an assignment like this before! And for that amount of credits, we'll barely—"

"It's about establishing a reputation," I murmured, cutting him off. "If we consistently handle assignments faster and cheaper than everyone else, we'll be the go-to enforcer ship for this backwater planet."

That was what Endellion had done when she had been the captain of the *Star Marque*. She had done everything with a brutal efficiency—the superhumans *had* to acknowledge her. And when they had wanted something personal, they had gone straight to her for all their dealings.

If Endellion could do it, so could I. The *Star Marque* would become the top enforcer ship within the entire Vectin quadrant.

The captain of the *Scorpio* turned to face me. One of his eyes had been replaced with a mechanical sensor. I hated cyborgs. Every time I saw one, it reminded me of Endellion—and I swear the ice in my veins lowered the temperature of the whole fucking room. Probably irrational, but that didn't change the fact.

"What's that?" the captain asked. "Is that the new captain of the infamous *Star Marque*?"

The room went quiet and stiff.

Lysander whispered, "If you want a good reputation, handle this *diplomatically*."

Heh. I always handled my shit diplomatically.

"I'm Captain Clevon Demarco," I said to the cyborg. "Enforcer and starfighter extraordinaire."

That got a couple of chuckles throughout the crowd, but they went quiet again the moment Captain Tube-Neck opened his mouth.

"I'm Captain Lorenzo Varvont," he said. "And as a bit of

friendly advice, I think you should let *my* crew handle these wraith bugs. We know what we're doing. You're as green as they come, and it may be too much for ya."

I smirked. "If a guy with a coffee pot in his head can handle this, I'm sure I could genocide the whole damn wraith bug population with ease."

Lysander shook his head. "Goddammit, Demarco."

The rest of the room collectively held their breath as Captain Varvont turned his full attention to me, a forced smile set on his twisted face. Cyborgs never looked right after a few surgeries. Well, some could—Endellion always looked human—but the chumps who took cheap parts had the facial movements of a stroke patient.

"I guarantee the Vectin-10 mining operation will regret taking a bid like yours," Captain Varvont said. "And then they'll have to pay *my* prices to clean your bodies off the rocks of that hive. No one wants to deal with amateur hour, punk. You best back down while ya still can."

That thug placed his hand on his plasma rifle. He could've used a lesson from the gangbangers of Capital Station. I had seen far more intimidating men in my life—and this guy was so far beneath them, it was almost laughable.

I wanted to throw down, maybe knock a couple of his teeth from his machine-ridden head, but Lysander placed a hand on my shoulder. His fingers dug into my black enviro-suit. He didn't need to say anything. He wanted me to be *polite*.

The mining foreman straightened his posture, his brow furrowed.

Before he could say anything, I said, "The *Star Marque* has nothing but the best of the best. Our last captain went on to become the first human planet governor since the war, after all."

The mere mention of Endellion's successes got the room buzzing with excited whispers.

"He's right—Endellion did come from the Star Marque!"

"The Endellion Voight? Unbelievable."

"She's one of the best. Wasn't Captain Demarco her vice-captain?"

All humans knew about Endellion's accomplishments. Invoking

her name was like casting a spell of awe. To my disgust, they loved her. Thought the world of her. *She was the ultimate victor. A human with no equal.* If only they knew all the atrocities she had committed, then they wouldn't get so wet in their panties when they heard her name.

Nobody knew the real her. Not like I did. Everyone else just thought she was a prodigy and gifted leader beyond compare—someone working to help humanity rise to the same status as super-humans. She had only become a planet governor eight months ago, and already it was a thing of legend.

What a load of bullshit.

But no one would believe me if I told the truth. She had destroyed Capital Station and murdered millions. And she had made it personal when she had tried to kill me and the crew of the *Star Marque.* Did Endellion really think she could get away with it all?

No one wanted the truth, though. Then Endellion wouldn't be a *human* savior. Best to just use her name and reputation to my advantage.

I continued, "I'm the pinnacle of human fitness and reflexes, trained by Endellion herself. My doctor is famous throughout the Vectin quadrant. My vice-captain was trained at the Ares Military Academy. Trust me—if the Vectin-10 Mining Company has any brains at all, they'll take my discounted rate and thank their lucky stars I decided to grace this shithole with my presence."

Lysander slid his hand down his face, his eyes scrunched shut. "I can't believe you."

"Sounds like a bunch of upper crusts who think the titles before their names equate to experience," Captain Varvont said. He motioned with a hand, smirking the entire time. "Don't you fools remember the last enforcer ship who swooped in to do some *quick work* on Vectin-10? Where are they now? Corpses in the sand."

"I'm nothing like them," I said.

"Course. You're the idiot without any cybernetics. Probably genetically engineered, aren't you?"

The question unnerved me. On Capital Station, no one ever guessed I had been genetically modified. They all just assumed I was a standard human who had gotten lucky with genes. This guy knew? Just by looking at me?

Captain Varvont's slimy smirk never faded. "That's what I thought. Your superhuman master must've booted you from his ranks, and now you think you can lord over us with your *special talents*." He laced his words with venom and some people in the room chuckled. "Well, us *chumps* aren't the dolts you think we are. A few machines will even the odds, and I've got decades of experience dealing with arrogant trash like you and your whole *Star Marque* crew."

"I've still got the lowest bid," I said, my voice cold.

The mining foreman waited for a moment, as if to see whether or not Captain Varvont would make a counteroffer. When nothing happened, the foreman nodded. "That's right. The *Star Marque* has the lowest bid, so if we have no other takers…"

Captain Varvont stared at me, his machine eye pulsing with a faint glow. This wasn't over. I could tell by the confidence in his smug expression.

When the silence persisted, the foreman banged his hand on the steel desk. The clang betrayed the metal in his own hand. Another damn cyborg. They were everywhere. "We're finished here. *Star Marque*, I expect results."

<hr>

I STOOD at the head of the conference table, staring down the line at my handful of officers, four in total. There were more empty chairs than people, but I intended to fix that. Once I had a reputation, I would attract attention from everyone looking to join a good crew. Then I could pick from among the best—find the people I needed to help me bring Endellion to justice—and put this dark chapter behind me.

The void of space beyond the viewing window created the perfect backdrop for my mood. I wouldn't stop until this was done. I couldn't let go of my hatred for her. Endellion didn't know who she had wronged.

"I can't believe what you did," Lysander said, pulling me from my dark thoughts. He shook his head and leaned back in his chair. "There's a difference between *making a name for yourself* and *becoming a complete embarrassment.* Did you consider what will happen if we fail this mission? After a show like yours, we'll be laughed out of an enforcing license! And that's not even considering how many enemies we've made so far."

Noah, my temporary starfighter commander, glanced over with a half-smile. "I wish I could've seen you in action. Captain Clevon Demarco, the hard-ass. I bet it was hilarious."

"It was borderline infantile," Lysander said. "He made the whole bidding process a pissing contest."

"Really? What did he say?"

"*If a guy with a coffeepot in his head can handle this, I'm sure I could genocide the whole damn wraith bug population with ease,*" my own voice said over the speakers of the ship—an obvious recording.

Everyone turned their attention to my chief cyber operations officer, Sawyer. She sat in her chair with her legs drawn up, her chin resting on her knees, her pixie-short red hair disheveled. She had her PAD up with the audio recording of my taunts set to play. No matter where I went, or what I did, she listened to everything like a damn stalker—the PAD mounted to my arm was her link to my life, even off the ship.

"It was amusing to listen to," Sawyer muttered as she lowered her arm and went back to typing on her PAD. "Especially with Lysander's added commentary. The two of you could star in a sitcom."

"God, help me," Lysander groaned.

Sawyer offered a smile in response. Unlike the rest of us, who wore skintight enviro-suits, she sported a green jumpsuit, the type favored by most starship engineers. It made it easy for her to roll up a sleeve and use her PAD—the device was paper thin and wrapped around her arm, so it could fit under any piece of clothing. PADs were plugged into the arm and powered by a human's internal temperature, easily hidden within most clothing, even enviro-suits.

"I think it's best that we make an impression, even if it's negative," Noah said.

I'd expect nothing else from the youngest in the room. Even if he had become an accomplished starfighter, Noah still looked the part of a fresh-faced recruit. Gaunt like a teenager. Stubble on his chin like he had glued flakes of blond sprinkles in random places. Noah didn't have the toughness of his brother, Lysander, but he was trustworthy and loyal—two traits I valued more than any others.

Dr. Clay, my chief medical officer, scooted to the edge of his seat. He had a rod up his ass, and he moved like that wasn't a metaphor. "You don't want a reputation for being difficult, no matter how much your name gets out there. Trust me. None of the superhumans hire starships with a temperamental history."

I snapped my fingers and pointed at him. "You worked with a lot of superhumans, right? What *did* they look for?"

Homo superior—genetically improved Homo sapiens—ruled the whole goddamn galaxy. If I was going to get any sort of real work, I would need to show them what a genetically-modified human was capable of. Then again, Captain Varvont's words bounced around my skull. Homo superior always hired genetically-modified people, because they created them for that purpose. Servants.

I wasn't like that, though. No superhuman had made me to be their dog. My mother had had my genetics reworked while I had still been in her womb. Not because she had wanted to make me a one-trick flesh machine for superhumans, but because she had wanted me to have every advantage possible.

"Did you hear me?" Dr. Clay asked, snapping me from my musings.

"What?" I asked.

"I said, superhumans want people who are intelligent and discreet. The exact opposite of how our crew conducts themselves."

How pleasant. It was like Dr. Clay had his own special game to see how fast he could irritate everyone else in the room. His lack of charisma matched the sharp angles of his face and his slicked-back black hair. If he had said his life-long passion was to become an evil vizier, I wouldn't have been surprised.

"It doesn't matter anymore," Lysander said. "We need to focus on the task at hand. What do we know about wraith bugs?"

Sawyer brushed some of her vibrant red hair out of her eyes. "They form colonies around a single fertile queen. The drones, fertile males, build the nest and produce saliva that is acidic for a few seconds before it rapidly hardens into a solid wax. On average, you see about 50 of them per hive. The workers, sterile females, gather resources. We should see about 300 of those."

"300?" Noah balked. "Aren't they huge?" He held out his arms at full length. "And we're gonna kill them all?"

"They're *insects*," Dr. Clay snapped. "We have plasma rifles. Use your brain."

"But I heard they have venom that can melt through enviro-suits, and they attack in swarms. Plus, we'll be in a mine, so we'll be in close quarters."

Sawyer shook her head. "We don't have to fight each one. Killing the queen will disperse the hive. She'll be protected in the center of the nest, typically so bloated with eggs, she'll be unable to move. Most exterminators focus on drilling a hole straight to her."

Dr. Clay lifted a manicured-to-perfection eyebrow. "How do you know all of this? The encyclopedia entry I read didn't have much in the way of detailed information. It focused on the scientific classi-fication."

"I was born on Vectin-10," Sawyer drawled. "I've seen thou-sands of wraith bugs. They're passive until you start messing with their hives. We'll be able to walk straight to this hive with them buzzing around. But once the show starts… that's when they get real aggressive."

"I see."

"The wax the males produce is hard stuff, though. We'll need a powerful drill." Sawyer smiled. "Or explosives."

"Feh." Dr. Clay waved a dismissive hand. "I'm no ground enforcer. I'll leave the logistics to the grunts."

The grunts. Dr. Clay had a way with words.

"All the assignments we take on Vectin-10 will be terrible," Noah said. He turned to me and sighed. "Are you sure you want to stay here? I mean, I thought you and Endellion had a falling out. Why pick the planet she was given to govern? What if she finds out we're here?"

"I want her to know I'm here," I said.

My statement ended with a long stretch of silence. My tiny crew of officers replied with questioning glances.

Of course, I had picked the planet Endellion was governing. I wanted a reputation here. I wanted a reputation where she could see it. I wanted her *to worry I would come after her*. And when I had the favor of superhumans in this quadrant—when I could call in favors and make the deals like she did—I would be that pistol lurking in the shadows, waiting for her to make one wrong move.

If I were on some other planet, far from her seat of power, I wouldn't have the opportunities I needed. I had to stay here. I had to hound her every step.

While everyone else thought she was a perfect human role model, I knew otherwise. She *would* make a mistake. And I would be the one to kill her.

TWO

The Hive

The mines of Vectin-10 ran deep.

Four and a half kilometers beneath the surface and I could understand why some guys got nervous. If an accident happened down here, you were fucked. The miners said they had medical personnel, and high-tech equipment to detect hazards, but if the whole tunnel collapsed, what good would any of that do? At least when I was on a space station, there were escape pods and ships at every dock. It was more like living on an island than living in a subterranean hellhole.

Rock floors, wires on all the walls, and a ceiling covered in pipes gave the whole place a gloomy feeling. Still better than Capital Station, though. Here, all the equipment looked cared for, and none of the wires were broken or frayed. Unlike my home space station—rotting and damaged everywhere you looked.

The mines would've looked great if the wraith bugs hadn't been crawling all over everything.

And Noah was right. The bugs were big. Thirty-six kilograms of pure disgusting.

They had spines on the underside of their abdomens, and they curled up on themselves to create little spirals of protruding weapons. To make things worse—or perhaps more bizarre—the exoskeleton was transparent. It made keeping an eye on the spines difficult. I could see the bugs' damn intestines better than the outside of their bodies. And the insides were a dark blackish-purple, right down to the beating heart.

"Repulsive," I muttered.

"The bugs?" Sawyer asked over the comms of my enviro-suit.

Even with my helmet folded down like the unused hood on a hoodie, hanging limply between my shoulder blades, I heard her clear as though she were next to me.

"Yeah, the bugs," I said. "They make strange sounds."

The insects walked on four of their six legs, creating a constant clicking noise since their "feet" were as hard as stone. The other two legs they held up, like hands, and poked at the walls. Their giant purple eyes shook and glistened whenever they found something. Then they'd dig at the hard rock, using a weird acid spit to get deeper until they managed to eat something. Their corrosive saliva would rapidly calcify and form a new piece of their hive. Then they shuffled to the next location.

Weird.

"I find them interesting," Sawyer said.

"Yeah, well, you have a fish for a brother. I should've known you'd like the bugs."

"That fish has a name, thank you. And that name is Blub."

"Right," I said, waving away the comment. "I forgot the flying sushi had a name."

She laughed. I loved the sound of it. Feminine and genuine. I wished she did it more often. Then she abruptly stopped.

"Demarco," she muttered.

"What is it?"

"I need to talk to you about the people on this planet. It's important."

"You can tell me anything," I said. "I've got your back."

"I…"

"Demarco," Lysander called from down the tunnel. "What're you doing down here?"

"Checking out the area," I replied.

Sawyer went silent, no hint of a breath that she would continue. What had she wanted? She didn't open up that often, and ever since Endellion had left, I hadn't felt right with Sawyer. Like she had shut herself off from everything and refused to feel.

Lysander approached with his enviro-suit helmet up. The suit hoods hardened when secured in place, the flexi-glass becoming a tinted visor that hid the face of the wearer. Lysander's voice was distinct enough, though, and I could recognize it through the suit's speakers.

"Why didn't you command one of the ground enforcers to handle this?" he asked.

"We don't—"

"And why don't you have your helmet up?"

I yanked my helmet over my head and allowed it to suction in place. The visor screen pulsed to life, giving me readouts of the sedimentary material and the temperature of the tunnels.

"We don't have enough ground enforcers," I said over the personal comms. "But once we get this payday, things will be different. We'll finally get the crew we need."

It was long overdue, but I never had enough credits to hire everyone the *Star Marque* would need. This payout would be enough to start us on the right path.

Lysander motioned to one of the far tunnels. "Let's patrol together. I have things I need to discuss with you."

I walked with Lysander, my attention more on the bugs than him.

He began with, "Do you see these?" He pointed to fist-sized canisters glued to the wall with quick-drying adhesive. "These are the remote blast charges we're going to use to blow holes in the hive. If we set up everything ahead of time, we can blow a hole straight to the nest and then crawl down later, when the swarm has gathered around the queen."

"Uh-huh."

"We're setting them up in specific locations to create an opening without damaging the structure of the mine."

"All right."

"The adhesive attaches quickly, so don't get any on your skin for longer than a second."

I swear Lysander wanted me to stop paying attention. He had a voice that grated on my patience. I shifted my full focus to the wraith bugs that skittered by.

There were hundreds moving around, and the more I stared, the more I realized their calcified hive structure spanned down multiple tunnels. Some were so blocked up with the milky-white material that no person could get through.

While I walked over uneven flooring, I couldn't even see the steel grating underneath.

"—which is why I think we should focus on ground assignments for the time being," Lysander said, his voice barely registering in my thoughts. How long had he been talking? Probably the entire time we had been walking. Too long.

"Why is this hive so huge?" I asked.

"Are you paying attention?"

"No. I'm not talking to you. Sawyer?"

Lysander snapped his head in my direction, no doubt pissed, but I ignored him.

"The hive is this big because it's years in the making."

"Yeah," I murmured. "That's what I thought. What the fuck? I thought these bugs were a problem that *sprang up* out of nowhere?"

"It only became a problem when the Vectin government decided to reopen this half of the mining facility," Sawyer stated. "Funding to the mines had been cut under the last planet governor. It seems Endellion has reversed that. Most mines are planning expansions to their operations."

Goddammit.

I almost wanted the whole mine to go up in flames after that revelation, but I held back the urge. Whatever Endellion wanted, my default was the opposite. Why did she care about mining? I knew she didn't—that bitch only cared about herself—so there had to be some benefit to her. But what?

The floor beneath my boots quaked. I kept my balance, but the tremor persisted for a full ten seconds. Dirt and crust from the insect hive rained down around us, creating a thick fog of debris. My visor blinked with several warnings, including an increase in temperature.

"Demarco," Sawyer said over the comms. "There was an explosion in tunnel 3-B."

"Why?"

"Someone detonated a crate of mechanical explosives. Those aren't ours. I think you should—"

Her communication cut out, replaced with an eerie static.

"Sawyer?" I asked.

Nothing.

They weren't our explosives? Was someone trying to sabotage our extermination?

Lysander yanked me by the arm as another tremor hit. The wraith bugs in the area rushed down the tunnel, two of their arms up like knives, the spines on their abdomens flaring. They didn't attack me or Lysander, though. They rushed past, making an odd hissing noise the entire way.

"We have enforcers in tunnel 3-B," Lysander said, our local comms still functioning, even if the ship comms couldn't cut through the interference caused by the explosion. "C'mon!"

We both hurried down the tunnel, though I pulled ahead. Hot air rushed out from a distant corridor, carrying with it a cloud of dirt. My visor immediately outlined the area for me, giving me sight despite the terrible conditions. The moment I entered the affected tunnel, shouting drowned out all other commotion.

At least a hundred wraith bugs had rushed in, each spitting their acidic saliva. My enforcers fired lasers and plasma rifles left and right, the light show enough to pierce the dirt fog. My visor informed me of everyone's positions, including the insects', and the information covered the flexi-glass from top to bottom.

It didn't matter. I lived each moment in slow motion, absorbing information and calculating my next move as though I had four seconds when everyone else had just one.

With unparalleled speed, I fired fifteen of my plasma bolts, killing eighteen bugs. Those superheated plasma bolts melted straight through flesh and bone. Every bolt sailed through the body of a wraith bug and slammed into the wall, burying itself a few centimeters deep before the heat dissipated.

I ripped a laser rifle out of the hands of a nearby enforcer. Unlike plasma guns, which needed bolt ammunition, the lasers fired until they ran out of juice and their shots had no kickback. The giant insects swarmed for me. Perhaps they would've overwhelmed a normal man, but I was genetically modified. I tracked their movements without trouble, shot each right through the eye, and managed to keep a meter away from their spit at all times.

My visor beeped in warning—movement detected in the walls. I leapt away as more wraith bugs crawled out of the cracks in their hive, each hissing louder than the last. My enviro-suit started blocking out the sound, the warning on screen read: *Decibel level of 85. Permanent damage may occur. For your safety, sound dampening has gone into effect.*

Lysander shot a bug digging its way out of the floor—one that had almost caught me by surprise. I nodded to him, and he rushed in to help enforcers who were struggling with the threat.

"Help!" someone shouted over the short-distance comms. "I'm trapped!"

My visor outlined a body trapped under broken bits of the hive, one the size of a small vehicle. I effortlessly jumped over a pile of debris and lifted the rock-like structure from the enforcer's legs. It didn't strain me. I could bench press 191 kilograms without a thought—the benefits of being genetically modified.

"Thank you, Captain," the enforcer breathed. "Thank you."

He crawled from the wreckage, and when bugs came for him, I fired my laser rifle and wrecked their disgusting heads. They popped if I hit them just between the eyes. Two other enforcers ran over and helped the first guy to his feet. Once I was sure he would make it, I turned back and focused on culling the infestation.

Fortunately, technology had an advantage over nature. Vents opened in the tunnels, sucking out the debris and replacing it with fresh air. With the chaos under control, my remaining enforcers— those uninjured from the explosion—went to town on the wraith bugs. They killed them by the dozens until the remaining insects fled to the cracks in the wall. Those with missing limbs crawled, and I crushed a few under my boot, their giant eyes popping like grapes.

The ambient noise died down.

"Good riddance," I muttered.

The long-distance comms flickered back to life. Sawyer's exhale went straight to my ear, and I smiled.

"Everything okay?" I asked.

"The wraith bugs are gathering at their queen," she said. "The injured ones will rest, the dying ones will become food for the babies, and the rest will hole up."

"Fuck'em. They weren't difficult to kill."

Well, they hadn't been difficult for *me*. The rest of my enforcers were in various stages of injury. Some had been hurt by the tunnel half-collapsing. Some had acid burns from the bugs. Others had been hit by stray laser fire. Luckily for them, our enviro-suits were top of the line.

"You don't understand," Sawyer said. "Now that we've agitated the bugs, they'll build a wall around their inner sanctum. If they feed off the dead, they can survive for months. And if we want to blast them out of there, it'll take three times as many explosives. *This* was why we had to be careful how we went about bombing the place."

Goddammit.

Lysander placed a heavy hand on my shoulder. I focused my attention on an area in the tunnel where the dirt had cleared. An entire portion of the mine had collapsed. That meant even more digging.

Another tremor went off underfoot, and I held my laser rifle close. Then the shaking stopped.

"What was that?" I asked.

"Another explosion," Sawyer said. "This one in tunnel 1-A."

"More sabotage?"

"From what I can tell, it was our own blast charge."

Another round of debris fell from the roof, but much less than the last time, no doubt a smaller explosion. Still—what the fuck was going on? Someone had messed with my operation, and now my own crew was setting things off before the signal? If the wraith bugs hadn't been holing up before, they were now.

"What happened?" I asked over the main comms. "Someone better fucking answer me."

"We had an accident," a woman replied, her voice shaky.

"We're in the middle of an emergency," I barked. "What *accident*?"

"One of the charges went off. We h-have it under control now, sir."

Now they have it under control? Out of all the times to mess up, this wasn't one.

"I'm getting reports," Lysander said. He tapped the side of his helmet. "The tunnels have been scanned. No one died, and there don't seem to be any miners in the area. That means the first detonation must've been remote. Or perhaps timed."

"Damn," I said with a huff. "Now what?"

"We should regroup on the *Star Marque* and discuss how we're going to handle the situation."

"Fine."

"What should we do about the second explosion?" Lysander asked. He shook his head. "Apparently, it's damaged some more of our equipment."

"Figure out whose mistake it was, and I'll deal with it."

If someone from my own crew had helped in this sabotage, I'd make them regret it.

MY EXPLOSIVES EXPERT, some young woman fresh out of heavy weapons certification, stood on the other side of my starship's conference table, her eyes down. Most of the *Star Marque's* old crew had left when Endellion had. She had given them planetside property on Vectin-10 for their years of service, which had been enough for most of the old crew to retire. Lysander had scraped together credits to hire a few replacements, but nowhere near what we needed.

This "expert" had been one of the new hires. I couldn't remember her damn name, though, even if my life had depended on it.

"What happened?" I asked.

She flinched. "One of the blast charges went off accidentally, Captain."

"Because of the first explosion?"

"N-No, sir."

Lysander stood next to me, his expression stern. He glanced at me to continue, and I huffed.

"Then, *why*?" I asked. "What the fuck happened?"

"W-Well, I placed the charges correctly," she said. "But the adhesive we used started a chemical reaction in the calcified hive. It became acidic again, and corroded away the casing of the blast charge, and then the detonator inside—"

"Why did you allow that to occur?" Lysander asked, cutting her off.

The woman lifted her gaze to meet his, more confident than before. "I had no idea the adhesive would react like that! We were on a tight schedule, and we had to place the charges."

"Not counting the devastation caused by the first explosion, we have three crew members with injuries, as well as severe equipment damage from where your blast charge went off. Were we in such a hurry that you couldn't check the blast charges after they were placed? This all could've been avoided with a simple inspection."

"Yes, sir. Sorry, sir."

She lowered her gaze again, her jaw clenched, her shoulders bunched at the base of her neck. Everything about her appearance was unremarkable. A green jumpsuit for engineer types. Her brown hair tightened back in a scalp-straining bun, highlighting the features of her face—and it wasn't anything to write home about. Small eyes that weren't aligned. Thin lips. Three moles. A face made for radio. Hell, her face had been *hit* by a radio.

When I glanced through her history, though, it was a different story. She was only nineteen, and had already been certified for heavy explosives, plasma canister maintenance, and biochemical waste. A lot of shit for someone her age. More education than I'd had at nineteen. And she had never had any trouble with the law, which was *also* much better than me at nineteen.

I tapped the screen of my PAD, scrolling to the top of her background report until I came to her name. Vera Shanina. She didn't seem like the type to help in a sabotage, not with a record as clean as hers. It meant her accident had likely been genuine—just poorly timed.

"Vera," I said as I glanced up from my PAD. "You cost me 50,000 credits in equipment repair."

She exhaled. "Yes, Captain."

"Do a goddamn check next time. We might be under a time crunch, but that doesn't mean you half-ass the explosives. Understand?"

"Next time?" Vera asked. She chanced a glance at me and then at Lysander. "I'm not… fired?"

"Fuck, no," I said. "I just spent 50,000 teaching you a lesson you'll never forget. Why would I fire you now?"

Both Lysander and Vera gave me odd looks, their eyebrows high. Was it really that surprising? The woman had demonstrated *some* talent with her overachieving history, she just didn't have any experience. Now she did. And she probably wouldn't be asking for a raise any time soon, so this was a win-win in my opinion.

"Th-Thank you, Captain," Vera muttered. She took a step away from the conference table, shaken, but clearly more relaxed. "I'll return to my station, if that's acceptable."

I motioned to the door. "Go on."

She hustled away from the conference table as fast as she could without breaking into a full-blown sprint. The automated starship door slid open, allowing her into the corridor, but she stopped in the doorframe. After a shaky breath, she faced me.

"Thank you so much. I… really need the credits. You don't know how much this job means to me and—"

"Too much," I snapped. "Get out of here."

Vera nodded and leapt into the corridor. Once the door slid closed, I sat down in one of the conference room chairs and swirled around. One problem dealt with—now I just had to figure out what else I was going to do.

"Why didn't you fire her?" Lysander asked.

I shrugged. "Eh. She has potential."

"Well, it might not matter."

"Why's that?"

Lysander glared. "This sabotage has cost us. That first explosion mangled ten of our enforcers. They would've died had they not gotten treatment in our healing vat. But those canisters of mother-cell fluid aren't cheap. It was either save their lives or our money."

I kept quiet, my teeth gritted.

"And we lost a ton of equipment," Lysander continued. "We have enough credits for repairs, but we won't finish this job on time, which means we get paid a fraction of the agreed amount, maybe nothing. That'll mean we'll be broke by the end of the month."

I ran a hand down my face. Who would want to cause me problems? My first thought went straight to Endellion, but she was more sophisticated than a random bomb in the mines. And we had just received this assignment ten hours ago. I knew she was good, but she wasn't *that* good. So, who else could it have been?

"Captain Varvont," I said as I glanced up at Lysander. "He's the only one I've had a problem with since I got to Vectin-10. It has to be him."

Sawyer replied with a chuckle over the comms. "I could see it."

"Do you have any proof?" Lysander asked.

I shook my head. "But you know it's true. You saw the way he tried to punk us. He doesn't like new enforcers outbidding him on assignments."

"Without proof, there's nothing we can do about it."

"Let's pretend we had proof. We could turn him in to the Vectin-10 justiciars and he'd be sent straight to some prison station. Maybe even Ucova."

"Again. You have no proof." Lysander shook his head. "I swear you sometimes ignore the fact that I'm speaking to you."

I stared out into the depths of space, focusing in on the stars that twinkled within the blackness of the void. Endellion wouldn't have allowed some piece-of-shit cyborg to defeat her right out the gate. Captain Varvont thought he could mess with me? I would make sure everyone on this sad sack planet knew they couldn't mess with me and get away with it.

"We can get proof," I said. "That won't be hard."

"You're *assuming* he was behind the explosion," Lysander said. He walked around to stand in front of my view. "And what're you planning on doing?"

"Sawyer is a coding genius. I'm sure the captain has damning evidence on his ship's systems. Some communication or payment record. All it would take are a few facts to line up and the justiciars would have to act."

"I can't access their ship's system from here," Sawyer said, chiming in. "I know you think I'm a computer wizard, but technology isn't magic. I'd need to be on the ship, or at least have a proxy on the ship."

Lysander nodded. "And it's not like you can traipse onto the *Scorpio* without hassle. We can't break into another enforcer starship. *We'll* be the ones arrested by the justiciars, then."

"That's not entirely true. Enforcers can break some rules if in the pursuit of lawbreakers. Almost killing ten of our people means we have the authority to investigate nearby starships."

For a long moment, there was silence. I mulled over the statements, my gaze distant. It wasn't just the money or the setbacks. I absolutely refused to allow Captain Varvont to get away with harming my crew. And I bet that was his plan, too. Kill my enforcers and scare me a bit.

But no one did that without paying the price. It didn't matter what rules were in place. He would be made to pay.

THREE

Payday

____

A space elevator stretched from the surface of Vectin-10 all the way past the stratosphere.

All space elevators looked alike—a giant duralumin wire with a donut-shaped compartment that slid up and down all day long. The elevator could carry hundreds of tons, and transported materials from the planet's surface to the attached space port. The place bustled with life—*human* life. Superhumans didn't frequent the elevators. They had their own transports, and most wouldn't want to mingle with Homo sapiens in a cramped elevator, even if it was the only choice.

I waited at the top, near the docking ports. The *Star Marque* and the *Scorpio* weren't far from each other physically, but the circular structure of the space port meant they were a thirty-minute walk apart.

I craned my head back and stared out the transparent ceiling to get a better look at Vectin-10—it looked like it was floating above me, a bizarre tan-colored moon. It was mostly a desert. I never understood why everyone described deserts with such disappointment in their voices until I'd actually set foot on the planet myself. Deserts were the armpit of terrain. A sweaty, disgusting environment made of heat and exhaustion. Nothing like the lush planets in the rest of the system. Especially Vectin-14, the capital.

"Demarco."

Sawyer spoke through a small comm I had inserted in my ear, her comforting voice going straight to my thoughts. I wore my planetside casualwear—a tank top and cargo pants—to avoid my obvious enviro-suit. And to give me better access to my PAD mounted on my left arm.

"The *Scorpio* has a crew complement of 345," Sawyer continued. "After that last guy leaves, 273 of them will be away on leave. With only 72 aboard, there's a decent chance you won't get caught."

Perfect. From what I had gathered, Captain Varvont and his crew frequented the local entertainment. They would be busy with the local hotel bars for hours.

The last man leaving, the *Scorpio's* petty officer, walked with a slight sway, a brandy pouch still clutched in his hand. Must've started his drinking early. Short guys like him never handled their alcohol well, and it was clear he had spilled some on his gray jumpsuit. He moved at a slow pace, bags under his eyes. I waited until he left the port before I stirred from the shadows.

"You sure about this?" Sawyer asked.

"Of course."

"Lysander still disapproves."

"He'll be fine." I pushed away from the bulkhead of the space port and headed straight for the *Scorpio's* loading ramp. "I know what I'm doing." I'd go in, get the information, and leave. If there wasn't any information, no harm done.

Besides, as enforcers, we were allowed to bend the law a bit. Normal civilians weren't allowed to trespass, but enforcers were given a special exception so long as criminals were being brought to justice. Technically, if I *didn't* find anything, and I was discovered trespassing, this would lead to a whole host of complications. I'd likely lose the *Star Marque* if someone could prove I was abusing my privileges.

That didn't matter. I knew I'd find something. I was law, and I was going to wield it like a weapon.

No one stood outside the *Scorpio*. I stopped at the entrance hatch and connected my PAD to the outer computer terminal. Words flashed across my screen, but I ignored them. Sawyer had remote access to my PAD so she could use her techno-magic on the starship.

"What's the holdup?" I whispered.

Other enforcers and dock workers patrolled the area. I didn't want to get caught with my PAD hooked up to a different ship before I had any evidence. Maybe I could feign being drunk. Worth a shot if it came down to it.

"I looped the internal security feed," Sawyer said, almost with disinterest in her voice. "Then I disabled the sirens and emergency communication channel."

"How long until I'm in?"

The entrance hatch slid open, answering the question with a whoosh akin to a long sigh.

"You're amazing, Sawyer."

She didn't reply. I liked to imagine the blush on her freckled face, though. I had always been in awe of her skills. My genetic engineering had improved my physical prowess and reflex time, but the people who had designed Sawyer had given her an uncanny ability to focus, multitask, and apply logic. The perfect computer engineer and coder—no standard starship programs would stop her from breaking in.

I crept into the main corridor of the *Scorpio*. Like the *Star Marque*, it was a vanguard-class starship, the kind of military vessel built before the United-Earth War. The guts of the ship consisted of capsule bunk beds, small lockers for storage, and steel grate flooring. Although there were weapon mounts by each door, they had been locked and secured. I crept farther into the starship, navigating my way to the lift despite the dull gray walls and dim lighting.

"Sawyer," I whispered. "You don't think I'm crazy, right?"

"I didn't until you asked that question."

I chuckled, but kept the volume to an absolute minimum. "You think Captain Varvont fucked with us, don't you?"

"Yes. If I didn't, I wouldn't have agreed to help you."

"Heh. I'm the captain now. You have to follow my orders."

"Careful, Demarco. I can reactivate the security and get you arrested."

I had to stop myself from laughing. What a ballbuster. That was why I liked Sawyer. She always got me smiling.

Once I reached the lift, I tapped the button for Deck One. All vanguard-class ships had five decks. Deck One housed the officers and everything of importance. When the lift doors opened, I stepped inside and waited. A few seconds later, the doors opened again, revealing a nearly identical corridor to Deck Three. I knew better, though. I went straight for the central database, my footfalls echoing in the empty corridor. I didn't want to thank my luck, but I couldn't help it. I hadn't run across a single soul from the entrance to my desired destination—exactly how I had wanted it.

I reached the central database and hooked my PAD to the computer terminal mounted next to the door. After a few beeps, Sawyer did her thing. The door hissed open. I stepped in and hooked my PAD to the main terminal. The spacious room, designed for four people to do their work, complete with individual stations and computer terminals, had a stink about it. Not much ventilation or perhaps IT officers didn't shower much. Either way, the place had a rank odor.

"You in?" I asked.

"Yes," Sawyer replied.

"How long will this take?"

"You sound like a woman on a bad date."

I smirked. "And you would know?"

"Oh, I know."

"Sawyer, baby, if we dated, you'd never have a bad night. You know that, right?"

Normally, I'd expect some sort of quip or comeback, but her end remained silent. I stared at the screen on my PAD, watching information fly by at an unreal speed. She was obviously working, but that had never stopped her from chatting before.

"Something wrong?" I asked.

"Demarco, I..."

I didn't like the quiet tone of her voice, or the way it wavered when she had said my name.

"We should talk at some point," she concluded.

"I agree."

"Alone."

"We're alone now, aren't we? Just you and me on this little excursion."

"You, me, and all this incriminating evidence," Sawyer quipped. "Hm… You'll like the results of this. Captain Varvont paid miners to blast the tunnels. And he's been selling plasma weapons to members of the rebellion. And smuggling out stolen equipment from multiple mines around Vectin-10. At least twenty felonies here. At least."

As if the universe wanted to hit me with a cruel punchline, the door to the central database slid open with a soft hiss. I whipped around, tense and loaded with adrenaline.

A man stepped into the central database. No, not a man—a monster made of machine with flesh stretched over it. He was a cyborg, through and through, with enough cybernetics for three people, most of which protruded at odd angles, betraying the handiwork of terrible surgeons.

His jumpsuit didn't fit right. The sleeves had been ripped off to accommodate his jagged shoulders, and seams had come undone around the sides of his gut. He must've weighed three times my weight—close to 320 kilograms, for certain.

The hideous cyborg stepped into the room and stared with prosthetic, corpse-blue eyes. He didn't blink as often as he should have, and it gave him a robotic quality that matched the cogs in his guts.

The door hissed shut behind him.

"I locked it," Sawyer said into my ear. "He can't go get help."

I couldn't escape, either.

"Security," the cyborg said, his voice modified by the machines in his neck. "Call the captain."

The computer didn't respond, and it never would, not with Sawyer in the ship's system.

The freakish man realized something was up at the same

moment I reached for my belt and pulled out a duralumin knife. At 13 centimeters long, it could flay a man fast, but I wasn't so sure it could deal with layers of metal and wire.

The cyborg glanced at my weapon and smirked. He pulled out his own knife—a plasma blade—and ignited it. The edge, made of whitish-blue ionized gas, seared the air and created a sizzle similar to water sprinkled across a hot pan. The scorching ionized blade could reach temperatures of 2,700 degrees Celsius—more than enough to cut clean through steel.

"I can take you to the brig or I can take you to the morgue," he said, his smile growing wider.

I liked his attitude. Too bad he worked for Captain Varvont.

"I came for evidence that you all tried to kill members of my crew," I said. "And I have it. Let me go, and we won't need to see which one of us is better with a knife."

"Morgue it is."

Corpse-Eyes slashed wide, his glowing-hot weapon coming within centimeters of my chest. I leapt back, slammed into the computer terminal, and then stumbled to the side. After a quick yank of my arm, I detached my PAD from the ship's computer.

"I hope you got what you needed," I murmured.

"I did," Sawyer replied. "Kill this guy fast."

The machines in the man's body whirled and hissed. When he attacked a second time, it was faster and stronger, his slash powerful enough to whoosh as it flew by my head. I jumped away and crashed into another workstation, my heart pounding with enough force to drown out all other noise. When Corpse-Eyes swung a third time, I ducked and came up with my own blade, hoping to catch his throat.

He pivoted at the last second, and my blade hit his shoulder. While I cut flesh, and blood leaked over the steel protruding from his body, I didn't get deep enough. He punched and clipped my side, right on my floating ribs.

I grunted, leaned into the blow, and staggered back. He must've broken a few bones. I smiled, surprised he had gotten a hit in, and also excited by the fact. Not many people were fast enough to get me.

Corpse-Eyes chuckled. Sweat rolled off him at a fierce rate, despite the fact we had only been going full-tilt for about ten seconds. His overclocked machines obviously couldn't handle sustained power. I would win if I dragged the fight out—he'd gas and I'd cut him up—but I didn't have time for that.

I leapt in. His disgusting eyes went wide.

Apparently, he hadn't expected me to get aggressive.

I didn't go for his neck. I went for the hand holding the plasma knife. With as much strength as I could muster, I cut into his wrist—the thinnest part of his arm—and slashed it open.

Blood gushed to the floor, and he dropped his weapon.

We both went for it, but I rolled and snatched it first.

Corpse-Eyes stomped, centimeters from crushing my head under his steel-girder foot. I leapt up with enough grace to get back into a combat stance. He drew back, telegraphing a fight-ending punch. I knew better. I kept away, and he swung with all the speed his cybernetics could dish out. If I had gone in for a stab, I would've been caught before I could duck out. But once he swung, I side-stepped his metal knuckles and went straight for his chest with his own plasma knife.

It cut deep into his lungs, melting through the metal casing in half a second. My hand slipped into the guy's body, and when I pulled away, I cut my wrist on jagged steel jutting out of the man's injury.

The cyborg threw an arm wide. I ducked under as he staggered backward. He wheezed and hacked up a mouthful of blood, staining his worn jumpsuit. When he placed an unsteady hand over the injury, I rushed him. He swung with his other arm, hard enough to shatter a man's skull. I dodged and then slashed at the duralumin floor. The plasma blade cut into the metal, and when I brought the blade up in an arc, sparks sizzled through the air. Corpse-Eyes looked away—a terrible mistake.

That was the end.

I slashed into his neck while he was momentarily distracted and damn near severed it.

His body spasmed. I stepped back, deactivated the plasma knife, and wiped my own sweat from my brow. As the electricity of the fight wore off, the pain from my ribs set in. I needed to get back to the *Star Marque*.

"Take the weapons with you," Sawyer said.

"I will."

"And hurry. We don't want to give Captain Varvont any time to retaliate."

ENFORCERS WERE mercenaries hired to fill in the gaps of law enforcement, bounty hunting, and general manpower. *Justiciars*, on the other hand, were the official law enforcement branch of the criminal justice system. They were the ones who handled disputes between enforcers, high level military, and political figures, and they also protected those who had been publicly elected.

When I walked into the Green Lane Resort—a casino and bar located at the top of Vectin-10's space elevator—accompanied by a handful of justiciars, I got everyone's attention. The justiciars wore their black enviro-suits with their helmets on. The visors reflected the patrons of the casino like perfect mirrors.

It didn't take long to locate Captain Varvont. He sat at one of the dice tables, his tube-neck cybernetics a dead giveaway. I pointed him out and waited by the door as the justiciars walked over to the table. The justiciars lifted heavy plasma rifles and Captain Varvont got to his feet.

"What's the meaning of this?" he asked in a raspy voice.

"Captain Varvont," one of the justiciars said. "You're under arrest for attempted murder, racketeering, arms dealing, grand larceny, and fraud. Any attempt to resist arrest will be considered deadly force."

Nothing soured the mood in a casino quite like a list of felony charges. No one took their turn in a game. No dice. No cards. No drinks. Everyone waited while Captain Varvont mulled over the situation. He glanced at the door and met my gaze, his brow furrowed.

He knew what had happened. I could see it in the anger that flashed across his face.

Didn't matter. I replied with a smirk and sarcastic salute. No one fucked with my starship or my crew. The moment Captain Varvont had put my enforcers in danger was the moment I had stopped caring if he lived or died.

And breaking into his ship and exposing his crimes hadn't been just an act of revenge. Turning in corrupt or criminal enforcer captains came with a sizable reward.

Basically, enforcers were encouraged to rat on each other—the superhumans loved to see us fight among ourselves. If I exposed a fellow enforcer for breaking the laws, even if I had to get that information through questionable means, I would be rewarded. If the crimes were egregious enough, and the fellow enforcer lost his ship, it would be sold at auction, and I'd get a portion of the sale.

Selling the *Scorpio* alone would net me far more than the half a million credits I would've gotten from the wraith bug mission.

So, in a way, Captain Varvont had helped me out. Now I would get paid. And I was sending a clear message to the other enforcer captains.

Don't fuck with my crew, or else.

Then again, I was also sending another message: I wasn't a friend to any of my fellow enforcers. Some of them might even think I was a superhuman dog, ready to rat them out for any amount of favor.

I didn't care what they thought. I had things to do.

NOTHING BEAT PAYDAY. Even the lingering ache in my side felt better after seeing all those credits in our account. Now I could pay everyone's salary for a couple of months, get repairs, resupply, and even hire a few more enforcers and officers. We were set long enough to have a little breathing room.

"Here's to our captain," Noah said as he lifted his rum pouch. "For gettin' us paid!"

"Hear, hear!" half the crew shouted.

The mess hall erupted into cheering and clapping. Alcohol always got people jovial, myself included. I threw back an entire rum pouch and smiled. Endellion had never mingled with the crew when she had been the captain. It had given her an air of mystery, but I wasn't like that. I liked my crew.

I genuinely liked my crew.

One by one, group by group, each of my enforcers came to the mess hall to greet me. They patted my shoulder, made some quick toast, and went off to drink their evening away. Noah and Mara sat on either side of me. The three of us occupied the main table in the middle of the room.

Mara, a short woman with chin-length black hair and a button nose, held her own shiny aluminum pouch close and offered me a smile. She nursed her drink and said nothing. It didn't bother me. I had known her for a while, and this wasn't unusual behavior since she didn't have an implant forcing medication in her head 24/7.

I returned to downing my drink, frustrated with the damn container. The pouches made it difficult to guzzle anything. They kept liquid safely contained, just in case of gravity failure, but I thought the secondary purpose was to prevent people from sucking down a stiff drink and moving on to the next. I wasn't some average schmoe, though. I could handle my liquor. I grabbed another pouch, sliced open the top with my steel knife, and threw back the contents.

Good stuff. Nice and fresh.

I glanced around, my thoughts turning inward. Most of the crew I had grown to love had left when Endellion had doled out her properties. Lee and Quinn, two of the older starfighters, by far some of my closest friends, had gone on to start a family. That had left me with five pilots—Noah, Mara, Hattie, Asahi, and Melba. I barely knew Melba, Asahi, and Hattie. They had been the last three recruited by Endellion herself.

The three sat off in the corner, drinking their rum, chatting among themselves.

I needed to train with them. Our starfighter team wasn't up to snuff, and it fell to me to make sure we could handle corsairs.

"Captain."

Vera stood next to my table, her odd face contorted, and her eyebrows knit together.

"Yeah?" I asked.

"I'm Vera, your weapons expert."

"I remember who you are." Who could forget a mug like hers?

"R-Right. I, uh, just wanted to apologize for what happened. It really was an accident that'll never happen again. I'll triple check everything. I've already made it a part of my procedure."

Eh. I didn't need *groveling*. I had thought I had made my position clear. She had fucked up. She shouldn't do it again. Everything would be fine. Why did she have to remind me it had even happened?

"Vera," I said.

She perked up. "Yes, Captain?"

"Sit down. Right here. Next to me."

Without a second's hesitation, she sat between me and Mara. I grabbed an unopened rum pouch and tossed it into her lap. She picked it up, flipped the pouch over to check the expiration date, and then gave me a nod.

"Thank you—"

"Don't talk to me again until after you finish that," I said. "That's an order."

Vera went to say something—no doubt *yes, sir*—but she stopped herself short and half-laughed. It wasn't a real order, obviously, but she complied nonetheless, which amused me. Girl needed to unwind. Plus, if we had a few drinks together, maybe she wouldn't look half bad, and who knew where that would lead?

"Demarco," Sawyer said over the comms on my PAD. "I need to speak to you."

I stood, threw down my empty pouch, and headed for the door.

Mara scooted closer to Vera and smiled. "Don't worry," she whispered. "The captain is always like this."

I was surprised Mara had spoken at all. Even Noah glanced over like Mara had yelled her statements.

I didn't bother listening to the conversation. Instead, I walked straight out of the mess hall and into the main corridor. The *Star Marque* was a vanguard-class starship, designed for military personnel. Everything was laid out in an efficient, albeit uncomfortable, style. I knew the guts of the ship like the back of my hand and navigated to the lift without much thought.

"You in your workroom?" I asked as I rounded a corner.

"No," Sawyer replied.

"Then where are you?"

"Your quarters."

My pulse quickened, and I couldn't help but smirk. She had never asked to meet me in my quarters before.

To my surprise, Lysander waited near the lift doors. He stood at attention when I drew close.

"Demarco," he said.

"What're you doing here, Sanders?" I asked.

He narrowed his gaze. "I told you I hate that nickname."

"Just get on with it," I said as I hit the button for the lift.

"I disagree with what you did to get that information. Captain Varvont may have wronged us, and several other people, but we could've caught him in a more honorable manner. You're going to give us a bad reputation. Or perhaps a *questionable* reputation."

"You and I both know it would've taken longer than a month to catch him if we had used *honorable methods*." I shot him a glare. "You wanted us to go broke? Is that it? Besides, I'm not going to let people hurt me or my crew. He almost killed ten of my enforcers. *Ten*. I won't be punked by amateurs like him."

Lysander returned my glare with one of his own. "Be careful. Some days you sound just like her."

Just like *her*.

He didn't have to say Endellion's name for me to know who he was referring to.

The doors to the lift opened, and I stepped inside. "I've heard your complaint. I'll try to curb my actions in the future."

"Where are you going?" Lysander asked.

"To get laid."

The lift door shut, but my irritation over the conversation lingered. I didn't want to become Endellion, but I kept deferring to her leadership style whenever I got lost. She had done it so well that it went full circle and went back around to being terrible. No, not terrible. *Evil.*

Was I really like that? Not yet. But perhaps Lysander was right. I couldn't do whatever I wanted, or else I would end up in Endellion's position. I had to keep that in mind.

After a few seconds in the lift, the doors opened, and I stepped out into the corridor. It looked similar, with a layout damn near identical to the last deck. I went straight for my quarters.

When I reached the door, I waved my forearm over the scanner. Buried deep between the ulna and radius sat a small identification chip that contained personal information—everything from my status as the captain of the *Star Marque* to my goddamn bank account. It gave me access to every room on the starship, even if people had settings to lock everyone else out.

My door opened and I glanced around.

Sawyer sat on the end of my bed, dressed in her normal engineering jumpsuit, her knees up and pressed against her chest. She tapped away at the PAD on her arm, her red hair unkempt—short and tousled, like she had just woken up.

I sauntered inside. "Well, this is unexpected."

FOUR

General Lone

S awyer lifted an eyebrow. "Excited?"

"To be here with you? Of course."

She half-smiled and continued to poke at her PAD.

My room—the captain's quarters—was the largest on the *Star Marque*, but that didn't mean much. Shaped in a perfect square, it held my bed against the back wall, a weapons locker, and a closet opposite that. I technically had my own shower stall, which was a disappointment. When I had been a starfighter, I would shower with the others, and that amused me in more ways than one. The position of captain came with a shadow of loneliness.

A koi fish floated down from the ceiling. Four bloated sacs of helium jiggled on his back, letting out a quiet *toot, toot, toot,* as he descended to head-level. The fish—*Blub*, as Sawyer called him— swirled around my shoulder, his mouth opening and closing in rhythm, like a heartbeat. I reached up and stroked his scales, admiring his shiny black eyes and the single red splotch of bioluminescence glowing on his forehead.

He had been genetically engineered for a specific appearance, like Sawyer with her red hair and gray-blue eyes, and while Blub's nibbling of my short hair could get annoying, I enjoyed him well enough.

"You brought your fish for this?" I asked. "Are you sure you want an audience?"

I ripped off my tank top and threw it to the floor. Sawyer didn't even look up. When I unfastened my belt, however, she stopped her work and glanced over.

"You giving me a show?" she asked.

"I hope you brought singles."

"I do like a man with scars."

Her comment almost didn't register. While I had run with gangs on Capital Station, I had avoided most injury due to my natural physical prowess. But after joining the *Star Marque*, I had run into a few scraps even *I* couldn't skate through. A large scar, smooth and straight, ran along my side, right between my ribs. It was deep and had been given to me by a plasma rifle while I had guard duty on Vectin-14. I had lived through the injury, but because I had exited the healing vat early, I'd never be without it.

I kicked off my boots and yanked off my pants. Sawyer, her face pink, lifted both eyebrows and returned her attention to her PAD.

"Oh, you *are* excited." She sighed. "Unfortunately for you, that's not why I came here."

"Don't lie," I said as I knelt on the edge of my bed. "We could've met in your workroom or in the officer's lounge if this was going to be chaste."

"Perhaps I wanted to speak with you in private. I have things I need to discuss."

Blub let out another *toot, toot* and dropped to the blankets of the bed. I pushed him aside and scooted over to Sawyer.

"Let's hear it, then," I said.

"General Lone is on Vectin-10."

I waited.

The person who had created Sawyer and Blub, the man who had "owned" her before she had joined the *Star Marque*, was none other than General Lone. I had never met him, but I already knew I despised him. He was a classic superhuman, the kind who flaunted his power over others in ways only properly described as *heinous*. A man who looked down on others for their genetic inferiority.

A small part of me knew he lived on Vectin-10—this was where Sawyer had grown up, after all—but I hadn't considered the fact that us being here would affect her.

"It's a big planet," I said. "We won't be running into him."

Sawyer held up her PAD. She had a list of assignments for enforcer ships, including calls from government facilities. Half the assignments came from *Tyndall Space Base*, located near the capital.

"That's him," Sawyer whispered. "If we stay here… we'll be working for him one way or another."

"Just because the asshole has assignments doesn't mean we have to take them." I scrolled through the list until I found something interesting. Then I flicked the paper-thin PAD screen. "Look at this. Bounty hunting. That's more up our alley anyway."

Blub squirmed around the bed, wrapping himself in my thin blankets. When he couldn't escape, I yanked him free and released him in the air. He twirled, confused, until he bonked into the wall and regained his bearings.

I returned my attention to Sawyer. She remained on the edge of my mattress, her legs tucked tight up to her chest. I positioned myself behind her, amused by our difference in size—she must've weighed a third of what I did. Whereas I had muscle to spare from years of weight training, she could've been made from paper and straws.

It didn't matter much to me. I wasn't picky, and I knew how to be gentle.

"What will I have to do to get your mind off him?" I asked, my breath on her neck. "I have lots of ideas."

Sawyer closed her eyes and bunched her shoulders at the base of her neck. "Don't act like it's that simple."

"It could be."

She stood and held her PAD close, her body trembling. "Goddammit, I thought you understood." After a few deep breaths, she continued in a steadier tone, "You've seen what he's done to me. This isn't something I can forget. He carved it into me, Demarco."

Sawyer pulled the collar of her jumpsuit higher, hiding her freckled skin. "He… carved it…" Her voice wavered.

"You said you liked a man with scars," I said as I rested back on the bed. "Maybe that's how I like my women."

"This isn't the same," she murmured. "I'm disfigured."

Disfigured? What an odd word choice. Had he messed with her that bad? I hadn't actually seen her naked, so I didn't know. All I had seen was a little bit beyond her collarbone, and just from that, I knew she had hundreds of scars along her body. General Lone had to have been a sadist of the highest caliber if he could bring himself to hurt someone like Sawyer.

But now I understood why she had wanted to talk in private. Sawyer had never told this to anyone. As far as I knew, I was the only one on the *Star Marque* who knew her history with the general. Endellion had been the one to save her back in the day—no one else had been involved. Sawyer wanted to keep her history as private as possible.

"I don't want us taking assignments from General Lone," Sawyer said. She didn't even turn around—she kept her back facing me the entire time.

"Fine," I said. "I already said we won't."

"Even though he could pay us well?"

"We can get pay elsewhere."

"So… So just like that?" She glanced over her shoulder.

"What? Isn't this what you want?" I shrugged. "Or do you want me to fight it?" I tucked my hands behind my head and stretched out across the cool sheets.

"Endellion would have—"

"Fuck Endellion," I snapped. "I don't give a shit what she would've done. If anything, that only makes me more certain. It's my crew, and I won't upset and betray them over some credits."

A long moment of silence passed between us. What would Endellion have done? I knew. She would've taken the highest paying job and rolled with it, regardless of anyone else's concerns. And although Lysander had accused me of becoming more like her, this was a line I knew I wouldn't cross.

Sawyer retook her seat on the edge of my bed, her presence barely disturbing the sheets or mattress. She poked at her PAD for a few minutes before scooting closer to me—never looking at me for longer than half a second, her face still pink.

"You said you wanted to hire more enforcers and officers," she muttered. "I found you places and people, if you want to look at them."

"Right now?"

"Yes."

"Eh." I exhaled and stared up at the ceiling. Blub floated by a few times before I said, "Fine. Toss me my shirt and pants. We can get some work done."

"You don't need to get dressed."

I shot her a sarcastic glare. When she offered nothing else, I smiled to myself. If she wanted to be a voyeur, that was fine. Who wouldn't want some of this? I was a good lookin' man.

"Show me who you found," I said.

Sawyer held up her PAD and scrolled through the lists. The most expensive personnel were at the top, with squads of mercs listed as single units for hire. It made sense to hire entire teams for ground enforcement. They had already trained together and trusted one another without any additional investment. If I hired individuals, I would need to give them additional training to get them up to snuff. Then again, Lysander was a fantastic instructor. He always made sure all the ground enforcers knew their shit before going into the field.

I scrolled through the list until I came to individuals and scoffed at the first guy who had an asking price of half a million credits for a year of service.

"What does this asshole bring to the table?" I asked with a laugh. "Can he turn lead into gold and resurrect the dead? Because that's what I'd expect with an asking price that high."

"He was an officer at the Ares Military Base," Sawyer said as she pointed to his credentials. "And he was the coordinating administrator for a fleet of ten starships. This is the kind of guy we would hire once we command multiple starships."

"Multiple?"

I hadn't considered the possibility of adding more ships. Wasn't the *Star Marque* enough? Not if I wanted to handle larger assignments. The *Star Marque* could hold a crew of 250, and if I pushed it, maybe 300. Not enough to handle city-level enforcement.

"Well, we can't afford him, or the next ten guys on the list," I said.

"You want a legitimate commander for your starfighters, right?" Sawyer pointed to a woman with an asking price of 200,000 credits. "She's had several engagements with rebellion fighters, and she has ten years of experience running on enforcer ships."

I sat up, held Sawyer's arm close so I could get a good look at the list, and huffed. How the fuck did anyone run a starship with these kinds of numbers? If I hired three more officers, I wouldn't have enough credits to pay the crew.

"Endellion didn't pay Lysander this much," I said.

"That's because Endellion revealed to the Navy HSN Corps that he had a genetic defect so he would be dishonorably discharged. When he thought he had no other prospects for employment, she swooped in and offered him next to nothing." Sawyer tapped the side of her head. "That's what Endellion did with everyone. She either found them at their lowest—"

"—or orchestrated their fall," I muttered. "I remember. But that's not what I want."

"There's nothing wrong with finding people at a low point. You don't need to be the one who destroyed their livelihood."

I scrolled to the bottom of the list, wondering if I could be so lucky as to find someone worthwhile among the chumps and schmoes of Vectin-10. To my surprise, the people listed at the bottom had an asking price of zero credits. Did they want to work for free? What did that even mean?

Sawyer must have read the confusion on my face because she said, "Those are people who either want an apprenticeship, have taken themselves off the market, or who have died."

"Why would someone take themselves off the market?" I asked.

"Medical problems. Too long without work. They got in trouble with the law." Sawyer shrugged. "Lots of reasons."

"Does that mean they're actually free?"

"They're not *slaves*. And if they're alive, it means there will probably be a problem with recruiting them straight away, but I suppose you could always talk to them."

Fantastic. Now I was bargain hunting for officers. Then again, I needed bodies more than anything else. I could train up people or fire the ones incapable of improving.

I stopped scrolling the instant I recognized a name. *Cai Qi*. It was short and distinct enough that it clicked in my memory. He had been on Capital Station on more than one occasion, each time on the trail of some high-profile criminal. No one in my gang had wanted anything to do with him—he was a bounty hunter extraordinaire. And that sounded right in line for my new crew.

"Is this guy dead?" I asked.

Sawyer poked his profile. "No."

"Then why is he listed for zero credits?"

"I don't know. It doesn't say."

"Find him for me," I said. "We'll hire this guy to be our ground commander." And if we went after a bunch of bounty assignments, I could get my money's worth out of him.

"Cai Qi, huh?" Sawyer asked. "I remember reading about him."

"Even *you've* heard of him?"

"It's odd a bounty hunter like him would be looking to join an enforcer starship," she said. "He worked freelance before, hunting individuals. I guess we'll find out why soon enough."

Blub floated into Sawyer's lap, his fins and mouth moving slower than before. The little fish was tuckered out, and he rolled onto his side when Sawyer went to pet him. I patted my own stomach and cocked an eyebrow.

"You could always pat *me*, Sawyer. You wouldn't even need to get undressed. I could lie back, give you all the access you want…"

"So generous," Sawyer said, her tone dry. "I'll keep it in mind." She stood, Blub in her arms. "But I need to find Cai Qi. Maybe some other time."

FIVE

Cai Qi

"Cai Qi must've made a lot of money if he once had a home planetside," Noah said.

I shrugged. "He rented. It's not the same as owning property."

"Still impressive. My father was a commodore for the Federation Navy HSN Corps, and he never rented property planetside."

"I bet you and Lysander lived in a posh station home," I said with a forced laugh. All the military guys did. Unlike on planets, the living quarters on a space station were cramped—unless you had connections. Then it was like having a mansion in space.

Noah walked next to me, his plasma rifle held loose in his hands. The narrow corridors of Trinity Station kept him close. Although he was younger than Lysander, I swear he stood a few centimeters taller. Maybe he had grown. I didn't remember him always being taller.

"I grew up comfortable," Noah said. "But I'd give that all up to have the genetic modifications you have."

"Oh, yeah?"

"Definitely. No doubt in my mind."

He said it so full of confidence, I almost laughed. But then I remembered—he was a defect. The membranes inside his body deteriorated under physical stress. That must've bothered Noah's father. I had never met the man, yet I could already tell. The HSN Corps had the worst anti-defect sentiment in the whole galaxy. They were the *Homo Sapiens Corps*, after all. They wanted perfect humans, free of abnormality, to stand side-by-side with superhumans. If Noah and Lysander had a father deep in HSN ranks, he no doubt had the same mentality.

"So, where does Cai Qi live now?" Noah asked.

"Sawyer said he's at a port stop."

Port stops were basically taverns on space stations. They were tiny tin cans packed together near the starship ports, most of which doubled as brothels. Not the kind of place someone made their residence.

Noah faced me with a raised eyebrow. "Did you ever live in a port stop?"

"Of course not," I snapped. "I may've been some thug on Capital Station, but that doesn't mean I was scum. I always had enough credits or friends for proper sleeping quarters."

"So, port stops aren't proper? Like, people aren't supposed to live there?"

"Not unless you're a whore."

"Cai Qi is a legit bounty hunter, right?" Noah frowned. "There's no chance he switched careers?"

I didn't answer. Sawyer hadn't found much information on Cai Qi. All she knew was he had once lived planetside, but five months ago he had lost his home and taken up residence on Trinity Station, the space port connected to Vectin-10 through a space elevator. His address had switched to a port stop. That was the same time his payment on the employment registry had gone to zero. Had something happened? But a man as talented as Cai Qi shouldn't have had a problem for long. Five months living in a port stop was the equivalent of giving up on life and sleeping in a dumpster.

Why not just get another job?

As Noah and I approached the address of the port stop, the corridors of the space station got narrower. And grimier. The denizens were chem addicts, the food from the hot plates would barely pass for edible, and the whole area smelled of rotting meat, no doubt from the shoddy cybernetics that were decaying inside the cyborgs we passed.

No one bothered trying to stop and sell us anything, probably because Noah and I wore enforcer enviro-suits. If we had been wearing casual clothing, we would've been bombarded with all sorts of bullshit—anything from knockoff PADs to blowjobs.

The port stop we wanted, amusingly named *The Last Stop*, had a red sign mounted to the bulkhead of Trinity Station. Noah motioned to the arrow, and we followed it to the entrance—a shitty door with a heavy lock and an ancient computer terminal.

Noah stuck close, never lowering his weapon, like we might get into a firefight at any second. He even tapped his fingers along the side of the grip, his whole demeanor jittery.

"Relax," I said. "You're making *me* nervous."

"My brother says this is the kind of place where your organs get stolen." His voice sounded more robotic when filtered by the helmet of his suit, but still shaky.

"No one is going to jump a pair of enforcers for their organs. Get your shit together."

"What makes you so positive?"

"Because *I* wouldn't have stolen organs from enforcers," I said with a chuckle. "If I needed a liver or a kidney, I would've gone after some runaway teen, passed-out drunk, or cracked-out-of-his-mind chem addict. They're a lot less trouble to get, and not many people will come investigating afterward, if any."

I tapped the control panel for *The Last Stop* and the door opened, but it took a good five seconds, and the hinges groaned the entire time, like an old man trying to get up in the morning.

I stepped inside and came face-to-face with a counter covered by a mesh wire barrier. Some fat cyborg with a tiny mustache sat behind the wire. He had a pipe between his lips, which explained the smoke hanging in the air. The whole place smelled of oil and burnt meat, but that didn't bother me.

"Can I help you, enforcer?" the cyborg asked. He had a rasp to his voice that lowered his tone by a few degrees.

"I'm here to see Cai Qi," I said as I stepped into the place. "Should be in Room 27, if my records are correct."

"Cai doesn't have any warrants for his arrest."

"I didn't say I was here to arrest him, *Tin Can*. I'm here to hire him."

The man sucked on his pipe for a moment. His cybernetics were centered around his collar and chest, giving him an even bulkier silhouette than his fat. His arms, tattooed from the elbow to his neck, had a visible bit of muscle, and it made me wonder if he used to be in good shape, but then had some operation that had rendered him sedentary.

"Let me scan your ID chip," the cyborg said, holding the pipe with his lips while he spoke.

I slid my arm under the grate barrier. The counter, while seemingly innocuous, lit up as it scanned the area between my ulna and radius. A screen mounted on the wall brightened with my information, including my title.

The cyborg stroked his blond mustache. "Captain, huh?" He poked at the counter, as if typing on an invisible keyboard, and another screen came on next to me. It highlighted the communication system for Room 27. "Cai," the cyborg said. "You awake?"

Several seconds passed with no response.

Then a crackle sounded through the building's comms. "What is it?" someone responded with a weak voice.

"An enforcer captain is here to hire you."

A single laugh sounded over the comms. "No captain is looking for me."

"I checked his ID," the cyborg said. "It seems real."

"Those can be faked, old man. How many times do I have to tell you that?"

"It says he's the captain of the *Star Marque*, though. You think someone would be ballsy enough to fake that position?"

"The *Star Marque*?" Cai asked. "The one on the news?"

On the news? I almost cut in to ask about the fame, but I held back. It no doubt had to do with Endellion, and I didn't want to talk about her right now.

The cyborg let out a puff of smoke and shrugged. "They look the part, Cai. Fancy enviro-suits. Kat-Tec Rapid-Shot plasma rifles. Want me to send them up?"

"No," Cai responded. "We can talk through the comms."

"This is a private matter of employment," I said.

"Jack can be privy to the discussion," Cai said with a cough.

"I'd prefer if we spoke in person."

"I'd prefer people to leave me the fuck alone, but it looks like neither of us will get what we want."

Noah scoffed. "Seriously?" he whispered. "What a jackass."

I leaned against the wire mesh barrier, slightly amused by this guy's lack of giving a damn. He wouldn't get along with Lysander, which was a strike against him, but if his price was right, maybe Lysander could be brought around.

"I'm Captain Clevon Demarco of the enforcer ship, the *Star Marque*," I said.

"So I heard," Cai replied, his voice an odd mix of breathless and distant.

"I'm looking for a ground commander. I saw your name on the list of potential hires and I thought you'd make a good fit."

"Why's that?" Cai asked.

"You're a bounty hunter, right? I intend on hunting down some known fugitives. Plus, I remembered your reputation from my time on Capital Station. All the thugs used to be afraid of seeing your name after them."

"That's it?"

"Well, you're cheaper than some of the other fuckers I could hire. We have to balance the books."

Cai laughed over the comms, but stopped after a couple of seconds when he started coughing up a storm. Once calm, he said, "Forget it. I don't have time for cheapskates."

"You don't have time, period," Jack the Tin Can Cyborg said. He inhaled on his pipe, blew out a long line of smoke, and shook his head. "You can't afford to be picky."

"You gonna kick me out?" Cai asked.

"Ya know I won't. But I'll have your corpse removed in one of those stink-proof bags once you're done rottin'. Maybe hear these enforcers out."

"I have it under control, Jack."

"You don't want work?" I asked.

"Not from you. Get out."

Noah turned to me, his helmet nothing more than a one-way mirror that reflected my own confused expression. The moment I started thinking about Cai's situation, I had a few theories.

"You have some sort of chem addiction or something?" I asked.

"What the fuck did I just say?" Cai growled. "We don't have anything else to talk about."

"Or maybe you got the wrong cybernetics?" I continued. "Those can really mess a guy up. And paying someone to fix a mistake can cost twice—no, *three times*—as much as the original surgery."

No one said anything, and I knew I had hit close to the truth. Cai was likely having debt problems brought about by some sort of medical condition. And that was one of the worst places to be on a space station. Good doctors were hard to come by, and if you didn't have credits, it was impossible to get anything done. Sure, Cai could go to one of the free clinics, but they were more likely to steal functioning cybernetics and organs and then replace them with junk rather than give actual service.

"Let me guess," I said. "You've been out of commission because your last operation didn't go so well. You probably tried to do some jobs to make some credits, but your condition is worse than you're letting on. Those piece of shit cybernetic parts really take a toll on your stamina. And you probably lost the rest of your money fighting the new planetside laws. Or maybe you blew it on chem and hookers."

"He's real bad at dice," Jack said with half a smile.

"Stay out of this," Cai snapped.

I chuckled. "I think you're overwhelmed and you're lying low."

"I'm not overwhelmed."

"You sure?"

"Well, perhaps *maximum whelmed*," Cai quipped. "But I'll get through this." He moved around on his side of the comms, causing a bit of white noise. "And it's not what you're thinking. Not entirely. I was huntin' down some rebellion fugitives, and one got a clean shot on my hip. I went to have surgery—with a trusted guy—but the parts he used didn't settle right. I didn't know that until after they had taken their toll."

"After you had already lost a ton to Briggsy and his crew," Jack chimed in. "And after you paid off those other hunters who were lookin' to take you in for evadin' taxes."

"Rough," I said. "Your life sounds more like *regret management* than *goal achievement*."

Cai snorted. "You can hike your happy ass out of here. I already gave you an answer."

"Do we even want him?" Noah asked. Then he pointed toward the front door. "There are other people we could hire. More competent, too."

No. I knew Cai Qi. He had caught tons of thugs and scum from all over the quadrant, including guys who jumped between space stations. He was plenty competent, even if this situation was dire. It reminded me of what Sawyer had said. I didn't need to bring people to their lowest point, I just had to scoop them up when I had the opportunity.

"You've heard the reputation the *Star Marque* has?" I asked.

The fat cyborg lifted an eyebrow.

Cai replied with, "Of course."

"I have a doctor from Vectin-14 on my ship. He specializes in all sorts of cybernetic parts, including the good ones the superhumans use on themselves."

No one said a thing, but I knew they were all putting the pieces of the puzzle together. This was how Endellion would have sold it— she would show people the thing they wanted, and then offer them the route to obtain it. People liked routes. They liked having hoops and guidelines.

Most people were sheep, and they wanted a pat on the back whenever they did something right.

Even *I* had fallen for it back in the day. Endellion had offered me a way to a planet, and a way to turn my life around, and then she had told me exactly what I had to do to get it.

"Join my crew," I said. "You agree to work for me for three years, and I'll have my doctor fix you up with the best parts we can get our hands on."

Noah fidgeted with his weapon, but he didn't offer any input. He didn't like Cai, but that didn't matter. They wouldn't be working together much.

Jack blew out a long line of his foul smoke. "Cai, you're not gonna get a better offer than that."

"Two years," Cai said.

I smiled. "Two and a half. You'll be getting room and board on the *Star Marque*, after all. I need to get my money's worth."

"Fine. You have a deal. I'll be your damn ground commander."

***

"WHAT CONDITION IS HE IN?" Dr. Clay asked.

I shrugged. I hadn't actually seen Cai yet. I had left Noah to help him pack and then returned to the *Star Marque* to get everything ready. Couldn't have been that bad.

The entire infirmary staff prepped for surgery. We didn't have much medical staff—eight people—but that was enough to handle one operation. And I had the funds to purchase medicine or cybernetics for Cai, so this would ultimately work out in my favor, but I was still nervous. If Dr. Clay fucked this up, and Cai died, I would be out a lot of credits in medical supplies.

The *Star Marque* had a healing vat, and if Cai had gotten in one before allowing his injury to fester, this whole problem would've been much easier. However, the mother-cell fluid of the healing vats only sped up metabolism to ensure a quick recovery. If someone was scarred or the wound had become infected and then healed, the vats wouldn't be helpful.

And they didn't help defects at all. I doubted Cai was one, but I didn't technically know.

The door to the infirmary opened. Noah walked in with a man hanging heavily on his shoulder.

Cai Qi—sweating from every visible pore on his body—held Noah like he would collapse if he let go for even a second. He wore a pair of cargo pants and a tight-fitting shirt, both of which were soaked with perspiration. Bandages around his gut poked out from under his shirt, the gauze yellowed and soggy. His black hair, scruffy beard, and bushy eyebrows were matted and crusty.

If Cai had said he had just escaped the morgue, I would've believed him. Although I suspected he normally had a honeyed complexion, all color had gone the way of his lunch.

Still, through all of that, he held himself mostly upright. He had muscle, and there was a **PAD** mounted to his right forearm. He also carried a plasma pistol on his belt, but I doubted he could shoot straight in his condition.

"You must be Mr. Cai," Dr. Clay said, not a hint of surprise or emotion in his voice. "I'm Dr. Clay. Please lie here, and I'll examine you."

Cai let out a long exhale as Noah helped him to the operating table. Although I wasn't needed for any of this, I stayed out of curiosity. Was Cai going to be okay? He climbed onto the table like every movement, even each breath, caused him a fair deal of pain. Once he rested back, he relaxed, but not much.

Dr. Clay used the table's computer interface to start a scan of Cai's body. It took a few moments, but then gave a readout of Cai's entire physical structure.

"Subject has a comminuted fracture of his left ilium, two nonfunctioning bone-mounted cybernetics, and a severe nostra bacterial infection. Abnormalities found in the bloodstream. Further diagnosis is required."

"We're going to remove your clothes," Dr. Clay said as he tapped away at the **PAD** mounted to his arm.

The nurses in the room gathered tools and materials. I stepped back, as did Noah, and allowed them to set up a small table next to the doctor. They pulled out a pair of scissors, and Cai grabbed the arm of the nurse, his grip tight.

"Don't touch me," he hissed.

"I need to examine you," Dr. Clay said, in the exact same monotone he had spoken in before. "Please remain calm."

"The fucking table said what was wrong with me."

"The *fucking table* doesn't have a medical degree, Mr. Cai. Don't make me sedate you."

"Damn you," Cai said through gritted teeth. "I don't want these scissors to touch me, not even for a second."

"We will give you something for the pain."

A nurse injected Cai in the shoulder before he had a second to react. He took in two breaths, and already, he rested easier. The first nurse cut at his shirt, then through his belt, then his pants, and finally through the bandages. A moment later, parts of Cai spilled out onto the table.

Cai's skin had split open like ripped seams on a pair of pants. Bits of bone poked through the carnage, like his hip had exploded.

Dr. Clay took a scalpel and jabbed at a giant red bubble of flesh. A chunky white substance oozed from the injury, like someone had hidden a tub of cottage cheese inside Cai's wound.

I almost gagged at the smell of rancid milk. I took a step back.

What the fuck was that?

"How is it?" Cai asked, his gaze glued to the ceiling, his words strained. "Give it to me straight."

"I've seen worse," Dr. Clay said as he poked at his PAD. "Everything will be fine."

"Even with… a severe infection?"

"I had feared you would have something untreatable. As it is, this will be a routine procedure. We're going to put you under."

A nurse moved in to administer the sedative, but Cai stiffened as though he would throw a punch, even in his weakened state. Would I need to hold him down? I had done it before—I could do it again.

"N-No," Cai said. "I don't want to go under. The doctors on the station said that bacterial infection w-would kill guys who went under. I want to remain awake."

Dr. Clay shook his head. "Those doctors are butchers compared to me. When I say you need to go under, that's the only opinion you need. And when you wake, the worst of it will have passed. Do you understand?"

His words, though lacking in any emotion, did seem to reassure Cai. The man closed his mouth and his eyes as the nurses went about their work. Within a handful of seconds, Cai fell unconscious.

"Clean this up," Dr. Clay said as he motioned to the mess on the table. "In five minutes, I'll adjust the cybernetics and then piece together his hip. After that, we can place him in the healing vat for post-op recovery." He took a step away from the table and continued to work on his PAD.

Noah let out a loud sigh of relief. "Wow. You've really seen worse than that, doctor?"

Dr. Clay didn't even look up when he shrugged. "Sure. Several times. On dead bodies."

Both Noah and I caught our breath.

I turned to the doctor, my eyebrows at my hairline. "Wait. Is Cai going to be okay?"

"I sure hope so," Dr. Clay drawled. "We'll see, though. He was on the verge of death. A few more hours and he would've passed out, no doubt in my mind."

"But… you made it sound like this was a normal problem."

"I was lying." Dr. Clay stopped his work and glared at me. "Did you see the way that man panicked at the slightest thought of operation? What he needed was someone to reassure him everything would be okay. I was that someone."

"What about going under?" Noah asked. "He said it would kill him."

"Our medication is better than what they have on Trinity Station. I wasn't lying about that. But it will be a miracle if he lives." Dr. Clay returned to his PAD. "Good thing for you, I'm a miracle-class doctor."

Heh.

Damn. Dr. Clay had one hell of a poker face. I'd had no idea he had been lying about Cai's chances on the table. I had thought he had it all under control. Actually, I would have preferred not to know the truth.

"Demarco," Sawyer said over the ship's comms.

"Yeah?" I asked.

"We have two urgent matters. First, an assignment came in to apprehend a rebellion starship. They're paying five times the normal rate."

"Let's take it," I said.

"Second," Sawyer continued. "Someone is here to search the *Star Marque*."

"Search it? Why?"

"They think a criminal is hiding aboard."

"We're not harboring any criminals."

"I told them that, but… We're not going to be able to tell her no. It's a superhuman. And she has a warrant."

SIX

Victtra Barten

"**A** *superhuman* is here to search the ship?" Dr. Clay said. He stopped typing on his PAD, his hand shaky. "What have you done?"

"I haven't done anything," I snapped. "Just focus on the surgery. I'll handle the damn superhuman."

My pulse quickened and my thoughts raced as I stepped out of the infirmary. The others watched me as I went, their eyes wide.

Superhumans didn't lower themselves to such menial levels. They didn't *physically investigate* things or sully their perfect hands with jobs that were classified as grunt work. So why would a superhuman come to the *Star Marque*? I couldn't think of a logical reason. My theories all revolved around Endellion sending someone to fuck with us, but she would never chance the crimes of the *Star Marque* going public. That wouldn't benefit her—so why was this happening?

I jogged down the corridor, my chest tight. I had told Sawyer we weren't harboring a criminal, but we both knew that wasn't true. We had helped Endellion kill millions, even if it had been unwittingly. The whole crew of the *Star Marque*, right down to the goddamn janitor, could be indicted for mass murder. *We* were the criminals.

I wiped sweat from my temple as I stepped onto the lift.

No one knew about what we had done to Capital Station. Except Endellion.

Was this warrant her doing? Had she sent people after me so I could be her scapegoat?

When the lift opened, Lysander stood on the other side. He gave me a formal nod and then motioned to the exit hatch. I took a moment to control my breathing before heading toward the exit. We went through decontamination, and then the exit lift lowered from the ship with a smooth *swish*.

I had expected a huge crowd. Superhumans didn't walk around without their manservants and entourage, or whatever they called them. To my surprise, there were only three people waiting on the dock outside the *Star Marque*.

I held my breath the moment I spotted the superhuman.

She was… a little girl.

Well, a preteen. Maybe. I didn't know superhuman ages very well. I knew they weren't human, and I knew they progressed through life differently since they lived much longer, so I didn't have much to base her age on other than normal human standards.

Still, what was this? Baby's First Private Investigation?

The superhuman pushed back her long, silver hair and stared at me with gray eyes—her expression so hard-set, it bordered on an accusing glower. Despite her youthful appearance, she still stood tall, similar to most superhumans, perhaps one and a half meters. All superhumans stood out like blood on white linen, their posture perfect, their skin two-tone, and their hair metallic in sheen.

The two humans next to her, some burly guys with their enviro-suits fully up and plasma rifles held in their hands, didn't have the same kind of commanding presence as the girl's elegance and composure.

I gave one of her bodyguards a quick reverse-nod. "Did you lose the girl's adult?"

"You will address *me* from now on," the superhuman said with a snap of her fingers, drawing my attention back to her. "I'm the one in charge. Not them."

The superhuman girl tapped on the collarbone of her own enviro-suit. Unlike the two men's, her suit had black scales, reminiscent of a fish, and they shimmered with an inner technology I wasn't familiar with. Her helmet hung loosely between her shoulder blades, like a hood, but the rest of it hugged her athletic frame.

Knowing a kid was in charge erased my building anxiety. I exhaled and offered her a smile.

"All right," I said. "What can I do for the girl in charge?"

"Are you Captain Demarco?" she asked, no pleasantries in her voice.

"That's right." I motioned to Lysander. "This is my vice-captain."

"Vice-Captain Jevons," Lysander said.

The girl gave me the once-over. "My name is Victtra Barten. I have a search warrant issued by the Vectin Ministry's Office to search the *Star Marque* for potential clues in a homicide investigation. I've provided your chief cyber operations officer all relevant information."

She spoke like she was a 30-year-old wearing the skin-suit of a child. And her sentences had the hard bite of someone irritated by the information they had delivered. Or perhaps pained.

"Okay," I muttered.

Superhumans were smart—too fuckin' smart—even at a young age. They could perform complicated tasks even as toddlers, and it wasn't unheard of for superhumans to handle investigations for complicated cases, even if it was their first day on the job.

Still, it was laughable that a pre-teen would be the one called in for a homicide investigation. Was it too tough for the local human authorities?

Lysander shot me a disappointed look before clearing his throat. "The crew of the *Star Marque* will do everything we can to aid you in this search. Can you tell us the name of the victim? And why you think the *Star Marque* would be involved in this tragedy?"

"The victim was my father," Victtra said. "Emissary Kayllin Barten."

"A superhuman?"

"Indeed."

Wait. *Emissary Barten?*

My heart stopped as panic set in. Half a second later, I recalled all the terrible details. *I* had killed Emissary Barten. In cold blood. We'd had no personal connection—his only crime had been standing in the way of Endellion's ambition. She had ordered me to kill him, and I had.

But…

There was a little girl who had seen me do it. I had been wearing a rebellion enviro-suit, but she had still *seen.* Instead of killing her—and removing all possibility of a witness—I'd rendered her unconscious and left. I had never thought a *child* would hunt me down with a search warrant. I figured she would've been traumatized or given to some relatives to recover. That was what humans would've done—long years of therapy. Superhumans, on the other hand, obviously didn't have time for any of that weak bullshit.

I stared at the superhuman, my hearing momentarily dulled as reality invaded my thoughts.

She had come to find *me.*

This wasn't a random investigation—this pre-teen had taken it upon herself to investigate her own father's murder. And being a superhuman, she could do whatever she damn well pleased.

"Investigators and bounty hunters alike have helped me piece together a series of complex contextual clues," Victtra said. "I believe the *Star Marque* may have been involved in the escape of the murderer. All my reasoning, and authority, can be found in the warrant I provided."

"Captain?" Lysander asked, dragging me from my thoughts. "Do you have anything to add?"

"No," I replied. "Let her on the ship."

There weren't any clues to my involvement. Not on the *Star Marque.* Endellion and I had taken rebellion starfighters to meet Emissary Barten. We had killed him on Outpost Station. Nothing linked me to his death. *Nothing.*

"Thank you for your cooperation, Captain," Victtra said.

"You're already shaping up to be a better host than the last starship captain I visited."

She held her head high as she walked onto the entrance lift. Her silver hair, glittering in the artificial light of the space port, flowed behind her as she walked. Her two-toned skin, going from dark on the back of her neck, and wrapping around to be light on her face, glowed with a healthy sheen. Little black dots—holes, actually—lined her face on the side, near the ear and neck.

Her two thug bodyguards followed closely behind, their mirror-visors hiding their expressions. Lysander and I joined them as we returned to the *Star Marque*. And while I was certain she wouldn't find anything incriminating, anxiety wouldn't leave me.

If Victtra found anything, I'd be put down like a rabid dog. A human who had killed a superhuman wouldn't be allowed the luxury of a prison planet, especially when that superhuman had been a prominent emissary.

The moment we entered the main corridor, I motioned to our surroundings. "My vice-captain will show you around. I have other things to deal with."

"Can I see the starfighters?" Victtra asked.

"Vice-Captain Jevons will handle it."

"Miss Barten," Lysander said as he stepped between us. "I can show you each starfighter individually. Why don't you follow me?"

When she offered no protest, I took off toward Sawyer's work-room. Technically, none of the crew even knew what I had done, so questioning them wouldn't yield anything. The only two people aware of the assassination were Endellion and Sawyer.

The instant I stepped onto the lift, I said, "Sawyer, is there any way she'll find something?"

Sawyer's lack of immediate response added to my dread. Although death worried me, it wasn't as bad as imagining Endellion getting away with everything. If I died, no one would go after her. That thought alone transformed my worry into rage. I wouldn't allow her to get away with anything else. I wouldn't.

"I don't think she'll find anything," Sawyer murmured, as though deep in thought. "But then again, I would have said we left no trace of our involvement at Outpost Station. The fact that Victtra Barten is here says I might've overlooked something."

"Maybe she's desperate," I said as the lift doors opened to Deck One. "The *Star Marque* wasn't far from Outpost Station. Far enough for an escape, but we still could've been in someone's scanner range, which would've put us on a list of places to snoop around. Plus, she mentioned another starship investigation."

"You may be right. Emissary Barten was killed over eighteen months ago. Given the girl is traveling light, this could indicate that she's lost support for a continued investigation. Still, you should be cautious. Her search warrant was authorized by Minister Ontwenty."

Tsk. The second person I hated hearing anything about. Minister Ontwenty might as well have been Endellion's handler. That superhuman bitch had betrayed us and forced Endellion into a tight spot.

Ontwenty was the one who had approved the search of the *Star Marque*? I wondered if she wanted us gone for her own reasons.

I walked into Sawyer's workroom without knocking. She sat at her desk, no boots on, her legs crossed in front of her, her eyes glued to the screens mounted to the bulkhead. "Hello, Demarco," she muttered as she typed away. The ship's computer code—which was nothing more than thousands of lines of gibberish—slowly scrolled down the screens.

"How can you be so calm?" I asked.

Blub let out a *toot, toot,* as he floated down to greet me. I let him nibble on my hair as I took my position behind Sawyer's chair.

"Nothing has happened yet," she said. "Besides, I'm more worried about this rebellion ship we're supposed to go after."

I had forgotten she had mentioned that. "You don't think we can handle some rebellion fighters?"

"It's not that. The bounty for the starship's capture is so high that I doubt we'll be the ones claiming the prize."

"What the fuck are we waiting for? The *Star Marque* is plenty capable of getting there first."

That was the whole point of a vanguard-class ship. Our speed should have been unrivaled by other starships of similar size.

"We have a superhuman aboard," Sawyer said. She spun her chair sideways to give me an odd stare. "She could take hours with her investigation, and we can't even start tracking our target ship until we get to the sector of space where we can look for a plasma trail."

Goddammit.

"Contact Lysander when he has a moment alone," I said. "Tell him to get the girl off the ship. She can search it when we get back."

Sawyer ran a hand through her disheveled red hair. "Are you sure you want to do that? She might get pissy."

"Who cares? She's, what, an eight-years-old? She can order her guards to change her diaper while we're gone."

BEFORE SUPERHUMANS HAD BEEN CREATED, the United-Earth Government had run all four massive quadrants that made up the Cygnus Sector. Their mismanagement had led to in-fighting and wars, and more defects and cyborgs than ever before. Once super-humans had gotten their hooks in power, they had straightened things out, but in the most tyrannical of ways. The United-Earth Government had been dissolved, and the Federation had formed to take its place. The biggest difference: only superhumans could rule.

The *rebellion* was just the leftover United-Earth faction—they were Homo sapiens who disagreed with the reworked Federation constitution and argued against superhumans' control. I didn't hate the rebellion, but they had tried to kill me enough times that I didn't think well of them.

And now we had to run down a corvette-class starship under the rebellion's control.

I poked away at the computer terminal in our deserted Central Data Room. All the information I could ever want was stored in our files, and I brought up the system schematics for corvette-class starships.

The bounty for capturing our target was outrageous. The bounty for destroying it… not so much. Apparently, the passengers on the starship were more important. We needed the rebellion officers alive. Which meant we needed to incapacitate the starship if we wanted the payout. Once I had a plan, I could send it to the other starfighters, and we could practice in our simulation pods.

Sawyer said it would take us eighteen hours to reach the section of space where the starship had last been seen. It wasn't much time, but enough to get some solid formation training in.

While sifting through the information, my thoughts drifted. For a distraction, I tapped on the ship's comms and sent them through to the infirmary.

"Dr. Clay," I said.

"Yes, Captain?" he replied, somehow sarcastic, even though we hadn't said much to each other.

"How's Cai?"

"He's been placed in the healing vat. The recommended amount of rest is eleven hours, but I set the machine for thirteen. After that, I suggest he get eight to ten hours of sleep. If all goes well, he should be back to 100%."

"There weren't any complications?" I asked. I couldn't get the image of Cai's ruptured hip out of my mind. The guy had looked like *man stew*.

"Oh, there were plenty of complications."

He offered nothing else.

"Thanks," I said. "For making sure he lived."

No response. I switched away the comms, almost irritated I had reached out. Sure, I had gotten the answer I wanted, but Dr. Clay had all the lovability of a smelly corpse. At least Sawyer would joke with me, even when making official reports.

I pushed away from the computer terminal, anxious and hungry. When I opened the door to head for the mess hall, I flinched back. Lysander stood by the door's computer terminal, poised to open it himself. Next to him—to my shock and irritation—was none other than that superhuman girl and her two bodyguards.

"What—" I began.

"Hello, Captain," Lysander said. He motioned to the girl. "If you don't mind, I'll be showing our guest to the central database."

Victtra greeted me with a slight bow of her head. "How are you, Captain Demarco? You seem surprised."

"Don't worry about me," I said. "I'm sure you have a lot on your mind."

"Yes. I do. If you don't mind, I'd like to take a look at your travel logs."

I motioned to the Central Data Room. "By all means. I hope you find your answers."

Most people never picked up on my insincerity when I wanted to lie to them. A part of my genetic modification involved heightened pheromones—chemicals produced by my sweat pores that affected the behavior of others around me. It was a slight influence, but it usually got people to be more trusting, or attracted to me.

The way Victtra looked at me, however… It was like she already knew my terrible secret, and my simple lie had irritated her. The expression faded in half a second, though. Perhaps I was paranoid and seeing things.

"Thank you," she said.

Victtra and her stooges walked past, not a word between them. I allowed them by, but when Lysander went to follow, I grabbed him by the upper arm and shoved him into the hall. Then I closed the door to the Central Data Room, separating us from the superhuman.

"What the fuck is your problem?" I asked. "I thought you were the guy who gave me a lecture about *insubordination* or some bullshit. Isn't defying my *direct order* against your military programing?"

Lysander jerked his arm from my grip. With a sneer, he said, "You obviously didn't read the supplemental information she provided with her warrant. If I had kicked her off the *Star Marque,* she could've gotten an arrest warrant—and then we wouldn't be working at all, now would we?"

I opened my mouth to offer a retort, but I opted to remain silent.

"I tried to contact you," Lysander said through clenched teeth. "But apparently you had my comms blocked."

Oh. Right. I had forgotten. That was from the day he had kept making a series of gripes straight to my personal comm. I still hadn't enabled him to speak directly to me.

Lysander exhaled. "Fortunately, Miss Barten said she could conduct her investigation while we flew to our destination."

"We'll be entering combat," I said. "You told her that, right?"

"When I told her we would be apprehending a rebellion starship, she practically jumped at the idea of watching us work. We have passenger quarters, you know. Endellion would often take individuals from one station to the other while performing her duties as an enforcer."

"Oh, yeah?"

Lysander shook his head. "Really? *That* surprises you?"

"Listen. I don't care. Just keep an eye on the superhuman. I'm sure we'll also get in a lot of trouble if she's hurt." I rubbed at the back of my neck and then stared at the ceiling. "And don't ever be alone with her. Got it? No one on the *Star Marque* should ever be alone in the same room with her."

"Is everything okay?" Lysander asked.

"Yes."

Then he stepped closer and lowered his voice. "We didn't have anything to do with Emissary Barten's death. Right?"

"Of course not, Sanders," I said with a smile. "What makes you think we would ever be involved in shady activity like that?"

The question lingered between us. Lysander didn't answer. If anything, he grew tense as he stepped back. What did he want me to say? I sure as fuck wasn't going to tell him what had happened. He didn't want to hear it, and I didn't want to relive it.

This was better forgotten.

SEVEN

Starfighters

I paced the training room as I waited for the other starfighters to arrive.

Apprehending a rebellion starship would require us to engage in combat. There was no way around it. The superhuman had me distracted, but once I had a few practice sessions under my belt, everything would be fine. Our simulation pods cut the pilot off from the world, creating a lifelike environment. Once inside, I knew I'd be able to focus.

The training room door slid open. Noah and Mara walked in, each in casual clothing—cargo pants, sleeveless shirts, and lace-up boots. Mara moved with energy in her step, a smile on her heart-shaped face. When she spoke, her words had a lighthearted edge, a hint of her old, medicated self.

"And then we stopped at this place at the base of the space elevator," she said. "It had all sorts of drinks I had never even heard of. We must've tried thirteen types. Planet booze is just better than the stuff they give us on the stations."

Noah shrugged. "My brother doesn't like drinking outside of the ship."

"Why have you been spending so much time with Lysander lately?"

"I'm the *temporary starfighter commander*." Noah brushed himself off as he opened the door to his simulation pod. "I have to make a good impression. That's what—" He cut himself off the moment he noticed me. "Demarco. You're here already?"

Mara glanced over, her eyebrows knit. "Captain, are you okay?"

"I'm fine," I said. "I've just been… reviewing tactics."

"Is the rebellion ship we're after that dangerous?"

"Nah. I just don't want to mess this up."

"Oh."

Noah and Mara exchanged quick looks. They hurried to their pods and climbed in. The inside of each pod was nothing more than a seat, and once each of them got in, the sides of the pods tightened on their bodies and legs, limiting the blood flow to the lower extremities. It was a safety precaution since the G-forces of starfighter combat put stress on a pilot's heart and circulation.

I rotated my shoulders, but anxiety burned my muscles.

If I managed to get this ship, I could hire more ground enforcers. If we didn't capture the ship, it wouldn't wreck us, but our progress would be delayed. One setback could cost us time I didn't want to waste. I *couldn't* waste.

The training room door slid open again. Melba, Hattie, and Asahi entered, none of them speaking. They stopped and regarded me with slight nods. Then they walked to their pods, troubled expressions on their faces.

Hattie, the youngest, was so thin, she could be half-human, half-curtain rod. Even her hair, straight and thin, hung limply, adding to her narrow silhouette. Asahi, the man of their group, kept his black hair slicked back, highlighting his clear gaze. He examined everything, missing no details. He was the first to notice me, and I understood why he made for such a talented starfighter.

Melba was the oldest, perhaps in her late forties, and she waited until the other two got into their pods before she opened the hatch of her own.

"Captain Demarco," she said. "It's a pleasure to have you training with us."

Melba had a plainness to her—drab brown hair that matched her khaki jumpsuit. If I didn't already know she was skilled, I would have mistaken her for some everyday food cart schlub.

"We need to be prepared," I said. "We'll be in combat in a few hours."

"Yes, Captain."

Melba slid into her pod and closed the hatch with a soft *swish*.

That was it. The last of my starfighters. Not the best group I had ever seen, but that was what I had to work with. If I lost any of them in combat, my fighting force would be devastated. Six fighters was hardly anything.

This would be the first combat where I took lead. The first time since Endellion had left—since Lee and Quinn had left. And Quinn had been the damn starfighter commander. She had known everything about our ship and tactics, and here I was trying to piece it together.

"Get a fucking grip," I muttered to myself.

It wasn't a complicated battle. One corvette-class starship couldn't have more than ten starfighters aboard. I could handle that myself, yet here I was, fretting like a child.

"Demarco," Sawyer said over the ship's comms. "Your starfighters are starting to ask about you."

"Tell them to buckle their damn seat belts and wait."

"It isn't like you to hesitate."

"Yeah, well, I have a lot on my mind." I paced the room once and then stopped in front of my simulation pod. The black duralumin exterior shone under the lights. "How close are we?"

"We'll be in the last known area within fourteen hours. After that, I'm not sure how long it'll take."

With a deep inhale, I opened my simulation pod and slid inside. The hatch closed, blanketing me in absolute darkness. The sides squeezed me tight and gripped my legs from the knee down, locking me in place. I grabbed the two side-sticks as the lights flickered to life. The view screen pulsed and showed me the virtual space we'd be practicing in.

An inky void surrounded me on all sides. The sparkle of distant stars didn't diminish my hatred of space. If anything, those stars were the flickering lights of bug traps, meant to lure life out into the unforgiving vacuum. Nothing unnerved me like the thought of dying outside a starship. You couldn't fight your way out of a black hole or train for a situation where you were floating through the unimaginable chill of a planet's shadow.

I shook my head and went through a round of controlled breaths. The fear of dying out in space wouldn't stop me.

The others were already accelerating through obstacles and using their hyperweapons. Unlike in real combat, where the number of hyperweapons was limited to the number of plasma carriages a single starfighter could carry, the simulation allowed for unlimited shots. We could switch the program to a more realistic setting, but I suspected the others wanted to get a handle on the devastation brought about by a single shot.

Sure enough, Mara launched one of her hyperweapons at a single asteroid. The superheated plasma lit up the area with the intensity of the sun. Starfighters had shielded tinting over the clear duralumin windows, but I still had to squint every time one was fired. Those damn hyperweapons were so hot, they melted through steel in a fraction of a second.

That asteroid didn't stand a chance.

"Demarco," Noah said through the comms. "You made it."

I slammed the starfighter into acceleration and shot into the group. "Enough messing around. We have work to do."

"Yes, sir."

"Heard," Mara said, her jovial attitude long gone.

Melba, Asahi, and Hattie all replied at the same time with, "Acknowledged."

The three of them flew around in a synchronized formation. Noah and Mara fell into position, but obviously not in line with the others.

"Let's go through some standard drills," I said. "Set simulation to Course Fifteen."

I had run through each course a dozen times. To prevent them from getting predictable, the computer tweaked the obstacles. Sometimes there was debris, other times it would be clear—the whole point of each course was to hone a specific skill. The point of Course Fifteen was to maneuver in tight formations. We would have narrow openings between ships and natural obstacles. If we flew poorly, there was a chance we could hit each other or the environment. Or, in the worst-case scenario, we would fly too close to an enemy starship and activate their *point-defense systems*—automated torpedoes that fired at speeds too fast to dodge.

Our starfighters were deadly, but fragile. Even a tiny rock could pierce the hulls at our top speeds, which meant everything was a hazard. You had to fly without error, or it was all over.

Which was why I wanted to practice Course Fifteen.

I took point. The others fell in line behind me, with Noah first, and then Mara. The last three moved together in a way that impressed me. Their dots on my viewscreen had a fluidity that betrayed their familiarity with each other. Melba, Asahi, and Hattie had all come to the *Star Marque* together, so it made sense.

Piloting a starfighter required a lot of concentration on surroundings. While I had plenty of instruments in the cockpit, I spent the majority of my time focused on the position of everyone, and everything, in relation to my starfighter. And in space, there were three dimensions to keep track of.

I could handle it. Ten obstacles, twenty obstacles, fifty obstacles —it didn't matter. I took in the information faster than any normal human. The screens displayed everything I needed, and I absorbed it like I had a sixth sense for piloting.

With a slight press on my side-stick, I accelerated through the first batch of hazards. Bits of shattered starship littered the battle-field. I wove through the chunks of metal and wire, avoiding even the smallest of pieces by tilting my starship around in half a circle.

Noah and Mara copied my path, but Melba broke off with the other two and took a different route. I almost said something over the comms, but the point of the exercise was to make it to the end of the course, so I dropped the issue.

Once we reached the second wave of obstacles—two enemy ships with a wide range of defenses—I decided to see how the others would handle the situation.

I clicked the comms on. "Mara, you take lead."

"Yes, sir," she said.

She shot forward, accelerating into the narrow space of safety between the ships. Noah went after, no problem. But again, when the last three went, they did something different. Melba, Asahi, and Hattie tilted their starfighters so that there was the maximum distance between them and the enemy starships.

Once everyone had made it to the other side, I accelerated, but not like normal. I went as fast as I could. My starfighter's screens blinked with a warning.

4Gs. 5Gs.

The increase in pressure pressed me back against the seat, but I had handled worse. Each G-force was a multiplier of gravity—1G the equivalent of home-world Earth gravity. If the G-force got too high, I could black out, or even die. I forced myself to breathe until I cleared the obstacle and then decelerated until the pressure returned to normal. The screen stopped its warning blinks, leaving me in the soft blue glow of the control panel.

"Captain," Melba said over the group comms. "I think we should go through that run a second time. We should be using the Witscale Maneuver for this situation."

I switched off the team comms. "What is that?" I asked, knowing full well Sawyer could hear me no matter how many instruments I cut power to.

She chuckled over the comms. "That's where you keep the bottom of your starship parallel to the least threatening enemy ship when caught in a pincer formation. Like this one."

"Why do you know that?"

"I'm the tactical coordinator, remember? I've studied a good deal of space combat, including famous historical battles during the Federation Formation War."

Damn. What *hadn't* she read up on?

Apparently, I had been quiet in the group comms too long, because Noah clicked onto the chat with, "I was taught how to pilot from some of the best at the Ares Military Academy. They said the Witscale Maneuver shouldn't be used in situations with enemy starfighters."

"This simulation doesn't have enemy starfighters," Asahi responded, his voice harsh and to the point.

"Y-Yeah, but the situation we're entering will have them. That's why Captain Demarco didn't order us into that maneuver. Rebellion fighters will know it, and they'll use that knowledge to their advantage. It's also faster to maneuver up or down in relation to the pilot, so you should always keep your escape in one of those positions. If an enemy starship is above *and* below, you're limiting your reaction time."

"That's right," Mara said, her jovial tone returning, even in a heated debate. "It's slight, but it can make the difference. Turning to the side is proven to be slower."

Melba huffed. "The Witscale Maneuver is safer. Having the least mobile and threatening target underneath you allows the pilot to focus more on their field of vision. That's how I was taught at the Ace Rangers Institute."

"Same here," Hattie said.

"Me as well," Asahi stated.

I hadn't been taught at any institute or academy. Hell, Endellion and Quinn were the only ones who had given me lessons, and neither of them had mentioned anything this specific. As a matter of fact, Endellion had wanted me to fly as though I were a rabid dog unleashed. I doubted she cared about formal formations. And Quinn had her own personal preferences for maneuvers.

"We'll be facing one starship," I said. "So it won't matter."

"It can help in other situations as well," Melba replied with an exhale. "This shouldn't be ignored. You can get yourself killed if you don't know the basics of starfighter engagements."

"I know the basics," Noah interjected. "I'm telling you—they're not useful here."

"Kid, I've been a pilot longer than you've been alive. Trust me when I say, this maneuver has saved my life *countless times*. I don't care what statistics you have up your sleeve. It was probably written by some twat in a fancy suit who never had any flight experience."

Tension grew so thick, I could choke on it.

I didn't need this.

"I already gave my order," I said, harsher than I had wanted to. "We won't be practicing that maneuver. We're moving to the next obstacle."

Everyone answered with muttered acknowledgements. I accelerated to the next area, unwilling to deal with petty shit. On the other hand, the conversation stuck with me like a needle hanging limp from the skin.

I hadn't been formally trained. And Noah *was* a novice, even if he had been trained.

I'd have to mull this over.

I SAT on the edge of my bed, my gaze glued to the PAD on my left arm.

Five hours before we reached our destination. Sleep eluded me. I could get drugs to help me, but I didn't want any. I had seen too many guys get hooked on chems in order to sleep. I'd just power through it and sleep once we captured the rebellion ship.

"You've been sitting on your bed like that for two hours," Sawyer muttered over the comms.

I exhaled and leaned back on my bed. The dull, gray walls and ceiling didn't improve my mood. "You saw our training," I said. "We're not coordinated. We're not a team."

It went beyond the one damn maneuver. The *Melba Trio* acted as one unit, and *My Trio* acted as another. I didn't have time to force us together, especially not in a single sitting. I had a job to do. Why couldn't they understand?

I missed Lee and Quinn. They both knew how to ease tensions, and they were perfect starfighters. Now I was stuck with a grandma and her two lackeys.

"You can't sleep," Sawyer said.

"What makes you think that?" I quipped.

"Maybe you need company."

I sat up and smiled. "Oh, yeah? You changed your mind about everything? My door's always open. You can come down right now. I promise to be gentle."

"I'm busy, but Blub has been awfully needy. I can send him over and the two of you could cuddle."

Eh. The idea of spending even one second with that sad sack fish put me back in a foul mood. I threw myself onto the bed and laced my fingers behind my head. "Sawyer, stop dicking with me. Tell me straight up—what's it going to take to be with you? I'll do whatever you need."

Nothing.

I waited a few seconds. Still, she didn't answer.

"You don't want me to see you without your clothes?" I asked. "We can turn out the lights. I don't need to see to get things working."

"That's not enough," she murmured.

"Okay, okay. I'll gouge out my eyes."

Sawyer snorted and laughed, more than I had ever heard her. I liked it when I caught her off guard with jokes.

"Demarco…" She calmed herself and let out a sigh. "Maybe one night, when we're not on a mission, we can turn out the lights."

I held my breath, waiting for her to finish. Would she really? The mere thought that it *could* happen got me more excited than anything else had in months. Sawyer didn't need to worry about what she looked like. There was something about her I admired that came from far deeper than her skin.

"I'm going to keep my clothes on," she continued. "That's part of it."

"What?" I said with a laugh. "That's no fun."

"You can take your clothes off, though."

"And then what? Me and Righty will get busy while you watch? How is that different than any other night?"

She huffed over the comms. "I was thinking *Righty* could take a break and… well… I could…"

She didn't go any further, but even a rock could imagine what came next.

A harsh buzz sounded over the ship's comms, signifying a message from the bridge. I jumped off my bed and grabbed my cargo pants.

"What's going on?" I asked.

The bridge comms clicked on. "Captain Demarco," Lysander said, curt and official.

"Yeah?"

"Captain Killian of the *Sun Surfer* has hailed us. She wishes to speak with you regarding the rebellion starship. Your presence on the bridge would be most appreciated."

I headed for the door, but stopped myself. Lysander would be irate if I showed up without the proper attire. With a sigh, I turned and gathered my boots and shirt. He could wait a damn minute if he wanted me looking presentable.

"Oh, and Captain," Lysander continued. "Our superhuman guest has requested she be able to watch the starfighters during the confrontation with the rebellion forces."

"Why?"

"She said, and I quote, *Nothing would please me more.*"

What a sadistic little kid. Then again, maybe I shouldn't talk. What if watching her father being murdered in front of her eyes was what had triggered this bizarre need to see violence? Or maybe all superhumans delighted in the harm of their lessers, like men who bet on dog fights.

"Whatever," I said. "I'm not her parent. If she wants to watch, fine. I'm sure Sawyer has some way to make this happen."

"I do," she said.

"There." Once dressed, I exited my room. "Now let's deal with the *Sun Surfer.*"

EIGHT

Rebellion Corvette

The *Sun Surfer* was nothing more than a clipper-class starship—the kind used for specialty merchant trading. Those starships could, in theory, have plasma weapon and starfighter capacity, and according to the *Star Marque's* readouts, that was the case with the *Sun Surfer*. Perhaps a merchant-turned-enforcer? Whatever the case, it was a smaller ship not built with combat in mind. The *Star Marque* could handle it in an instant.

Lysander motioned to the screens around the bridge. While some displayed travel information, others were held for communication between ships. The *Sun Surfer* had hailed us, and the enforcer at the operations station waited for me to give the signal before he answered.

"Do you want me to escort the superhuman girl out before we make contact?" Lysander muttered under his breath.

Victtra stood off to the side, her two bodyguards never more than a whisper away.

My meager bridge crew, three enforcers in total, kept giving her brief glances. I doubted a superhuman had ever set foot on the bridge of the *Star Marque* before. I was surprised to see her whenever I looked over.

"She can stay," I said. "I don't give a damn." Then I motioned to the operator. "Connect us."

"Yes, Captain," the man replied.

The screens flickered to life. Captain Killian appeared a moment later, her features so harsh and rugged, I thought she was a grizzled scrap of leather for half a second. Thin scars lined her jaw, and her short hair had been pulled back tight enough to emphasize her large forehead.

"Captain Demarco," she said, her voice as gruff as her appearance.

I smiled. "Captain Killian, to what do I owe the pleasure of your beautiful visage?"

Lysander shot me a glance as he murmured, "Rein in the sarcasm."

"Let me get straight to the point," Captain Killian said. "I saw the warrant for the capture of the rebellion corvette. You and I are the closest starships, and of the two of us, you're the faster vessel."

I crossed my arms. "And?"

"And *I* want the bounty. My ship took unexpected damage a month back, and repairs will bankrupt me. If I get these rebellion traitors, however, I'll have more than enough to get back on course."

"So, you want me to back down?" I almost laughed. "You have to be joking, lady. You just want a favor? Who says I don't need the credits?"

"Hear me out," she said. "I'll give you a fifth of the bounty to simply stand aside and allow me to do the job."

I lifted both eyebrows. Lysander leaned forward and stroked his chin, an intent look on his face.

Captain Killian continued, "Four fifths of the bounty will be enough to repair my starship. There's no risk to you, and you'll still make a hefty chunk of credits. And if I do fail, you can always swoop in to capture the starship yourself."

Damn. I hadn't realized so many enforcers were hard up for credits. No wonder she hadn't gotten upset when I had been snide with her—she had basically come here to beg for the job. But I could handle this, so why would I give it to her? I could collect the full bounty or get a small portion—what long-term advantage was there to take less?

"Can we speak in private?" Lysander asked.

I motioned to the operator to cut the comms. "Give us a second, Captain Killian."

The screens flickered to the standby mode. Lysander took me by the upper arm and turned me away from the rest of the crew.

"I think you should take this offer," he whispered.

"Why?"

"It'll breed good will between the *Star Marque* and other enforcers."

"I don't care about that. You saw her starship. She's small time, and on the verge of collapsing. This doesn't benefit us."

Lysander mulled over the comments for a moment. Then he said, "Fine. Perhaps she isn't a great ally, but Noah told me about your training. I don't think it's a good idea to go into combat with a bunch of starfighters who don't know how to fly together."

"You think it's too great a risk."

"Yes." Lysander met my gaze. "Let the *Sun Surfer* do the heavy lifting. A fifth of the bounty is more than enough for us to get other enforcers and more work."

Lysander wanted to take the safe route. No risk, moderate gain. But I could see Endellion's reaction in my mind's eye. She wouldn't have hesitated. She would have taken this mission, and a hundred more, and always come out on top. I could handle the rebellion fighters. I had done it dozens of times in the past. Even if we risked losing a starfighter in the process, the rewards were high—and this was the point in my career where major successes counted the most.

A piece of me knew why Lysander was concerned. He didn't give a shit about Melba, Asahi, Hattie, or Mara. Hell, he probably didn't care much about my life, either. But he did care about Noah. Lysander was too overprotective for his own good.

"Listen," I said. "I've heard your concerns, but I think right now is the time we strive for excellence. Noah can handle it."

The moment I mentioned his brother's name, Lysander tensed.

After a second of contemplating my words, he shook his head. "I didn't mean it like that. Noah made it clear he can take care of himself. My other points still stand."

"And I want to take the risk." I placed a hand on his shoulder. He gave me a stern look as I continued, "The *Star Marque* can handle it. *I'll* make sure this is a success."

He relaxed a bit. "All right. Fine. You have my support."

"There you go, Sanders." I tapped his shoulder and half-smiled. Then I barked at the operator, "Bring back the other captain."

The guy switched the screen back with a shaky hand.

Captain Killian waited in the same position in which we had left her, the same harsh look she'd had throughout the prior conversation still etched into her face.

"All right," I said. "My vice-captain and I had a chat. I'd love to help you out, but the *Star Marque* needs its own credits."

Captain Killian gritted her teeth.

I smirked. "After you file for bankruptcy, tell your crew I'm currently hiring, will ya? That'd really help me out."

Lysander waved his hand, and the operator killed the comms. Good thing, too. It had looked like Killian had been taking in a breath to unleash an epic tirade I just didn't give a damn about.

"You know what?" Lysander asked, his tone on the edge of furious. "You should hire a Public Relations Officer next. That's my official recommendation."

"Is that right?" I said with a laugh. As I turned to leave, I patted Lysander on the chest. "You handle the bridge while I'm out killing those rebellion idiots."

"We should give them a chance to surrender," he said.

I ran a hand along my side. My rib scar had come from rebellion lunatics. "Do they really deserve mercy?"

Victtra perked up and stared at me, a slight smile on her face. She was a little *too* happy.

"Let me at least make the offer," Lysander said.

"Fine. But if they offer even the slightest hint of resistance, we're engaging in combat."

"Yes, Captain."

THE *STAR MARQUE* shuddered as we decelerated.

"I found the corvette," Sawyer said over the comms. "All starfighters should get into position."

I ran down the corridor and got to my starfighter hatch. Just like the simulation pod, the cockpit didn't have a speck of light. I sat down, allowed the seat to suction me in place, and then grabbed the side-sticks. The readouts flared to life, and the screen gave me a list of all the fighters currently online.

SF-1 [Captain]: Clevon Demarco
SF-2 [Subcommander/Starboard Leader]: Noah Jevons
SF-3 [Starboard Fighter]: Adachi Mara
SF-4 [Starboard Fighter]: Unlisted
SF-5 [Port Leader]: Melba Bennett
SF-6 [Port Fighter]: Hattie Andler
SF-7 [Port Fighter]: Haruto Asahi
SF-8 [Support]: Unlisted
SF-9 [Open]: Unlisted
SF-10 [Open]: Unlisted

I MISSED old lucky number eight. That had been my fighter while Endellion had been captain, but it was foolish to attach superstitions to anything. With or without a lucky number, I would make these rebellion assholes regret they had ever crossed paths with the *Star Marque*.

The comms clicked on. A message was coming in from the bridge, broadcasting to all ships in the nearby area.

"This is Vice-Captain Jevons with the enforcer starship, the *Star Marque*," Lysander said, stiff and formal. "A warrant has been issued for your capture. I'm transferring the details now. Surrender your starship and this whole procedure can happen without incident."

He really was more diplomatic than I was, but his civilized tone wouldn't work in every instance. If I had used something so pleasant back on Capital Station, no one would've taken me seriously. There was an advantage in aggression, especially when dealing with belligerent assholes.

The rebellion corvette gave no response. My chest tightened, and I gripped the side-sticks of my starfighter.

Lysander continued with, "This is your final warning. Prepare your vessel for boarding or we'll be forced to disable your starship."

Red dots appeared across my screens as the rebellion corvette released ten starfighters, the sudden flash of crimson adding to the icy adrenaline in my veins. I checked their weapon capacity, half-hoping they would come at me with everything they had. Hyper-weapons were canisters of plasma gas, ready to become ionized and superheated in an instant. Scans could detect plasma in large quantities, so when my readouts showed nothing, I bit back my irritation. All they had were torpedoes, and while they could tear a starship to shreds, they weren't as devastating or as efficient.

It was stupid of me—I should've been delighted to see they were weak—but it disappointed me more than anything.

Just as I was about to give the command to disengage, I caught sight of the enemy corvette on the readouts. Instead of turning to engage the *Star Marque* with weapons of its own, the plasma engines flared to life.

"Sawyer," I said. "What's going on?"

The rebellion starship made a hard jump away from the area, leaving the starfighters.

"They're running," Sawyer muttered.

Goddammit.

"And they've abandoned the starfighters to slow us."

Lysander clicked into the conversation. "Captain, the enemy has fled the area. Am I cleared to pursue?"

The enemy starfighters shot straight for us.

"Port leader," I said over the comms. "You stay docked to the ship." I slammed my main screen, starting the undocking process.

"*Disengaging*," the computer intoned.

My starfighter detached from the *Star Marque*. As I pulled away from the docking port, Melba connected her comms to me, one-on-one.

"We can handle the fighters," she said.

"Stay docked," I barked.

The enemies fired weapons. Ten torpedoes rushed into the area. Two were shot down by Mara and Noah, and six sailed off into space, but two hit the hull of the *Star Marque*, damaging minor systems and Deck Two.

Starfighters couldn't survive long without their starship. They didn't have the fuel capacity to maintain life support for longer than a couple of hours, and their original design had aimed to accommodate as many weapons as possible, not to keep someone comfortable. If the rebellion corvette left, that meant it was leaving these starfighters to die—either in combat or through the slow chokehold of space.

"Lysander," I said. "You run down the corvette and disable it with our port team starfighters."

"By your command," Lysander said.

Melba didn't have anything else to add.

But I didn't have time to worry about that. I accelerated toward the enemies, my thoughts narrowing in on my sole purpose: *destroy the starfighters*. My readouts gave me suggested courses of action, as well as maps of the surrounding area. I took note of the obstacles and sped forward, my focus and reaction time in leagues of their own.

"Noah, Mara," I said over the comms while I readied torpedoes. "Protect the *Star Marque*."

"Yes, Captain," they replied in unison.

Three starfighters versus ten wasn't fair odds, but I knew what I was doing. Melba and her crew had trained in precision and textbook stunts. *My* crew knew their way around combat. Instead of forcing them together without any time to acclimate, I would keep them separate. Melba and her port team would easily incapacitate the rebellion corvette. My starboard team could handle the enemy.

No conflict or bickering this way—everyone would get the job they were best suited for.

When the rebellion fighters fired ten torpedoes, I whipped around, shot one midway through its course, and then flew straight for an enemy. The rebellion fighter swirled and turned, but I was faster. I launched a torpedo, jerked the side-stick away, and took off toward the next target. My readout showed I had hit the first guy—his red dot disappeared from the screen, fueling my ever-increasing heart rate.

5Gs. 6Gs.

As long as the enemy starfighters were firing at the *Star Marque*, it was too dangerous for it to leave. We had to cull their numbers, or at least distract them.

"Careful," Sawyer warned. "There are lots of smaller obstacles. Too fast and you might not be able to dodge in time."

I saw them.

With twitch-reflexes, I flew through a cluster of deadly rocks. 10-degree tilt, slight acceleration, 15-degree turn—the numbers and movements happened without much conscious thought.

As I turned wide, my attention caught on the specific alignment of objects and enemies. Watching as the rebellion fighters flew in a tight formation, I prepped a hyperweapon bolt as they moved into position.

"Demarco?" Sawyer asked. "Those aren't necessary for starfighters!"

I fired the *instant* three enemy starfighters were aligned. I caught them, and four bits of rock, all in one blinding shot. The brilliance of the attack caused our enemies to scatter in all directions. The hyperweapon blast didn't faze Lysander, however. The *Star Marque* took the opportunity to hard jump after the corvette, leaving me, Noah, and Mara to deal with the remaining starfighters.

Two more red dots disappeared from my screen, and it added to the pulse of electricity running through my system. I had caught three of them in one shot, and now they were unfocused and unco-ordinated, like bugs fleeing a bright light.

Lysander had to deal with the rebellion corvette before *our* life support gave out, or else we'd be in the same situation as the others. I had faith in him, though. He'd get back to us—we just had to make sure the enemies were dealt with.

When two more enemy starfighters came for me, I accelerated harder, adding to the pressure of the cockpit and restricting my breathing.

7Gs. 8Gs. 8.2Gs.

While it hurt to take half a breath, I moved three times faster than the enemy. I whipped around them, launched a torpedo, and then sped after the second guy. When he tried to turn, I was already on top of him, my heart beating fast as I fired another torpedo.

Both their dots vanished from my screen.

The enemies were losing quick, and it was more than a differ-ence in skill. Rebellion forces didn't have the equipment to stand against outfitted enforcers. They lacked hyperweapons *and* the ability to accelerate at even half my rate—humans just weren't built to handle the heightened G-force. But I wasn't a normal human. My genetic modifications allowed me to handle the intense G-force pressure of acceleration.

Not only were the enemy starfighters using older model ships, but the pilots probably weren't genetically modified, like I was.

With only two of their force remaining, I swear I saw demoral-ization in their tactics. They disengaged and flew for Noah's starfighter, no doubt hoping to take down at least one of our forces before getting destroyed. When I moved to pursue, however, they scattered a second time. Did they fear another hyperweapon blast?

Of course they did. Nothing but cowards.

Smiling wide, even if it hurt from the mounting pressures of accelerating, I enjoyed this game. Each destroyed ship added to the thrill. These dogs had come to kill me, and I had torn their whole force apart. I was a goddamn enforcer captain—and they were space dust.

Whatever anxiety and tension I'd had before, it melted away when the last of the red dots disappeared from my screen. I relaxed my grip on the side-sticks, my palms sore from the force I had applied over the entire fight. After a few flexes, everything felt right.

"I need a smoke," I said with a smile.

Sawyer snorted. "That good, huh?"

"Have you ever—"

"Demarco," Noah said over the comms. "What should we do while we wait for the *Star Marque* to return?"

Mara clicked in, her voice breathless as she said, "That was intense. I can't believe you got *three* in one shot. We have to celebrate later with drinks. And the whole crew!"

Noah laughed. "No one will believe us."

"They will! Don't you remember Sawyer saying she would set up the tracker in the mess hall? For that superhuman girl? Everyone on the ship probably watched the whole fight."

"Oh, yeah… But that only shows readouts. They probably just saw a few dots disappear at once."

"Still," Mara said, her voice filled with a smile. "That's enough proof."

"Let's group up and conserve fuel," I said as I turned toward the other two. "I'm sure Lysander will be back any moment to pick us all up."

And if he came back with the corvette in tow, I'd have to give him a raise. The man had handled that exit perfectly.

NINE

Interrogating The Enemy

D ocking onto the *Star Marque* had long since become second nature. I didn't even pay attention to the readout as my starfighter fit into place with the fasteners. While it had taken Lysander fifty minutes to get back to us, our life support could've lasted a few hours longer. We had never been in any danger.

Once I stepped into the main corridor, I tapped on my PAD, bringing the thin screen to life and scrolling through the officers' logs. Reports indicated the rebellion ship hadn't put up much of a fight. Our ground enforcers had boarded the vessel and installed our remote piloting program without issue.

I smiled to myself. The Federation required all starships to have similar system coding for the sole purpose of controlling ships if they got out of line. Their wireless aura of control stemmed from any powerful emitter, but it only affected ships with the proper programing. Endellion had had Sawyer modify the *Star Marque* to get around that issue—and the rebellion assholes used an outdated system code to avoid the control as well.

The rebellion starship code was vastly inferior. I didn't even know anything about ship coding, and I knew that much. Rebellion humans had written their own code, and there was no doubt in my mind that it paled in comparison to superhuman work.

I headed straight for the bridge, intent on praising Lysander for his accomplishments, but when I entered, there were only three enforcers at the helm. They turned around and stared. The comms operator stood a second later, a little shaky.

"Captain, what can we do for you?"

I ignored him and left, my thoughts a tad scattered. I entered the officers' lounge a second later, but Lysander wasn't there, either.

"Sawyer," I said. "Where is my vice-captain?"

"He's in the infirmary," she replied from the comms.

"What?"

In an instant, I was ready to fight again, my muscles tense. Had those rebellion thugs gotten the drop on him? Had they somehow overpowered my enforcers? Was it because I had sent them with half the numbers needed? As the captain, I was the one responsible for—

"He's not injured," Sawyer quickly added. "Lysander is overseeing the recovery of the injured rebellion soldiers."

I ran a shaky hand down my face, cursing my mind's ability to run away with a thought. The information relaxed me, though. Lysander was too much of a professional to get taken down by some schmoes who had decided to take off instead of fight.

"I'm going to the infirmary," I said.

Sawyer didn't respond, but I knew she wasn't gone. She was never gone. With her tech-presence embedded in the bulkhead of the ship, I headed to the lift. My dogfight had left me confident. With this rebellion ship in tow, I should've been riding an all-time high, but I wouldn't get there until I knew we had succeeded in our assignment.

I reached the infirmary, barely seeing my surroundings, and waited until the door parted with a quick *swoosh*. To my shock, all five of our medical beds were occupied with people. Dr. Clay stood between them, barking orders to the medics. Lysander stood at the end of the first medical bed, his arms crossed tight across his chest.

"Demarco," Lysander said the moment he spotted me. "What're you doing here?"

"I was going to ask you the same thing."

The individuals on the tables wore standard olive jumpsuits, none of them stained with blood. None of them had bruises or twisted limbs, either. If anything, they were all perfectly healthy, just sedated.

Lysander walked around the table and stood by my side. "These are rebellion officers. After we boarded their vessel, they attempted suicide. I brought them onto the ship, and Dr. Clay has been able to resuscitate three of them."

"Suicide?" I asked. The asshole on the table looked like a chump I could take while half-awake. He'd had the stones to kill himself? "I don't see a pistol hole."

"They took chems." Lysander pointed to the dead stiffs. "They took the hard kind. Melted their insides. These three took the sleeping kind. Dr. Clay thinks one will have permanent brain damage, but the other two will be fine."

Chems. The coward's way out. What a bunch of weak-spined idiots.

"Why are they still unconscious?" I asked.

"Dr. Clay thought it would be safer if they were asleep for the ride back."

"If they tried to kill themselves once, they'll do it again," Dr. Clay said. "And we need to turn them into our *superhuman masters*." I appreciated the fact that he never hid his sarcasm.

I had almost forgotten the warrant required the rebellion officers to be alive. It made me curious. Why all this fuss over a couple of rebellion losers who couldn't even kill themselves properly?

Lysander must've read my mind because he narrowed his gaze. "I don't know what you're thinking, but I don't like it."

"What's so important about this starship and its crew?"

"The warrant didn't say." Lysander stepped closer. He lowered his voice as he added, "And we should leave it that way. If you interrogate these men without the proper authority, we can get fined. Or worse."

I knew he was right, but still. Endellion would've dug through this mess. She always knew what was happening, and how to twist it to her advantage. If we questioned these rebellion punks, we could learn something. Maybe they had secrets, or maybe they had stolen something from the higher-ups in the sector government. Perhaps I could use the information.

Lysander grabbed my upper arm. "Demarco. Let's do things by the books. This once. Please."

I scratched at my neck, mulling over the plea. "Fine," I said. "We'll leave them alone. We'll do things by the book." Then I smiled. "You think they'll give us a hard time for two dead officers and a vegetable?"

Lysander let go of my arm and chuckled. "Probably. But we'll cross that hurdle when we get there."

SIXTEEN HOURS until we made it back to Vectin-10.

Space travel took time. Starships propelled themselves with powerful plasma engines, accelerating faster and faster until speeds reached that of light. The slow build of speed prevented G-forces from killing everyone in the starship, unlike starfighters. Those tiny starfighters sped up so fast that the G-forces threw the pilot back against the seat.

I preferred starfighters. I could handle the stress, and I liked the speed. Sixteen hours was too long. All I wanted was to keep advancing and improving my starship crew, but now I would be forced to wait, trapped in my own thoughts, dwelling on future hypotheticals.

The officers' lounge didn't have much in the way of amenities, but it did have booze. Aluminum pouch booze, but still booze. I leaned back on one of the couches, an empty pouch in one hand, my gaze on the ceiling.

The click of the comms returned my focus to the immediate.

"Your new officer will be exiting the healing vat soon," Sawyer said.

"Shouldn't he have been out of it long before now?"

"That was the schedule, but Dr. Clay removed him from the vat halfway through, did a minor surgery, and put him back in."

"Why?"

"Cai has some advanced cybernetics in his leg, apparently. They were broken and malfunctioning. Dr. Clay fixed them with the second surgery."

That was why I had kept Dr. Clay aboard the *Star Marque*. Endellion had hired him because of his extensive research on genetically defective humans, and because he was a master of cybernetic augmentation. From what Endellion had said, Dr. Clay was the best human doctor you could ask for. I was glad to have him among the crew, even if we didn't get along.

I stood, grabbed two more aluminum rum pouches, and headed for the infirmary. Anything was better than staring off into space. Sure, I could train or read up on some starships, but right now I wanted a distraction.

The gray corridors made the trek one long blur. I entered and exited the lift without much thought. Our infirmary had four rooms —one for surgery, one for recovery, an office, and a healing vat room. I went straight for the healing vat, uninterested in seeing the rebellion officers a second time.

I stepped into the room, my attention caught by the window that looked out into the vastness of space. The black tide all around us never made me feel secure. Part of me was tempted to order shutters for all the viewing windows.

The *Star Marque's* healing vat sat in the back corner, extending from the floor to the ceiling. Its shiny metal exterior had no view windows. Right as I was about to walk over and check the computer readout of Cai's progress, a loud click and slush echoed throughout the room. I smiled and leaned against the wall.

After a few moments, the side of the vat lowered, revealing a naked Cai. He stumbled out of the vat, yanked out the breathing tube lodged in his throat, and then proceeded to hack up the mother-cell fluid. The contents of the vat had a jelly-like consistency —mother-cells—and with each wheeze, he left a glob on the floor.

"*Rejuvenation complete,*" a feminine machine voice said. "*Four lacerations have been mended. The iliotibial band has been reconstructed. Please, speak to a physician if any pain persists.*"

Once Cai's nose and mouth were clear, he stood and pressed his back against the door of the vat, his expression one of vague confusion.

"It's usually me in that vat," I said. "Nice to be the one on the outside for a change."

Cai rubbed at his eyes, then his temple. "I'm just glad I'm not in a body bag."

I shook a rum pouch, and Cai glanced up. I tossed him the drink, which he caught without a problem.

"You brought me liquor instead of a towel?" He ripped open the pouch, not even bothering with the straw. "I already love this ship."

We shared a laugh. Then Cai downed his rum.

"But I will need a towel at some point," Cai said.

Although he still had the thick goo of the mother-cell fluid on his body, nothing was left to the imagination. He had a gnarly scar on his hip, one that flared outward, like a star. It was clear he had been struck with a projectile of some sort, and while the skin looked twisted, it didn't seem to impair his movement.

His lithe frame, etched with defined muscle, had to be the product of rigorous training. I was surprised how well Dr. Clay had fixed him up. Cai had been panting and sweating enough for six people, but now his honeyed skin appeared healthier than ever.

"When can you start training the ground enforcers?" I asked.

Cai tossed his empty rum pouch onto a nearby crate of medical supplies. "Eager, huh? I'm out of the recovery tub for thirty seconds and already I have to get back to work?"

"Those mother-cells aren't cheap."

Cai laughed again. "Nothin' worth havin' is cheap." He shrugged. "Give me an hour or two."

"Good. We still have plenty of time before we get back to Vectin-10. You can get to know the enforcers and set up a routine."

He rubbed at the scars on his hip, his fingers tracing the bits that wrapped around his side. He didn't have scars anywhere else on his body—at least, not from what I could see—and I suspected it bothered him. He did have tattoos, though. Thick, black ink ran from his shoulders to his elbows, creating bizarre designs I wasn't familiar with. They reminded me of the mustached cyborg I had spoken to when we had recruited him.

Cai was good looking. I enjoyed staring at the complete package.

"Are you gonna keep starin', or are you gonna get me a towel?" Cai asked.

I glanced around. The rest of the room acted as a storage closet. When I opened the crates, I found medication, but not anything to wipe down with.

"Sawyer," I said. "Where are the towels?"

"You have company," she said from the comms, ignoring my question altogether.

"What? Who?"

The door to the infirmary opened. Cai and I both turned to face the newcomer—Victtra Barten, the superhuman girl. I jumped up and stepped between her and Cai, unsure if the sight of a naked man would disturb her or not. She was young, wasn't she?

"You needn't worry, Captain," Victtra said as she brushed her long, silver hair over her shoulder. "Superhuman anatomy is far more *intimidating* than a human's."

"What was that?" Cai barked. "Who the fuck is she? Why's there a superhuman here?"

I stepped closer to the girl, blocking more of her view. "I want to know that, too. *Why* are you here?"

"To speak with you," Victtra said. "You've been in the officers' lounge for the last hour, which is an area restricted to me."

"Okay. You have my attention, kid. Why don't we speak out in the corridor?"

Victtra nodded, turned on her heel, and walked right back out of the infirmary. As I followed her, Cai huffed.

"I still need a towel," he said just as the door shut.

Alone in the corridor, away from the other enforcers, and with a half-meter of duralumin between us and everyone else, I met the girl's eyes. She really wasn't much shorter than I was, and it irked me. I never appreciated how tall superhumans were.

"Where are One and Two?" I asked.

Victtra lifted an eyebrow. "Who are *One and Two?*"

"Your bodyguards. The two assholes who might as well be twins."

"Oh. You mean the genetically-modified men my family hired." Victtra shook her head. "I told them to explore the ship. I wanted to speak with you in private."

Away from even her bodyguards? What could she possibly want from me?

"Go on," I commanded.

"You have several rebellion officers in your custody."

"What of it?"

"I want to interrogate them," she said. "And I was wondering what it'll take to convince you. Credits? Favors? You must want something I can provide."

I almost laughed. She was trying to manipulate me? With credits? Who was this girl?

"Why?" I asked.

Victtra glowered. "My father was an emissary—a diplomatic representative sent on a mission to end the conflict between the Federation and the rebellion. He was murdered on the eve of this negotiation, in his private quarters."

I held my breath and controlled my heart rate. Was she going to explain my own deed to me?

She continued, "The leader of the rebellion, a human woman by the name of Meina Kinski, has four children, so my father wanted me to accompany him to the peace talks. He thought there could be common ground between parents who wanted nothing but the best future for their children."

The best future for their children.

I crossed my arms, my grip tight on my biceps. My mother had wanted the best future for me. She had given up everything to have me genetically modified in the womb. I wouldn't have been the same man I was today if it hadn't been for her efforts. Had Emissary Barten been like my mother? I hadn't known the man when I had killed him—all I had known was what Endellion had told me.

Well, she and Minister Ontwenty.

As a matter of fact, it was Minister Ontwenty who had *really* wanted Emissary Barten dead in the first place. Minister Ontwenty had engineered several medications for individuals with genetic defects, but she didn't want her medication going to humans in the rebellion. The rebellion called for a superhuman genocide, after all. I could understand why she wouldn't want her life's work going to save their lives.

"I was there when my father died," Victtra said, her words devoid of emotion. "The killer wore a rebellion enviro-suit and flew a rebellion starfighter. It was concluded then that the assassin had to be a member of the rebellion, but every human I've spoken to, even rebellion thugs in custody, don't seem to have any information on the planned assassination."

"You think the men I have in custody might know what's going on?" I asked.

"If such an urgent warrant was placed on their heads, I imagine they aren't low-ranking terrorists like the scum I've spoken with in the past. They may know something substantial."

That wasn't a terrible conclusion to draw, but I didn't want to help her get any closer to the truth. If these rebellion officials said there had been no plan to assassinate Barten, then Victtra might start looking elsewhere for answers.

I couldn't let that happen.

Under no circumstance would I allow her to speak to the men in my custody.

"My speculation leads me to believe the rebellion was used as cover," Victtra said, her intense gaze matching mine—like she fucking knew the truth. "I think my father was assassinated for polit-ical reasons. But I can't be certain until I've questioned the vermin you have in your infirmary. Will you please allow me to interrogate them?"

"Sorry, kid. I don't have that kind of authority."

"Under Federation criminal code 20, section 4, paragraph 16, enforcer captains can interrogate captives if they think they're linked to an outside crime, or if they're still a threat to the ship, or if they know of a future threat to the ship." Victtra smoothed her metallic hair. "This is obviously related to an outside crime."

I was starting to dislike this girl, not because she was annoying, but because of how *competent* she was. I had never met a human child with such skill. Were all superhumans like this? What precocious little fucks.

"Ask my vice-captain," I said. "He'll get everything sorted out. And he'll check up on your penal code statement." And while that was happening, I would make sure Sawyer put an end to this. Even if she had to make up some sort of law or addendum, no one would question the rebellion officers.

"I'm starting to think your vice-captain is the one with all the authority," Victtra replied. "You defer to him for all matters of decision-making."

Maybe I had given her too much credit. This was infant-level manipulation.

I stepped closer to her and lowered my voice. "I defer to Vice-Captain Jevons whenever I want something handled with kid gloves. He'll get emotionally invested in your sob story and help you however he can—he's a nice guy like that. In the meantime, I'm going to run this ship, because that's what captains do. Understand?"

Victtra replied with a curt nod.

"Good."

I stepped around her and headed straight for the officers' lounge. This bitch needed to get off my starship. She was getting too close to my crime for me to rest easy, and I knew the moment I slipped up, she'd be all over me.

TEN

Accolades

Ten hours until we reached Vectin-10.

I walked the corridor of Deck Three. I should've been resting, but the excitement of the starfighter battle raged through my system. Waiting forever wasn't my style. I hated the time between space stations—the dull ache to get things accomplished burning me from the inside out. But in a fight? Everything happened so fast, and the thrill of coming out on top almost rivaled the excitement in the bedroom.

Nothing else was happening on the ship. Lysander had managed to deny the superhuman's request to interrogate. All we had to do now was get back to Vectin-10.

Two enforcers headed in my direction, their chat echoing through the corridor. The moment they spotted me, they smiled.

"Captain," one guy said.

"Carry on," I muttered, intent on going about my business.

"Oh, uh, is it true?"

I stopped and faced the guy—a man so tall, it looked like he had been stretched out. Even his Adam's apple bulged, as though it couldn't fit into his thin neck.

"Is *what* true?" I asked.

"We have a superhuman aboard the ship?"

I chuckled and shrugged. "Yeah. So?"

"We've never met a superhuman before." The skeleton of a man elbowed the other enforcer. "Right? Not in person? Just on vids?"

The second guy, built like he was hoarding muscles under his clothes, nodded along with the sentiment. "Right. I've never seen one. What's it doing on the ship?"

"Investigating," I said. "Just leave her alone and—"

"It's a woman?" they both asked in unison.

"—don't go near her," I finished.

The enforcers exchanged curious glances. I knew the excitement. Before I had joined the *Star Marque*, I had never seen one, either. Superhumans were weird, exotic—more creatures of legend than actual people.

After I had killed one and scrubbed his blood from my enviro-suit, the exhilaration of seeing a superhuman had disappeared.

"I mean it," I said to the men. "If you see her in the corridor, great. Get an eyeful. But don't go searching for her. Understand?"

They nodded.

"Yes, Captain," the tall one said.

I patted the man on the shoulder and resumed my course. The last thing I needed was a bunch of enforcers trying to get a quick picture or vid with the superhuman. She'd cause a fuss, and I'd have to do something like throw them in the brig—Lysander would make me do it. I really didn't want to do that to my own crew.

Wait.

I glanced over my shoulder. The two enforcers were marked as part of the ground unit. Weren't they supposed to be in training? Why were they walking around the ship? I decided I'd solve this mystery by going to the source.

It didn't take long to get to the training room for ground enforcers. The massive entrance door, constructed to allow for five men walking side by side, was set to remain open. Lysander typically ran the ground enforcers through drills, but today the room sounded empty.

I glanced in.

Cai stood near the back, his hands tucked into his armpits. Lysander was opposite him, glowering. None of the ground enforcers were in sight.

"Am I in charge, or do I need a babysitter?" Cai asked, sarcastic.

Lysander took in a breath—I knew his signs of irritation. "Captain Demarco may have asked you to start working, but you need to fall in line with our procedures."

"I thought I was brought on to train these sad sacks in the art of bounty hunting? That's what I was showing them."

"We have tactics we run through. Teambuilding."

"Bounty hunting doesn't involve that paramilitary bullshit. Informants don't talk to enforcer thugs." Cai ran a hand through his short, black hair, combing it back. "Providing cover fire isn't going to help our enforcers question the locals. Those are two vastly different skill sets."

I strolled into the room. "What's going on?"

They locked up as they turned to face me. I didn't know Cai as well, but Lysander exhaled in relief.

"Demarco," he said. "I'm glad you're here. Before we have our new officers start working, I think we need to review procedures. That's why I canceled the training."

"You canceled it?"

Lysander nodded. "Officer Cai was attempting to teach the ground enforcers how to *shake down a thug for information*. His words, not mine."

I had never been a ground enforcer. Even when Endellion had taken me on ground missions, I had stayed with her, or worked as a guard. One time, I had found a group of drug dealers for her, but that wasn't anything special. I had just known where they had been.

"How *do* you shake down a thug for information?" I asked Cai. "Enlighten me."

He cocked an eyebrow. "You make them think you're searching for someone other than your target." Cai smirked. "My go-to strategy involves getting a list of my target's enemies—rival drug lords, smuggler captains, whatever. I make everyone think I'm hunting *them*, and I let my target find his way to me."

Interesting. The target would *want* to help in order to get rid of a rival. Made sense, in a twisted sort of way.

Cai continued, "First I go into the area asking questions. Then I start offering credits and favors to anyone who has any information. Maybe I bust a few low-level thugs—to prove I have the skills to be credible. But I let a few go. The ones who give me a bribe. That way, everyone knows I'm willing to take a deal. Thugs like it when enforcers take deals. It makes those lowlifes think they can keep control of the situation with enough money. And once they're confident they have control, that's when the real information starts to flow."

"This is fascinating," Lysander said. "But not how enforcers should work. We keep the peace. We don't stir up gang rivalries."

I mulled over the information, practically giddy. It wasn't a bad plan. It was a damn good plan, actually. I knew a lot of thugs back on Capital Station who would've fallen for it in a heartbeat. Sometimes people got so caught up in their own bullshit that they forgot the bigger picture—that was when they started trusting famous bounty hunters to help them out.

"I like this," I said.

Lysander snapped his attention to me. "Demarco?"

"Cai made a name for himself doing this kind of business. I think it would benefit the ground enforcers. Not all of them, mind you. I love everyone in my crew, but that doesn't make them conversational geniuses." I clapped my hands together once. "I got it. Let's make a special task force for this bounty hunting operation. The rest of the ground enforcers will handle grunt missions. Easy stuff."

"Do I get to pick the enforcers for the task force?" Cai asked.

"Of course. You'll be in charge." I motioned to the training room. "But you've got to keep doing Lysander's drills. I've gone through them myself. They're good. And everyone needs to know how to assemble and disassemble their plasma rifles."

Cai narrowed his eyes. "Do I have to participate?"

"You're the ground commander, jackass. What do you think?"

"Tsk."

Lysander shook his head. "We can't do this. We can't be taking bribes from criminals just to prove we have *street cred*. It'll come back to haunt us, I guarantee it."

I had known enforcers who had done far worse. Since enforcers were granted the right to kill in the line of keeping the peace, often they would shoot first and ask questions later. Capital Station had the worst offenders, and everyone knew it was a risk interacting with them. Taking a few bribes wasn't anywhere near that level of incompetence, but Lysander was right. It was a gateway.

"Having undercover enforcers will help," I said. "And we can make rules and guidelines for them to follow. Some bribes in the line of work to catch high-profile thugs are worth it. We just need to curtail any major offenses."

"Who's going to write up these rules?" Lysander asked. He pointed with a thumb at Cai. "This fine, upstanding gentleman?"

I shook my head. "*You*, Sanders. And once you're done, I'll go over it with you. We can set our own parameters, and Cai can teach our new task force how to make it happen. This can work."

Cai chuckled. "Ha. *Sanders*. I'll need to remember that."

"It's *Vice-Captain Jevons* in front of the enforcers," Lysander said, his tone harsh. "I know this isn't the Navy HSN Corps, but maintaining a strict sense of hierarchy is good for morale, organization, and efficiency. Our past captain was too loose with titles. I'm hoping we can correct that."

"You were in the HSN Corps?" Cai asked.

"That's right."

"My father served." Cai relaxed as he gave Lysander the once-over. "And it explains a lot. Nobody has posture like those naval officers."

"Good posture also helps with morale, organization, and efficiency."

"Heh. Yeah, my old man said it also helped with takin' a deuce."

"One of many hidden benefits," Lysander sardonically quipped.

TWO HOURS before we reached Vectin-10.

I still hadn't slept. Didn't matter. Soon we'd be back on schedule. I paced the bridge, giving serious thought to our next moves. How could I accomplish my goals in the shortest time frame possible? Growing a starship required more effort than I had thought, but it wasn't something outside of my capabilities.

The comms screen blinked with an incoming message. I stopped my pacing and stared at the sender—Vectin-10 Judicial Command. They were the ones in charge of the warrants and writing my paychecks. What could they possibly want?

"Demarco," Sawyer said over the ship's intercoms. "This message is being sent through a priority channel. I think you should take it."

I shrugged. "Fine. Allow it through."

The guy at the communications station didn't even get a chance to act before Sawyer had the screen light up with the vid message from Vectin-10.

Some wrinkled man in an enviro-suit stood on the screen, his hands behind his back. His body looked like someone had tried stuffing loose skin into a pair of black leggings. I tried not to cringe, but it was difficult.

"This is Captain Clevon Demarco," I said. "What can I do for Vectin-10's Judicial Command?"

The man frowned, his light blue irises nearly the same shade of off-white as the rest of his eye. "Hello, Captain. I'm Lieutenant Laron. Our long-range scans indicate you've managed to capture the rebellion corvette. Is that correct?"

They could scan out this far? It surprised me for a moment, but just a moment. This entire area of space, from Vectin-14, the capital, to Vectin-10, had tons of orbiting scanners and ships. Someone had probably reported the ship I had in tow.

"You're correct," I said. "It'll be docked in roughly two hours."

"Did you manage to capture the rebellion officers?"

"Yes. Two of them are alive, but sedated. We'll hand them over as well."

Lieutenant Laron's bushy white eyebrows rose to his disappearing hairline.

"Is something wrong?" I asked.

"It's excellent news, Captain. The corvette was part of a trio of ships, you see. All three of them have been apprehended, but only *you* have captured any of the rebellion officers."

I wouldn't have gotten paid without them. Still, it made me curious. Maybe I should've used that superhuman's excuse to interrogate them. I could still do it—say I thought there was still a threat to the ship—but I doubted it would work. Best to leave it.

"I'm glad I could help," I said.

"You'll be happy to hear the rest of my message, then, Captain." The lieutenant smiled. "Governor Voight has asked that all ships who have apprehended rebellion starships come to the parliament building for accolades and further career possibilities. We have an assembly scheduled for the day after tomorrow. I'll be transmitting the date and time in just a second."

I caught my breath. After a moment of silent recovery, I forced half a smile. "Will the governor be there herself to offer these accolades?"

"Yes, Captain. The entire assembly will be there."

There was no way.

Endellion wanted to meet me in person? No. It had to be a mistake. She probably didn't know the *Star Marque* had been one of the starships chasing the rebellion corvette.

But what if she did? What if she was specifically calling *me* to this assembly? Why would she do that? What could she gain from this?

I rubbed my sweaty palms on my cargo pants, my thoughts going to dark places. What if I met her alone in a hallway, behind closed doors? What would I do then? Killing her in the parliament building would result in my immediate execution, no doubt in my mind. But was it worth it?

"Captain?" the lieutenant asked.

"Yes?"

"I assume you'll be in attendance?"

"Yes, Lieutenant."

"Fantastic. I'll let the dock master know of your trajectory and expected arrival. We'll have a detail of soldiers waiting to receive the rebellion traitors."

Whatever. I didn't care about that. I nodded and agreed to everything the old man had to say, my thoughts dwelling on Endellion. Maybe I could end this all quick. Then again, perhaps this was a trick. Endellion could just as easily get some thugs to murder me in a back alley—and then she'd pardon them or some bullshit, just to add insult to injury.

"Thank you, Lieutenant," I muttered as I signaled for the communications guy to cut the transmission.

The second the screens flickered off, Sawyer said, "I don't think you should go."

"I already told them I would. It'd be rude to back out now."

"Demarco, you shouldn't go anywhere near Endellion. She… isn't the forgiving type."

I knew that more than anyone. She was insane, and she'd stop at nothing to get what she wanted. But what did she want now that she was governor? To keep her governor status.

"Killing me would be suspicious," I said. "And you know Endellion isn't the reckless type."

"But she *is* the type to scheme. If you go into her territory, you're risking everything. Endellion can get creative when it comes to—"

"I can handle it," I interjected.

"Demarco, please. I don't think this is a good idea."

I didn't care. If Endellion wanted to face me, so be it.

ELEVEN

Assembly Meeting

The parliament building on Vectin-10 was one of the oldest in the quadrant. Sure, it had been rebuilt a few times, but they had kept the same odd architecture choices as the original building. Unlike modern designs, which were sleek and mostly constructed from metal alloys, Vectin-10's parliament building had an abundance of stone and glass. The computer consoles spouted tourist information nonstop.

"The building design was taken straight from the pages of our origin world ancestors. Everything from Rococo to Classical techniques were used."

I really didn't give a shit. Government buildings were where taxpayer money went to die.

Also, I had little love for our *origin world* ancestors. I didn't know them, and they sure didn't know me. Their accomplishments, while grand back in the day, were so far removed from my life that I found it difficult to care. All I needed to know was that they had somehow gotten us all to the Cygnus Sector on their mass transport ships.

I walked the halls with my attention set on the windows. The vast lawn and water fountains entertained me, especially considering Vectin-10 was a desert mining planet. Still—I had a fascination with all things nature. I would never grow tired of seeing a planet up close and personal.

The inside of the building had pale brown walls, red carpets, and black steel accents on the furniture and baseboards. None of it intrigued me. It felt old, in every sense of the word.

Lysander walked alongside me, his enviro-suit all the way up, including his helmet.

"Nervous?" I asked.

He shook his head. "I was born on the Ares Military Base. The one that orbits the planet. I suspect there's a slight chance someone here might know who I am."

"Your father's a big shot, right?"

"If by *big shot*, you mean *officer in the HSN Corps*, then yes."

I probably should've brought someone else, but the assembly called for captains and vice-captains only. On the upside, Lysander knew his way around bureaucracy, a skill I lacked. As long as he wasn't discovered, this was for the best.

The other captains and vice-captains littered the hallways. They didn't offer any greetings—probably because of what I had done to the last captain who had crossed me—and it was probably for the best. These enforcer groups were in my way.

But their words and conversations caught my attention.

"Governor Voight will be giving the address," one of them said, their voice as rough as jagged metal. "Isn't that something?"

Another chuckled. "She's already causing trouble. The superhumans hate her."

"A real inspiration."

"She's got enough balls for the whole damn universe."

"Humanity's come a long way since the war. Maybe we can start buying land soon. Wouldn't that be somethin'?"

They had nothing but admiration for her.

Their words got under my skin and crawled around. I wanted to grab the next guy to speak and throw him against the wall. These dumb fucks didn't know what was happening; all they saw was a human in power, and somehow—because *they* were human—this translated to their success as well.

Nothing could be further from the truth.

Lysander turned to me, his enviro-suit mask hiding his expression. "Demarco? Are you okay? My readout says your heart rate went up."

"I'm fine," I said. "Let's just get this over with."

We reached the assembly room with the awe for Endellion following us like a shadow. The rational part of me knew these other captains weren't excited about Endellion specifically. They were excited because her successes meant it was possible for others. Even with that reasoning, I still hated their logic. Sad sacks liked to delude themselves. Someone destined for greatness didn't care if others came before them—they forged their own paths, no matter the obstacles. Anyone who needed to be shown the way, who needed an example to follow, had already failed the test of brilliance.

Everyone here wasn't worth my time.

The assembly room, shaped like a half-circle, had stadium seating all the way down to the central podium and raised platform. Tables and computer terminals were positioned between each grouping of four seats, no doubt to provide accommodations to the planet ministers who regularly attended. There were no windows, but the artificial lighting kept the place evenly lit.

Today, the enforcer captains and their vice-captains were given the highest seats, while a few ministers took up the front, closest to the platform. Monitors were built into the walls, showing everything happening at the front of the room.

This place was large enough for a thousand people, yet only a couple dozen haunted the area. Some party.

Lysander and I took a seat at the back corner. It gave us a good angle on the assembly room platform and a large monitor. The others made their way inside, past the sturdy locking doors and genetically engineered guards. We weren't allowed projectile weapons inside the parliament building, but those thugs at every door had heavy plasma rifles. Although I didn't think Endellion was out to kill me with this stunt, the weapons got me nervous.

The captains and vice-captains took their seats while the planet ministers discussed things near the podium. The planet ministers were mostly superhuman and taller than any of the humans in the room. To my surprise, military commanders also made up some of the people in attendance. Their advanced enviro-suits carried all the decorations of generals.

I kept my eyes on the central platform, not because I cared about the genetically superior politicians and their military brethren, but because I wanted to see Endellion.

She had yet to arrive, and every second that she delayed her appearance, I grew tenser.

Conversations echoed around the room. I ignored them. It took me a few minutes to realize my jaw hurt from grinding my teeth. I tapped my fingers along the edge of the small assembly room table. There was a button and a microphone built into the piece of furniture, no doubt to allow people seated in the back rows the ability to speak up during official assemblies.

"You should relax," Lysander said. "You're making *me* jumpy."

"I can't—"

Endellion walked into the room from a side door near the platform, and I caught my breath midsentence. Like Lysander, she wore an enviro-suit with the helmet up, covering her face, but the insignia on the shoulder of her outfit marked her as the planet governor. I'd have recognized her regardless. She had a distinct gait—confident, powerful, and lacking in hesitation. And I recognized the curves of her body, as well.

I couldn't believe it. There she was. *Right there.* But I couldn't do anything. Not yet. Not here. Had she summoned me just to taunt me with her presence? I wouldn't have put it past her.

When Endellion walked across the assembly room platform, everyone went silent. Some of the captains pointed and whispered, but otherwise, there was little commotion. Ministers stood and welcomed her, but the three generals barely acknowledged her presence.

Endellion took the podium and activated the audio and display for the entire auditorium. The monitors flared to life, the overhead lights dimmed, and the platform elevated slightly. The atmosphere of the whole building seemed to shift.

Lysander tapped my shoulder and pointed to the ceiling. "We're being monitored," he whispered. "Please, don't do anything you'll regret."

I glanced up. I hadn't noticed before, but the ceiling was covered in utility fog—a swarm of nanomachines that stayed connected through a static wave. Those damn tiny machines could do everything from regulating temperature to taking continual video footage. And they could move about with ease, almost as easily as mist. They looked like mist, too. They hung around like smoke with no scent.

"Greetings."

Endellion's voice reached the four corners of the room, dominating everyone's attention. She spoke through her mask, her voice slightly artificial, but no one demanded that she remove it.

Why keep it over her face? It seemed like a faux pas, yet in my gut I knew the answer. The last time we had interacted, it had been a fight to the death. Both of us had gotten roughed up, and Endellion had taken a cut to the face.

She was scarred. I knew it.

Any normal person would've been happy to have their life after escaping a falling space station, but Endellion couldn't tolerate her own imperfection.

She wore the helmet to cover the scar—so that no one would know it was there.

"I've summoned you today to discuss a bounty hunting proposition," Endellion said, regal and authoritative. "As approved by the Vectin-10 governing board, and signed into effect under my rule, we will be paying triple the bounty on all rebellion outlaws in the Vectin sector."

Triple the bounty?

The expressions on people's faces spoke louder than trumpets. Some bounties for rebellion thugs could reach the millions, which meant cutting down specific terrorist leaders would result in an early retirement for some.

A few of the other enforcer captains tapped the buttons on their tables in order to speak. The lights flashed on the main monitor—at least seven of them had questions or comments.

A military officer, a human man slightly shorter than Endellion, stepped forward and raised a hand. "Hold your inquiries until the end." He gave the command with irritation in his voice. Six of the lights on the monitor flickered off. One remained. "If you can't follow instructions, you will be removed from the assembly!"

The bark at the end of his words screamed of a man who didn't really have control over the situation. His bald head reflected the lights on the podium, making me hate him even more.

"Who's that?" I asked Lysander.

"It's Commodore Grayson," he replied. "He worked for my father for many years, but later transferred to General Lone's division."

Commodore Grayson waited until the last light went off before shifting closer to Endellion. He stood behind her, with his hands behind his back, and a look of contempt on his flushed face.

He was Endellion's dog, I could tell.

Lysander sighed. "The man's quite full of himself."

"Heh." I rubbed at my chin. "He probably masturbates to a heroic degree."

Normally, Lysander didn't care for my crude humor—and he even tried to stifle his chortling—but I heard it through his suit's speaker system nonetheless.

"There have been threats against my life recently," Endellion stated, drawing me right back into her speech. "Rebellion assassins have been arrested at several space stations in this quadrant, and our intel indicates they're becoming more brazen."

Everyone in the room remained still and quiet. While the rebellion was a small organization, they had been known to kill prominent humans every now and again. They wouldn't kill Endellion, though. No matter how hard they tried. I bet she didn't even really fear them—so why call us all here?

Endellion glanced between each Homo superior in the room, and then to the Homo sapiens. "The rebellion hopes to cause another war for control of the Cygnus Sector. They see my accomplishments as a mending of old wounds, and they'd rather end the Federation as soon as possible. For the sake of stability, and prosperity for all humanity, no matter the genetic branch, it would be best if we stopped them."

Ha! Turning this into a moral cause. How manipulative—just like her.

"I've summoned you enforcers specifically," Endellion continued. "While the navy will continue their efforts to curb rebellion activity, I want smaller teams hunting down leaders and political influencers within the rebellion. Each one of you here has demonstrated a high degree of skill when it comes to handling rebellion insurgents."

Commodore Grayson coughed and then lifted a hand. "If you have questions, you may ask them now."

One light flickered on, and Endellion transferred it through to the comms of the massive assembly room.

Some captain sitting in the far back spoke into his mic. "Even if you increase the bounty by three hundred percent, it still takes time to hunt down some of these bastards. I don't have the resources to stop what I'm doing to prance around every space station in the quadrant. Fuel ain't cheap."

Endellion clicked off the comm before addressing the entire assembly room again. "Those concerns have already been taken into consideration. All enforcer ships that accept this long-term assignment will be given a quarterly stipend determined by the size of their starship and crew."

That news sent waves throughout the room. The captain and vice-captain sitting next to us even smacked each other on the shoulder, each smiling.

"I told you," the captain said. "Look around. She only brought *humans* here for this special assignment. She's trying to help us. She's giving us luxe jobs."

His vice-captain, some short woman with a shaved head, smiled. "She's giving us a chance to prove ourselves in front of those pomp military assholes."

It did appear that way. I didn't buy it, though.

"All those in favor can confirm through their computer terminal with their starship routing information," Endellion said. "Once confirmed, any and all intel on rebellion leader whereabouts will be transferred to your navigation systems. It should go without saying, but I'll say it anyway—any ships found in service of the rebellion, or aiding them in any way, will be convicted of treason."

There weren't many questions after that. One by one, the enforcer captains in the assembly room confirmed their participation through the computer terminals. Lysander turned to me, his expression still hidden, though his fidgety body language told me he wasn't happy with the situation.

"What will we be doing?" he asked.

I tapped the button prompt to speak to the assembly. Lysander slammed his hand down on my forearm and squeezed tight.

"*Don't.* You shouldn't speak to her."

I shot him a glare. "She knows I'm here. I just need to give her what she wants."

Endellion clicked me through to the comms and the room went silent. I stood—my blood still hot, my muscles unbelievably tense.

"As captain of the *Star Marque*, I formally reject your offer."

That got everyone's attention.

Endellion, unfazed, replied with, "Formal rejections are not necessary, but if you have concerns, the assembly would like to hear them."

I couldn't help it. She had *invited me* to speak openly to her —*daring me to say something*.

"You can lie to everyone here," I said as I fought with myself to keep my words precise. "But I know what you've done. I know what you are. If it weren't for the justiciars, and the guards with their rifles, and these superhumans who are duty-bound to protect you… I'd rip every machine from your body until I reached that cold, black heart rotting in your chest. Get yourself another pawn for your games."

An uproar happened the moment I finished. The guards at the doors stepped forward, their weapons hefted, no doubt waiting for orders, but they didn't walk over to me—yet.

"Archivist," Endellion said, speaking to the archiving computer systems. "Strike Captain Demarco's words from the record."

The assembly room computer system beeped in compliance.

I slammed my hand back on the comm button. "Should I repeat myself? Because that's my official fucking position."

Some of the captains shouted slurs at me, no doubt disgusted with what they perceived as a slight to the human race. I couldn't care less. They were ignorant blowhards who only saw what Endellion wanted them to see.

Commodore Grayson lifted both his hands and called out to the room. "Order!" When the ruckus quieted a bit, he snapped his fingers. "Threats against the life of the governor are punishable by up to twenty-five years in prison."

"Goddammit, Demarco," Lysander muttered as he stood. "This wasn't necessary!"

The guards moved closer, and I knew I couldn't fight my way out of here, but I was sure as hell going to try.

Endellion shook her head. "Stand down. There's no need for threats. I won't be pressing charges."

"Governor?" the commodore asked.

"I've worked with Captain Demarco in the past. He has a colorful way with words due to his background. I'll accept his rejection and allow him to leave so long as he does so immediately."

I had hoped to sway at least some of the other enforcer captains and get them to reject as well. That wasn't what had happened, however. Anger had gotten the better of me. If I had been smart, I would've articulated my exact displeasure with her—though any specifics would implicate me in crimes against humanity as well.

Still. I should've tried harder. Instead, I turned on my heel and headed for the assembly room door.

As I went, I noticed the military officers—the superhumans specifically—staring at me the entire way. They didn't offer looks of disgust. The opposite, in fact. Some of them smiled and nodded, like I was the only hero in the room, and I needed acknowledging.

Odd. But I pushed it from my mind as I slammed my way through the doors and out into the parliament building's long corridor.

TWELVE

Alliance

———

It took until I reached the front steps of the parliament building before I felt calm enough to speak. Lysander didn't bother trying to engage me in conversation. We followed the long walkway toward the gates, the pristine landscaping lush and green all around us. The sound of water trickling mixed with the harsh click of our enviro-suit boots.

Lysander's steps slowed. I stopped and faced him.

"I'll never work for her," I said.

He also stopped. "The stipend would've been nice, but—"

"The last time I worked with that bitch, it ended with us trying to kill each other. I don't need to be under her command a second time to learn my fucking lesson."

"—but I agree with you," Lysander drawled. "I'm just curious as to why she bothered to ask. Endellion must've known you'd say *no*. Why did she go out of her way? It only makes her look bad. The *Star Marque* was her old enforcer ship, and the new captain—her old vice-captain—rejected the first offer that came his way. I'm sure there will be word of it all over Vectin-10 within a couple hours. A political nightmare."

We stood around for a few minutes while the hot wind rushed

by. Every space station I had ever lived in had temperature-controlled environments. Planets, on the other hand, fluctuated wildly. I found it both fascinating and irritating. The heat made me sweat more than sex, and I swear it altered my mood.

Lysander remained quiet.

"What is it?" I asked.

"I'm curious about my father. He would visit the surface of Vectin-10 from time to time."

I glanced over my shoulder at the soldiers by the gate. "Ask one of them if they've seen him lately."

"You don't want to hurry back to the ship?"

I rotated my arms, my muscles still tense. "No. I want to get rid of this excess energy before we return to the *Star Marque*."

Lysander replied with a single nod. Together, we walked over to the gate. There were at least four human soldiers, two automated plasma turrets, and no doubt aerial surveillance. I wasn't a fan of everyone carrying weapons when I had none, but now wasn't the time to complain.

"Excuse me, ma'am," Lysander said to one of the soldiers. "I'd like to ask a question."

The soldier, a woman in a reinforced enviro-suit, turned around and glared. Her helmet's visor was clear, so we could see her face, and she offered us both a contemptuous sneer.

"You may address me as Lieutenant Commander Swart, enforcer."

I almost laughed, but I held it back and rubbed at my jaw to hide any hint of a smile. Humans who worked under Homo superior always got this weird complex—they needed everyone below them to know who they were, and why they were important. Super-humans liked to flaunt their status, after all. I was certain that habit rubbed off on everyone they fucked over.

"I'm sorry, Lieutenant," Lysander said. "I was just curious to know if you had seen Captain Jevons of the HSN Corps."

"I'm a *Lieutenant Commander*," the woman corrected.

And she didn't answer the question.

The other soldiers glanced over, their helmets hiding their

mouths, but their eyes told me they were just as amused. Was the lieutenant commander waiting for Lysander to say it?

I stepped around the soldier and grabbed Lysander by the upper arm. "Let's go."

The soldiers said nothing as we left the parliament building's premises. It wasn't a long hike to the mag-lev train. Halfway there, I slowed my pace and gave Lysander a playful shake of my head. "That was painful to watch."

"What?" he asked. "The way those soldiers treated us?"

"No. *You.* No wonder you're single."

Lysander stutter-stepped to a halt and stared. His helmet visor—reflective and dark—didn't reveal his face, but I could imagine the shock and incredulous expression.

"Are you serious?"

I shrugged. "You could've tried some verbal maneuvers on her."

"I wasn't picking up ladies at a bar, Demarco. I was asking about an officer in the HSN Corps. You realize there's a difference, don't you? Not everything has to involve your sexual organs."

He was mad. His stiff speech gave it away.

I was thankful, though. It helped bring me down after the half-confrontation with Endellion. Riling up Lysander always had a way of making me laugh. The man was just an easy target to mess with.

"And aren't *you* single?" Lysander asked as we started our walk again. "Perhaps you should mind your own business."

"Heh. Sawyer and I have this awkward back and forth. She wants me—who doesn't want me, am I right?—but she's worried about something else. She's never really told me."

"Not everyone wants you."

I hit Lysander on the shoulder. He cringed away. I chuckled and continued with, "Did I ever tell you I was genetically engineered with pheromones? If you weren't such an icy corpse, you'd have loved a night with me. My thick musk would've guaranteed it."

"Please," he muttered as he dragged a hand across his helmet. "Never utter the word *musk* in my presence again." He motioned to our surroundings. "And do you really think this is the place to have such a discussion?"

We entered the platform station for the mag-lev train. There weren't many visitors, just soldiers, transporters, and planet miners. The place had a utilitarian feel—it wasn't for people taking a vacation. I didn't care about the crowds. I wanted to feel like my old self again. Anything to distract me from Endellion.

"You're too picky," I said with a sigh. We stopped at the edge of the platform and waited for the next train. "That's your problem, Sanders."

"I see you're going to force me to have this conversation against my will."

"I mean, look at me. I'd be a vacuum-sexual if it meant getting my dick sucked. You need to lower your standards. Maybe we should hit a bar before going back."

I laughed at my own joke, but I stopped the instant someone threw a hand down on my shoulder. Ice returned to my veins as I turned around. Maybe someone wanted a fight. I'd welcome it at this point.

Some human—a man, brawny, like me, perhaps genetically engineered—in a full enviro-suit, and carrying a plasma rifle, looked me up and down. "Are you Captain Clevon Demarco? Of the *Star Marque*?"

"Yeah. What of it?"

"Come with me." He motioned to the security station. It took me a moment to realize the guy wanted me to follow him there.

"What?" I barked. "I didn't do anything."

Lysander stepped forward. "If this station has speech restrictions, we were unaware. The *Star Marque* is docked at the Vectin-10 Eastern Hemisphere Space Elevator, Dock 14-B, if you'd like to issue a fine. We'll maintain cordial conversation from here on out."

They were going to arrest me for my crude speech? Was that even a thing?

"That's not why you need to come with me," the man said, his voice gruff. "Vice-Admiral Valfive wishes to speak with you in private. He's waiting in the security station."

Valfive? That was a superhuman name, no doubt in my mind.

Although I didn't like the thought of speaking to a random

superhuman, I was also somewhat intrigued. What did he want to speak to me about? Perhaps he wanted to hire me for a mission.

I half-shrugged. "Fine. Lead the way."

Lysander gave me a quick glance, his rigid mannerisms betraying his disapproval. Now wasn't the time to act like a street thug—that was exactly what he would say. He wanted me to conduct myself with all the prim and proper authority of a starship captain.

He was right, so I used the short walk from the edge of the platform to the security station to calm myself.

The door slid open with a *whoosh* akin to a gentle sigh. We stepped in, and I marveled at the clean floors, high-tech computer terminals mounted on the walls, and guest counter that had an automated system for reporting crimes.

The genetically engineered soldier strode to the back door and held his left forearm to the scanner. It opened, revealing private offices in the back. Lysander and I followed.

Some of the rooms weren't for pleasant meetings. They reminded me of the interrogation rooms I had seen back on Capital Station. They had chairs, tables, and anti-riot warnings on the doorframes, which meant the rooms could be blasted with high voltage to subdue anyone inside.

We didn't enter one of those, lucky us. Instead, our quiet friend led us to the main office—the fancy one meant for the superhumans. The moment we entered, it reminded me of the landscaped gardens around the parliament building. Lush plants grew in pots around the room. The plush carpets sprang back into position after each step, and the chairs had cushions on them with enough down to get lost in.

One of the Homo superior stood behind a desk, his scaled enviro-suit marked with the insignia of a vice-admiral. His metallic hair shone in the artificial lighting, and his two-toned skin, going from dark in the back, to light in front, had a healthy glow to it. Extra breathing holes—small black dots—lined the side of his neck and stopped just below the ear.

"Ah," he said, his smile and teeth perfect. "If it isn't Captain Demarco."

I glanced around the room. Besides the guy who had led us here, there were two other soldiers, both genetically modified to be buff and tall, both carrying rifles. I returned my attention to the superhuman.

"Ah. If it isn't Vice-Admiral Valfive."

"You've heard of me? Good. This will make our meeting go a little faster." He took a seat and motioned for me and Lysander to do the same. "You see, I didn't want to attend our new planet governor's meeting with a gaggle of enforcers. No offense meant to you, of course."

I took a seat. Lysander sat in the chair next to me.

I leaned back. "Okay?"

"I did enjoy your speech," Valfive said with a chuckle. "You made me regret missing out on all the fun. I would've loved to see Voight's expression."

"Okay. Why am I here, then?"

Unfazed, Valfive replied, "I'm sure you've already reasoned this out, but hiring a bunch of enforcers to handle rebellion threats is more a political move than anything else. If Planet Governor Voight had really been afraid of the rebellion, she would've used her newfound authority to command the military in the region to act." He continued smiling—to the point that it grated on me. "But due to her *suspect* rise to power, she obviously believes the military will either drag their feet or publicly make a commotion over the matter."

There were very few superhumans who had wanted Endellion to rise to power. She had allies, but none of them had ever been friends. Even Minister Ontwenty, the superhuman woman who helped Endellion secure her position as planet governor, had betrayed her at one point.

It wouldn't surprise me to hear Endellion was afraid the superhumans would ignore her orders. It would be an embarrassment, and it would obviously diminish her perceived authority.

"It's all a show," Vice-Admiral Valfive said. "Especially her decision to hire Homo sapiens enforcers to handle the situation. You understand how this is a PR move, don't you? Of course. You were the only one smart enough to call her out and leave the assembly room."

Ah. It all made sense, then.

He knew I hated Endellion, and now he wanted to strike some sort of deal.

Interesting.

I moved to the edge of my seat. "Go on."

Vice-Admiral Valfive snapped his fingers. "Planet Governor Voight has been involved in some questionable activities. I don't trust her, I don't like that she has authority over me, and I'm intrigued that her previous second-in-command doesn't want to play her games anymore."

I gave his soldier-thugs another quick glance before returning my attention to the vice-admiral. "So, what do you want from me?"

"I want you to help me expose her for the fraud she is."

"How?"

"Let's say you'll act as my *special agent*. I know people and places that'll have information, and I want you to collect it. Also, I'd like it if you… helped out a few people that Governor Voight would disapprove of."

At first, I was prepared to make a joke, but the seriousness of the situation kept me from being my sardonic self. Why did Valfive want this? Did he want the rebellion to get closer to Endellion? I supposed it wasn't a terrible plan. Maybe an assassin would get lucky.

"I can pay you," Vice-Admiral Valfive said. "More than the pathetic stipend Voight was going to offer you. You'll only take orders from me and my superiors. No need for odd jobs—I just need you and your crew at your best."

Lysander turned to me. When I stared back, it was at my own reflection on his helmet. I could see my own determination. Vice-Admiral Valfive wanted to fuck over Endellion's political career. That didn't interest me as much as her life, but it would be a start.

Then again, it was clear this asshole wanted Endellion gone

because she was *human*, no other reason. He might've known about her past deeds, but not all of them. He just didn't want to be a superhuman taking command from a lesser. It embarrassed him. I could tell by the eagerness in his voice to get this over and done with.

Did I really care about that, though?

"What do you say, Captain Demarco? Will you help me?"

I stood and offered my hand. "You've got a deal."

THIRTEEN

In Service To General Lone

I never grew tired of using a space elevator.

The donut-ring lift would travel at 3,700 kilometers an hour, straight through the atmosphere, all the way to the space station in orbit. It took ten hours to go up or down, which was three times longer than the space elevator on Vectin-14, but the capital planet always got the best shit. Regardless, the view of Vectin-10 during the long ride was second to none, so I didn't mind. The deserts—arid and flat—had a golden glow from up high enough. Sawyer had said the minerals in the sand had a natural refraction that caused the effect.

The moment I thought of her, I pulled my enviro-suit helmet over my head. It hardened and clicked into place. Once the visor pulsed to life, I switched the comms to her personal channel.

"Sawyer?"

But she didn't answer. That was odd. She typically responded within seconds—but everyone had to sleep eventually. Perhaps I had caught her at a bad time.

I turned around. The space elevator was partitioned into four compartments, three of which were for the 50,000 tons of cargo. Our passenger compartment reminded me of a waiting station for a mag-lev train. Seats and entertainment stations were placed in perfect lines to accommodate as many people as possible.

Lysander sat on an end seat, his head back and his arms crossed tight. His helmet remained up, so I couldn't see his face, but his even breathing betrayed the fact that he was sleeping. I hadn't slept in twenty hours, but I didn't want to miss the view from the elevator, so I hadn't planned on resting until I got to the *Star Marque*.

Alone in an elevator with thirty other people, I returned my attention to the window. The vastness of the planet dwindled the higher we climbed. After a few hours, the clouds and the haze of the stratosphere blocked most of my view. Despite that, I stayed and observed the transition into the thermosphere, and then the exosphere. The layers of the atmosphere reminded me just how small I was. The thought still shook me, no matter how many times I had experienced it.

Lysander woke a few minutes before we reached the space station. Once the elevator stopped, we exited and headed straight for the docks.

My comms beeped with an incoming message the moment I stepped foot on our starship platform. I figured it would be Sawyer, but Dr. Clay's name flashed across my visor instead.

"What is it?" I asked.

With the helmet up, the voice went straight into my ear. "We got our first assignment. We're waiting for you in the conference room."

"Already?"

"That's right."

Eager to get straight into the action, I boarded the *Star Marque* and took the lift to Deck One. Sawyer still hadn't contacted me, however. In theory, she'd be waiting with the other officers in the conference room, but it still bothered me.

Lysander and I arrived in record time. Cai, Noah, and Dr. Clay were all there, but not Sawyer. And it was apparent that something was amiss. Noah didn't look at me when I entered—he tapped at the computer terminal built into the conference table, his hands unsteady, and his eyebrows knit.

I ripped my helmet off and allowed it to fall between my shoulder blades like a hood. "What's going on?"

Dr. Clay sat up straight. "You're asking *us*? We were informed you struck a deal with Vice-Admiral Valfive. Please tell me this isn't a surprise to you."

"It's not," I snapped. "What's with this mood? What's our assignment?"

"Valfive wants you to meet him at General Lone's planetside villa for a private discussion." Dr. Clay motioned to the screen on the table. The briefing information plainly stated I was to return to Vectin-10 to have face-to-face discussions with the military leaders stationed there. "It's marked urgent," Dr. Clay continued. "And you're supposed to be there with your vice-captain in twelve hours."

I barely heard the last of the words.

Now I knew why Sawyer wasn't here, and why she was upset. She had only ever asked me for one thing—*not to work with General Lone*—and his name was the first thing that had popped up on our assignment.

With a curse on my breath, I crossed my arms and stared at the dark gray of the duralumin flooring. I should've known a vice-admiral would have to answer to a general, but I didn't think we'd have to directly interact with the one man Sawyer wanted to avoid.

Then again, there weren't billions of superhumans like there were humans, and only superhumans held the top positions in all branches of government. Perhaps I should've known.

Lysander stepped to my side. "Demarco? What's wrong?"

"Did you know Vice-Admiral Valfive works for General Lone?" I asked.

"Yes."

I gritted my teeth and forced myself to take a long inhale. "Why didn't you tell me that?"

"Why would I?" He stared up at me, his blue eyes groggy. "All the superhumans stationed around the Ares Military Base answer to General Lone. He's in charge of Vectin-10's security and has the highest rank. Of course, Vice-Admiral Valfive answers to him."

"There isn't an admiral who Valfive answers to or something?"

"I don't think any are in the area. Last I heard, Admiral Vanine died with the collapse of Capital Station, and Admiral Lone—who is General Lone's nephew—was put in charge of the cleanup, so he's on Galvis-4."

Noah glanced up from the computer and glared at his brother. "General Lone will recognize you."

Lysander nodded. "Probably."

"You can't go down there," Noah said. "He'll probably arrest you or something."

"He knows you're a defect?" I asked.

"Of course," Lysander drawled. "He was part of my disciplinary hearing and signed off on my dishonorable discharge. Although General Lone isn't a man to remember individual Homo sapiens, he opposed my father's rise in the military, and used my discharge as a reason to deny him all further advancement. I have a feeling he'll delight in seeing me on an enforcer ship."

I almost asked how Lysander got around with a reputation like his, but I already knew the answer. It was the same reason nobody knew of my criminal history. Sawyer had rewritten his ID chip—the only way to identify him now was to see him.

"Well, you park your happy ass on the starship while I handle this," I said.

Dr. Clay stood. "You should take someone with you. I've seen these meetings take place hundreds of times, both for politicians and military officers. The villa was likely constructed without the standard surveillance that most modern buildings require. What is said in there, stays in there. I suspect they want to question you regarding Endellion."

I turned to Lysander.

He replied with a curt nod. "They're called *dead zones*. It's illegal to send signals in or out of them. They're underground penthouses, basically. Homo sapiens aren't allowed to get permits for them, but Homo superior are. They justified the construction by saying that some military secrets were classified, and in this age of technology, they—"

"I don't need a damn history lesson," I snapped. "I just need to know what I'm getting into before I go down there."

"Dr. Clay is right. They likely want to discuss Endellion without the chance of their conversation getting back to her. They'll probably ask why you opposed her in the assembly room."

Although Cai had been silent since I had entered the room, he cleared his throat and got everyone's attention. "I know I'm new here, and I'm not sure how you all operate this starship, but I've had plenty of dealings with those two-toned freaks who think they're superior. Trust me. They won't just be asking questions. They're going to demand you do something, and then they're going to threaten you if you don't comply. You better be agreeable long before you get there. They like genetic scum like us—but only if we play by their rules."

Oh, I knew.

This was how Endellion had gotten herself in trouble. She had "played the game" with Minister Ontwenty, and then the minister had taken advantage of her whenever she could. But even knowing all these facts, how could I use them to my advantage? What could I do to keep myself from repeating all of Endellion's mistakes?

"Cai," I said. "You're coming with me when I go back planet-side. You can be with me in this *dead zone*."

Noah slumped a bit in his chair, but he didn't say anything. If his brother would be recognized, there was a chance he would be, too. And I didn't want to go anywhere with Dr. Clay. At least Cai had done this before.

And there was a benefit to keeping Lysander on the ship. Lysander wasn't the type of man to play games. He'd be upset with whatever happened at the villa, but this way, I could just give him a report, rather than have him try to sway me. I knew what needed to be done in this situation, and Lysander's methods wouldn't help me.

"Be ready to go in an hour," I said as I turned and left the conference room.

———

I COULDN'T FIND SAWYER.

She wasn't in her workroom or her personal quarters. She wasn't the type to socialize, either. Clouded by my frustration, I almost forgot that the ship could locate personnel. I jogged to the nearest computer terminal and slammed my hand across the touch screen.

"Locate Chief Cyber Operations Officer Sawyer Coda," I said.

The screen flickered with a detailed map of the *Star Marque*. It took me a moment to scan through the decks until I came to her location—my personal quarters. That surprised me, but I got over the shock a moment later. She wanted to speak to me.

I didn't slow or stop until I got to my quarters. I walked straight in, determined to explain my mistake, even if she yelled or accused me of ignoring her request. I hadn't thought about the vice-admiral's connection to General Lone, but we probably wouldn't have to work with him directly. Why would the general get his hands dirty by ordering around an enforcer starship? This would probably be a one-time visit to his villa, and then we could work with Valfive instead.

When I entered my room, I found Sawyer sitting on the edge of my bed, just like before—her knees up to her chest, her eyes glued to her PAD. It felt surreal, like walking into the past. The door shut, and she offered me a quick glance before returning to the work on her screen.

"Sawyer," I said.

"Demarco."

"You didn't answer any of my communications."

"I was trying to display anger," she said, monotone. "Or maybe disappointment. It's hard for me to distinguish between the two."

I stifled a laugh. Of course she wasn't very upset. Sawyer never felt much emotion over anything. Apparently, it had been written into her genetics long before she had come into existence. I wondered for a moment—what it must have been like to live in a state of near-apathy—but I knew she felt *something*, or else she never would've left Endellion to save my life.

I walked to her side and stood next to her. "I didn't know General Lone would be involved."

"Is that right?"

"If you want, I'll call off this whole arrangement."

Sawyer stopped working and tilted her head back enough to stare up at me with her gray-blue eyes. "This is a good deal. You should meet with them. This was how Endellion got her chance to become a planet governor. She worked directly with superhumans and collected favors like currency."

I didn't sit on the bed. Instead, I knelt on one knee in front of her. I was tall enough that I matched her eye height. "I can't do this without you."

Sawyer caught her breath. Then she exhaled and whispered, "Endellion said the same thing." She continued to stare, but I saw she wasn't seeing me, but rather, something distant. "Sometimes I wondered if she saved me from General Lone just so she could use me. That's the obvious logic—that's what Endellion did with everyone—so now I wonder if that's why you keep me around as well."

I took her hand and held it in my own, tighter than I should have, but it was hard enough not to yell. "I'm not like her. What do I have to do to prove it to you?"

Her hand trembled in mine, but Sawyer didn't pull away. She forced an inhale and exhale, her gaze on our hands. The extended physical contact was something we had never done before.

"I don't have anyone else besides Blub." Sawyer relaxed after another round of forced breathing. "That's why I dedicated myself to Endellion. She was the only one who ever helped me. She was my family. And now... I don't even have her. I asked you for one favor, and you've already broken your word."

I took her other hand and held them both. "You've seen me at my worst, you've seen me at my best—you've seen me standing at death's door begging for a second chance, for fuck's sake. You know me, Sawyer. No one else knows me like you do. I swear I didn't know about any connection to General Lone. And I promise I'll tear down this whole arrangement if it'll make things better between us."

For a long moment, we sat in silence. She didn't answer right away. Instead, she rubbed my knuckles with her thumbs, her skin soft—more than I had imagined.

"Can we lie next to each other?" Sawyer whispered.

The question caught me off-guard. "Wait, what?"

"Like couples do. On the bed. Side by side."

Although tense, I couldn't help but smile. "We can lie together literally anytime you want." I got up and on the bed in a matter of moments. Then I rolled onto my back and motioned for her to come closer. "Normally, people don't cuddle during an argument, though."

"Are we arguing?" she asked as she scooted closer to me.

"Heh."

Sawyer rested her tiny body next to mine. She curled into the fetal position, her knees against my rib cage. When I went to wrap my arm around her, she jerked away.

"No. Don't."

"You don't want me to hold you?"

"I hate feeling like I'm restrained."

The statement chilled my blood. I tucked both my hands behind my head and laced my fingers together. Sawyer scooted close to me again and tucked her head into the crook of my armpit.

"You should speak with Vice-Admiral Valfive," Sawyer said. "For many reasons. If he's an opponent to Endellion, he'll make for a good ally, even if only for a short time. Additionally, when we received the message to meet, that superhuman girl, Victtra Barten, went straight down to the planet to also have a few words with Valfive."

"She's not here?" I asked, almost tempted to sit up. "As in, she's off the ship for good?"

"No. Apparently, she wants to tell them about your performance as a starship captain. She specifically stated she'll be returning."

That news shocked me more than anything else. Was she trying to get me in trouble? Was Victtra going to report some sort of breach in code? Or perhaps she was going to complain that I hadn't let her interrogate those rebellion officers…

Dammit.

"And you should at least offer a counter interpretation," Sawyer continued. "Just in case she has something slanderous to say."

"And you don't care that I'll be speaking with General Lone?"

"I only care because he's a man with little empathy. He's willing to torture and kill, and he's done it so often that I doubt he'll bat an eye at it in the future. Please don't have him come aboard the ship— and whatever you do, don't work for him directly."

I turned my head to the side. "Want me to kill him for you?" I had meant it as a joke, but my tone came out with an icy seriousness.

Sawyer shook her head. "You'd never get away with it. The Lone family is the oldest and most powerful group of Homo superior. He has connections everywhere. He's a military hero. He's the best of his peers."

"Don't suck his dick too hard," I quipped.

"Just avoid him," Sawyer replied, her voice so cold and dead, it might as well have been a fish sandwich. "General Lone has nothing to do with you or Endellion, other than the fact that he's stationed here."

"But what if we dropped a space station on him?" That came out lighthearted and comical, just as I had intended.

Sawyer chuckled. "Traitorous speech like that is normally automatically reported to the authorities by the starship's computer systems. You're lucky I've modified the ship's recording and reporting processes."

"I'm lucky in a lot of ways," I said.

FOURTEEN

Dead Zone

————————

Vice-Admiral Valfive left me no fucking time—I had twelve hours to get to General Lone's villa, but it took ten hours to ride the damn space elevator, not to mention the time it would take to travel across land. The only thing I could do on the ship was change into a fresh pair of cargo pants and a tank top. Then I headed out with Cai.

I didn't know much about Cai outside of his professional career. He stood next to me on the elevator, staring out the windows, watching the atmosphere whip past us. He wore the same kind of casual outfit that I did, his tattooed arms out for everyone to see. The designs intrigued me, but they were mostly lines and abstract symbols—no solid pictures from which to draw interpretations.

"What's with the tattoos?" I asked.

Cai flexed his arm. "When I was younger, I ran with a crew where people inked up. Everyone just kept getting more the longer they were there. I left before I got the full-body experience."

"Is that what you like to do for fun? Get some ink?"

"Nah. It was fine, but I eventually got tired of it."

"You into *other* types of fun?" I asked.

Cai glanced over, obviously confused by my vague wording. "Huh?"

I tugged at the crotch of my pants and smirked.

The puzzle pieces visibly clicked in Cai's mind as he narrowed his eyes and slowly turned away. "Nah. Sorry. Not into that kind of fun, either."

Of course he wasn't. Just my luck.

Frustrated, and no longer in the mood for conversation, I fixed my gaze on the bright white clouds. *Nimbus* clouds, according to the materials I had been studying. Normally, I didn't find academics interesting—not in the slightest—but I absorbed every fucking piece of information when it came to planets. I still couldn't believe I was able to step foot on them as often as I did.

I had Endellion to thank for that. It was probably the only memory that wasn't tainted by her vile actions. She had delivered on her promise to me.

"You okay?" Cai asked.

His voice brought me back to the present. I glanced over and nodded. "Yeah."

"You seem tense."

"I'm fine." We still had six hours before we reached the surface. I had already had a short nap—what else was there to do? After exhaling, I asked, "So, tell me about yourself." It wasn't the smoothest conversation starter, but I wasn't in the greatest of moods.

"My mom operated a piece-of-shit food stall on a space station," Cai said. "She made me work with her, even when I was young. We were at that food stall so much that I thought my name was *Spicy Meat Bowl.*"

I chuckled. "Is that right?"

He shrugged. "Whaddaya want from me? I also like long walks on the beach. Is that what you wanna hear?"

"Now I understand why you worked alone," I quipped.

Cai cocked a brow. "Hey, it's a lot easier to get shit done when you don't have to check the pecking order every time you have to take a piss."

"I'll agree with that."

"Your vice-captain wouldn't."

"Well, that's one reason why my vice-captain isn't here," I said as I rubbed my jaw.

"Oh, I see." Cai half-smiled. "All that bickering between you two was real. I just figured it was some sort of lovers' quarrel. Glad to know you're not as military as Sanders."

Ha! *Sanders.* I'd get that name to stick.

And I realized then that I really liked Cai. He was the perfect person to accompany me into the den of our enemies. Just the right amount of sardonic to keep me sane.

AFTER THE SPACE ELEVATOR, we took the mag-lev train south. The desert landscapes never ceased to amaze me. Sawyer had said they were dangerous—that the heat and light created a terrible combination that killed life—but I loved the golden dunes and glitter of sand whenever the wind picked up. The train cars were temperature-controlled, so I couldn't feel the heat, but I tried to imagine it.

Once we arrived at our destination, my imagination was no longer needed. I stepped out of the car and into a wave of invisible lava. Heat rushed up from the ground, and I immediately regretted not wearing my enviro-suit. This was what they had been made for —to protect the wearer from all the elements, including the harsh vacuum of space. If I had kept my suit, this heat would have been nothing. As it stood, I would now be wearing fresh sweat stains into this meeting with General Lone.

Cai wasn't any better. His black hair stuck to his forehead, clumped from the beads of sweat rushing down his face. He had all the excitement and exuberance of a drowned rat.

"Let's get this over with," he muttered.

We headed for the private shuttle to the villas on the edge of General Lone's property. His security force—made up of genetically-modified humans—all looked identical when it came to height and brawny build. That was supposedly a benefit of the genetic engineering: everyone was nearly identical.

Even though I had also been genetically modified, I was different—my mother had ordered DNA modifications to improve me in every way she could think of. These guard-post punks were engineered to follow orders and be tough. At least, according to Sawyer. She had said their purpose had been baked into their biological coding, similar to how she had been made physically weaker, and designed with an unreal ability to multitask.

"I'm tempted to just stare into the fuckin' sun and dare God to kill me," Cai said, tugging at his sweat-soaked shirt.

"You'll be fine."

The shuttles were tube-like vehicles hooked to tracks. They looked like mini-trains to me, but I didn't comment. Cai and I stepped into one, and then immediately relaxed. The cold air was a sweet relief.

Each shuttle only carried four people, but the seats had been designed to accommodate the large size of the superhumans, which meant Cai and I were more like children sitting in Daddy's recliner than full-grown adults.

Once the shuttle door closed, the vehicle zipped off down the tracks. To my surprise—since we had tiny windows by our seats—I watched as the shuttle tracks took us into the ground. That made sense. The *dead zones* were underground, apparently. Lucky us.

The electric hum of the shuttle was quiet. When I zoned out, and stared at the ceiling, I couldn't hear it at all.

Cai leaned back in his seat, and then laced his fingers together and placed his hands on his head. "So, what's the deal with your cute red-head officer?"

"She's taken," I snapped.

"By who?"

"By *me*." I glowered at him, ready to throw the bastard from the shuttle if he thought he could argue his way out of this.

"I thought you were into men?" Cai asked, obviously baffled. "Didn't you want to hook up on the elevator?"

With a chuckle, I shrugged. "I'm into whatever has a pulse."

Then I gave my statement more thought. "Maybe… more than that. But I'm gonna stick with what I said."

"Oh, you're one of *those* guys." Cai scoffed and leaned farther back in his seat.

"I give you permission to pursue Sanders."

We both got a good laugh at that statement.

Lysander had a good chance of dying alone. Man was too uptight for a broom. Then again, perhaps as his captain, I should make it a priority to make sure he had time for personal fulfillment. Or maybe it was none of my business.

What would Endellion do?

She would ignore him.

Which meant… I should probably help.

I cursed under my breath. Fortunately, the cursing didn't last long. The shuttle came to a halt at the end of the tracks. And although we were underground, the tunnels had been outfitted with some of the best lighting fixtures I had seen in my life. The shuttle doors opened, and I stepped out into a cool and well-illuminated tunnel, complete with green plants on both sides of the walkway.

The genetically modified human guards motioned to the tunnel. "You want Villa 1. Head straight down until you see the door on your right."

Cai and I barely acknowledged the men. We headed down the path, and the first thing I did once I was out of sight was check my PAD. I poked at the paper-thin screen and noticed that it wasn't receiving any comms signals.

"It's a dead zone," Cai said, staring at my PAD. "You're not gonna get anything."

"I just wanted to check."

"Yeah, well, once we're in the villa, play it cool. If you don't want to answer a question, feign stupidity. Trust me—these two-toned dogs think we're barely evolved rocks. Play the dumb card whenever you want. Works like a charm."

I nodded along with his words.

Two-toned. Everyone always said that. It was because of the superhumans' skin. They were colored like lions—dark golden brown on their backs, and paler gold on their stomachs, chests, and faces. Apparently, it helped their bodies regulate temperature better than humans, but I doubted it amounted to much. Whoever had designed the superhumans had probably just thought it had looked cool.

The underground villas intrigued me. Cai and I reached a giant set of double doors marked with the number one, but I noticed a few other doors farther down the walkway. How many superhumans lived here?

A single guard stood watch at the massive double doors. His enviro-suit was all the way up, no doubt to protect him just in case something happened. Even though this was a well-worked villa, and constructed to last, what if there was a gas leak? The enviro-suit would protect the wearer from any accidental deaths.

The punk guard opened the villa doors.

Another wave of cold air washed out, and I was drawn in by the pleasant aroma of flowers. I'd never get tired of that scent. It was everything a space station wasn't.

That didn't help calm me, however. Everything about this felt like a trap. The temperature, the smells, the location—Cai and I were cut off from everything, and the superhumans around here didn't give a shit what happened to us.

Still, I wouldn't let it frighten me.

I stepped inside. Cai followed suit.

According to the central database on the *Star Marque*, a *villa* was a luxurious country home away from the cities. We hadn't had anything like that on Capital Station. Everything we'd had was a dumpster fire. But this… General Lone's villa was everything I had imagined.

The gigantic entrance room was lined with "windows." They were digital displays, showing an artificial exterior, but it was damn convincing. The "landscape" consisted of rolling emerald hills, pink trees, and small fields of blue flowers. A distant lake reflected the white-and-blue sky.

It was beautiful.

The actual villa interested me a lot less. It had carpet—I was a fan—and the massive couches with pillows the size of a fully grown man were interesting. Quiet music played through speakers built into the villa. The pleasant songs eased my anxiety. The white, pale green, and soft yellow color scheme was… not my style.

Then I spotted Vice-Admiral Valfive walking out of the nearby hallway. He was followed by a second superhuman, and for a brief moment, I felt sorry for Valfive. This new man was the epitome of *superior*.

General Lone.

The general carried himself with confidence and authority. His muscles practically prevented him from putting his arms all the way down against his sides, but despite that, he moved with the agility of someone with excess energy. When he spotted me and Cai, his attention homed in on our location, and he smiled a predator's smile.

"Our guests," Lone said, causing me to shudder.

Valfive nodded. He was shorter than Lone—which was shocking, considering they were both about three meters—and his smaller physique just didn't help him maintain a presence. "As you requested—Captain Clevon Demarco. Of the *Star Marque*."

"Excellent."

General Lone strode away from Valfive and approached me specifically. To Cai's credit, he didn't move away. He stayed next to me, even as the superhuman loomed over us.

"Captain Demarco," Lone said with a slight smile. "Why don't I show you around my villa? Your man can wait for us in the theater room, just beyond the bar."

Cai's eyebrow lifted at the mere mention of a *bar*. But then he turned to me, his expression just as serious as it had been when he had been getting the infection in his hip dealt with. "You want that, *Captain*?"

I nodded once. "I wouldn't want you to miss out on a drink."

Although our conversation was casual, Cai's stiff movements

and odd expression conveyed a lot more. Did I really want to be alone with the most powerful superhuman on Vectin-10? Or *any* superhuman, for that matter.

I smiled as Lone motioned to the long hallway.

Hopefully, I wouldn't regret my decision.

FIFTEEN

The Enemy Of My Enemy

Lone was just like all other superhumans. Silvery-white hair. Two-toned skin. But his eyes were unique. They were a striking shade of indigo, and his pupils dilated and constricted enough that it fascinated me. I didn't stare long, however. I was sure this bastard would take it as some sort of insult.

We walked the long halls of his villa. The artificial windows almost made me forget we were underground, but every time I glanced at my PAD, I knew better. This dead zone was like sitting on an island with no boat.

"Tell me why you and Planet Governor Voight had a falling out," General Lone said, no preamble or small chat.

I preferred it that way.

"She's a power-hungry lunatic who endangered *my* crew in order to fulfill her own selfish desires," I said. Which wasn't a lie—it just wasn't specific details.

"It wasn't just your crew, was it?" Lone turned to me, never blinking as he added, "A man doesn't go on record with a threat unless it's personal."

He had gotten me there.

"She risked my life as well." But I knew that wouldn't satisfy Lone. He wanted some juicy details—some secret information no one else was privy to. With a smirk, I stopped walking and faced him. "But it was more than that. We were partners. Lovers. Then she threw it all away and tried to kill me like a psychotic bitch."

Again, I wasn't lying, per se. I just wasn't giving away the biggest and best details.

Lone stopped and regarded me with an expressionless glance. The light from the fake windows glittered in his short, silvery hair. The man stroked his chin, contemplating the information.

"And you want her dead?" Lone asked.

"I said so on record," I quipped. "It's not really a secret anymore."

"I'm glad we have something in common, then." Lone crossed his arms over his brawny chest. "If we have a similar goal, we should work together on this matter. My money and power—your connections. This won't be a long operation."

"My *connections*?"

"Human connections." Lone motioned to the hall, and then resumed our walk. I hurried to his side, a little confused. "You see, I don't just want Voight dead. I want all of her efforts to fall apart. I want to make sure everyone knows she *failed* in her duties."

To make humans look incompetent.

"And how can I help with that?" I drawled.

Lone tapped the side of his head. "I'll give you resources, and you take them to some key human personnel. Use the resources to convince the Homo sapiens to side with us. The more you warp Voight's operations, the more people will lose faith in her. Once that happens, her downfall is inevitable. And then her death will soon follow."

The way he spoke left me feeling slimy, and I had run with dozens of gangbangers in the past. Lone was just as calculating as Endellion, perhaps worse. Or perhaps he delighted in it more. Every word he spoke was laced with a self-assured smugness that made me think he was playing a game of chess with a corpse.

He knew he would win. Now he just wanted to sit back and watch the pieces fall.

"What do you mean?" I asked, feigning stupidity, just as Cai had recommended. "Resources? People? Like what?"

As if expecting I would need more clarification, Lone quickly replied, "Planet Governor Voight has reopened several mines. I want you to speak with some of the foremen and workers. Convince them that a bank account full of credits is better than doing a good job. Have them wreck their operations—slow down Voight's attempt to industrialize—and get it on the news by greasing the hands of those who can report on it."

Lone had thought of some specific details.

He continued, "Those miners won't trust a superhuman, no matter how many credits I offer them. But they'll trust a fellow human. Especially one with your history. It'll be the same with all the others."

"And that's it?" I asked, almost sarcastic, but I held it back.

"After that, we'll deal with the rebellion." Lone shrugged with one shoulder. "Voight claims they're making assassination attempts. Perhaps one of them is successful." He smiled. "All you need to do is bring rebellion criminals to *me*. I'll make sure they eventually escape their cells. They won't even know it's my hand helping them. Their guards will be sympathizers, and I'll conveniently leave weapons for them to steal. They want Voight dead—which makes them quite useful."

Then General Lone could blame the violence on human infighting. He had this all mapped out.

I wasn't necessarily against it—tearing Endellion down was my top priority.

"I want you to help me," Lone said, pulling me from my musings. "Valfive will send you messages, resources, leads… And in exchange, you'll be generously compensated. Not to mention you'll have a chance to see everything Voight built burn to the ground."

We turned down a corridor and then came to a large room with a pool in the center. The giant tub of water was shaped like a natural lake, with inclined edges so that someone could gently walk in. The still waters had no ripples or waves, but the bottom of the pool had been decorated with gem-like tiles that glittered beneath the surface.

We didn't have pools on space stations, not when the gravity generator could fluctuate. Seeing them planetside was always a shock. This amount of water—wasted—for some assholes to dunk their bodies in for a short period of time.

To my surprise, a woman sat on a couch by the edge of the pool. After a moment of staring, I recognized her. But… it was impossible. *Sawyer* was here?

It looked like her. Red hair—longer, though. Down her shoulder. Blue-gray eyes—brighter, though. No sleepless bags. And freckles. Cute little freckles. Exactly like Sawyer's.

She wore a semi-transparent white dress that went down to her knees and a pair of shorts underneath. But nothing else. I wasn't complaining, but it startled me a bit. *This* Sawyer wasn't covered in gnarled scars. Her skin, breasts, and fine features were blemish-free.

"Good afternoon, General Lone," Other-Sawyer said. She smiled and tossed her red hair with her fingers. "I was just about to go for a swim. Care to join me?"

The forced joy in her words unsettled me. I stared—I couldn't help it—and my breath remained trapped in my lungs. What was this? It obviously wasn't Sawyer. She'd never be here. Which meant… This was some *other* genetically altered human. A clone? A little project?

"Is something wrong?" Lone asked, one eyebrow lifted.

I offered him a half-smile. "Of course not."

"You're aware that Homo superior was created with an ampullae of Lorenzini, aren't you?" Lone ran a finger up his neck and over one of his ears. "It's a specialized organ that senses electric currents. That's why we superhumans have such an easy time with advanced computer technology."

He spoke like a parent lecturing a small child. I was well aware of the ampullae of Lorenzini. It allowed superhumans to "see" in the goddamn dark, basically. They sensed electricity even in the muscles of people around them.

"Electric currents are in nearly everything," Lone said, practically parroting my thoughts. "And when someone lies, their body reacts in subconscious ways. When you're hiding things from me—like in the hall—or when you're flat avoiding a question, like right now, I can sense it. Your heart rate, your muscles, even your *breathing*. Everything betrays you."

I snorted and turned away from the prick. "All right. Your lady reminds me of someone. It was a little creepy at first."

Lone faced the Other-Sawyer and then snapped his fingers. "Helia, come here."

Without a second's hesitation, the girl bounded over to Lone's side. She was so much shorter—damn near half his height—and she had to stare up at him. The girl's eyes were large and focused, and bright with intelligence.

Just like Sawyer.

"This is my personal assistant," Lone said as he stroked her hair —like someone petting a dog. "Helia handles all my household affairs, including the maintenance of the computer systems." Then he nudged the girl in my direction. "Helia, be a good girl and entertain our guest."

She didn't complain or offer any resistance. Helia hugged one of my arms, proving to me just how *thin* her clothing really was. I didn't know what to say. Sawyer had told me that Lone had tortured her like a sick sadist.

This…

What was this?

How could I even articulate the right questions without giving away the fact that I had Sawyer on my ship? Hadn't Sawyer said, *Endellion saved me from Lone?* What did that really mean? I hadn't asked any follow-up questions, like a fucking idiot.

"You seem disturbed," Lone said, a hint of amused curiosity in his tone. "Should I send her away?"

I tensed and then shook my head. "Nah. I'm just processing everything."

No matter what I tried, I couldn't take my eyes off Helia. She stared up at me with a brighter smile than Sawyer ever had. When Helia squeezed my arm, I shuddered. She was so soft—so fragile.

"Then we should continue on our way." Lone motioned to another door. "I have a bar and theater, and I wanted to speak to you about the specifics of our arrangement. There are special comms channels reserved for the highest levels of the military. Your starship will need to be outfitted with the right equipment to even join in on these conversations."

I nodded along with his words, still engrossed with the girl.

We walked out of the pool room, Helia on my arm, quietly giggling whenever our eyes met. Lone continued his discussion, but I barely heard anything.

GENERAL LONE'S theater room was gigantic. It had three large screens, two massive couches, and four tables positioned around the room for food and drink. A personal bartender, a chef, and a musician all stood in their own corner around the room, waiting to be given instructions, like sentient pieces of furniture.

Helia and I sat on one oversized couch, and Cai sat on the other. There was at least seven meters between us. Who needed a room this large? It took me a while to crane my head around in order to absorb all the details. The art on the wall reminded me of blue blood splatters. The carpets were in the shapes of animals. The edges on the couches were sharp enough to cut.

Was Lone trying to intimidate us with his interior decorating?

"So, the big shot wants us to work as instigators, is that it?" Cai asked. He patted some of the nearby pillows. "Little dogs for his games?"

"Something like that," I muttered, my attention returning to Helia.

She nuzzled against me and smiled whenever I moved, including taking a deep breath.

I forced myself to turn to Cai. "I'm thinking it might be too much. I don't want to wreck this whole system or orchestrate some sort of propaganda against Homo sapiens."

Cai scoffed. "Too late now, chump."

"Why's that?"

"Because you're in too deep." Cai waved his arm around, motioning to the room. "You don't get brought into the inner sanctum only to ultimately say *no*. These assholes expect something from you. If you turn them down now, they're going to add *you* to their shitlist, do you understand?"

Damn. He made a lot of sense.

Lone had me in a tight spot. I could say *yes* and then half-ass everything, but if I straight up told him to go to hell, I'd just be making a powerful enemy.

"Fine," I said. "I'll take this deal."

Helia giggled and ran her hands over my arm. "That's amazing. I'm sure you'll love working with General Lone. He's so talented. Beyond compare."

"Who's this?" Cai said with a reverse nod at Helia. "I didn't want to say anything at first, since, uh, she looks like that other dame, but this is just getting awkward."

"You've seen the thug bodyguards around here, right?" I asked.

Cai nodded.

"They all look alike, yeah?"

"Yeah. So what?"

"It's because they're all genetically engineered to fulfill certain roles. The tubes they were baked in have a few settings always checked, so it results in people who look like twins." I tilted my head, motioning to Helia. "Let's just say the same thing happened here."

"She and Sawyer could be twins?"

I held up a hand, anger lancing through my system. There was no reason to mention Sawyer's name. Not here. Not ever.

Helia didn't seem to recognize it, though. She tilted her head from side to side, her eyes wide. "Hm? Is something the matter?"

"Nah, babe," I said with a smirk. "We're gonna work with Lone. Everything will go smoothly."

"Excellent." Helia jumped from the couch and then clapped her hands together. "Let me get you both drinks."

The bar wasn't far. "We can get them ourselves," I said, half-wanting to pour myself something stiffer than reasonable.

"N-No." Helia hurried for the bar just beyond the theater room. "General Lone would be furious if I allowed you two to get your own drinks. Please wait here! I'll be right back."

The bartender in the corner coughed, and I almost shit a brick. I had forgotten all about that guy. Helia shot the man a glare as she left the room, and I wondered if there was something there. Was it some sort of game between them? Who would get to serve who?

Or perhaps Lone had some sort of weird hierarchy they had to follow.

"How long are we gonna be here?" Cai asked.

I shook my head. "They didn't say. I assume a few more hours, since Lone said something about eating, but I'm not about to ask."

"Good call. Just wait until he dismisses us. Less of a chance we'll get punked."

When Helia returned, she had a whole damn tray filled with treats, drinks, and ice. Some of the cookies were shaped like koi fish. Helia handed one over to me with a genuine smile, like she was proud of it.

"You make these?" I asked, my voice low.

She nodded. "Aren't they cute? They make me happy when I look at them." Then she shook her head and laughed. "I'm sorry. That must sound childish."

"It's fine," I whispered, staring at the treat. It reminded me of Blub.

Had Sawyer been forced to do this, when she had been with Lone?

Helia served Cai and me with a smile, her thin dress a distraction the entire time. She was mostly flat, but she had enough jiggle to be fun when she bounced around. Most women hated the staring —even if they wore something to draw the eye—but Helia neither said anything nor attempted to hide. Was this her idea of fun? Or was it Lone's?

I already knew the answer.

With gritted teeth, I pulled off my tank top.

Cai's eyebrows shot to his dark hairline. The bartender in the corner of the room leaned over to get a better look. The chef and the musician were in the corners behind me—who knows what they thought? But Helia reacted only the slightest bit.

"Are you warm?" she asked. "Or would you like me to show you to one of the guest roo—"

I grabbed her, and then pulled my tank top over her head and onto her body.

Everyone…

Their expressions were priceless—although clearly baffled.

I didn't care. I continued with my work. I pulled Helia's arms through the holes and then secured my black shirt in place, making sure it covered everything. Her cheeks grew red, and her eyes got wide. When Helia glanced up at me, it was with the most confusion of anyone in the room.

"You… want me *more* dressed?"

"What? You hate clothing or something?" Then I motioned to the couch. "C'mon. Sit with us. You have to entertain me, right? Or else Lone will get mad?"

Helia slowly nodded.

"Then enjoy how good my tank top smells and have a drink. *That* will entertain me the most."

The silence that followed irritated me. Why were these instructions so difficult to understand? Fortunately, Helia did as she was told. She took her seat, got herself a glass of whiskey, and then settled in next to me.

I preferred her without my tank top—obviously—but not if she was *forced* to dress that way. I liked my partners willing. Actually, I preferred them *excited*. I wanted them to want me. Anything short of that irritated me.

I was a fuckin' catch. No one compared to me in the sack. And if I wanted, I could get Helia out of her clothing the old-fashioned way. I didn't need Lone's disgusting tactics.

Cai shifted around his couch, his eyes narrowed in bemused curiosity. "You're the weirdest starship captain I've ever interacted with."

I raised a glass to toast his statement. "I'm the *best* starship captain you've ever interacted with, just you wait and see."

SIXTEEN

New Officer

Although General Lone had mentioned food as a passing comment, he hadn't meant we'd *eat together*. No, that was far too beneath him, apparently. Instead, Cai and I got to remain in his plush theater room. We had food brought to us, but we ate without the general.

The food wasn't bad—the opposite, really. He'd said we'd be eating some sort of genetically engineered desert buffalo. Apparently, those were *large* animals, because I had never heard of them. Space stations didn't have room for animals that size.

Regardless, whatever the hell a buffalo was, it was also fucking delicious. I practically moaned as I ate the piece of steak that Helia served me. She giggled as she watched me consume everything, to the point I thought she might have voyeuristic oral fixation.

Sawyer was somewhat of a voyeur as well...

I watched Helia with a bit of fascination.

"Were the cookies good?" she asked.

I nodded once. "Yeah. I didn't like the thought of eating koi fish, though."

"Oh." Helia's expression dropped for a moment, then she artificially returned it to her force-happy attitude. "I apologize. I'll make sure I make them different shapes for your next visit."

I shook my head. "Don't. I like them. I just like the live fish more." Then I leaned back on the couch and smiled. I wanted to say something more to her, but I couldn't find the words. What would Sawyer have asked her?

"You're staring," Helia whispered as she cuddled close to me on the couch. She poked at the empty plate on my lap. "General Lone said that if you were fascinated with me, I should take you to the pool room and make sure you had a wonderful experience here."

She said everything with a sheepish smile and hesitation.

I didn't like it.

Thoughts of Sawyer continued to rattle around my skull.

Cai sat across the room on his own couch, practically orgasming every time he took another bite of his meal. He wasn't even concerned with us. I could probably leave and enjoy a dip in the pool, but...

I leaned in closer to Helia. A part of me wanted to ask her if she was in danger, but I knew that wouldn't get me anywhere. Even if this place was a *dead zone*, there were eyes all around us. She couldn't say she was in distress. She couldn't ask for help.

But perhaps I could still get answers.

In a gruff whisper, I asked, "Lone wants me to have a good time?"

Helia nodded against my shoulder. "Anything you want, I'll provide it."

"I don't know about that. I'm sure Lone wouldn't want me damaging his property."

She tensed, but the tone of her voice never changed. With a soft touch of her fingers across the back of my hand, Helia said, "The villa can easily be repaired."

"I wasn't talking about the building."

A period of silence stretched between us. I didn't mean it—I wasn't a sadist—but if *she* thought I was, I knew she'd be willing to answer a few more questions. Helia eventually replied with, "General Lone has the best healing vats on all of Vectin-10."

That explained why Helia didn't have any scars. Even if she was being torn apart every night, so long as she was dipped in mother-cell fluid, she'd be good to go again. The thought sickened me.

"You used healing vats before?" I asked, trying my damnedest to conceal my anger. "Perhaps the general and I have similar tastes, then."

"It has been my experience that *all* powerful individuals have similar tastes to General Lone." Helia said everything with a sultry and alluring tone. When she smiled, though, it wasn't genuine. I knew Sawyer enough to recognize the signs. "Perhaps there's something intoxicating about blood and control."

All individuals? More than just Lone?

Did that freak just loan out Helia like a vehicle people could use for a quick ride? Was that what he had done to Sawyer as well? Every detail of this encounter added to my building rage.

"I don't think you've ever been with someone like me before," I said, unable to keep some of the hate from my voice. It made me sound like a psychopath, but I supposed that was what I was going for. "I might break a bone or two."

Helia shivered and then shook her head. "You needn't worry. General Lone designed me without the ability to feel the worst of pains. I won't… I won't lose consciousness or fall into shock."

I stood from the couch.

Helia flinched back, her eyes wide.

Cai stopped mid-chew. Once he got a good look at my face, he also stood. With all the grit of a street kid, he spit his masticated meat onto the floor.

"What is it?" Cai asked.

"I need to speak to General Lone," I said as I headed to the door, my vision practically tunneling. The urge to rip somebody apart was overwhelming. I didn't care about Helia—I barely knew her—but she looked so much like Sawyer. All I could think about was her.

And all her scars.

I slammed my way out of the theater room and strode down the long corridor, my body practically operating on autopilot. What the fuck would I say to that monster? Could I kill him in a straight fight —in his own home—without my weapons?

Probably not.

Superhumans were stronger and faster than any human, even genetically-engineered humans, like me. I'd be at a terrible disadvantage.

And if I lost, I'd never get my revenge against Endellion. That fact alone chilled some of my anger. So, what was my alternate plan? Dick-punch this lunatic and steal Helia? That would still result in me being banned from this quadrant of space.

It made me wonder how Endellion had gotten away with rescuing Sawyer…

Cai jogged to catch up to me, then he matched my gait and snorted. "What're you doing? The food give you a stomachache or something?"

"I just need to clear a few things up with him," I said, my words heated and terse.

"Did that girl tell you something shocking or what? You two were whispering for a long-ass time."

"Forget about it. I'll handle everything."

"You're not normally this cold," Cai said as he gave me the once-over.

I forced a smirk. "You're not normally this inquisitive. Unusual circumstances require unusual responses."

Although I didn't know exactly where Lone was, I listened for voices and echoes. When I heard something beyond the corridor, I headed for it. We entered the main room, and then passed through without incident. I headed for another hall, and then slammed through another door, irritated this place didn't have automatic opening mechanisms.

For some forsaken reason, it was "fancier" to have compounds and buildings with antiquated building design. This was a "classical abode" complete with round handles on the doors and visible hinges.

I hated it.

Without seeing much of my surroundings, I entered another

room and then came to an abrupt halt. Cai practically ran into me, but he narrowly sidestepped and then glanced around.

An underground greenhouse.

Plants of all shapes and sizes were arranged in a park-like fashion, complete with a beautiful stone walkway and cushioned benches for sitting and enjoying the scene. I inhaled deeply to absorb the fragrance of the many flowers, tiny pine trees, and leafy ferns. The place looked like it had been finished yesterday—immaculate and well cared for. There wasn't a single leaf on the ground, or a bush that hadn't been trimmed.

How did this oasis exist under a desert?

Thankfully, General Lone was here.

And so was someone else. That precious little girl, Victtra Barten. She wore the same high-tech enviro-suit and stood next to Lone with a sense of belonging and purpose. Although I thought she was tall, she didn't compare to Lone's three meters.

Her silvery hair matched his, though. They looked like they had been cut from the same cloth, but I knew that wasn't the case. All superhumans had bizarre surnames. They weren't descended from any humans—the first superhumans had been created in test tubes in some lab hundreds of years ago. The first batch that had lived had each been named after the test tube they had emerged from.

The superhumans with the last name *Lone* were from test tube *one*. The number was in their name.

Victtra Barten had obviously descended from the superhumans who had emerged from the tenth test tube.

Separate families.

They all still looked alike, though. Same two-toned skin. Same weird hair stylings. Same freakish size, growth, and intelligence.

"If it isn't Captain Demarco," General Lone said before I could open my mouth. "What perfect timing. Come. I have one last thing to discuss with you." He beckoned me with a wave of his hand.

The plants in the room did wonders for my rage. Although I still felt the sting of anger on the edge of my thoughts, I managed to calmly cross the greenhouse. Cai shadowed me the entire way, his movements more tense and awkward than my own. I wanted to touch the nearby plants as I walked by—plants were rarely seen on my "hometown" of Capital Station. They were almost magical in my mind.

General Lone didn't waste any time. The moment I got close, he said, "Victtra told me of your command style. She was impressed with how you handled the rebellion."

Impressed? The information caught me off guard. I figured she would've bad-mouthed me the entire time.

"That's nice," I said, far more sarcastic than I should've been. "I'm glad she enjoyed her time on my starship. I don't normally take passengers."

"She wasn't keen on how you handled the law, however."

The law?

"I'm going to interrogate the rebellion leaders you captured," Victtra said matter-of-factly. "I told you there were loopholes that would allow me to investigate them. I'm rather disappointed in your overall knowledge of the legal system."

Every word she said cut into my confidence. What if those rebellion officers knew that Endellion had stolen their starships and enviro-suits? Then Victtra would know *for sure* that someone had impersonated the rebellion during the assassination.

I shot her a sidelong glance, and Victtra replied with a smirk.

Something told me this wasn't going to end well.

Before Lone could get into some other topic, I interjected with, "Listen, I know we already discussed compensation for my work." I kept everything vague, just in case Victtra wasn't in on plan. "But I don't just want credits and resources. I want something else. Something specific."

"Is that right?" Lone drawled, the corner of his lips curling upward into some sadist grin he just couldn't hide. "I'm anxious to hear what you want."

"Helia," I stated.

My request seemed to confuse him. For a moment, he just regarded me with a long stare, as though he thought he heard me wrong.

"The woman I engineered?" Lone finally asked. "You're *that* fascinated by her?"

"What can I say?" I grabbed the crotch of my pants and adjusted it. "Clearly, I'm ruled by baser instincts. I get obsessed with specific women."

That wasn't true—but Lone didn't know that. All he knew about me was that I wanted to kill Endellion, and I had a "crush" on his clone-servant. I probably *did* look like someone with an obsession problem. Better to lean into it than correct him.

"Interesting," Lone said. "But I prefer to keep my personal assistant to myself." Before I could protest, he held up a hand. "But don't worry. You also have something I want, and perhaps we can make a trade."

"A trade?"

Lone motioned to Victtra. She straightened her posture and stared down her nose at me, like she couldn't wait for the announcement.

"Miss Barten wishes to join the crew of the *Star Marque* for a short period of time while she investigates the murder of her father. I told her that you would be hunting down rebellion criminals, and she wanted the opportunity to interrogate more of them."

I was about to launch into an epic tirade against the whole suggestion, but Cai grabbed my arm and dug his fingers into my flesh. I whirled on him, my rage transferring to him in an instant. He didn't back down. He met my glare with one of his own.

"*Think about this,*" Cai hissed under his breath.

Even Lysander would be berating me here, I knew it.

When I went to face Lone and Victtra again, I forced myself to take a breath. "I can take her on as a guest, I suppose… But not a member of my crew. We have standards."

"That's not acceptable," Victtra started, cold and precise. "I'm a licensed starfighter, and I know your crew is understaffed."

"*You're* a licensed starfighter?"

I wasn't even licensed. I had been taught by members of the *Star Marque* as a side gig.

"I completed my courses at *Starfield University.*" Victtra squared her shoulders and held her hands behind her back. "I was second in my class—my scores are higher than any human could possibly hope to achieve. I graduated on the accelerated track, along with the other superhumans. It took us a fourth the time of the normal trainees."

"This line of work is dangerous."

"I know the risks. I'm old enough to accept responsibility."

"Aren't you *young?*" I balked, struggling for *some* reason to deny her. "I thought… you were a superhuman *child?*"

Victtra waved away my comment. "I may be a child, Captain Demarco, but unlike with humans, that isn't as much of a disadvantage. I'm a member of Homo superior. You see, humans require a lengthy period of time after they're born for their brains to develop. This process is called *synaptic pruning.* Human children have excess synapses firing in their brains, which cause them to act out in an immature manner. The older humans get, the less these synapses interfere with their rational thoughts."

I… didn't know that.

"But when superhumans were designed, that *synaptic pruning* was removed from our developmental cycle. Most superhuman children are fully capable of mature thoughts and actions at a very young age. Our brains are mature long before our bodies. It helps us develop skills faster. You'll find I'm more educated than most human adults."

General Lone gave me a smile—it seemed charismatic, but I knew better. It was a threat. "A superhuman on your starship will increase efficiency. You'll take Miss Barten and aid her in any way possible. I doubt this will lead her to a murderer, but I want to support my brethren. If you do this for me, once everything is said and done, I'll make sure Helia is stationed on the *Star Marque* for your pleasure."

"I want her *now,*" I stated, irritated that these freaks would tell me who I could and couldn't recruit.

Cai tightened his grip on my arm again. I didn't care.

"You're more than welcome to use her while you're here," Lone stated, no hint of giving-a-damn in his voice. "But she isn't to leave the villa. You're lucky I'm willing to part with her at all—the only way she leaves is if you do as I say."

There wouldn't be any arguing with him.

I swallowed hard, burying my pride and anger. When I glanced over at Victtra, it was like she was reveling in her newfound position of power over me. I wouldn't give her the satisfaction of complaining. She wanted to be a member of my crew? Fine. I'd stick it out for Helia's sake.

No one deserved what Sawyer had gone through.

"You're right, having a superhuman crewmate will be a great boon," I said with a smirk. "I can't think of another enforcer ship that can boast that."

"Perfect," General Lone said. "Then I'll assign her as one of your starfighter officers."

"Officer?" Cai interjected, almost offended.

"Miss Barten wasn't lying about her accomplishments. And I've read over the *Star Marque's* crew complement. She far superior to anyone you have. It's only logical she would be given an officer position."

"But officer pay is much higher," I said, trying to find that magical loophole.

"The armed forces of Vectin-10 will be picking up the bill." Then General Lone motioned to the far door. "And as long as you have nothing else, our meeting is over." He turned on his heel and headed for the opposite end of the greenhouse. "I look forward to reading your reports, Captain Demarco."

SEVENTEEN

Bounty Hunting

The shuttle ride to the surface was as silent as a well-shaken baby.

Cai sat on his own bench, peaceful and content. But Victtra had an issue. She had positioned herself on the same bench as me, mere centimeters away. She was close enough that I could smell her—the faint musk of pheromones, the kind that were sweet and enticing.

All superhumans had the ability to alter their chemical scents. Hell, even I had it—it was one of the first things genetic engineers had truly mastered. By altering chemicals that were excreted from the body, someone could "smell nice" or "smell aggressive." Most people couldn't articulate that, though. The scents would just *make them react differently*.

Like smelling freshly grilled meat caused people to get hungry.

But superhumans—and genetically-modified assholes, like me— could detect the difference if they knew what they were looking for.

And for some reason, Victtra had chosen to smell pleasant.

I faced her with a half-smile, and she returned it in kind.

"I'm the captain," I stated. "What I say goes. Understood?"

"Perfectly," Victtra replied.

"If you disobey even a single command during a firefight, I'll have you sent straight to the brig. I don't care how smart you think you are. You follow orders."

Superhumans had tiny holes on their necks—from their ears down to their collarbones. They were like extra little noses. They allowed superhumans to breathe faster and better, and to prevent them from being choked if someone had a hand around their neck. Extra oxygen in the blood meant they were naturally more athletic and could recover from fatigue easier.

And the little holes flared when they got really angry.

It amused me.

Victtra placed her hands in her lap and then threw some of her metallic hair over her shoulder. "You sound jealous, Captain Demarco. I know it's easy for you Homo sapiens to look upon your superiors with envy, but I thought a man of your position wouldn't have that problem."

"I'm not jealous. I just know your kind gets heads so big, you need a lift to carry them around."

"We are better than you," Victtra said matter-of-factly, all ice and no warmth in her voice. "You'd be wise to remember that."

"Yeah, but the difference between us can be bridged," I said with a shrug. "I've seen it."

"No human ever really gets the best of us."

"Is that so?" I leaned back on the bench, anger driving my decisions. "Remind me again—a *human* killed your father, right?"

Cai must have been listening to the conversation, because he suddenly got up from his bench and moved to the farthest bench away, a good three meters from me and Victtra. What a sad sack. He didn't even have the balls to face our direction.

I probably shouldn't have provoked her, but sometimes I couldn't help myself.

Victtra held her breath for a long moment. When she answered, her voice remained calm, but her scent was laced with anger. "I would kindly ask that you leave my father out of our discussions. He was a dignified emissary for the Federation, cut down before his time." She hardened her gaze. "Please don't drag his name into a dick-checking contest. Thank you."

I admired her ability to restrain herself, but I still didn't care for her.

"How about you focus on finding your father's killer, and I'll focus on finding us rebellion sad sacks?" I turned away from her, done with this. "We don't really need to interact under any circumstance."

"I'm your new starfighter officer."

"Yeah, well, we'll be taking a lot of bounty hunting requests for the near future, so fighting in our starfighters won't be necessary."

That fact must've bothered her. Victtra went silent.

I stared at the side of the shuttle, my mind on everything but our current ride to the surface. Could I kill Victtra and get away with it? I hadn't wanted to eighteen months ago, because she had been an innocent child wrapped up in a war of ambition.

Now she was an obstacle to my goals. That changed things.

It was dangerous being an enforcer—especially on some of the space stations. It would be easy to kill her and shift the blame. Or maybe seriously injure her, so she had to leave the *Star Marque*.

Then again... if Victtra was hurt, it'd be on me. They'd have my ass so fast, I wouldn't have time to ask for lube. Which meant I couldn't actively do anything about her.

What would Endellion do? She'd have some sort of convoluted plan that would involve the superhumans accidentally harming Victtra—or something equally crazy. How could I do that? How could I have her death be *someone else's* fault?

I rubbed my chin and stared intently at the shuttle wall, not even seeing my surroundings.

There would be an opportunity in the future. I would just need to recognize it when it happened.

THE *STAR MARQUE'S* conference room made it easy to see the void of space. One wall was completely made of transparent dura-lumin, like a glass window, but a thousand times sturdier. Even docked to Vectin-10's space elevator, the window offered a view of the black tide.

I stood at the head of the conference table. All my officers were gathered—including Victtra. She sat on one side, and everyone else had sat on the opposite side, like they wanted to get a good look at her, and this was the only polite way to do so.

Her two bodyguards stood behind her, looming like the thugs they were. Their muscle and weight were impressive—like mine— and while they were physically superior to most in the room, their genetic codes had been altered to make them more obedient by nature.

They wouldn't leave Victtra's side unless she wanted them gone.

"You need to send away One and Two," I said, giving Victtra a sidelong glance. "This is a meeting for officers *only*."

Both bodyguards had their enviro-suits on and their helmets up, completely masking their faces. The man closest to me turned his head until my face reflected directly on the visor of his helmet.

"Who are *One and Two?*" the bodyguard asked, his voice machine-like, filtered by the enviro-suit.

"*You*, asshole. You're *One*." I pointed to the other guy. "That's *Two*." Then I motioned to the door. "Now get out of here."

The bodyguards turned their attention to Victtra. They needed her command to leave, it seemed. Just as I had thought.

She nodded once, her movement so precise, it almost looked unnatural. The two genetically-modified men left the room without another word. One of them glanced at me—I think it was Two— but it wasn't for long, and I couldn't see his face.

It would make my day if he started a fight. I really wanted to kick someone's ass.

But I had work to do.

"Everyone, I have to introduce our newest officer." I motioned to our new superhuman. "This is Victtra Barten. She's no longer a guest on the ship, but our resident starfighter expert." Then I gestured across the conference table. "Victtra, this is Dr. Clay, my chief medical officer."

The man's narrow face scrunched as he awkwardly forced a

smile. "It's a pleasure to have a member of Homo superior with us. I used to cater to some prominent members of your species before I was employed on the *Star Marque*."

Victtra nodded but said nothing.

I briefly wondered if having her species pointed out nonstop bothered her. Probably not. She likely enjoyed it.

I went down the line of seats and motioned to Lysander. "You've interacted with my vice-captain enough to know him well, right?"

Again, she nodded.

Then I got to Noah and hesitated. "Yeah, well, Noah is now your vice-starfighter officer. He'll be showing you how we operate."

Noah leaned on the conference table, his tall and lanky frame similar to Victtra's young superhuman body. He smiled—probably genuine.

"It's a pleasure to meet you," Noah said. "I, uh, didn't do anything famous before the *Star Marque*. I've been part of this crew for a few years now."

Cai—knowing I was about to introduce him—sat straighter in his chair. "I'm Cai Qi, the ground commander. I'm in charge of training a special squad of bounty hunter types." He rubbed at the tattoos on his arms. His tank top made it easy to see the details from his wrists all the way to his shoulders.

With a sarcastic huff, he said, "And before this *prestigious* job, I was a bounty hunter. And before that, I helped run a daycare."

I snorted and laughed. "The kids you kept trapped in a basement didn't count as daycare."

"Keep it professional," Lysander said through his gritted teeth.

"I was just joking, of course." I rolled my eyes and waved away the comment.

Cai shrugged. "I was tryin' to say that I helped my mother run this daycare, and at some point, Federation officials got involved, and they demanded my mom work in a specific section of our station, and it happened to be near some Homo superior kids."

"Very entertaining," Victtra drawled. "I'll log that information away for further use in the future, I'm sure."

She had a bit of sarcasm in her. Maybe we could get along after all.

"And last, but not least, this is my chief cyber operations officer, Sawyer." I motioned to her, but I knew that wasn't necessary. Victtra had been giving Sawyer odd looks since we had entered the conference room.

I didn't blame her.

Sawyer and Helia could be twins.

Genetically, they *were* twins.

"I see you have a collection going," Victtra muttered under her breath. Then she offered Sawyer a tight smile. "A pleasure to make your acquaintance."

Sawyer said nothing. She kept her head down, her intent gaze glued to the PAD on her forearm. She typed away on the thin screen like she couldn't hear a damn thing. I knew better, though.

This was my fault.

We were now neck-deep with General Lone, and we had a superhuman in our midst who wouldn't hesitate to have us all arrested. This wasn't my best performance, and Sawyer was irritated.

I'd have to deal with that later, though.

I slammed my hand on the conference table, and everyone flinched. They turned to me and I pointed to the computer screens on the table in front of them. Everyone glanced at their individual lists of information.

"Those are the potential bounties in the whole quadrant," I said. "Most of them are chumps who simply didn't make it to their court appointments, but some of those assholes are murder-gangsters on the run."

"Is *murder-gangster* an official term?" Dr. Clay asked, snide and condescending.

Noah—who probably hadn't caught the sardonic tone—chimed in with, "Actually, three of these guys are classified as *mass murderers*, which means they killed more than three people in the same geographical location, at the same time." He pointed to his screen and highlighted the people at the top. "These ones are classified as *serial killers* because they killed three or more people at different locations and different times. Technically, you can be charged with gang affiliation *and* murder so long as—"

"Enough," Cai said, snapping his fingers like he was trying to get the attention of an untrained dog. Then he pointed to a specific name on the list. "This here. This is the guy we want."

Everyone glanced at their screens as Cai highlighted it for the group. It was the fourth name on the list—a man by the name of Horas Hines. His crimes were listed as: TToS tampering, three counts of murder, and illegal surveillance.

His bounty was worth a surprising two million credits.

"Why this guy?" I asked.

"You said you wanted to go after rebellion guys, right?" Cai double-tapped Horas's name and brought up more information on his screen. "See this? He's one of them."

"How do you know he is rebellion?"

"That crime—TToS tampering—is when people mess with the Federation mandated codes of a starship."

Like Sawyer was doing all the time.

It wasn't a crime until we got caught, right?

"All the rebellion chumps do it," Cai said with a smirk. "And that surveillance crime means he was probably the fall guy for some sort of rebellion operation. I guarantee."

"What do you mean?"

"I mean, these rebellion guys go to a space station in small teams. Maybe three or four. If they're going to kill someone, they make sure one of them is caught for the crime so the others can escape. The one *caught*—" Cai used air-quotes, "—makes a break for it while the others get away clean."

"You're saying this man is an assassin?" Victtra asked, her voice practically a whisper. "You're certain?"

Cai nodded once. "I've rounded up a dozen of these guys before. I know their tricks."

I stared at the bounty next to his name. Two million. He was also listed as *highly dangerous* and *elusive*. That meant we'd be chasing him for a long while… But maybe Cai's smarts would help cut down the time.

If he didn't, this could all be one wild chase through space, though. The rebellion had friends on every space station. Horas could hide from us for a long time, in theory. Only *we* were on a time crunch, not him.

Victtra scooted to the edge of her seat, her back straight. "I vote we pursue Mr. Hines."

"It's not really a voting situation," I said. "This isn't a republic. I'm the captain."

"But you take input from your officers, don't you?" Victtra glanced over at Cai. "And your ground commander articulated the best course of action, didn't he?"

The others at the conference table exchanged nervous glances. Well, except Sawyer. She still hadn't looked up. I doubted she even cared who we went after.

Dr. Clay cleared his throat. "I agree with our new starfighter officer."

Of course he did. He wanted to kiss her ass so hard, he was preparing his nose for the eventual brown smears.

"Are there any other people you suggest?" Lysander interjected. He stared at the list, thorough in everything he did. "We could at least pick three and then narrow down our options."

"No," Sawyer said. She barely made a noise, but everyone else stopped what they were doing. We turned to face her. Sawyer didn't even look up from her PAD. "We should go after Horas Hines."

I walked around the conference table—it was large enough for twenty fools, but we barely had seven. It didn't take me long to reach Sawyer.

"Why this one?" I asked in a casual volume and tone.

She briefly paused her typing to answer, "Because we won't have to chase him far. I know he's here on Vectin-10."

EIGHTEEN

Horas Hines

"How do you know he's here?" I asked.

Sawyer's cold, almost robotic movements confirmed my suspicions. She hated everything about this mission and case. I didn't even need to ask.

She replied, "There's a message in the junk code of the space elevator's main programming. It's from Horas Hines. He wants a ship off the planet, and he's asking for assistance."

"Junk code?" I leaned on her chair, honestly curious. "What's that?"

"I don't think I have enough patience, or crayons, to explain it to you," she said, curt.

Normally, I wouldn't fucking take that—but this was Sawyer, and all her quip did was drive home the guilt. Part of me wanted to send General Lone a message and tell him I wouldn't be part of his operations, but Cai had been right. I couldn't back out now. Best I just do as he wanted, and get what I needed from him, before angering any more of these "superior humans."

Noah sat a little straighter in his chair. "Junk code is the part of a program that doesn't actually do anything." He answered the question with the enthusiasm of a school kid. "It's usually left in the program because the programmer wrote the code poorly."

"Or in this case, *intentionally put it there*," Sawyer said, tapping at her PAD. "Instead of sending a message the old-fashioned way, someone wrote a message through the space elevator's coding, and when our ship docks to the space elevator, we can access that part of the code."

"How has no one caught this?" I asked.

Sawyer shrugged. "Maybe someone has. I just did. I'm sure Horas wants to find some rebellion guys to help him."

Cai shot out of his seat. "We should go right now." He hustled around the conference table and headed for the door with a spring in his step. When he noticed no one else had jumped up, he stopped and faced us. "Well? Get your asses movin'. If your engineer is right, that means our target is definitely preparing to leave. We should catch him *before* he gets off planet."

It also meant he was on the move. He'd likely have friends by now, or potentially someone who was going to give him a ride.

"Is this how you always conduct your officer meetings?" Victtra asked, her judgmental gaze lingering on Sawyer and then slow-panning over to Cai. "Everyone gets their insults in before rushing out the door?"

I could practically hear Lysander's teeth grinding.

"This is unorthodox," Lysander said before I could answer. "We're usually much more professional."

Dr. Clay shook his head in sardonic disagreement.

"*We need to go.*" Cai slammed his hand on the bulkhead of the starship, gaining everyone's attention. "Traveling anywhere on a planet takes time. We shouldn't be wasting it on etiquette."

"Is it really imperative we all jump up right now?" Lysander asked, probably because he wanted to do some sort of "official end" to the meeting.

"*I was a bounty hunter for most of my life.*" Cai held his hands out like a man begging for a scrap of food. "Do you think a guy with a two-million-credit bounty on his head is gonna take his *sweet-ass time* gettin' to a starship?" Then he made some motion like he was mock-slapping Dr. Clay across the face. "Of course not! In order to make money in this line of work, you have to seize opportunities when they come your way. *Get up. We're leaving.*"

I pushed away from Sawyer's chair and walked around the conference table. "He's right. Let's get going."

Our ground team wasn't really skilled at the moment, but I trusted Lysander and Cai—even if they seemed to hate each other's guts. To my surprise, Noah jumped up from his seat and hurried over to me.

"Can I join you on the planet?" he asked. "I'd love to help catch this guy."

I shrugged. "Fine."

"I'll join you as well." Victtra stood from her chair.

I pointed at her. "No. Not you."

"You're allowing the *other* starfighter officer to join you." She said everything with a hint of anger. "And I assure you, I'm more skilled at locating people. My eyesight is superior, my—"

"And you stick out like a corpse in a nursery." I gestured to everyone else. "*Homo superior* don't go walking around with the rest of us chumps. You'll get us caught in no time."

With quick wits, Victtra replied, "Then take one of my bodyguards to the surface. Both of my men are skilled combatants. They'll be a valuable asset."

She wanted eyes on our activities. That was the only reason she wanted one of her bodyguards to go with. But what did it matter? I wasn't about to do anything incriminating. And her goons *would* come in handy.

"Fine," I said. "I'll take Two."

"He has a proper name."

"I don't care," I said as I followed Cai out of the conference room.

<hr>

OUR BOUNTY HUNTING team consisted of five people—me, Noah, Lysander, Cai, and Two. In order to blend in with the workers of Vectin-10, Cai had said we couldn't wear enviro-suits, which meant we each had casualwear. My cargo pants and tank top had seen better days. Lysander, on the other hand, had creases across most of his outfit, like it had been folded so tight and perfectly that the edges could now cut a bitch.

"Your mom teach you how to put away your clothes?" I asked him with a half-smile.

He eyed my clothing. "It's called *discipline*, Demarco. You'd be respectable if you could master it."

The hot wind rushed by, carrying trace amounts of sand. The glittering desert in the far distance hurt my eyes. I held a hand on my forehead, shielding my vision from the oppressive heat. The Vectin star burned with an unrivaled intensity.

I glanced down at the PAD on my left forearm.

Sawyer still hadn't messaged me. She had left us all the information she had on Horas Hines and then hadn't said a word afterward. It irritated me.

Thankfully, she had told us Horas would likely be near the storage facilities. From there, Cai was confident he could find our target. He took us straight back to a loading platform connected to a gigantic warehouse. Trucks and mag-lev trains could load and unload goods from the massive dock, and hundreds of workers were busy using the machinery to lift and haul two-ton crates.

Food and supplies, most likely. It had to be.

Cai wandered into the massive warehouse to get information, which left the rest of us to mill about the place. I didn't like it. We hadn't told anyone we were enforcers—Cai had gotten us into the storage facility through unknown means. Well, we had walked to the front gates, and then he had spoken to some people, but I still didn't understand how he had gotten us all inside without many questions.

What secrets did he have? Why not just tell us?

Or perhaps these were tricks of the trade.

Noah walked around with his thumbs hooked on the top of his cargo pants. "Wow. That desert is amazing." He also shielded his eyes as he stared out beyond the fence on the north side of the facility. "I've seen it from space tons of times, but up close, it's completely different."

"Stay close," Lysander said as he grabbed his brother on the shoulder. He yanked him back as an automated scanning bot drove by and examined the crates.

Noah shook off his brother's hand. "What was that for? The bot would've driven around me."

"Those things scan for defects," Lysander said under his breath, his eyes narrowed at the robot. "If you're accidentally scanned... It could cause trouble."

After a short sigh, Noah rubbed at his upper arm. Then he replied with a single nod before returning his attention to the distant horizon.

It surprised me how often Lysander thought about his status as a 'defect.' Did he worry about it all the time? Or just in public? How often had he and his brother been denied service because their genetics marked them as *unsuitable?*

The thoughts reminded me of Endellion...

No one knew she was a defect.

That was probably her biggest secret of all. If anyone found out—even other humans—they'd be disgusted. Which was a shame. It wasn't the fault of humans.

It was the fault of our quadrant's three stars. The radiation from the stars was far worse for humans than the single star we had been born under on our home-world planet. The triple radiation caused birth defects at a hideous rate, most of which were genetic, which meant they'd pass down to children.

I glanced over at Two.

The man returned my hard stare. He was here to rat me out to Victtra.

We... looked a lot alike.

He was tall, muscular, and his skin was a dark tan. His black hair was cut short, and his eyes were quick to pick up any movement.

Genetically modified. Just like me. The first people to alter themselves had done it to prevent the negative effects of radiation. But then humans had decided to make *superhumans*—far better at resisting genetic mutations and with perfect immunity to solar radiation—and the rest was history.

"What're you staring at?" Two asked, keeping his voice low.

I ran a hand over the stubble on my jaw. "Trash."

He tensed, and for half a second, I thought he'd be dumb enough to throw a punch. Then he relaxed and rotated his shoulders, defusing his own anger. "Workin' for the girl is just a job. We all gotta earn a livin'."

I didn't say anything.

That was a good answer, I had to admit.

A group of warehouse workers walked by, each wearing a dark red jumpsuit that marked them as employees of TransSide, some sort of shipping company. They eyed me as they went, their gazes lingering on my outfit.

We probably didn't have much time before someone threw us out of here.

Normally, I'd be afraid of getting caught—since trespassing could result in jail time—but we were technically enforcers. We carried immunities that would allow us to get away with trespassing, so long as it was in the pursuit of a criminal.

I still didn't want to deal with the hassle, though.

Noah looked away from the desert. "What's this Horas guy look like? Do you think he'll be dressed as one of these workers?"

"Probably," I muttered.

Then I poked at my PAD and brought up a picture of Horas. The man was whiter than pus, and his blond hair matched his sick complexion. The pink rings under his eyes told me he liked chems. Although he wasn't smiling in the photo, I would've put money down that his teeth were fucked.

He probably used stimulants. They were the only kind of chems that heightened someone's capabilities, at least for a short period. Those stims could make a man smarter, quicker, tougher—but they wrecked the human body more than unchecked maggots.

Horas probably used some stims to get all his jobs done, and now he was on the run.

Two glanced over and stared at my PAD. Lysander—not to be

left out—came around my other side and got another look at the man. Everyone had already seen the picture, but I guessed everyone wanted to see him again.

Cai strode out of the warehouse, wiping at his nose. He squinted his eyes as soon as the hot wind rushed him.

"Demarco," he called out. "We should check the transport gate." Then he snapped his fingers and pointed at the other three. "You all should follow one of those scanner bots around. If the little robot skips a box, check it manually. It might've been reprogrammed to intentionally miss something."

Noah jumped to the task like he had been born to it. "Yes, sir! We're on it." He turned on his heel and headed for the far crates, his gaze set on the one bot scanning the goods.

"We should regroup here in ten minutes," Lysander said. "Just to make sure nothing has happened."

I replied with a nod.

Two gave me another odd glance before heading off with Lysander and Noah. He didn't talk much, but for some reason, I liked him a lot more without his enviro-suit on. Maybe it was because *I* was so amazing. Why wouldn't I love someone like myself?

Cai crossed his arms, his tattoos visibly on display. He watched Lysander go, and then smiled. "Sorry about that. I just didn't want to get paired with that guy, so I figured I should call the shots."

"I don't care," I said with a shrug. "You know what we're doing down here."

"You have a lot of faith in me."

"I remember your work from Capital Station. Every fool I ran with was scared of you."

For a long moment, Cai didn't say anything. Then he turned his narrowed eyes on me. "Were *you* worth a bounty back in the day?"

"Don't we have to find Horas before he loads his body into a box?" I grabbed Cai by the upper arm and turned him around. "By the transport gate, right?"

After a couple of chuckles, Cai went silent. No more questions. No more looks. We just walked over to the gate in silence. Since Capital Station had exploded on Galvis-4, it wasn't like anyone would ever remember all of my terrible deeds, but there was always a possibility that some planetside computer would be dug up and my name would be on some list. It was better not to give Cai any terrible ideas.

"You think Horas is going to be in a crate?" I asked.

The transport gate was massive. Trucks the size of small starships drove through the opening, each hauling hundreds of tons. They needed to drive supplies all over Vectin-10. The desert planet didn't take kindly to those with low amounts of water.

"No," Cai muttered. "Too many guys die in those things. You wouldn't believe how often supplies are delayed. And if you're in there too long, you eventually dehydrate or suffocate or get sick—nasty business. Our guy will be driving the truck. Guaranteed."

Once we got closer to the gate, I scanned the drivers who went by. Most had tanner skin—too dark for our target—but their uniform-red jumpsuits did make it hard to distinguish one sad sack from the other. How many drivers were here? Thirty? Fifty?

I turned my attention to the men manning the gate. There was a security station behind a wall of transparent aluminum, with at least ten workers staring at computer screens, their gazes half-dead.

But then I saw him.

That pus-white complexion and sickly blond hair were undeniable.

Horas stood in the security station, sipping a drink like he had worked here for decades. Although I was outside the security station —and across the road, on a small walkway meant for truck drivers —my enhanced sight picked up every detail.

I turned around to grab Cai, but I was confronted by a man in a black jumpsuit.

His chest and legs were thicker than the rest of him—which meant he wore body armor—but his half-helmet didn't quite cover his fat head. The man held a little laser rifle. Plasma had too much of a kick. Lasers were easier to wield for a man of his… physique.

"Excuse me," Fat-Head said as he gave me the once over. "What's a dog like you doin' here?"

Cai glanced over and frowned. "Hey. We're here with Trans-

Side's worker union. Leave us alone while we do our assessment." He held up his arm with the PAD and pointed to the thin screen.

Most of these planet workers didn't have the funds to buy themselves a fancy PAD. No one here—not all the men in jumpsuits in this entire facility—had one. It was a good disguise, since most government workers were issued PADs, but why hadn't Cai just revealed our identities now that we knew Horas's location?

I'd let him make the decisions.

"But do you have a permit on that thing?" Fat-Head asked. Then he motioned to me. "Is this your bodyguard or somethin'? We don't let these ones loose around here."

All of us "genetically modified humans" worked for Homo superior. That was the myth, anyway. We were traitors to our kind. No better than scum. I understood—it was the reason I hated Two.

"Back off," I growled, gaining Fat-Head's full attention. "We're busy. Go deal with real problems."

"If you don't have a permit, I'm gonna throw you outta here."

I grabbed the man's squishy arm and hauled him closer to me. Fat-Head uttered a soft gasp, like he hadn't expected that at all, and I almost laughed. This man wouldn't have lasted long on Capital Station.

"Listen—talking to you is killing brain cells so fast, I'll be dead by the end of this conversation. Take your happy ass out of here and leave us to our work or else things will get rough for you."

Before he could answer, I shoved the man away.

I hoped he would decide to go get a manager or something. That way, I'd have enough time to grab Horas before any sort of commotion broke out.

Fat-Head hesitated. He held his laser rifle close, like it would protect him. I turned away, unconcerned. He would be sorry if he stayed. His one and only hope of making it home without any broken bones was to leave now.

"Cai," I said. Then I jerked my head in the direction of our target. "There he is."

"No kiddin'." Cai rubbed his hands together and smiled. "Perfect, perfect." Then he ran his hands down his sides, his smile barely restrained. "This is the most exciting part of the job, kid."

"*Kid?*" I balked.

"Everyone younger than me is a *kid* now." He shot me a glare, his expression more than serious. "Pay attention. We're going to surround the security station. I'll take the left door, you take the right. When we enter, we have to—"

Fat-Head pointed his laser rifle at me. "You two aren't goin' anywhere. I'm taking you both into custody."

I shot him a glower and then glanced back over at Horas. Our pasty target was shuffling between the other workers when he finally lifted his gaze and caught sight of me and Cai. We looked like thugs—I couldn't deny that—but it must've been the way we were staring at *him* that tipped Horas off.

He shot for the far exit, running faster than I thought he would.

"We're going to lose him," Cai growled under his breath.

Not if I could help it.

NINETEEN

Under Arrest

Fat-Head stepped forward. "Get on the ground."

"We're enforcers," I growled, holding up my PAD. "Leave us!"

Cai leapt onto the road and dashed after our target. I figured I could cut Horas off if I went out the front gate and headed for the main road. There was only one way out of here, after all. That punk would have to come to me.

The guard probably didn't believe us—not when Cai had offered him a completely different story for our presence. Fat-Head, in the most foolish move he could've made, shoved the tip of his rifle into my shoulder.

Which was going to cost him.

I grabbed the laser rifle and slammed it back into Fat-Head's face. I broke his nose, and blood exploded out his nostrils and onto his jumpsuit. Then I jerked his weapon out of his grip.

"Step off, asshole," I said as I threw his weapon to the ground.

Fat-Head stumbled back, his eyes watering and his hands up over his busted face. Crimson soaked his chin and palms. He didn't say anything—a smart move—and instead, turned and ran off.

I gritted my teeth as I returned my attention to the security station.

Horas was already gone.

And so was Cai.

Cursing under my breath, I stepped onto the road, dashed in front of a moving truck—the bastard honked—and stepped around another vehicle before reaching one of the security station's doors. I touched the handle but shook my head.

I could stop to question the guards. But would they know anything valuable? They could just be rebellion sympathizers.

"Why are you hesitating?" Sawyer said over the comms of my PAD.

Her voice was like a cold drink in all this desert heat. I smirked to myself as I leapt away from the guard station and headed for the gate.

"I'm not hesitating," I said as I clicked on communication. "I'm strategizing."

"That doesn't sound like you."

"Maybe I'm learning new tricks."

"That doesn't sound like you, either."

The snark.

To my surprise, Cai had sent an emergency message to everyone involved on the ground. It detailed Horas's sighting and explained that Cai and I were in pursuit. I hadn't thought to inform anyone else of our operations—that wasn't something I had done on Capital Station—but it made sense here.

I should utilize my team more.

Right as I exited the gate, I noticed a truck pick up speed. The giant hauling vehicle wasn't fast, but it was so large that even at twenty-five kilometers per hour, it would do significant damage. The damn truck probably weighed sixty tons all by itself.

Horas sat in the driver's seat. Two others were in the cab, one with a laser pistol.

They sped for the gate, and the idiots in the security station released all barriers so that the truck could roll out. I stepped off to the side, to allow the truck to pass, but the moment it went by, I grabbed on to the passenger side door and lifted myself up.

The trunk continued to pick up speed.

The window slid down, and the man in the passenger seat gave me a hard once-over. He was human—probably in his forties—with a scar over his forehead. I'd seen the straight-line scars before. He had been in an accident where the visor of his helmet had smashed inward. The injuries from that were always the same.

Scar-Head held up his laser pistol, his grip firm, and his expertise on display.

But he made his first mistake when he rolled down his window.

I punched inward, much faster and stronger than the man could ever hope to be. I clipped his chin, sending him into slumberland. The second passenger—another gunner in the middle seat—opened fire. Laser guns had no kick, so he fired with his arm outstretched, as fast as he could pull the trigger.

Unfortunately for him, I saw the world differently.

My mental processing power was so fast, I saw everything that was happening as though it were in slow motion. For every second a normal schmoe got to comprehend something, it felt as though I had four. I saw the gunner reach for his weapon. I knew when he was pointing in my direction.

And I had plenty of time to grab Scar-Head and yank his unconscious body forward, shielding me from the laser blasts. The super-heated rays of light burned Scar-Head enough that the cabin of the truck smelled like a barbeque plate, but I wasn't complaining.

The truck swerved as Horas tried to shake me.

"Demarco, be careful," Sawyer said through the PAD, her voice tight.

I appreciated her concern, but I held on to the door with ease.

Then the gunner lunged for the door controls, and the window zipped up with factory-efficiency. The window wouldn't shut with my hand on the top of the glass, but it did limit my ability to throw a punch.

The truck reached the empty main road. Not a lot of traffic out by the desert warehouses. A satellite tower was positioned not too far from the concrete pathway, and we sped toward it.

Horas—that clever fucker—angled the truck so that the satellite tower would peel me off the vehicle. I wouldn't die that easily.

The gunner shoved Scar-Head to the side and fired again. This time, I was distracted. The laser shots burned the side of my arm. I gritted my teeth and grimaced as I flung half my body onto the front of the truck. I slid onto the grill just in time—the satellite tower was three meters thick with steel and wires, and if I had been hit by that, I would've splattered across the golden sands that lined the road.

The truck continued to accelerate.

Horas swerved again, but that was useless. I kept my grip on the vehicle, even though the flesh on my right forearm was burning.

The truck was too large to tumble over, but I feared we would destroy whatever we hit. Myself included.

Before I could formulate a plan, I spotted Cai on top of the truck. The wind whipped over him, causing his black hair to tangle in front of his face. He held on to the roof with an expert grip, and although he had been sick for months, the man still had it—this was the bounty hunter everyone had feared on Capital Station.

The gunner shot at me again, this time by leaning out the passenger window.

I half-slid down the grill of the massive truck. The engine inside was something electric, it purred, almost silent, but up close, I could feel the vibration of its power. I slid to the side, out of the gunner's view, angling myself toward the driver's side.

With one hand, Cai withdrew a plasma knife and lit it up. The "blade" contained ionized gas that super-heated in an instant. He stabbed it into the roof of the truck, slicing through the metal at a slow, but steady pace. He wasn't cutting into the cabin—he was ripping a hole into the storage.

I cursed myself for not bringing a plasma blade of some sort. Instead, I just had a duralumin knife. Still strong, but it wouldn't cut through steel without considerable strength—the kind I didn't have.

Gunner-Boy opened the passenger door and leaned out in order to get a better angle on me.

I pulled out my knife, and with frightening accuracy, I threw my only weapon. Since I saw everything in slow motion, I could make out the details on the guy's face as the blade punctured his neck. The man's mouth fell open in some sort of shout, but the knife was so far into his esophagus that no words could be formed.

In his panic, Gunner-Boy let go of the truck door. He hit the concrete and then went off the road, rolling like a tumbleweed.

The truck turned, and I used the momentum to help swing my body back to the passenger side door. Another satellite tower was up the road, and so were a few vehicles—all military-grade planetside cruisers. They were the kind with hover capability, but they also had tread tracks that allowed them to scale the most difficult of terrain in any kind of weather.

What were they doing here?

But I pushed that from my thoughts as I swung myself into the cab of the truck.

Horas was no fool.

The moment I got inside, he fired a laser pistol. Fortunately, his eyes were half on the road, and not fully on me. He missed—his final mistake. I lunged forward and grabbed his outstretched arm before he could shift his focus.

Then I punched him straight in the throat, bruising his windpipe in one brutal blow.

The pasty sad sack definitely hadn't seen that coming. He dropped his pistol and it rolled to the floor.

Then I grabbed his collar and slammed his head into the glass of his door.

Damn.

I hadn't realized how reinforced it was. That window hadn't even been crack, but Horas's skull... It hadn't been as lucky.

Banging echoed in the truck's trailer. I knew the sound of fighting when I heard it, but Cai was on his own. I had to deal with the whole fucking cab by myself—he could handle whatever was waiting in the back.

I had thought Horas was down and out, but he pulled out his own steel knife and swung for my face. I saw it coming, but I wasn't fast enough to fully avoid it. I turned my face, and the blade sliced my cheek from the ear to the chin. I barely felt it—not through the sheer excitement of the moment—but the slick heat of my own blood wept across my face and neck, soaking into the straps of my tank-top.

Horas slammed the wheel to the right, and I lost my balance. I hit the cab seat. Scar-Head tumbled around like a sack of cooked meat.

I kicked Horas before he could slash at me again. My boot connected with his chin, but that didn't knock him out. I ripped his skin and revealed the metal plating underneath.

A cyborg. No wonder he wasn't a chump like the rest. He had machines hardwired all throughout his body.

Horas threw his knife—just like I had done—and I had a fraction of a second to react. I tilted my head to the side, and the blade slammed into the cab cushion, ripping through the fabric. Which was unfortunate for him. Not only was I still alive, I now had his knife.

Two military vehicles sped down the road toward us. A blaring alarm sounded from one of them, and I figured they had come to stop the commotion. Horas had likely stolen this truck, and that security guard back at the warehouse had probably contacted the authorities.

"Just give up," I said, some of my own blood creeping into the corner of my mouth. I smirked—and I probably looked sadistic.

Horas shot me a desperate glare. "I won't be taken alive."

"I'm afraid that isn't your decision."

He continued to accelerate the truck—this time heading for the military vehicles. A crash would likely damage everything involved, but I suspected the truck would ultimately be okay afterward.

Just not us.

Then Horas scrambled to grab the laser pistol on the floorboards near his feet. That was when I had him.

I couldn't kill the bastard—not if I wanted the bounty—and he was obviously a lunatic who would kill himself rather than be captured. I'd have to subdue him, but his cyborg parts would prevent most attempts to knock him unconscious.

Those machines kept the body functioning properly no matter what. Well, so long as they were *good* parts, and since I hadn't been able to tell Horas was a cyborg until just now, it was safe to say he had nothing but the best.

I lunged for him.

Instead of punching or striking, I wrapped one arm around his neck and then used my other to hook everything in place. I squeezed his throat, cutting off his air. Horas clawed at me, and his nails ripped up my skin, causing me to bleed, but that didn't matter.

I was cutting off the blood to his brain with this hold.

Normal chokeholds—that cut off air—could take a full minute or longer to lead to unconsciousness—but blood chokeholds worked in a matter of seconds. Horas's head went bright red, then purple, like a bruise developing at a breakneck pace.

The truck drifted to the side and crashed into the sand.

I'd had no idea that sand acted like a damn wall, because the truck jerked to a fucking halt faster than I had anticipated. Horas and I were thrown into the windshield. I hit side-first, shielding Horas as best I could. The man went limp in my hold, and I knew I had him.

My ribs felt like they had cracked, though. With each breath, it felt like someone was pushing dagger into my side.

I'd have trouble walking after this, that was for sure.

But I hadn't even broken a sweat. The truck rocked and settled into place as I caught my breath, hoping the stabbing sensation would ease up for a moment. The military vehicles came to a screeching halt, surrounding us in an instant. I wasn't familiar with military proceedings—I knew enforcers weren't part of the official hierarchy, but we were close, like the deformed cousins of the armed forces. Would I have to submit to some sort of search or identification?

This was a moment I wished Lysander were here.

I dragged Horas up and then kicked open the door to the truck. Whatever happened, they couldn't have my bounty.

Although my body was numb and stiff, I hefted Horas onto my shoulder and stepped out into the desert air. The concrete shimmered with heat. I waited with my eyes squinted as soldiers surrounded the truck.

They wore full enviro-suits, each one black and green. I envied them. The temperature inside their suits was likely cool and comfortable.

The trailer doors opened, and Cai hopped out. Parts of his cargo pants was soaked in crimson, but he didn't walk with a limp. That was someone else's blood.

He jogged over to me, but the instant the soldiers lifted their rifles, Cai threw his hands into the air.

"It's fine," Cai called out. "We're with the *Star Marque*. You can check our identification." He motioned to Horas. "We were in pursuit of a dangerous criminal. He's subdued now."

For some reason, that didn't pacify the soldiers.

"Clevon Demarco," one soldier said, his voice filtered by his suit. "Get down on the ground. You're under arrest."

Cai's eyebrows shot to his windswept hair. "Wait, what?"

"Cai Qi, you're to come with us as well. Both of you get down on the ground."

I tensed, unsure of what to do.

"Listen to them," Sawyer said over my PAD, her voice quiet. "They have an arrest warrant for you."

"For what?" I muttered under my breath. "Breaking the guard's nose? I can get him fixed within a few hours."

"No. The arrest warrant is for theft."

That didn't make any sense. Theft of what? I hadn't stolen jack shit.

"It's obviously incorrect," Sawyer muttered. "Maybe someone is using your identity, or someone made up a charge to get you behind bars."

Who would do that?

Twenty soldiers pointed their plasma rifles at me. Unlike lasers, which were weaker weapons with light-based shots, plasma bolts could melt even the strongest of metals. One plasma round from these soldiers and I'd have a hole the size of my fist through my body.

I set Horas on the ground. His limp head tilted to the side, and his whitish-pink tongue lolled out of his mouth.

"On the ground," a soldier commanded.

Cai did as he had been told.

My body felt... like it had gone through a human blender. I got myself onto my knees, and then onto the ground, nice and slow so that I didn't agitate anyone.

Once down, the soldiers rushed over and handcuffed me and Cai. Then they ripped the PAD from my forearm—the wires embedded in my arm came out like tendons in meat. They burned the whole way, causing me to grit my teeth.

I wasn't sure what they were doing, but my gut twisted in dread.

What if... this was Endellion's doing?

TWENTY

Jailcell

Our holding cell smelled of cleaning chemicals.

I knew why. They had machines in the corners of the room that sprayed down the cell after the inmates were removed. The machines worked automatically. It didn't matter how much the cell reeked of artificial scents—the damn machines would squirt down the entire cell from corner to corner.

The cell was larger than most I had seen. It was three meters by three meters—a perfect little cube. Two walls had benches. One wall had built-in cuffs. That was *my* wall. They had my hands cuffed above my head, and my feet cuffed near the floor. I would've said it excited me to be in that position, but none of our guards seemed up for some erotic disciplinary action.

I missed Capital Station. I had gotten to know one guard *really* well…

The military police hadn't locked up Cai, though. He paced the cell with his hands behind his back.

"Vectin-10 is fuckin' crazy," he muttered, his tone heated. "I've *never* been placed in a high-security *holding cell* when running down a bounty. Never. *Never.*"

I tugged at my restraints. The duralumin was too tough to force my way out of. I *could* harm my hand—ripping the muscles in my thumb to dislocate it—but the one time I had done that, I had been out of commission for an entire week due to the pain. I had only gotten over it once a buddy of mine had gotten me some mother cell fluid and a doctor.

The last wall was open and consisted entirely of bars and the door. I could see into the wide corridor, but what worried me was the absence of anyone else. We had one guard to watch us. The other holding cells were empty.

The dull gray floor, steel-colored walls, and dark ceiling made for an oppressive atmosphere. The overhead lights were bright—too bright. They added to my anxiety.

Cai wheeled on me, his tattooed arms crossed over his chest. "*Well?* What's going on here? Is Vectin-10 so different that we aren't given proper due process? Normally—even if I break a law—I'm let out on bail, for fuck's sake."

I smirked. "It's because they want me here. They're going to kill me."

Every fiber of my being told me it was true.

Cai scoffed and then offered a forced laugh. "Who is *they?*"

"The planet governor and her goons."

Cai mulled over my comment, then he laughed again, this time genuinely. "I didn't take you for a conspiracy theorist quack. The *planet governor* isn't going to kill some lowly starship captain. That's insane. She's got bigger problems to worry about."

As if the world had a sense of humor, the lights flickered once, and then went out.

There weren't any windows in this room. We were shrouded in a thick darkness that stank of chemicals and burned my nose. The sole guard on duty turned on a flashlight, but then he stormed out, grumbling something.

"What the hell is going on?" Cai asked as he stumbled over to a bench and sat down. "These buildings are powered by some amazing reactors. *And* they all have backup generators in case something happens. The lights shouldn't be off like this."

"Unless the planet governor wants them off," I muttered.

"Pfft. Please. You sound like a drunk. There's another explanation for this."

What if they pumped gas through the vents? Cai and I were dead. No way around it.

Fuck me.

Again, I tugged at my restraints. What was I going to do? I couldn't go down like a chump. I refused. No matter what happened, I'd make sure Endellion remembered it.

But I did regret the fact that I couldn't speak with Sawyer. I would've loved to hear her snark one more time. Maybe stroke her hair, and say goodbye to Blub. Anything. My chest hurt just thinking about it—she was the only one who ever made me feel that way.

The main door in the central hallway opened. A bright slice of light cut through the room, illuminating the area just beyond our bars. The footfalls of half a dozen men bounced off the walls as they marched in.

Soldiers—elite men in scaled enviro-suits, the most expensive kinds—stopped in front of our cell. They each held a plasma rifle close, like they might need to use it at a moment's notice. Lights at the end of their rifles lit up our holding cell.

And then Endellion walked into view. Even with her helmet up, I recognized her. She looked just like she had in the assembly room —tall, commanding, and with her helmet up. She even had a damn cape that went to the floor. It was a ceremonial part of the outfit reserved for military officers.

Planet Governor Endellion Voight.

Cai slowly stood from the bench, his body stiff. "Oh, shit," he whispered. "The planet governor really *is* going to kill you."

I said nothing. I couldn't. I just kept my gaze on Endellion. Her reflective visor kept her expression hidden, but I imagined she had a smug little smile on her face. She had done it. She had caught me.

Now what?

Endellion motioned with her head. Two of her goons stepped forward, opened the door to our cell, and then grabbed Cai, one on each of Cai's arms.

Cai said nothing. He allowed himself to be led out of the

holding cell, but he did shoot me a concerned look over his shoulder. This was for the best. Perhaps Endellion would take him someplace safe, and *then* she'd have her thugs gun me down like this was an old-timey firing squad.

Fun.

Once Cai had been taken away, Endellion lifted her arm. "Out."

The four remaining guards turned their attention to her, obviously taken aback by the command. They didn't argue, though. They simply took a moment to process the order, and then headed for the door.

Except one. A man lingered behind and stood close to Endellion. "Are you sure, Governor?" he asked, his voice familiar, but obscured by the speaker system of his suit.

"*Out,*" Endellion repeated. "I'll call you if I need you."

The man nodded once and then left with the others. When the door shut, the room returned to utter darkness. That wouldn't matter to Endellion—her enviro-suit could easily help her see in these conditions. Not only that, but she had an artificial ampullae of Lorenzini, which would allow her to sense my heart beating and always know my location.

Alone with Endellion.

I had fantasized about this moment for longer than I cared to admit to anyone.

Now it was a literal nightmare.

I struggled with my restraints. With deliberate intention, I jerked my thumb into the cuff, prepared to rip every muscle in my hand to free myself, if it came to that.

"Clevon," Endellion drawled as she walked into the holding cell. Her movements were slow—cautious. Was she afraid of getting too close? "It's been a while since we've had a chance to speak like this."

"You're a sadist bitch." I smirked, more nerves than confidence, but she didn't know that. "If you want to kill me, get it over with. Save your world domination speeches for someone who gives a shit."

She continued forward, closer to me with each step. I held my breath when I heard her footfalls get close. Endellion was only a meter away.

"You disappoint me, Clevon," she said, a hint of amusement in her voice. "I have no desire to kill you with my own hands. If I wanted you dead, I'd send someone to do it for me."

I almost laughed aloud. Instead, I bit back my mirth and asked, "Oh, then you just wanted to see me, is that it?" I leaned my head against the unforgiving wall. "I was the best you ever had, and you want one more tryst?"

"Ah, there's the same ol' Clevon Demarco I know. You're just the man I need to speak to."

I twisted my hands around in the cuffs, my blood hot. "If you came to speak to me, you don't know me at all. There's nothing I want from you but your beating heart."

"So dramatic." Endellion chortled. "So predictable."

"What was that?" I asked, my tone icy.

"You didn't wonder why I called you to that assembly room? You didn't think it suspicious that I waited nearly nine months into my governorship to hire starship captains to patrol the area for rebellion thugs?"

I held my breath, just waiting to hear her explanation for this.

"I waited for *you*," Endellion stated. "I knew you'd never control your temper if we were in close proximity." When she laughed this time, it sounded mechanical and sardonic. "You're as predictable as death and just as boring as taxes. Your rage—*your tantrum*—was exactly what I wanted from you."

"You wanted me to call you out for being a mass murderer?" I asked, more curious than ever before.

"I knew you wouldn't give away the details." Endellion swished her cape—the rustle of her heavy clothing the only other sound in the room besides our voices. "You wouldn't ever tell anyone what *really* happened at Capital Station. But I knew you'd try to sully my name, and publicly condemn me. You're too wild and defiant to stay quiet. It's not your style."

Endellion always had known me well. I didn't keep my personality hidden.

"So?" I barked. Then I glanced around the darkness, unable to see. "You got what you wanted. I publicly told you to go fuck yourself. *What a masterful plan.* What did that accomplish, huh? Just cut to the chase. I'm sick of hearing your voice."

For a long moment, Endellion remained quiet.

The deafening silence unnerved me. I shuffled around in my restraints just to hear something other than my own heart.

"General Lone contacted you, didn't he?" Endellion asked, her voice a mere whisper of what it was before. "Don't worry. I had the power cut to this facility so that we could speak—if only briefly."

General Lone?

"What does he have to do with this?" I asked, my anger waning.

"I knew that if I called you to the assembly room, and you directed a public outburst at me, eventually General Lone would contact you for some jobs. You see, General Lone has been staying on Vectin-10 longer than planned in order to *watch over me.*" Endellion chuckled. "I'm the first human governor since the formation of the Federation, and that's the justification he gives for his presence."

Endellion…

She always had plans and schemes.

Endellion continued, "In reality, General Lone wants me out of the picture. He's here to watch my every move, and to swoop in the moment I make a big enough mistake. He's already turned several political allies into enemies. He's been contacting and hiring everyone in the area to expose my mistakes or blow them out of proportion. A hundred people question my every move, and a hundred more report every suspicious activity. It took a great deal of effort to even arrange this meeting without tipping off one of Lone's lackeys."

"And?" I asked, honestly curious now.

"And I wanted you to be one of the people General Lone contacted to help." Endellion took another step closer, limiting the distance between us to a few centimeters. "Something tells me that Lone would love the poetic irony if *you* were the one to take me down. He wouldn't pass that opportunity up. Which means he probably brought you into his inner circle—his villa somewhere beneath the sands."

I wasn't surprised she knew about that. I was certain Endellion had spies of her own.

"Clevon, listen carefully." Endellion took a moment to inhale and exhale. "General Lone is more of a monster than I ever could be. Ask Sawyer. She'll confirm all the terrible things Lone has done—especially to her."

"I know," I said, curt. "And?"

"And you… care about Sawyer, don't you?"

The way she asked put me on edge. She wasn't jealous, was she? No. That wasn't Endellion. This was something else.

"I care about Sawyer," I said, knowing Endellion already knew that.

"Then you know that she'll never really sleep right while her creator and abuser lives."

That had crossed my thoughts a few times, but I didn't know how I would go about solving it. General Lone was the most powerful superhuman in the quadrant. He could clone girls and abuse them to his heart's content. Who was going to stop him?

Endellion unfastened her helmet. Although it was too dark to see, my mind's eye pictured everything. The rustle of the helmet becoming a hood and falling on her back was clear in my imagination.

"Clevon," Endellion whispered, her unfiltered voice sending a shiver down my spine. "What if I told you that I could get you alone with Lone? *Isolated.* Away from everything. So alone that you could kill him, and no one would ever be the wiser?"

TWENTY-ONE

A Deal With The Devil

I opened my mouth to speak, but Endellion beat me to the punch.

"Lone won't truly trust you until you've been tested," Endellion stated. "But if you work with me, I can make that process effortless."

"*Work with you?*" I hissed.

Endellion didn't even acknowledge my rage. "All the enforcers in the sector will be feeding me information on the rebellion. I can give *you* the accumulation of their knowledge. You can use it to catch the most wanted criminals or bust the most heinous of rebellion operations."

"There's no way—"

"*You'll have all the credits you'll need from these jobs,*" Endellion said, speaking over me, her voice heated. "You'll have fame. Power. And then Lone will trust you. He'll come to you with plans. He'll outline my death."

I held my breath.

Endellion waited, the dramatic timing of her argument eating at my resolve. I wanted to know. What did she think would happen?

"When Lone comes to you with all the details, that'll be the moment," Endellion said, calm and cold—her normal demeanor.

"That will be the time that I get him into a dead zone, and you'll be with him. His most trusted *dog*. You could kill him then. When no one is around."

I clenched my jaw, the visuals of her plan bright in my mind.

"And just like with Emissary Barten, you'll get away with it," Endellion concluded.

I scoffed. "Have you heard? Barten's daughter is chasing me."

"And whose fault is that? I told you to make sure there were no witnesses. I told you to kill everyone there. If you had listened, then you wouldn't be in any danger now. Just like if you follow my plans, you can kill General Lone without any repercussions."

I hated her insistence that she knew what was happening. But at the same time—this felt like the old Endellion. Sounded like her. Smelled like her. Plans, schemes, contingencies. I should've known she had sent for me specifically when she had called for the crew of the *Star Marque* to attend the assembly.

"Clevon," she said, hard and distinct. "This is a symbiotic relationship. General Lone will destroy me if I don't deal with him. He'll also destroy several of his Sawyer-clone toys."

"You know about that?" I asked.

"Of course. I rescued Sawyer from that sadist, didn't I?"

"Why did you?" I asked. "Because she's useful?"

Endellion sardonically laughed. "Yes, Clevon. I needed someone who could circumvent the Federation coding. And then I heard Lone bragging about his genetically engineered *little girls*. He kept them to himself, using their technical skills during the day, and using them in other ways at night. I figured a person like that would *want* to be rescued, and the price for my kindness would be their skills."

She recited everything with a distant chill. "You didn't care about Sawyer at all?"

Endellion took in a breath, but no words followed. Then she finally said, "Clevon—when I went to destroy Capital Station, I planned to save the only two people I care about. I brought them with me. I kept them close."

Her words brought back every detail of that encounter. Endellion had brought Sawyer and me to the main computer system of

Capital Station. We were supposed to destroy the station and escape together. Just the three of us.

"I saved Sawyer for selfish reasons, but she eventually grew on me." Endellion exhaled. "Same with you. But now we have to look past that. Lone's death is my current desire. I want him dead more than anything else. And consider this—I can't betray you until Lone's gone, so you know I won't come for you in the meantime. If we work together, you can focus on rebuilding the crew of the *Star Marque*. And with all the money and fame you'll have at the end, you'll be in a better position to return your focus to me. Do you understand now, Clevon? Everyone wins."

I hated it when she made sense. Absolutely hated it.

Every fiber of my being wanted to refuse her offer. I wanted to break my restraints and then break her face. But she was right. I knew. If I went with her—if I helped in her schemes—she would deliver. Somehow, someway, she'd get Lone in a dead zone, and I'd be there with him, plasma knife in hand.

Endellion pulled her helmet back over her heard. I heard the hood secure itself into place, snapping into a solid form around her head. "I have Horas in custody," she said, her voice robotic. "I'm going to release him to the *Star Marque*. Think of it as a show of good faith. You take him, question him if you want, and then collect the bounty. Report to Lone, and make sure you're excited to speak with him. Lone is used to suck-ups trying to get his attention. Pretend to be one of them, and you'll blend right in."

"What if I refuse to help you?" I asked.

"Then you'll be making a mistake," Endellion said matter-of-factly. "But don't worry. If you refuse, I'll find another way. And then you'll have nothing. So it'll still work out for me."

"Then why come to me?"

"Because." Endellion waited for a moment before adding, "You were the other person I took with me to Capital Station, Clevon. Perhaps I can't shake my sentimentalities."

When I said nothing, Endellion turned and strode out of the holding cell, the click of her fancy enviro-suit boots echoing in the large, empty space. My heart thumped loud enough to drown out the sound.

Her words rattled in my thoughts, making it difficult to focus. Was she manipulating me?

Yes.

She would say anything—*do anything*—to get me to fall in line. She wanted me to stop chasing her. She wanted me to stop smearing her name. This was all a ruse. A distraction. *Another con.*

But…

General Lone was a monster. I knew. Sawyer knew. Everyone knew. And he was far above the law. Far above authority. Untouchable and secure. I'd never be able to handle him on my own. But with Endellion…

I shook my head as the lights flickered back to life.

No matter what happened, I'd let Sawyer decide this one. Whatever she thought was best, we'd do.

That way, there would be no chance I'd fuck this up.

TRUE TO HER WORD, Endellion released me and then gave the *Star Marque* custody of Horas Hines. All charges against me and Cai were dropped. The mysterious "theft" had been meant for someone else, and it had been a "glitch in the system" that had gotten me locked away for ten hours.

I didn't care.

Once all that was behind me, I had Cai and Sanders handle turning Horas into the authorities. I headed for the mess hall. Normally, we'd get food and drink inside aluminum pouches. It prevented the food from getting everywhere in case of gravity failure.

Today, I had some supplies sent to the mess hall from the planet's surface. Raw ingredients—something I had never dealt with before. Fresh cuts of meat? Vegetables that weren't blended and frozen? Fancy shit. The *Star Marque* had a hot plate, and I knew that could cook raw ingredients, so that was what I was going to do.

Well, my body would do that. My mind dwelled on the conversation with Endellion. It was all I had thought about during the ride on the space elevator, even while Cai had shouted about the injustice of our confinement. Lysander, Noah, and Mara had all contacted me through the ship's comm systems, asking about the arrest.

Even *Melba* had contacted me—we had run in one starfighter battle together, and she had to know what had happened.

I barely heard them. All I could think about was Endellion's plans. She was right, Lone wanted her dead—for the crime of being human. If Lone's reasoning had been different—if he had known about her past atrocities—this whole situation would've been different. But instead, my choice was between two monsters. Help the sadist superhuman rid the universe of Endellion, or help the sociopathic human rid the universe of General Lone.

The people speaking to me through the comms wanted to know the details of my trip. I didn't mind telling them about the holding cell incident.

But I didn't tell anyone about Endellion. I'd even had Cai swear to me that he wouldn't mention that part.

I shook my head, forcing myself to return to the present. What was I doing? Right. Cutting up vegetables. One was an onion. I thought. Another was… a differently shaped onion. And the last… was a root that looked like an onion.

They weren't all onions, but I didn't know the names for them. I didn't care either.

They all bled when I cut into them. Watery. Smelly. The onions took their revenge on my eyes. Fuckers.

Then I cut up the meat. I didn't trust the meat that looked pink, so I only purchased red and blackish-red meats. They were from different animals, but I didn't care. Meats were meant to be mixed, right? I cut everything into cubes and threw the mix onto the hot plate. The sizzle was satisfying, and the smell dragged me out of my own head for a moment while I admired my "cooking."

I was damn good. The vegetables turned colors. The meat

oozed tasty juices. Who said this was hard? They had no idea what they were talking about.

Although…

My onions became flabby. Were they supposed to do that? What did I care? I took everything off and placed it all on two plates. Then I shut down the hot plate and exited the mess hall. Some of my ground enforcers gave me odd looks while they sucked down their alcohol pouches. I gave them a jut of my chin—a reverse nod —and kept going.

Then I entered the hall and went straight for Sawyer's work-shop. She'd be there, or my room. It was 50-50 these days. After a short elevator ride, and a quick stroll down the main hall, I stopped in front of her room and gently touched the door's computer. After a soft swoosh, the door slid open, and I stepped inside.

Large engine blocks were around on the ground, some machines plugged into the wall and sparking. Sawyer handled all minor repairs for the ship. She was a mechanical engineer, as well as a coder, apparently.

I wasn't well versed in any of this.

Sawyer was near the opposite wall, sitting next to her computer and typing away at a furious rate. She had three monitors, all glowing a soft orange, that lit her workroom with a sinister hue. Two monitors were for the cameras positioned around the *Star Marque*. She watched everything, even while she worked.

The last monitor was covered in a wall of text so thick and confusing that it might as well have been a snowstorm.

After I stepped into her "office," the door closed automatically behind me.

Blub descended from the ceiling with a *toot, toot, toot*. He released helium from his body in order to adjust his flight, and I always found the little farting fish to be amusing. The koi fish nibbled at my crew cut hair.

"Hey, Sawyer," I said as I stepped around a machine in the middle of the room. It appeared to be a heater, but I wasn't certain. It was large enough to be a person. "I brought you something."

"Hm."

That was all she offered me.

Once I reached her desk, I plopped down the food. "Here. I made it just for you."

She slowly—and dramatically—turned her head. With a lifted eyebrow, she examined the meal and then glanced up at me. "You… cooked food?"

"That's right." I motioned to the monitors, pointing at the security feeds. "You didn't see that?"

"I don't normally watch the mess hall."

Damn. I had hoped that she would've seen it.

"Well, I know you." I sat on the edge of her desk and leaned back. "You probably haven't eaten in the last couple of days, right? You're too pissed at me."

Sawyer's expression settled back into a neutral *don't give a fuck*. She picked up her plate and held it close. "Where are the eating utensils?"

I laughed once as I stared down at my plate. "I forgot them."

"Ah. How gentlemanly."

"Hey, if you want, I can feed you." I slid closer, plucked up a piece of meat from my plate, and held it out for her. "It'll be sexy, I swear."

"You think eating from your hand like an animal is sexy?"

I shrugged. "Me putting anything in your mouth is sexy."

From any other person, that would've gotten at least *some* reaction. Disgust. Interest. A laugh. But Sawyer was hard to read sometimes. She just stared at me like I was a broom closet without enough brooms.

"I think I'll feed myself," Sawyer eventually said as she turned away. With delicate movements, she picked up a cooked onion and a slice of meat. Then she wrapped everything together and nibbled at the edges. "Hm. Do you also have a grudge against seasoning?"

I plopped a piece of meat into my mouth and chewed.

Sawyer was right. This was… good. But not really. The sensation of actual meat elevated it to "interesting."

I took another bite. And then another. We ate in silence for a short while, until Blub floated down and tried to snack on my meal.

I gave him my onions, because for some reason, half of them tasted strange. The damn fish slurped up one and then burped himself away.

Finally, I set my plate down.

"You know I went to a holding cell, right?" I asked.

Sawyer took another small bite of her meat, her eyes on her coding. "I heard everything you said over the comms."

"Endellion was there."

"That doesn't surprise me."

I waited for her to say something else, but it never happened. I exhaled and leaned against the wall.

"Hey. If I told you I could kill General Lone, would you want that?"

Sawyer stopped everything—no eating, no typing. She turned to me, her shoulders stiff. When her gray-blue eyes met mine, I was frozen in place. "Yes."

The word hung between us.

I understood how she felt. I wanted Endellion dead, after all.

"Endellion made me a deal," I said, my voice low. "If I help her, she'll help me get Lone."

"Why? That's not like her."

"Because *she* wants Lone out of the picture."

"Ah." Sawyer tore her paralyzing gaze from me and returned her attention to the computer. With angry keystrokes, she resumed her coding. "That sounds more like her."

"She had me cuffed to a wall," I said. "She spoke to me with the lights off, so I couldn't see her."

Sawyer didn't reply.

"I wanted to ask your opinion before I decided anything. Do you think I should listen to her? Do you think killing Lone is worth her eventual double-cross?"

Blub floated around my head. *Toot, toot, toot.* I waved him away, trying to understand Sawyer's thought process, but failing to grasp her feelings on the matter. She remained quiet as she typed, the reflection of the code covering her glassy eyes.

In a whisper, Sawyer said, "I think if Endellion went out of her way to speak with you, she definitely wants you to help her. But you're right. She won't ever fully trust you, and you'll never drop your grudge against her, so you'll have to be cautious. Once everything is over—and I mean *the second Lone's heart stops beating*—you'll be fair game. Do you really want to risk that?"

"If *you* want Lone dead, I'll do it."

Sawyer snapped her attention to me.

That must've surprised her.

"I'm sorry," I said, never looking away. "You asked me not to take jobs from Lone, and I did. On accident—but still. I want to make everything right with you. And he's an asshole worthy of a plasma bolt to the back. I know what he's done. Like Endellion said… Everyone wins here."

Sawyer ran a shaky hand through her short, red hair. When she turned away, her gaze was on her desk—and then it lingered on her meat-covered plate. "All right. Let's make this deal. But we should have a few plans of our own, okay? Just in case something goes south."

I nodded along with her words. "Right. That's not a bad idea."

TWENTY-TWO

Travel Wise

I left Sawyer's workshop after a few hours. Speaking with her always put me in a good mood. It was a shame she never got randy.

The moment I reached the lift, however, all joy was sucked from me. The door slid open to reveal Victtra and her two goons, One and Two. The three of them had obviously been waiting, and when I stepped inside, Victtra placed her hands behind her back and offered me a smile.

"I spoke with our captive," she said.

I held my breath as I hit the button for Deck One. "And?"

"Horas was well-informed when it came to superhuman operations."

A part of me wanted to ask her what that meant, but another part of me was just glad she hadn't discovered anything about my involvement in her father's death. I said nothing, and just waited as the lift moved us from one deck to the next.

Victtra decided she would fill the silence, however.

"Do you know Minister Ontwenty?" she asked.

My heart nearly stopped.

It was Minister Ontwenty who had asked Endellion and me to

kill Victtra's father, Emissary Barten. Apparently, Barten was going to make a deal with the rebellion thugs. They would stop hostilities in exchange for medication that could correct several common genetic deficiencies. Those medications had been developed by Ontwenty herself—and she didn't want them going to outlaw humans.

But that wasn't all.

Ontwenty hadn't wanted anyone to oppose her Stellar Engine project—and Barten had been threatening to slow the whole operation down. The Stellar Engine was a megastructure built around a star in a chain-link fashion, closer than a planet in the garden zone, but far enough away not to be damaged by the star's blaze. The engine captured heat, radiation, and solar flares, and then converted it all to energy.

Apparently, the energy created by this process could power more than a dozen space stations, or even create a "Dyson sphere"—some sort of structure that fully encased the star.

It sounded like a fairy tale to me. Barten had thought the same.

And now he was dead.

Superhumans didn't play nice.

"I've never heard of Ontwenty," I said with a shrug.

Victtra narrowed her eyes at me, but she didn't press me for details. "Minister Ontwenty is in charge of the sector's Medical Research. I assume you at least know what that is?"

"Sounds familiar."

"It seems she and my father had a dramatic falling out."

Fuck. Here came the meat of it.

Fortunately, the door to the lift opened. I stepped out, fully intending to leave Victtra and her two bodyguards behind. They followed me, unfortunately, and I headed to my quarters with haste in my step.

"Captain Demarco," Victtra said, keeping pace. "I'd like to accompany you down to the planet's surface when you bring Horas to General Lone."

"Why's that?" I drawled.

"I want to ask Lone's opinion of the minister."

I slowly came to a stop in the middle of the corridor. I turned to face her, torn between actually helping, or sending her after a false lead. In the end, I decided it was better Victtra focus her hatred on Ontwenty.

"Don't ask Lone about the minister," I said.

She ran a hand through her silver hair and then stepped out into the corridor. With keen and intelligent eyes, she focused on me. "Is there a reason?"

"You're old enough to understand power blocs, right? They're groups of people who use their political power to *get things done*."

Victtra waited in patient silence.

"Lone and Ontwenty are friends," I said. "Political friends. Whatever you say to him, will eventually go straight to her."

"And why does that matter?"

"I thought you said you wanted to catch your father's killer?"

That question shook her. Victtra's eyes went wide. Even her bodyguards grew stiff and still, like they wanted to hear more.

But it wasn't like I could tell her the whole truth.

"Captain Demarco, I thought you said you didn't know anything about Minister Ontwenty? Yet here you are, telling me all about her power bloc with Lone." Victtra smiled a little tighter. "Don't you realize that superhumans can sense the heart beats of others? And that when you lie, your body betrays you?"

"Oh, yeah? Then tell me—was my heart rate fluctuating when I was telling you not to mention any of this Lone?"

Victtra said nothing.

"Then maybe you should think long and hard about the reality of the situation." My tone had shifted to a quiet seriousness. "Ask yourself—who has the power *and* the motives to hide the murder of an emissary?"

She said nothing. Neither did her bodyguards.

I continued, "Sure, the rebellion thugs have a motive. They hate superhumans. But you've seen their operations. They aren't sophisti-cated. A wanted man was just hiding out in a storage facility." I threw a hand up and shook my head. "But… superhumans always have the resources to get things done."

"I saw the man who murdered my father," Victtra said matter-of-factly, her volume louder than before. "They weren't a superhuman."

"Of course not." I sarcastically laughed once. "If you got shot, who would you blame? The gun, or the fool pulling the trigger? Sometimes Homo superior just like to use people as tools, if you catch my drift."

One of the bodyguards—Two—shifted his weight from one foot to the other. "You should be careful with what you say. That's practically treason."

"I don't give a fuck," I said. And I meant it. "I'm just tired of watching the three of you flail about for clues." I shot Victtra a glare. "You might be *hyper smart* and *have the brain of an adult human*, but you're clearly lacking experience and common sense." I tapped the side of my head. "Think about what I said."

Victtra remained silent as I turned and headed down the corridor. She never called out or said anything—I just left her with her bodyguards, no words between us.

Hopefully, she'd stop sniffing around me and aim her sights at bigger stars.

IT HAD BEEN a while since I had exercised.

Apparently, the captain had a personal area in the ship's gym, but I didn't want to use that. The whole room reminded me of Endellion. It was secluded from everything, and I swear her scent still lingered there. I had locked the door and never intended to use the space ever again.

Instead, I lifted weights out in the main room with the rest of the ground enforcers. A few of them shot me smiles and offered congratulations for catching such a high-paying criminal, but I didn't have much to say. I just wanted to get my workout in while I had a chance. In a couple of hours I'd have to return to the planet's surface, which didn't leave me much personal time.

The *Star Marque*'s workout room was mostly dedicated to

firearms and reflex training. Only a small corner had been set aside for improving strength. I sat at one of the strength machines—where I could program in the weight I wanted to use—and started up my normal routine.

I set the machine to 220 kilograms. I needed to move up from there.

Cyborgs inserted machines into their bodies in order to improve strength, but I wanted to do it the old-fashioned way.

I thrust both arms forward, straining against the weight machine until I touched both palms in front of me. Then I relaxed at a slow pace, allowing the cords to pull my arms open. Nice and easy. One set at a time.

Noah walked up to my machine, his scrawny form easy to recognize. Especially with Mara by his side. They had become quite inseparable.

"Hey, Demarco," Noah said. "Melba was saying we should practice more of our starfighter maneuvers together. Did you not get her message over the comms?"

I thrust my arms forward again. When I relaxed, I shook my head. "I haven't answered any of the comms yet. I don't have much free time."

Mara tilted her head. Her cute little heart-shaped face didn't look good with a frown. "You don't want to practice?"

"I need to get my strength training in." I thrust my arms out again.

"Do you think Mara and I should go?" Noah said, motioning to himself. "If you think we should stay here, that's fine. I will."

I stopped using the machine to face him. With a lifted eyebrow, I asked, "Why wouldn't I want you to train with her?"

"I-I don't know. Maybe you didn't want us to make her feel welcome? Or maybe you only wanted us to train with you, since you and Melba don't agree on starfighter tactics."

Damn. Nothing could be further from the truth. I didn't give a shit about Melba or her two little lackey buddies.

"What makes you think I care?" I asked with a chuckle. "Do whatever you're gonna do. I'll join you for some training once I'm done here." I returned my focus to the machine and thrust my arms forward.

Mara lowered her voice as she said, "I thought that maybe you didn't like them because they were the last people who Endellion recruited."

I almost released the strength cord too early. With a jerk in my movements, I relaxed and rested my back against the machine. "Everyone here was recruited by Endellion."

"Not Cai."

"Fine. Yeah." I shot her glare. "Don't be a smartass. You know what I meant. Most people here were her recruits. Melba is no different. I just… don't get along with the woman. That's different. And it's on me. I should fix that—but first, I have to make sure I'm fit."

Apparently, I had to kill General Lone at some point.

If I was going to a fight a man of his skill and training, I had to be prepared.

Noah nodded once. "Right. Then, Mara and I should make friends with the other starfighters?"

"Yeah." I placed a hand on his shoulder. "And make sure you invite Victtra."

"The superhuman?" Mara whispered. "You're sure?"

"She's the new starfighter officer, right? Maybe if you all train together for a short while, you'll become friends." Or several of them will kill each other. "Captain's orders. Include Victtra in your comms conversations about training."

They must not have expected that, because both Noah's and Mara's eyes went wide. It only took them a moment to calm down, though. They exchanged curious glances and then offered me reassurances.

"Okay," Mara said.

Noah patted my shoulder. "I won't let you down."

"Good." I motioned them away. "Now get out of here. I have to focus."

ONCE UPON A TIME, I had loved the space elevator. Now it was losing its luster.

I went to the planet's surface again. Apparently, weather changed all the time. I had known that from my brief trips to other planets—weather had a mind of its own—but I had never known it was such a fickle bitch. Everything had been fine when I had taken the elevator up to the *Star Marque*, but a few hours later, on the way down, there were warnings about a sandstorm.

Wind and sand mixed together to create a haze of gold. The entire ride down, I couldn't see anything. It irritated me, but after a while, I enjoyed the golden dust as it sailed by the windows.

"I hate everything about travel," Dr. Clay muttered.

He stood a good three meters from me—he probably didn't want people to think we were associated.

I would've taken Cai, but apparently Lysander wanted to go over procedure. The way we had apprehended Horas hadn't been to his liking, and the only way to solve that was through rigorous discussions.

Victtra opted not to join me to see Lone, and I wondered if that was because she had taken my speech to heart. Would she suspect Lone and Ontwenty now? Only time would tell.

Noah, Mara, Melba, Hattie, Asahi, and Victtra were all training with the starfighters in the simulation pods. That was their task for the couple of days I'd be away. It would do them good—at least, I hoped.

And Sawyer would never set foot on Lone's property ever again, that much I was certain of.

Which meant, if I was going to take someone with me to the meeting, the only officer on the *Star Marque* left was Dr. Clay. It was the most unfortunate thing to happen to me since Endellion had almost killed us all.

Dr. Clay crossed his arms and stared out the space elevator's windows, directly at the raging sandstorm. He glowered, like the winds owed him money he knew he'd never see.

"Do you enjoy *anything*?" I quipped.

"I enjoy reading in my quarters." Dr. Clay narrowed his eyes and slowly turned his attention to me. "When I'm researching cybernetic enhancements, I'm also enjoying myself. But since our starship has *baby's first research microscope*, I don't get to do a lot of that."

I huffed out a laugh. "Is that your way of asking for credits?"

"You're getting a sizable chunk from your bounty, aren't you? New medical equipment—including the ability to make implants—would be appreciated."

"For what?"

"So we could enhance or repair our own crew," Dr. Clay snapped, his tone shifting to that of a parent. "Think about it. We could augment our own people. A few spinal reinforcers could allow our ground troops to wear heavier armor or jump from higher heights without damaging themselves. I've also read a few articles on the ability to change a person's range of hearing to include color."

I stared at him for a long moment, thinking he was joking.

I should've known better. Dr. Clay had as much humor as a bloated corpse.

"Hear color?" I asked.

Dr. Clay nodded. "Fascinating, isn't it?"

"Yeah. It'll really help us apprehend rebellion scumbags if we can all hear how loud the yellow of his suit is."

Dr. Clay rolled his eyes and turned away. "I wouldn't expect someone like you to understand. You're the type of man who wants jaw enhancements for better *phallic capacity*. My genius is wasted here."

I wanted to dig at him again—Dr. Clay was so easy to rile—but a terrible thought struck me. What if… someone on my ship turned traitor? Dr. Clay was the perfect candidate. He obviously didn't like our work environment, and he didn't like *me*, specifically. What if one of my enemies approached him with a deal?

The dark thoughts caused my chest to tighten.

"I'll get you the medical equipment," I said, never allowing my anxiety to show. "Just send me a list, all right? And prices."

Dr. Clay rubbed his smooth chin. "You mean it?"

"Yeah. You convinced me. We definitely need to offer the

ground enforcers augmentations. We can write it into their contracts —they serve us longer, but in the end, they get to keep the cyborg enhancements.”

“That’s a wonderful idea.”

“Your idea.” I offered him a forced smile. “Obviously a sign of your genius, right?”

Dr. Clay slowly nodded. “You’re serious.”

“I’m not talking to hear my own voice, that’s for sure.”

With a much merrier tone to his voice, Dr. Clay replied, “Well, I’ll get a list together right now. We still have another hour before we get to the surface.” He turned and headed for one of the public benches, his attention on his PAD.

I smiled to myself. One crisis averted. And improving the *Star Marque* was one of my ultimate goals.

Now I just had to face Lone again.

TWENTY-THREE

Genetic Clones

Dr. Clay and I rode the shuttle to the villa in relative silence. I already missed Cai. He was a man I could spend weeks with and never get bored. Dr. Clay sucked the happiness out of the room faster than the stench of a rotting corpse.

The underground dead zone got me nervous. Endellion was right. Someone could easily be murdered here, and no one would know.

Once the shuttle stopped, Dr. Clay and I exited and were escorted straight into Lone's private abode. The fake windows scrolled through several pleasant landscapes as Dr. Clay and I made our way down the hall. The "windows" settled on an ocean scenery, and soon the villa was filled with the scent of sea salt.

The vibrant blue of the waves matched the white and pale green of the carpet and decorations.

A few thug-guards waited for us inside the villa. They motioned to a massive study, and I momentarily wondered what they were busy guarding. It didn't matter. I went into the study like an obedient servant.

Now I had to put my game face on. I had to be the eager kid on the playground who wanted recognition.

Which was fine. I always loved praise.

I walked into the room with both my arms held wide. "General Lone," I called out. "Your favorite human is back, and I've brought along a gift."

The study looked like a mix between an oasis and an old-world library. A fountain was set up in the middle of the damn room. Who does that? Vectin-10 was a desert, and here we were, looking at water splashing over marble stone. Tall shelves covered three of the four walls, all of which had trinkets, awards, and decorations. Old pistols. Military uniforms. A model of the Vectin Solar System.

I hated this place.

Except for the floating fish that hovered overhead. They were koi fish—white, black, and speckled a bioluminescent red. They were genetically engineered to be attractive, and I agreed with that design. Four little helium sacs protruded from their backs, some inflating, some deflating.

They were just like Blub.

With a soft *toot, toot, toot,* one "wandered down" from the ceiling and approached me with its fins waving.

My eyes were on the animals, not Lone.

"Thank you for welcoming us into your villa," Dr. Clay said with a deep and formal bow.

He was the perfect man to bring with me. If my job was to convince Lone that I was loyal to him, no one would sell it better than Dr. Clay. That man already loved the superhumans more than he loved himself.

I finally dragged my attention away from the fish and met Lone's gaze.

He sat on a long chair in the corner of the study, his left arm up and the screen of his PAD glowing. Lone offered a smile as he quickly stood. "Ah. I'm pleased you already have good news to report."

With a dismissive wave of my hand, I walked over to the fountain. "I already apprehended one of the rebellion thugs before any of Endellion's men could get to him." I held up a finger. "And you're going to love this next part. The wanted criminal was hiding here on Vectin-10, right in Endellion's jurisdiction. I can't wait to see how she deals with that kind of news spreading around the planet's cities."

Dr. Clay turned and gave me an odd glance.

I didn't reply.

"Excellent," Lone said as he, too, approached the fountain. "I'll make sure the details are disseminated to all the local reporting networks."

The floating koi fish…

They all moved away from Lone. Even the one that had floated near me—it tooted several more times until it was on the ground, practically hiding from Lone's line of sight by tucking its body under the bowl of the fountain.

Lone didn't seem to care or notice.

"I'm impressed," he said as he poked at the PAD on his arm. "This is a highly dangerous individual. You're the type of man who enjoys a challenge."

Although I didn't appreciate the man trying to guess at my personality, I did appreciate the fact that he recognized my ambition. I wasn't about to disappoint—just like Endellion, I didn't want to be second at anything.

"I want to make sure Governor Voight gets what's coming to her as soon as possible," I said.

Lone couldn't stop himself from smiling. When he did so, he flashed his perfect teeth—it disgusted me. "I'm glad to hear that, because I have the perfect assignment for you." He stepped around the fountain and approached me with careful steps. "I'm going to recommend that the *Star Marque* escort Administer Twoine to Vectin-10. He's filed official complaints about rebellion thugs following him. He's been afraid of space travel ever since Capital Station crashed."

"What will Administer Twoine do once he gets here?" I asked.

"He's part of the delegation that will assess Endellion's competency as the planet governor. He had postponed his visit, because he hadn't felt safe enough to travel via official starships, but I told him I could get him a vanguard-class vessel that could get him to Vectin-10 without issue."

Ah. I was going to play babysitter for one of the high and mighty superhumans. That amused me more than anything else.

"And Administer Twoine will make sure Endellion is removed from power?"

"I doubt it," Lone said, narrowing his icy-blue eyes. "Endellion has yet to blunder as the planet governor. But his constant presence and judgment will add a strain to her day-to-day operations, I guarantee it."

"And once she's pushed, you figure she might break?"

Lone chuckled—dark and with way more delight than necessary. "I'm going to make sure her run as planet governor is the worst in recorded history."

I held my breath, trying to contain my irritation. Endellion didn't deserve to be a planet governor—I knew that better than anybody—but *this* was shameful. Lone hated humans. He wanted to make an example out of Endellion. He wanted her to break on the world stage so he could say, *See? Humans can't handle the pressure. This was a heedless experiment gone bad.*

To my consternation, if there was any one human who could handle the pressures of being a planet governor, it was Endellion Voight. Too bad she had done herself the ultimate disservice of betraying her allies.

"I'll escort Administer Twoine," I said. "Where's he currently staying?"

"He's residing on Breakaway Station. Not too far from here."

I nodded, vaguely aware of Breakaway Station's location. Technically, Trinity Station was connected to Vectin-10 via the space elevator —that was where Cai had been living—but most space stations used the gravitational pull of a planet to maintain their locations.

Breakaway Station wasn't tethered to a planet. It was attached via mining cables to a metal-dense moon. Apparently, this was the *second* time the station had had to be repaired. It had "broken away" from the moon several decades back, killing hundreds of miners who had been in the cables at the time. Since its repair, everyone swears it's one of the safest locations in the system.

Perhaps that was why Administer Twoine had taken up residency there.

Dr. Clay stepped forward—I had almost forgotten he was in the room with us. "I'll make sure Administer Twoine is given the royal treatment while he stays with us on the *Star Marque*."

"Thanks," I said to Dr. Clay.

The man shot me an irritated glance.

"I'm glad I have your full support," Lone said as he moved away from the fountain and returned to his corner seat. "I could've asked a military vessel to escort Twoine, but the man is paranoid it will attract too much attention."

Too much attention?

I didn't say anything, but my mind wandered. Surely, Twoine wasn't worried the rebellion would overtake a military cruiser? No. That would be preposterous. So what *was* Twoine afraid of?

Assassination by someone close.

Clever man. Emissary Barten had been taken down by Ontwenty. These superhumans didn't play nice when they conducted their politics. It was all or nothing.

"I'll get him," I said as I turned for the door.

Lone waved a hand. "The elevator likely won't be ready for several more hours. You should feel free to stay here. I have fresh fruits and vegetables. Nothing synthesized. Enjoy them while you wait, and then head out."

But he waved his hand a second time, like he wanted to make sure we understood he didn't want us *here*. We could wait in the kitchen, or the lounge, or at the pool, but not in his presence. Anything to keep us separated.

I nodded, muttered a *thank you*, and then headed for the door, my vision swimming in red. I hated this man more and more. He thought he was giving me a *treat* by allowing me to stay in his house? Like an animal?

He could fuck himself.

Dr. Clay hustled to match my pace as I stormed out into the corridor.

"What's wrong?" he asked. "Your heart rate has obviously gone up."

"Nothing is wrong," I said in a forced-calm tone. "This is how I normally look."

"I know. It's a shame there isn't a workout routine for your face."

With a slow turn of my head, I offered him a glower. Then I came to a stop in the middle of the hallway, trying to rein in my fury. While I didn't want to stay here, I *did* want to see Sawyer's genetic twin, Helia.

"Help me find someone," I muttered as I headed for the main lounge.

"Find someone?" Dr. Clay hurried along and walked by my side. "You know people here?"

"Just one. A genetically designed human."

"Ah. Yes. Those are common on the planets." Dr. Clay glanced away from me, his gaze almost vacant as he stared straight ahead. "It was determined to be *more efficient* to create humans with *aptitudes* for certain menial positions."

"I know."

"Did you know engineering and computer work in general are considered some of the menial tasks? Apparently, superhumans are more designers and theory crafters than they are the people who type out millions of lines of code."

"Yeah," I muttered. "I'm aware of that, too."

We made it to the lounge—the place with the musician and a bar—but I didn't see Helia. She looked just like Sawyer, so I'd recognize her anywhere, but I just hadn't seen red hair or freckles anywhere.

When we entered the gardens, I glanced around. Nothing. When we went to the dining room and kitchen—a lavish and expansive couple of rooms fit to feed forty people—I still couldn't find her.

There were house workers, including a couple of chefs, and someone fixing machinery, but they didn't offer anything helpful. As a matter of fact, they tried to avoid making eye contact with me whenever I entered a room. I had no idea why.

"Why are you so panicked?" Dr. Clay asked as we hurried down another hall. "We haven't eaten a thing. I'm starving."

"I don't care."

"Obviously."

I let out a short exhale. "I still haven't found her."

"*Her*? Is this some sort of booty call?"

"*Listen*," I said through clenched teeth. "Why don't you go back and—"

"Ah. Look here." Dr. Clay interrupted me by stopping dead in his tracks and staring at a plaque on the wall. "A medical facility. I was wondering if the superhumans would bother keeping something like this in a dead zone."

I stopped and turned around. Sure enough, the plaque on the wall read: *Infirmary*.

Would Helia be there?

I tapped the computer panel next to the door. The screen flickered to life, bright and blue. A pleasant melody played for a few seconds, followed by a feminine voice. "*Good day. Do you need assistance?*"

It wasn't a human. It was some sort of machine-voice meant to direct me to the correct location.

"Yes," I said. "I need to get into the infirmary."

"*Can you describe your ailment?*"

"My stomach hurts."

Who cared if I lied to a machine?

"*Please head down the hall and take a left. You will find a physician who can better assess your condition.*"

"Are you serious?" I barked. "You're not going to let me inside?"

"*Several individuals are in recovery. Only medical emergencies are permitted at this time. All other ailments must be treated by the on-site physician.*"

I was about to punch the goddamn computer, but Dr. Clay stepped forward, the smuggest expression a douchebag could muster plastered all over his narrow face. "Please, Demarco. You're embarrassing yourself." He touched the computer screen. "Hello. My spleen has ruptured. I have persistent blurry vision, and I have confusion that lasts between five to ten seconds. I need immediate medical attention."

The door whooshed open without another peep from the computer. Dr. Clay strolled inside, but when I went to follow, the door slammed shut. It had force behind it—the damn thing could've hurt me.

I tapped the computer again. "Hello. My spleen has also ruptured."

"*Can you describe your symptoms?*"

"My vision is also blurry. And my confusion lasts way longer than ten seconds. It lasts a good *thirty* seconds. My whole inside is a fountain of blood." I motioned with my hand, making exploding gestures. "Pew. Pew. Pew."

The door slid open with another whoosh.

With a smirk, I stepped inside. The sterile environment left me frowning. Plain white tile floors, eggshell white walls, and a ceiling done in a dull gray gave the place the feeling of a morgue.

"*We have a stage five emergency,*" the computer system said as a dim blue light shone over the entire infirmary. "*The physician has been called. If you are in pain, please position yourself by the healing vat and prepare to be submerged.*"

Dr. Clay and I were the only ones in the infirmary. There were empty beds, empty countertops, and four advanced healing vats in the back, but nothing else. A single door nearby on the western wall was likely the supply closet, but no one emerged, not even with the soft alarm ringing.

"What did you tell the computer?" Dr. Clay snapped. "It shouldn't be that insistent."

I shrugged. "I told her I was sicker than you."

Dr. Clay pinched the bridge of his nose. "What in the name of gossamer's rings did you do that for? Was it your need to compete? You needed to be *more sick* than me? What's wrong with you?"

When he said it like that, I chuckled. "Yeah, well, I guess I did want to be sicker than you."

"Congratulations. You just won that prize."

Although the blue lights continued to bathe the room, the doctor had yet to arrive. I glanced around, disappointed by the empty environment. I had thought I'd find Helia here for sure.

"The spleen has been mended," Dr. Clay said to the ceiling. "Run a diagnostic on all patients in the infirmary."

The lights shifted from blue to red. In the next few minutes, the lights danced around the room, like some sort of strobe effect. I shielded my eyes and backed myself up against a wall. "You know how to command the infirmary?"

"I've worked as a physician and surgeon in superhuman hospitals for over a decade," Dr. Clay drawled. "I know the standard voice inputs for their medical facilities."

The dancing red lights abruptly ceased. I tensed as I waited for some sort of confirmation.

"All three patients have been diagnosed," the feminine computer stated. *"Patient one has recovered from their splenic rupture. Patient two has recovered from their splenic rupture. Patient three requires additional time in the healing vat to fully recover from their lacerations."*

Patient three?

Again, I glanced around.

"All healthy patients may leave."

But I ignored the computer and headed straight over to the healing vats. The vats on the *Star Marque* were metal and without windows. These were fancier—a small rectangular window was built into the side, and lights were built into the casing on the inside, so that the patient could remain illuminated.

The first vat was empty. As was the second. But the third…

That was where I found Helia.

TWENTY-FOUR

Out Of Sight

I didn't look long—I had seen enough.

Helia had been injured pretty severely. I didn't know the medical terms for it all. All I knew was it made me sick. And I had seen tons of thugs get offed in all sorts of disturbing ways. Hell, I had even seen Endellion decapitate a man.

But this was different.

She looked so much like Sawyer…

"Are you feeling well?" Dr. Clay asked, no concern in his voice.

I didn't answer him. I poked at the vat's computer, going through the menus until I came to the *disengage* function. I clicked to have the vat opened, despite the many warnings flashing on the screen. Lone would be upset, but I didn't care. Helia had to come with me.

The thick, gel-like fluid in the vat swirled and headed for the drain that had opened at the bottom. Helia had tubes in her mouth and nose—for a steady supply of oxygen—and otherwise wore nothing else. The mother cells were semi-transparent, but it was like looking through clear slime. Once some of it had drained, I got a better look at her. Lacerations covered most of her body, from her shoulders down to her ankles.

They were so neat and straight—the work of a sharp blade.

The moment the gel lowered to her waist, Helia's eyes fluttered open. She braced herself on the inside of the vat, her arms shaky. Without the mother cells, her open wounds began to bleed once again.

"What're you doing?" Dr. Clay snapped. He stomped over and pushed my hand away from the computer. "You shouldn't be interrupting someone's healing."

"We're taking her," I said, a hint of finality in my tone.

Dr. Clay glared down at the readout on the screen. He tapped a few areas, expanding the medical history. Then he glowered up at me, his expression hard and neutral. "If you take her, she's going to die."

"Bullshit."

"*It's true*. Are you doubting me? Which one of us has a medical degree?"

"What's wrong with her?" I asked, damn near shouting.

"Several of her organs have lacerations. If we take her out now, she has less than thirty minutes before she's dead." Dr. Clay ran a hand through his black, oil hair. "What's wrong with you? Is this the girl you wanted? You can come see her once she's recovered."

The round trip from here to Breakaway Station was practically four months. Could Helia live through four more months of *this*? Constant trips to the infirmary? I was disgusted with myself just thinking about leaving her.

"Is there no way we can carry the vat?" I asked. I already knew the answer. The vat was several tons, and it needed power to keep the mother cells from dying off.

Dr. Clay shook his head. "The only way I could see getting her out of the vat is if she needed a medical professional to stitch her up by hand. Unfortunately—or *fortunately*, if you're a sane person—the mother cells will heal all her injuries with enough time. No need to risk surgery."

No way to safely take her. I shook my head, my teeth gritted. I wanted to rip her out of this hole in the ground and fly off with her, just like Endellion had done with Sawyer. But how would I get away with it?

I already knew how.

When I killed General Lone.

Dr. Clay poked the computer screen and stopped the mother cells from draining farther. The healing vat opened slightly—the glass window rolled down halfway, allowing fresh air into the container. Helia leaned on the glass, her eyes sunken in and her complexion paler than normal.

She had lost so much blood.

With tubes in her nose and mouth, she slurred out, "Wut's happening?" With unsteady hands, she wiped away goo from her brow and red hair.

"Nothing," Dr. Clay coldly stated. "Your recovery is going smoothly. Please step back so we can refill the vat with fluid."

I stepped closer to Helia and reached into the vat to help her clear some of the gel from the sides of her eyes. When she looked at me, it was with the same gray-blue gaze that Sawyer had. Almost apathetic, borderline uncaring. She was bleeding from dozens of cuts, yet it didn't seem to disturb her.

"Everything is going to be okay," I said.

Helia took in a ragged breath. "Captain Demarco?"

"Yeah. Sorry about this. I got worried about you—came to see where you had gone."

She blinked at me, her eyebrows knitting together in confusion. "You were w-worried about… *me*?"

"Yeah." I tried to offer her a comforting smile, but it probably came across forced. "I know your sister. I'd hate to have to tell her something bad happened to you."

"My sister…" Helia rubbed her cheek with the back of her hand. "Please make sure… she's okay. I don't care what happens to me."

The request struck a chord with me. Did Helia know of Sawyer? Or was she groggy from her time in the vat and just spewing words? Her disregard for her own life hurt, and I wanted nothing more than to take her from this place.

"Your sister will be fine," I said.

"Thank you…"

Dr. Clay pointed at the screen. "*Hurry*," he practically hissed. "She needs to go back under."

I stepped away from the healing vat and responded with a sarcastic salute. The doctor rolled his eyes, closed the vat, and then started the process all over again. New mother-cell fluid flooded the vat, engulfing Helia in the rejuvenating goo once more.

She closed her eyes, allowing the sweet numbing agents of the fluid to put her into a comfortable sleep.

I watched her until the vat was full, but my chest hurt the entire time. If I could have, I would've taken her. Instead, I had to get to Breakaway Station as fast as possible. Once I returned, this would be a different story.

***

"YOU COULD'VE EXPLAINED the details a little more thoroughly," I said, talking at my PAD. "I know it must be hard to talk about the times Lone hurt you, but I think I need to know all the gory details now."

The sandstorm had lessened, and the view out the space elevator had returned to golden landscapes and blue skies.

"Why do you *need to know?*" Sawyer asked through the PAD, her voice on the edge of sarcastic.

"I found one of your genetic clones down in Lone's villa, and when I visited just now, she was in a healing vat."

"Well, he likes to harm things weaker than him." Again, no emotion. Just a statement. "What more do you need to know from there?"

"How often did he hurt you?"

"All the time."

I waited, but she offered nothing else.

Sawyer obviously didn't want to discuss the details. Maybe that was enough. If it had been so horrible that *Sawyer* couldn't express the pain with words, I probably shouldn't push. To this day, she was scarred so deeply, she wasn't even comfortable with her own body.

"Why didn't you tell me about my genetic twin?" Sawyer asked.

With a sigh, I replied, "I didn't want to upset you."

"I'd rather know these details, Demarco."

"Fine—you want to hear? She's a mess. Ripped up, disgusting. Bleeding everywhere." The other passengers on the elevator gave me odd looks. I shot them glares that said, *you can go fuck yourself.* I held the PAD closer to my mouth and lowered my tone. "When I spoke to your twin the last time, she seemed to think the abuse was all okay and normal. It was unnerving. I mean, I've known night-walkers who will take twenty credits and let you do whatever you want for an hour, but I've never known any of them to think it was *normal.* They know their clients are freaks."

"And you're surprised she thought it was normal?" Sawyer asked. "Lone owns several organ farms. He uses their tech and vats to genetically engineer people all the time."

"Isn't that illegal?" I asked. "I thought you weren't allowed to mass produce—"

"There are exceptions to human cloning," Sawyer interjected in a matter-of-fact tone. "Homo sapiens can be produced for military purposes. And spoiler alert: General Lone is a *general.* There's almost nothing he can't do with those cloning vats. And once he has the people, he takes them to his dead zones, and does whatever he wants to them. I doubt *my twin* has ever known life outside of his captivity."

I leaned against the railing that prevented people from touching the glass of the elevator's window. Although Sawyer rarely showed any emotion whatsoever, I could feel the subtle difference in her word choice and voice.

This upset her.

"Hey," I said. "Everything will be okay. I'm going to make sure of it."

"Don't say anything incriminating over the comms, Demarco."

"I haven't slipped up yet."

"I'm just reminding you." After a short pause, she added, "And thank you."

With a smirk, I said, "Everyone has a vendetta, right? Once this is over, I swear you'll feel better."

"I hope so."

IT WOULD TAKE us thirty-eight days to reach Breakaway Station.

Before we had left Vectin-10, I had Sawyer send a coded message to the planet governor's office. Endellion would understand what it meant. We were giving her a heads up that Administer Twoine would be on his way.

It almost killed my soul to help her, but one problem at a time.

I sat in the captain's room, staring at the computer mounted to the desk. The screen had a display of everyone's training schedule. The ground enforcers. The starfighters. Even the protocol seminars were listed—I knew what everyone was doing at every point of the day.

The captain's room was spacious for a starship, but cramped for a planetside dwelling. I had a desk—a wall-sized window that peered out into the cold void of space—and a few cushioned chairs to entertain with. Nothing else.

My mind wandered for a bit, but I eventually returned my focus to the infirmary listing.

Lysander had been in to see Dr. Clay several times in the last week. I tapped on the screen, pulling up the details. Everything was listed as *Defect Surgery*. I held my breath and tapped a finger on the desk.

I knew Lysander had a genetic defect, but I hadn't realized it affected him that badly.

With a tap on the screen, I opened his personal comms. "Lysander," I said. "Report to my room, would you?"

"Demarco," he responded, a sigh on his breath. "How many times do I have to tell you it's inappropriate for a captain to engage in this kind of activity with his commanding officers? Besides, I've made it clear I'm not interested. Very clear."

I ran a hand down my face. "Not my *bed*room, asshole. My official *captain's room*."

"Oh." An awkward silence came between us. "You hardly use that room."

"Yeah, well, we have time before we reach the station. I figured I would perform my captain's duties while we flew over there."

"I see. I'll be there in a moment."

I waited in silence, almost angry he had thought I had been hitting on him. I had learned my lesson. Few people on the *Star Marque* wanted to tumble with me. I didn't know why—they were clearly missing out. I was probably too intimidating, which was a shame. It had been a while.

The door opened with a soft *whoosh* and Lysander stepped in, his hands behind his back. He looked ready for a dressing down—his square jaw tight and his blond hair slicked back with sweat. He had been working out.

I leaned on my desk and offered him a half-smile. "What's wrong with you?"

My question must've been in a foreign language, because it took Lysander a full minute to process everything. "What're you referring to?" he finally responded.

"You never mentioned any of your surgeries to me."

His eyes grew a little wider. "You mean… with Dr. Clay?"

"That's right." I tapped at the edge of my screen. "They've been happening more frequently lately."

"You do understand that an officer's medical information is private, correct?"

I laced my fingers together and tilted my head. "Yeah, well, here we are. Why don't you tell me what's going on? Maybe not as your captain, but as a brother-in-arms."

Lysander relaxed a bit. But only a bit. He kept his hands behind his back, even as his shoulders slumped. "Listen," he said, his voice quiet. "You already know I don't have that much time left. Even with Dr. Clay's expertise, I still suffer from cell deterioration. It's gotten worse, but the doctor has helped slow the situation."

"What can we do to reverse it?"

"Dr. Clay is working on some things, but he hasn't been successful." Lysander hardened his expression. "I'll let you know when there's news."

That was it? He had said everything as if it was a report to his commanding officer, and not the personal tragedy that it was.

Why did I work with a bunch of robots?

"When we get to Breakaway Station, I'll see what we can do about getting better equipment and supplies. I owe the doctor a bunch of shit anyway. Make a list. Price doesn't matter."

Lysander narrowed his eyes. "Demarco, you can't use the ship's funds to treat my illness."

"Who's going to stop me?" I quipped.

"Everyone dies. It's a fact of life. Getting emotional about it won't help anything."

I stood from my chair, both irritated and amused. Did people just want to suffer in silence? Or did they just not trust me to get things done?

"Look, Sanders. I don't need your permission. I'm going to tell Dr. Clay to get whatever medication you need to keep you alive as long as it takes to cure you." I snapped my fingers once and pointed at the door. "You're dismissed. Next time, tell me about your medical problems or I'm going to write you up for it."

Lysander glared. "*What?* You can't do that. That's not—well, it's not standard protocol. It's actually a violation of—"

"I don't care," I said, cutting him off. "Who're you going to report me to?" I sarcastically shrugged. "You going to tell them you're a defect and I'm mistreating you by making sure you live a long and healthy life? Fine. Whatever. Be my guest. Just get out of my room. I have other things to do."

My vice-captain grew slightly red in the face. With an awkward nod, he said, "You... have an odd way of expressing concern, Demarco. But I get it. Thank you."

Again, I waved him away.

Lysander turned on his heel and exited the room without another word.

A few seconds later, Sawyer spoke over the ship's comms. "You're so soft sometimes."

I scoffed and laughed. Then I glanced up at the ceiling—the speakers and microphone were there somewhere. "I'm not going to be like Endellion."

"Oh, you're definitely not."

"What does that mean?"

"I mean, she only helped people if it served her somehow. She wouldn't dump credits on anyone unless it served a purpose. Helping Lysander… That had never been on her agenda."

I turned my gaze down to the steel floor. "I know."

"I really appreciate that you're going to help him."

That helped my mood. I smiled and said, "Then I'm on the right track."

TWENTY-FIVE

A Race

Thirty-six days until we reached Breakaway Station.

Now was the perfect time to train with the starfighters. I sent a message through the ship's systems to meet in the training room, and because I was the captain, I was there an hour early. The others filtered in closer and closer to the meeting time, and I took note of who and when.

Melba and her two buddies, Asahi and Hattie, arrived first. That fact interested me, but only because I had a better grasp of their personalities now. I had watched them the last two days—in the mess hall, in the lounge areas, and around in the halls. They were old-school soldiers.

Melba was older, a little overweight, somehow, despite the near flavorless food they served in the mess hall, but she held herself with a stiff and serious demeanor. She reminded me of Lysander. Prim. Proper. Never late, never unprepared.

Perhaps that was why we didn't get along.

Asahi was the second-in-command. A tall man with thick, black hair and a piercing gaze. He didn't speak much, but that was because he let Melba do the talking for him. A follower, but cut from the same military cloth.

The last one—Hattie—was so thin and rigid, she might as well have been a steel rod. To make things worse, she had the personality of nutrient paste. A terrible combination for social situations, but it made her precise when it came to getting the job done.

I stared as Melba, Asahi, and Hattie went to their training pods. Melba and Asahi gave me polite nods, but Hattie broke the mold a bit by waving slightly—she didn't even bring her hand up all the way.

With a smirk, I gave her a reverse-nod, a jut of my chin.

Hattie blushed, for some reason, and for the first time in a while, I thought she might have been into me. Lysander always discouraged me, but perhaps after training, I could have a talk with Hattie and see where things went.

But Sawyer…

Wasn't sure how she'd feel about that.

I cursed to myself.

The next person to arrive in the training room was Victtra, followed by her thugs, One and Two. The two beefy men escorted her to her training pod. She offered me a smile before settling into the pod and shutting the door.

The two guards stood outside the pod, their hands behind their backs and their enviro-suits all the way up. The reflective visors shielded their faces, but I liked to assume they were bored out of their minds.

The last two to arrive were Noah and Mara—technically one minute late.

They were deep in conversation, smiling and laughing the entire way into the room. Noah, so tall, and Mara, so short, had an opposite's thing going on. Mara's subdued melancholy melted away when in the presence of Noah's exuberance. Her cute, heart-shaped face was more likely to be alight whenever Noah was around.

"Sorry we're late, Captain Demarco," Mara said to me as they walked by. "Noah made a mess in the gym, and I helped him clean it up."

Noah rubbed at the back of his neck, his face so red, it made his blond hair even brighter. "Yeah, uh, I might've run into someone. It won't happen again." As he opened the door to his training pod, he waited until Mara was inside hers before he turned to me and said, "Don't tell my brother, okay? Lysander will be upset if he knows I was in the gym today."

Just like his brother, Noah had a genetic defect. He shouldn't exercise too frequently, or the membranes inside his body would break. He still liked to train, regardless, but Lysander was a fussy mother with too much free time.

"I won't tell him," I said.

Noah gave me a thumbs up and then dove into the training pod.

I climbed into my pod and shut the door. The machine clamped down on my lower legs, restricting my blood flow. I grabbed both of the side-sticks as the screen of the pod flared to life. Lights filled the inside of the pod—bright, sharp, red-and-blue—and the screen displayed the view from a starfighter, complete with all the data readouts.

Hull integrity.

My position on the Vectin star map.

Our comms were also connected. Noah, Mara, Victtra, Melba, Asahi, and Hattie all displayed on the edge of the screen, the details of their starfighters listed for my convenience.

"We'll pick up from where we left off," Victtra said, her voice practically in my ear. "Our hit percentage was unacceptable. I recommend we go back to the targeting obstacle program."

I hadn't practiced with these guys since Victtra had joined. It didn't surprise me that she had tried to take charge. It was probably baked into the genes of Homo superior.

I switched to a private comms channel with Melba. "Hey—you agreed to have Victtra lead the training?"

"I didn't have much of a choice," Melba replied, her tone neutral. "She came in the first day and outflew everyone here. She made it *very clear* that she was better in every regard."

"Why didn't you just say you had more experience?" I asked.

"Listen, my options were, *get in a fight with a superhuman*, or *let her run the training.* I picked the path of least resistance. I don't want any trouble from those two-toned freaks."

When I switched back to the main comms, Victtra was still giving orders.

"I'll take it from here," I said, interrupting her.

A short stretch of silence was the only reply I got.

"Heard?" I asked.

"Acknowledged," Melba said, a smile in her voice.

Asahi and Hattie both replied, "Understood."

"*Wait,*" Victtra said before anyone else could say anything. "We're in the middle of a training regime. Changing our practice—when you're not planning on being with us every time—will mess with our starfighters. I recommend you allow me to continue with the scheduling. That way, when you occasionally train with us, we don't need to change everything to accommodate you."

Her condescension, mixed with her matter-of-fact tone, grated on me. I could understand why Melba had been argued into a corner. "Who says I won't be here every time?"

"You haven't been. Sometimes the duties of the captain call you away from the mundanity of formation practice."

I hated to admit it, but she was right. I would sometimes be absent. But part of me didn't want to put her in charge. Sure, she had been trained at a special school, but she was young. And if I put the superhuman in charge—from day one—what kind of message did it send? Homo superior always had the advantage, and while I did think they were talented, Victtra still needed to prove herself. Just *showing up* wasn't good enough.

"When I'm here, we'll do things my way," I said. "You're my starfighter officer—*this* is your job. Come up with flexible training schedules to accommodate the needs of the *Star Marque's* captain."

"Yes, Sir," Victtra said, her voice smooth and betraying nothing.

"And today, we'll be running some of the obstacle courses."

"Awesome," Noah said over the comms.

Melba and her two lackeys replied in unison with, "Understood." They all sounded ten times happier than before.

"I'm ready," Mara chimed in.

"Yes, Captain," Victtra finally said.

I poked at the screen of my training pod and input a custom design for a course—something with a lot of tight spaces. Then I made it a race. While that would never happen in real life, that didn't matter. I wanted our training today to be interesting and fun, so that I got everyone at their best.

Plus, I wanted more camaraderie. Would a race do that? I hoped so.

The instructions for the race flashed across everyone's screens.

"A race?" Melba asked.

"That's right." I rested back in my seat. "Don't worry about winning—I'm going to come in first place—just focus on making it through the course without crashing."

Noah half-laughed. "That's it?"

"You heard me."

"All right. I can do that."

The screen flickered, and the course appeared before us. I tilted my side-sticks, and I sped forward. When I customized our training, I removed all our torpedoes and hyperweapons, to prevent anyone from altering the obstacles with their weapons. It would just be our ships and our skill.

Our obstacle course was through two porous asteroids. The giant space rocks were large enough for us to fly through. The tunnels had sharp turns and narrow corridors, but they were easy if flown at slow speeds. If anyone tried to rush through, they'd likely smash into the walls.

Everyone flew their starfighters to the start of the track.

A giant red star hung in the distance. A purple nebula marked the darkness of space, giving our racetrack an interesting flare.

Once everyone was in position, Noah chuckled as he turned his comms back on.

"What do we get if we win?" he asked.

Asahi—who rarely spoke—interjected with, "For the first time ever, the respect of your peers."

"Oh, really? This coming from the guy who's planning on letting Melba beat him because he's always number two."

"Ha," Asahi sardonically replied. "I'll have you know, I've won a few races in my day."

"The ones Melba let you win."

Despite their harsh quips, laughter remained in their words. Even Mara giggled into the comms, the sweet noise a pleasant addition to the conversation.

"All right," I said. "Everyone ready? On the count of three." I tapped on the computer, and large numbers appeared in everyone's pods.

3.

2.

1.

Go.

I pressed forward on my two side-sticks and accelerated fast. The pressure from the speed crushed me back against my seat.

2Gs. 3Gs.

I shot straight into the asteroid and controlled my movement with slight adjustments to the side-sticks. The starfighter was nimble. As long as I reacted in time, I could turn on a thumbnail.

4Gs.

I stared at my screen, my whole body flattened against my seat. Melba was behind me. Then Victtra, then Asahi, then Hattie, then Mara, and finally, Noah. They weren't too far behind, and I didn't like that.

I sped through the tunnel of the asteroid, turning whenever needed and keeping my focus sharp.

5Gs.

Some people got lightheaded when the gravity pressures became too high. Sawyer always warned me about my vision tunneling, but I had been genetically altered to handle the crushing forces.

6Gs.

That was as fast as the training pod could simulate. Although I had flown faster in a real dog fight—all the way beyond 9Gs—I'd never be able to do that here.

Melba fell behind. So did Asahi, Hattie, Mara, and Noah.

But not Victtra.

She sped through the asteroid tunnel, closing the distance between us. Halfway through the first asteroid, she was on my tail, a mere meter away, despite our ridiculous speeds. Damn Homo superior could do anything. Even a prepubescent kid was practically showing me up.

"I think we should get something if we win," Noah said over the comms, his voice strained from the pressure.

I smirked. "If someone actually beats me, you can be captain for a day." Even my voice was strained—this wasn't an environment conducive to talking.

Victtra cleared her throat. "If *I* win... will you allow me to control the training, even when you randomly attend?"

The others forced out a few chuckles. Victtra clearly couldn't move past this issue. It almost made me laugh.

"Sure," I said through gritted teeth. "If you win, you can be in charge of all the scheduling and training—I won't say a damn thing. But if you crash..." I smiled to myself. "If you crash, you have to admit to everyone on the ship that I'm the better pilot."

Victtra scoffed.

We continued through the asteroid until the tunnel ended. We shot out into space, avoiding bits of rock that twirled around the exit. The second asteroid wasn't far. Victtra and I entered the gigantic rock at nearly the same time.

The second tunnel was narrower than the first. My starfighter flashed proximity warnings across the screen.

"Do we have a deal?" I asked, my jaw clenched from the pressure.

Our starfighters couldn't accelerate any faster, so winning would come down to who could pilot their craft the best. Obviously, Victtra thought she could beat me.

She thought she knew everything. It would be her arrogance that caused her to lose—I knew it in my gut.

"Deal," Victtra said in a sweet, but forced, voice.

With a hard jerk of my side-sticks, I smashed my starfighter straight into hers.

The training pod was undamaged, of course. The screen

beeped twice—highlighting where I had crashed with Victtra on the obstacle course—and then gave me my average stats for the exercise.

My chair shook.

The screen went black.

The lights powered down.

Then the lid to my pod opened and the cushions around my lower legs relaxed. Once free, I stepped out of the pod with a smirk.

Victtra leapt out of her own pod, so angry her nostrils were flaring. And not just her nose. Superhumans had holes on the sides of their necks—starting just below the ears—and they used them to breathe. I hadn't known those holes flared with anger until Victtra strode over to me.

She brushed back her silvery hair, a glare fixed on her perfect face.

"*You cheated*," Victtra practically shouted. "You *caused* me to crash."

I leaned against the side of my pod and laughed. That only got her angrier. "All I said was *if you crash*. I didn't say how." I tapped the side of my head. "I know you think you're the smartest person in the room, but if you underestimate everyone around you, this is the consequence. You'll lose."

Victtra stopped dead in her tracks, a mere half-meter from me. She gave me this look like I had slapped her in the face. With a deep breath, she turned on her heel and flounced away. No words. No acknowledgement. Her face was red, and I suspected I had damaged her pride.

Her bodyguards turned to follow her. One went out the door with Victtra, but Two lingered behind. He glanced over his shoulder.

"Did you really beat her?" he asked, his enviro-suit filtering his voice to make him sound machine-like.

I nodded once.

"Heh. I never thought humans would ever beat someone like her."

Then Two turned and walked out of the room, taking his awe with him.

I hadn't come to training with the goal of taking Victtra down a peg, but it did feel good. Perhaps she'd insist on leaving the *Star Marque* after this little stunt. I could see her preferring that over admitting I was the better fighter…

TWENTY-SIX

Logic Dictates

I sat in the captain's room, waiting for Victtra. With my fingers laced in front of me, I relaxed against my chair, trying to look as *captain-ly* as possible. When the door whooshed open, I held back a smile.

Victtra walked in with her bodyguards, One and Two. They stayed by the door as she approached my desk. I motioned to a chair, and she took a seat, her posture stiff. Despite that, she offered me a tight smile.

"You wanted to speak to me, Captain Demarco?" she asked.

"That's right." I leaned forward, my elbows on the top of the desk. The computer screen on the desk flared to life because of my touch, but I ignored it. "Listen, I'm sorry I did that during the starfighter training, but you needed it."

Victtra's smile and calm demeanor vanished.

"I *needed* to be humiliated in front of the others?" She balled her hands into fists and then gripped the armrests of her chair, her nose and neck holes flaring. "This is because I'm a member of Homo superior, and we both know it. You—and the others—are frustrated with your own inadequacy and *genetic problems,* and your jealousy causes you all to lash out against me. It's a flaw of your species."

Tsk.

I didn't even want this bitch here, but here we were. If I didn't fix this damn problem fast, it would cost us a life.

"I *needed* to humiliate you because you let the enemy dictate the terms of the engagement," I said, no mirth in my voice. "You were so fucking arrogant and cocksure that you would beat me at a stupid race, you let me pick the terms of the arrangement. I said, *if you crash, I win*, and you just agreed."

Victtra went to open her mouth, but I slammed my hand on the desk. She flinched, her eyes wide.

"The second reason I *needed* to humiliate you is because your entire team was rooting for you to fail." I glared at her, hoping this would stick in her super genius head. "They only knew you for a few days, and already they wanted to watch you fail. You think that's going to help in a dogfight? You think you're a good leader? Hubris is the problem here, not your fucking species, little girl. You want to be a starfighter officer? Put your maturity panties on and listen."

Her stunned expression softened into something more serious and focused.

"You need to have the respect of your team," I said.

"*You* don't conduct yourself like you deserve respect." Victtra huffed and crossed her arms. "You conduct yourself like an oaf. You're late for training. Foul mouthed. Insulting."

I smirked as I rubbed at my chin. "You just don't get it. Everyone here knows I'm going to go down with the ship. They can count on me. I'm skilled, I care about them, I'm willing to bleed on their behalf." I pointed at Victtra. "You're not here for them. You're here for yourself. You fucking pushed your way onto the ship, and you have no interest in the *Star Marque* or her crew."

"And my motives matter?" Victtra shot back. "You've never just hired some officers to do a job for you? You only take on people who will die for the ship?"

"Don't fuck with me," I said, angry all over again. "I know how smart you are. There's a big difference between someone who joins the *Star Marque* willingly—and as an equal—and someone who strong-arms their way into every situation. No one trusts you. You're out for yourself, and you look down on everyone else the entire time. Don't deny it."

The silence between us wasn't as satisfying as I would've liked. Victtra… She had an expression that was a mix between a child and an adult. Her lip quivered, but the rest of her face remained strong.

She had said that superhumans had brains that were more mature than humans', but that didn't provide her with experience.

"Look, I'm willing to look past the fact that you forced yourself on my ship," I said. I leaned back and kicked my feet up on the desk, my boots clean. "You *are* talented, and the *Star Marque* is understaffed."

Victtra took a moment to compose herself. She brushed her silvery hair with her fingers, and then straightened her posture. "I'm listening."

But this was the moment I dreaded. Were we going to have an actual partnership? Seemed like this whole thing would bite me in the ass if I weren't careful.

And I wasn't known for being cautious.

"How about this—let's make a deal." I lowered my voice, though I knew it didn't matter. Sawyer was listening to this whole damn conversation. "I'll help you track down the people responsible for your father's death, and in return, you'll listen to what I have to say, treat my crew with respect, and work with us for at least a year. Sound good?"

Victtra didn't even hesitate before saying, "You know what happened to my father, don't you?"

I didn't answer. Hell, I didn't even really breathe. I just stared her down, my mind on the rhythm of my heart, hoping it didn't give anything away like the traitor it was.

"The real question," I said, slow and calm, "is do you want to catch the man who physically killed your father, or the people who ordered your father's death? Because those goals are completely different, kid. The killer could be anywhere—and anyone—with no real hatred for you or your family. But the people behind everything…" I took in a deep breath and held it. "We might figure out who it is and be unable to do anything about it."

This question was the worst of all, because if she wanted the killer—me—I needed to make sure she died in a dogfight we had with the rebellion. But if she wanted Minister Ontwenty, I had lots of good news.

"I can't want both?" Victtra asked, cold and calculated. "I can't want everyone involved in my father's death dead?"

I just waited, unwilling to add anything more to the conversation. I suspected she didn't know it was me, but at the same time, she knew I was hiding information. Too much information.

"I see." Victtra tensed again. "The *Star Marque* was nearby when my father was murdered, and I thought there might have been a reason. I'm right, aren't I? I'm probably right about all of it. This ship was used to harbor my father's killer, or maybe even took the orders for the deed."

I said nothing.

She continued, "And you don't want to out any fellow Homo sapiens, but you'll more than happily point me in the direction of the Homo superiors, hoping I'll leave your little crew alone."

She wasn't wrong. I just wasn't going to confirm or deny anything.

"I understand," Victtra finally said.

"You do?"

"You'll help me track down superhumans, but not anyone else. Well, I don't need your help finding the killer. I'll do that on my own time. However, the members of Homo superior will not be as easy to deal with. I... I will need help with that."

She wasn't going to give up her investigation.

But at least she wasn't going to ask me—or the crew—for help. Which meant there was a good chance she'd never do it.

"My father's work was dedicated to bringing human defects supplies and medicine." Victtra sighed. "He... He cared about them. About *you*." She rubbed at her face and then regained her composure. "I always figured his enemies went to the highest levels, but he never wanted to discuss it. I was too young, but now... Now he's dead. And I'm the only one left who cares."

"Do we have a deal?" I asked, ignoring her morbid musings.

Again, without hesitation, she replied with a curt nod. "Yes. I want to find the people responsible for my father's death. The *real* influence who ordered the hit. Captain Demarco—if you know where to start, I implore you to tell me."

I stood from my chair and walked around the desk. Victtra didn't get up. She just stared at me, unblinking.

"I think we better figure this out together," I said. "We need proof, after all. And if we can't get that, nothing can be done about anything."

"But you'll point me in the right direction?"

"When we pick up Administer Twoine, I have a few ideas."

Victtra stood and smiled. "Excellent."

WE STILL HAD thirty-six days until we reached Breakaway Station.

This day dragged. Starfighter training. My talk with Victtra. I went to the mess hall, grabbed a pouch of flavored paste—and a few fish flakes—and then headed for Deck One without so much as giving anyone else a second glance, even though Hattie tried to approach me for casual conversation.

I wasn't in the mood.

When Lysander sent me a message request through my PAD, I sent him a command as his captain to let me have the next eight hours to myself. For some reason, Lysander liked this more than my usual conversation with him. He replied with *official communications* and stated he would let the crew know I was unavailable.

I swear that man got excited about all things protocol. It wasn't healthy. If he could do the Devil's Tango with a rulebook, he would.

After a short ride on the lift, I reached Deck One. Then I sauntered over to Sawyer's workroom and entered, my mind on distant things. Sawyer was the only one I wanted to talk to.

Once I opened the door, Blub spotted me and *toot, toot, tooted* over in my direction, his fins fluttering through the air like a veil caught on the wind. I patted his koi fish head with two of my fingers and then dug out the fish flakes from my cargo pants pocket. Blub shuddered as he nibbled them out of the palm of my hand.

Sawyer sat at her computer, typing away faster than ever, her multiple screens bright with text and camera feeds of the ship. Her olive green jumpsuit was stained by cleaning fluid.

"Demarco," she said, no emotion in her voice. "You've been busy today. That's new for you."

"What's that supposed to mean?" I dropped a handful of flakes on top of a broken piece of machinery and then made my way over to her desk. Blub stayed behind, gobbling up the food as fast as his little fish mouth could handle. I would've made a prostitution joke, but I doubted Sawyer would've been into it.

"I'm just giving you a hard time." Sawyer glanced over her shoulder for a short second, her gray-blue eyes alight with interest. "What're you doing here? I thought you'd head straight to your room for some *alone time* with your hand."

I leaned against the wall near Sawyer and flashed a smirk. "Oh? Disappointed you're not getting your nightly show?"

"It's more like bi-daily show at this point," Sawyer drawled.

I knew she watched—she had since I had first joined the *Star Marque*, but I didn't know she kept a damn schedule. I didn't really care, though. Not much interesting happened on the ship during these long treks through space. If I had the power, I'd probably watch everyone in the capsules as well.

I reached into my pocket and withdrew the aluminum pouch of nutrient paste. "Here." I placed it on her desk. "I figured you hadn't eaten yet today."

Sawyer glanced over at the pouch, a slight smile on her face. She took the "food" and hoarded it close to her keyboard. Then she resumed her furious typing.

"I was mad at you, I think," she said, smiling at the screen as she worked on the ship's code.

"Yeah. I know."

"I like this side of you—the kind side that's making things right."

I shrugged. "Well, I already promised I'd kill your ex-boyfriend and save your genetic twin—I'm not sure what else I can do to make you happy besides bringing you food and patting your fish brother."

Sawyer stopped typing. Then she swiveled her chair around. She sat in it like a lunatic—her feet on the chair, her knees pressed against her chest. She hugged her legs and then stared up at me through her lashes.

"You've made me feel better. I appreciate that."

"You sure you don't want to add a *beep boop* at the end of that statement?" I quipped. "You sound like a robot sometimes. And not the fun kind."

Sawyer brushed her red hair back. "Aren't you tired, Demarco?"

"What? You trying to get rid of me already?" I pushed away from the wall. "All right. I'll head to my room."

"I was hoping to join you," Sawyer said, all business. "Or are you too tired to try things tonight? Logic dictates that if we're to take this relationship further, we should be intimate."

It took me a quick second to fully grasp what she was implying. I *was* tired, but the instant I understood, I smiled. With an effortless motion, I leaned down, scooped her into my arms, and headed for the door.

Blub was too distracted by the fish flakes.

Sawyer didn't say a word. She remained stiff in my arms, her face pressed against my chest. I didn't hold her tightly—afraid she would feel restrained—and instead carried her like something delicate, my arms around her, but not curled too much.

"Any night you want to spend with me, just say the word," I said with a half-smile. "Even if I'm in the healing vat, I'll move over to make room."

"What a gentleman," Sawyer sarcastically said.

I chuckled as we made our way down the corridor. The captain's quarters weren't too far, but I took my time. Someone like me—genetically altered—had actual control over pheromones. With each step, I probably smelled sweet to anyone in the nearby area. More alluring. I was certain Sawyer knew all about my trick of biology. She laughed into my tank top.

When I reached the door, I tapped the computer screen with my elbow. The door whooshed opened, and I stepped inside, more excited than I had been in a long while.

The last person I had been with was Endellion.

With her, it had been a feat of athleticism. She had always been ready for more—and so had I. Only once, that I could remember, had Endellion wanted something more intimate and slower.

I had a feeling Sawyer wasn't the athletic type. That didn't matter. Sawyer had been the one to save me from a plummeting space station. Any way she liked it, that was what I'd give her.

With a few confident steps, I brought Sawyer over to the edge of the bed and sat her down on the mattress. Her face reddened, and then she glanced down at the sheets. With shaky hands, she smoothed them out.

She didn't need to speak. I was an expert on all things physical. I ripped off my tank top and threw it to the side. Then I did the same with my belt and boots. Then my cargo pants, until I wore nothing but my scars.

Sawyer watched with rapt fascination, though she never removed any of her clothing, not even her jumpsuit. I put one knee on the edge of the mattress, and Sawyer tensed more than she already had been.

"Can you turn off the lights?"

"You won't be able to see anything then," I said as I ran a hand over my muscled chest and stomach.

"You won't be able to see anything, either."

Tsk. I really didn't care that she was scarred. I wanted her to know that in her core, but I'd never be able to prove it if we were rolling around in the dark. She'd forever think I only stayed around because I never saw *the true her*.

Then again, I couldn't push her.

With a sigh, I got up and tapped the computer on the wall. I could've set up voice activation, but I had never gotten around to it. It was still set to Endellion's…

Once the darkness settled in, I turned around and climbed onto the mattress.

I had expected Sawyer to undress, but when she sidled up next to me, she was still fully clothed. That didn't ultimately matter. I crawled over her, and with soft hands, she gently touched my neck and chest.

When I leaned down to kiss her, Sawyer took a shaky breath before lightly pressing her lips against mine. She didn't feel emotions as strongly as others, so it was all the more exciting when she shuddered beneath me. She barely tasted like anything, but lust had its own unique flavor. Pleasant. Distracting.

I placed a hand on her side, ready to remove her jumpsuit for her, but Sawyer turned her head, ending our kiss, and then gulped down air.

"What's wrong?" I asked.

She said nothing, but I knew what she wanted. She didn't want me on top. She didn't want to feel trapped.

I rolled onto my back, and with one strong lift, I brought Sawyer on top of me. She gasped—a quiet noise—but she didn't dismount afterward. She waited with bated breath, but I just remained under her, my hands on her hips.

"Comfortable now?" I asked.

Sawyer took in a deep breath. Each second that passed, I felt her relax more and more.

"Thank you," she whispered.

"Anything for you."

A soft chuckle was my only answer, her voice a mix of amusement and affection.

It was too dark to see her exact reaction, but with shaky fingers, she caressed my chest and stomach. Her hand gradually went lower, but never anywhere that would be interesting. She made circles across my skin, following the grooves of my muscles.

Then she stopped.

"You're such a tease," I said, husky with excitement.

"I'm sorry." All remorse. No playfulness.

Sawyer was a little too serious sometimes.

I rubbed her legs and smirked. "Don't be sorry. I like it."

"You like everything."

"Which is why you don't need to be nervous," I quipped. "You can't go wrong with me."

Sawyer hesitated a moment. She placed her hand on my stomach, her fingers cool against my warm skin. "You don't mind... if I touch you?"

I bit back a laugh. "I ripped my clothes off the moment we were alone. That was my *please touch me* sign."

It took her a few seconds, but she moved her body so that she was sitting over me. Her jumpsuit was soft enough, and it eased some of my frustration. I could at least feel the heat between her legs through all the fabric.

I closed my eyes, content to lose myself in the sensations. "When you watch me at night, what do you imagine?" I asked. "We can do whatever you want. I'm easy."

She was a mere whisper away, yet I could barely hear her when she muttered, "I imagined... that you're enjoying yourself. That... we're doing what you and Endellion used to."

Ah. So she had watched all of that, too.

What a voyeur.

Still excited me, though. Probably a sign of how messed up I was.

Sawyer moved her hips, rubbing herself against me. I exhaled, still content with the situation. "I'm enjoying myself," I said, biting back a laugh.

That statement seemed to relax Sawyer the most. She placed a hand on my stomach, bracing herself against me. She continued to move against me, her hitched breathing and trembling hands telling me she was at least enjoying herself. I held her hips, keeping her close as I bucked against her.

Sure, I could have gone for more, but I hadn't been lying when I said I was easy. Whatever made her comfortable. There was always time later for other things.

I moaned with each of her small movements, and it must've excited her, because she picked up the pace and went harder. With a smile, I lost myself in the moment. Her soft noises were everything I wanted.

Sawyer was so lightweight. Endellion was a cyborg—filled with machines and wires—and she had weighed more than she looked. Sawyer was the opposite. I feared I would hurt her if I gripped her too hard, but at the same time, I just wanted the feeling of her body pressed hard against mine.

To my surprise, she shuddered and then sharply exhaled, her whole body stiffer than before. I opened my eyes, but it was still dark. All I could hear was her strangled breathing. She had stopped moving altogether, her hands trembling.

"You okay?" I asked.

There was a long pause before she whispered, "I've never felt that before."

With a smirk, I asked, "Pretty great, right?"

"I understand why you're constantly chasing people to get into bed with."

"It only gets better from here. Wait until you have multiple in one session."

She half-chuckled. "I don't know if I'll want to leave the room then."

"That's the goal, really."

Sawyer rolled off me and curled back up against my side. She tucked her head into my armpit, glued to my body. "Can we just lie here? I don't know how to feel about this."

"We can do whatever you want," I said.

"Do you want me to do something for you first?"

"Nah. It's more important to me that you feel comfortable. Just relax."

Seconds passed in silence, and while I wished she had waited until I had finished, I had gone many a night without the touch of another, I could do it again. Apparently, despite her time with Lone, this had been the first time she had enjoyed herself. I didn't want to ruin the moment by demanding she do more than she felt comfortable with.

I stroked her short, red hair, calming myself by thinking about anything else. Cold showers. Dead fish. The usual.

"Did you have fun?" Sawyer asked.

"You know I did."

"Even though I'm not particularly skilled?"

"I've got good news," I said, smiling. "I'm an expert enough for the both of us." I gently kissed her forehead. "You never have to worry with me. I'll make it fun."

"Always so confident," she muttered. "I remember when you first thought you could fly a starfighter, even though you had never been a pilot. You crashed on a stationary rock."

"Hey, look on the bright side. If I mess up my piloting here, we're just going to get sticky. No one's going to die."

Sawyer genuinely laughed. Then she held me tighter—enough that I could feel her heart beat. I paid attention to it for a prolonged couple of minutes, allowing time to pass between us. She fluttered her eyes shut, her lashes tickling my skin.

Eventually, fatigue got the better of me.

TWENTY-SEVEN

Travel Times

Twenty days until we reached Breakaway Station.

I sat in the training pod, helping the other starfighters get their maneuvers in order. We were practicing with hyperweapons, the super-heated plasma bolts that each of our tiny ships carried in a dogfight. They were powerful enough to break through the hull of a starship, but in order to get a good shot—and not have the bolt blasted out of space by anti-missile defenses, we had to get close.

But not too close.

Most starships had a *point-defense system*. The system was a series of torpedoes and lasers used in close quarters against smaller ships. At a far enough distance, anything could be dodged in a tiny starfighter, but when up close, the torpedoes traveled so fast that a starfighter pilot wouldn't have the time to react.

Not only that, but the point-defenses were automated, meaning they were triggered by proximity and not by the unreliable hands of people.

Get too close to a starship, get destroyed.

That was the lesson I was trying to hammer into everyone's heads.

The simulation had a single starship cruiser. The goal was to fly close to the engines—close enough to unleash a hyperweapon attack —but not so close that the point-defense system activated.

Mara flew in toward the starship, launched her attack, and then retreated.

The bright light of the hyperweapon was nearly blinding. It was like unleashing the power of the sun tenfold.

The cruiser was smashed, but since this was a simulation, it "fixed itself" seconds later, resetting for the next person to do their run.

Next up, Melba flew close to the ship. With textbook accuracy, she fired her blast and then turned away. Perfect.

Asahi went in and did the same—damn near the exact route that Melba had taken. He really was her little dog. I was almost impressed with his ability to mimic her. I supposed it came from years of training together.

"Watch this," Hattie said over the comms.

She accelerated her starfighter faster than the others. I watched with a half-smile as she shot for the engines of the cruiser, her little ship quickly maneuvering into place. With expert skill, she pulled up at the last moment and also fired off her hyperweapon.

The cruiser never stood a chance.

"Don't show off during a real fight," Melba chided over the comms.

"It's all right," I replied. "There might come a moment when we need that kind of skill in a fight. It's good to know Hattie can handle it."

Hattie breathlessly replied, "Thank you, Captain."

A piece of me knew she was showing off for my benefit. It wasn't a bad way to get my attention, but I probably shouldn't reward it very often.

When it came time for Noah's run, however, he was hesitant. I could already tell, just by the way he circled his starfighter around before diving in for the run. Had he been intimidated by Hattie's stunt? I didn't know. All I saw was his slow approach, his late shot, and his eventual triggering of the point-defense system.

He got too close.

The starship lit him up with fifty lasers and ten torpedoes, all so fast, he never had time to dodge. I cringed when I saw his starfighter disappear from my screen.

Thankfully, the simulation wasn't real, so he eventually returned to us in a brand-new starfighter.

"Don't worry," Mara said over the comms. "You'll get it this time. That's why we're practicing, Noah."

He didn't reply.

But then another voice filled the comms.

"You suffer from anxiety paralysis," Victtra said matter-of-factly. "If you let that control you, then you'll always fail when it comes to high-stress situations."

"Thanks," Noah shot back. "Real helpful."

I was about to step in and tell all the kids to stop bickering, but Victtra persisted.

"I had the same problem when I first started my starfighter course at the academy," she said, no hint of shame. "My instructors gave me several tools to help deal with the anxiety."

Noah hesitated before asking, "Really?"

"That's right. When I first flew a starfighter in a simulation, I crashed it into a stationary object because I was too frightened to move in any direction. My instructor gave me a meditation exercise to focus my thoughts on the immediate, rather than dwelling on possibilities or terrible outcomes."

"Oh, wow."

"Can I hear about some of those?" Mara whispered.

"Yeah, me, too," Asahi said, much to my surprise.

Victtra spoke with confidence over the comms. "Of course. My instructors told me to start with things you can control. Your breathing. Focus on your breaths. Take deep inhales. Count the seconds between each gulp of air. The more you focus on the *now*, the less you will focus on the *future*. Then, once you've grounded yourself, turn your attention to your target, and dive in. Don't give your mind time to wander."

That was solid advice.

Fighting in a starfighter was a lot like fighting in real life. Speed and confidence could win over raw strength and power, if you used them right.

"Thank you," Noah said over the comms. "I'll try that."

"I can show you all meditation techniques that my instructors perfected. They've helped me focus ever since I implemented them in my daily routine."

Everyone on the comms muttered their thanks and acknowledgements. I smiled to myself, glad Victtra was attempting to connect with the others. I doubted she would stay with the *Star Marque* for longer than our agreed upon year, but at least for now, we'd have the strength of Homo superior on our side.

On a private comm, Sawyer connected to my training pod and said, "You should probably take her training."

"Oh, yeah?"

"Sometimes you act rashly. So much so, that Endellion planned on it. And you never want to become predictable. That was what Endellion said multiple times."

I gritted my teeth, hating that—once again—I was following Endellion's lead. Would I ever escape her shadow?

"You don't think I'm running the *Star Marque* like Endellion, do you?"

Sawyer snorted and scoffed. "Oh, no. Endellion never would've had a superhuman on the ship. Not unless she had some sort of kill switch or dirt on the individual, that way she could always retain the power in the relationship. Endellion didn't trust anyone."

I smiled to myself as I remembered my time on Capital Station. Technically, Endellion had trusted someone. But just once. She had trusted me and Sawyer—and we had turned on her.

That fact stuck in my mind.

Endellion did have trust problems.

How could I use that to my advantage?

TWO DAYS FROM BREAKAWAY STATION.

I sat with Victtra, Lysander, Sawyer, Cai, Dr. Clay, and Noah in the conference room. While we still had empty seats around the table, it didn't feel as barren. Sawyer smiled at me from the opposite end, her demeanor a little brighter and more engaged. She still typed on the PAD attached to her arm, but she glanced up far more often.

"I've made sure that the administrator's quarters are prepped and prepared," Lysander stated. "We don't have much in the way of luxuries, so I suggest we pick up a few supplies while we're docked at the station."

Cai glanced at Victtra. "Do superhumans eat something special? You people have such freaky insides and organs."

Victtra didn't react to Cai's statement. Instead, she focused her attention on me. "Captain Demarco, I think it would be best if you left the accommodations to me. I can make sure Administer Twoine is taken care of."

"I would like to also offer my assistance," Dr. Clay said, leaning forward on the table. "I would love to speak with Administer Twoine about his thesis research."

"Thesis research?" I repeated, one eyebrow high.

"He worked in the Vectin Department of Medicine for a short period of time before being elected to the position of Vectin Administer." Dr. Clay narrowed his beady, over-calculating eyes. "Most superhumans graduate from their academies with multiple fields of interest. Twoine's other specialties involve medicine and solar radiation."

I didn't need to glance at Victtra for confirmation. I had met several superhumans—including Minister Ontwenty—and each of them was a walking university of information. And it didn't surprise me that Dr. Clay had done his research on our guest. Dr. Clay couldn't wait to get on his knees and praise our new guest for all his—

"Demarco," Lysander said, interrupting my internal tirade. "I would suggest we retrace our path back to Vectin-10. It's the fastest route, the least likely way we'll run across problems from outside forces."

"Fine," I said, waving away his suggestion. "Anything else? We're all prepared?"

Noah sat forward, like he would say something, but then he slinked back into his seat, as if realizing he had nothing. Lysander stood from his seat and tapped on his PAD.

"If we're finished, Cai and I need to train the ground enforcers."

Before everyone left, I said, "We have one more order of business. Victtra Barten."

The superhuman girl snapped her eyes wide open, like she had been prepared for my comment. I pointed to her, and then I tapped at my PAD.

"For the purposes of this trip, we're going to change your name."

"What?" Lysander asked, obviously baffled. "Why?"

I stared at Victtra, never acknowledging my vice-captain. "You want to discover more about your father's murder, right? Cai has a few interesting methods of gathering intel, and one of them involves misdirection. You should speak to Administer Twoine—not as the daughter of the murder victim, but as someone who thought your father's death was for the best."

While Noah stared at me in confusion, Victtra never lost the thread of my logic.

We would figure out if Twoine could be trusted by "testing" his loyalties. Twoine would likely speak to Victtra—whereas he would never speak to the Homo sapiens asking about the murder. Perhaps Twoine would lead Victtra straight to Ontwenty.

Or perhaps it would lead to nothing.

Either way, Victtra could get closer to her goals, and she wouldn't be looking in my direction. She would think I was her ally.

"Thank you," Victtra said, smiling. "I'll change my name in the computer's systems for the duration of the trek."

"I'll do it," Sawyer interjected. "No one should touch the computer's code but me. It's… complicated. I had to rearrange things."

"Very well. But once we reach Vectin-10, I fear General Lone might mention my presence on the starship, which will ultimately cause complications. I think I can speak to Lone ahead of time, however, and mitigate any problems."

"All right, everyone else just keep up the façade," I said to the rest of my officers. They all gave me slow nods, but I pointed at Dr. Clay. "Especially you."

"*Me?*" Dr. Clay said with a sneer. "You think I'm prone to mistakes?"

"No. I just think you're going to spend a lot of time with Twoine. Be careful."

"Tsk. There won't be any problems on my end."

Lysander placed a hand on the conference table. "Changing her name would probably be best for many reasons. Most laws still prohibit superhuman children from taking combat positions under the command of Homo sapiens. If we change her age on the file, we could avoid that."

Everyone was quiet for a long moment.

Then I clapped my hands together a few times. Lysander's face brightened to a pinkish-red.

"Congratulations, Sanders," I said to him. "That's the first time you recommended we break the law for the convenience of our mission."

Lysander clenched his jaw, his irritation growing faster than a microwaved marshmallow. He slammed a fist down on the table. "Dammit, Demarco. I'm trying to be serious. Victtra's position on this ship could put us all at risk. I'm looking out for the crew."

"Oh, I know. I was giving you a congrats because I liked it."

Sawyer nodded once. "You must admit, it's atypical behavior for you, Sanders."

"*You're* calling me that now?" Lysander snapped. He turned on his heel to face her. "I hate that nickname."

"You hate most things. And the nickname is cute."

Unable to combat that statement, Lysander ran a hand down his face. It made me laugh to think he would get embarrassed by it. But that didn't ultimately matter. We had an administer to deal with, and a general to kill.

And then a planet governor to overcome.

"This meeting is over," I said, waving them away. "Dismissed."

Lysander and Noah left the room together, neither saying anything else. Victtra gave me another smile as she left, her silvery hair fluttering behind her as she walked.

That left Cai and Sawyer. Before Cai headed out, he turned to me, his expression hard set.

He rubbed his tattooed arms. "We have a problem."

"What is it?" I asked.

"Your little plan about changing names isn't going to work."

"Why's that?"

"Most people forget this, but basic Federation computer and operating code, which is in every starship that docks at any port, has an automated system that records suspicious conversations and transmits them to investigation agents. The fact that we spoke about the administer, and then said something dubious about him, means our conversation will be sent to the station's authorities when we arrive."

"You don't need to worry about it," I said with a scoff. "We have it covered."

Cai narrowed his eyes, silently waiting for me to explain.

I didn't need to. Sawyer lifted her head. "I changed the coding of the *Star Marque*. Our conversations weren't recorded. We were a flying dead zone, basically."

"Oh?" Cai smiled wider than I had seen in a while. "I didn't know." He offered me a smirk. "First name changes, and now code tampering? You're getting damn close to being put on a bounty list yourself."

"Is that going to be a problem?" I asked.

Cai held up a hand. "It depends. How well do you know the rules? The difference between bounties and bounty hunters, is whether or not they got caught. *Every* bounty hunter I know breaks the law, but they keep it hidden better than light in a black hole."

"So, you're saying this is fine so long as we don't get caught."

"That's right." Then he pointed at me. "And don't tell anyone else about this. If one person knows your actions, it's a mystery. If two people know your actions, it's a secret. If three people know your actions, *everyone* knows about them."

"I got it," I said.

Cai said everything with the authority of a low-level cop warning some station thugs. I loved the man. He felt like a man I would've run with on Capital Station.

TWENTY-EIGHT

Administer Twoine's Advisor

Breakaway Station was just as I had imagined it.

Metal cables kept the station attached to a moon orbiting Vectin-12. It was for the convenience of the miners—they could walk through the cables to get to the mines, and then cross back into the space station once their work was done.

It was a rough life. Miners died all the time by bizarre means. Gas. Gravity failure. Structural collapse. Racketeering by local thugs. Miners had to rely on enforcers for protection, and if I were taking jobs for the *Star Marque*, I would look through their listings to see what was available.

That wasn't necessary for today, though.

We docked the *Star Marque* and I got dressed up in my fanciest enviro-suit for the meeting with Administer Twoine. Lysander and Victtra joined me as I made my way to the exit lift. We rode down together and stepped out onto the grimy dock as a gang of three.

With my visor up, I couldn't smell the filth of Breakaway Station, but my eyes did all the smelling for me. The gun gray metal of the hull was stained yellow and crusted brown from a lack of cleaning. The dock walkways were stained with various fluids. I wished blood comprised the majority of it, but I was pretty sure it was the *third* most common splatter mark.

Administer Twoine waited on the dock with his entourage of twenty genetically-modified humans. I stood stiff and still as they approached, my hands behind my back. Lysander took his spot at my left, and Victtra at my right. Of the three of us, Victtra was the only one to have her visor down.

Administer Twoine stepped forward. His golden hair matched half of his skin. The "backside" of his two-toned skin looked golden, and his frontside was a soft cream. Although I had never seen a lion, I liked to imagine Twoine as "lion colored."

He wore a tight enviro-suit with scale-like pieces along the outside. The expensive suit matched Victtra's, but Twoine's was marked with his position in the Federation government. Like Victtra, he didn't wear his visor. Neither did his twenty lackies.

When Victtra stepped forward to greet him, Twoine's eyes raised to his hairline.

"What a surprise," he said, his bright blue eyes locked on Victtra. He was half a meter taller than her—and nearly three meters in height himself—but rather thin. He held up an arm in a weak greeting. "I never expected a fellow member of Homo superior to be riding on this vessel with me."

"General Lone is a good friend of mine," Victtra said matter-of-factly. "I'm aboard the *Star Marque* for field training, and the captain invited me along to greet you."

"An intelligent decision."

The two of them turned to me, their superhuman visages strikingly similar.

"Captain Demarco?" Twoine asked with a tight smile. "Thank you for the escort. I appreciate your willingness to accommodate Lone's special request."

"Think nothing of it," I said. Then I motioned to the ship. "If you don't mind, we'll get you settled in, purchase some much needed supplies from the station, and then be on our way."

Twoine never stopped smiling as he headed for the lift. "Perfect.

I appreciate your business attitude. Keep this up the entire trek, and I'll give Lone a favorable performance review."

The man walked by without glancing in my direction. I bit back any sarcastic remarks, but I was plainly reminded of my status in Twoine's eyes. I was Lone's dog. A lackey who wanted the praise of his master.

Victtra glanced in my direction as she followed Twoine onto the ship.

Her expression…

She seemed sympathetic to my station, and I wondered if it was genuine, or if she was doing it because it was expected of her. I didn't know.

Lysander and I waited as Twoine's entourage boarded the *Star Marque*. They weren't all bodyguards, like Victtra's One and Two. This group was a variety of professionals, probably lower legislative workers and legal aides. All superhuman officials in the major positions of the Federation government always had service escorts. It was part of the job description, written by superhumans, to no one's surprise.

One of the women—her head shaved on one side, her black hair braided on the other—gave me and Lysander a quick smile and glance before heading onto the ship. Her eyes stared straight at my visor, her brow furrowed.

She mouthed, *I'm sorry*.

If I had to guess, she was some sort of public relations manager, but perhaps she was just friendly. I watched her walk by, hypnotized by her dress. It was so tight to her body I thought it was an enviro-suit from afar, but the moment she got close, I had to compliment the tailor. The decision to go with thin fabric was a gift to me.

I tapped the side of my helmet and switched to a private comm channel with Lysander. "Did you get enough rooms ready for twenty-one people?"

"No," Lysander drawled.

"Tch, tch. I'm disappointed, Sanders. As punishment, you have to talk to the lady with interesting hair and dress. She gives me a good feeling."

"The stirring in your loins isn't a *good feeling*."

"That's where you're wrong, Sanders."

I could hear him grinding his teeth over the comms. Lysander and I turned to head onto the ship, his movements stiff.

"Maybe some of them don't like working for the superhuman," I said.

"And?" Lysander snapped.

"And maybe you could seduce one away and have them join the *Star Marque* as one of our officers."

"*Do you even hear yourself?* Do you realize how preposterous you sound? Are you writing the script of an entertainment disc, or are you trying to run a starship?"

"I have faith in you," I said as we got onto the lift with the administer and his escorts. "Just talk to the woman, will you? You'll see. She's desperate to get away. I've got a hunch."

"What makes you so confident that she'll want to leave her position with the Vectin government?"

I chuckled. "You heard that pompous blowhard when he spoke to us. No human wants to serve under Twoine. Trust me. I'm right. I'm willing to bet anything on it."

"If you're wrong, you have to start running the ship with more class and authority," Lysander quickly said, like he'd had it prepared in case I ever offered him a bet.

"Deal," I said. "But if I'm right, you have to start seeing someone. You can't keep yourself *chaste and pure* just because someday you'll die."

"Fine. I'll take this bet."

Ah, Lysander. So straight-laced. So gullible.

He had also let me set the terms of this engagement. People should learn to never do that.

THIRTY-FIVE DAYS until we returned to Vectin-10.

Victtra spent all her time with Administer Twoine. I didn't call her away for starfighter training, or even for officer meetings. If she wanted to figure out more about the superhumans who had wanted her father dead, this was probably the best route.

And it kept her off my trail.

For the most part, Twoine stayed in his personal quarters and lounge, away from the crew. That was for the best. I didn't want any incidents. Twoine was an arrogant ass-wagon, and he would rub someone the wrong way, I already knew.

Dr. Clay had his new medicine and research material—he had the best money could buy on Breakaway Station, which wasn't saying much. It was better than we'd had, though. Now Lysander and Noah would have a better chance of living longer. And perhaps, if Dr. Clay had enough time, we could modify members of our ground enforcers.

If we had properly modified cyborgs—and not the butcher-shop jobs the "doctors" on space stations performed to create cheap cyborgs—we'd be one of the strongest enforcer ships in the system.

Noah trained with the starfighters.

Cai worked with a team of ground enforcers, creating a special team of bounty hunters.

I sat in the mess hall, watching Twoine's escorts. They mingled with my crew, never chatting too much. They mostly stuck to themselves, which I found unfortunate. Most of them had those nice dresses—some of them wore soft pants and close-hugging shirts. Again, from afar, I thought they were enviro-suits, but nothing they wore offered much protection.

They'd all die if a complication arose. Brave sons of bitches.

I sipped a rum pouch, wishing I had something stronger. My body processed alcohol far faster than the normal human specimen's. This would never get my buzzed.

"What're you doing?" Sawyer asked over my PAD.

I tapped on the volume, keeping her voice low. I wore my casual clothing—cargo pants and a tank top—and I was certain that Twoine's entourage had no idea who I was. They thought I was one of the crew.

"I'm winning a bet," I replied.

"Hm," Sawyer said. "This I have to see."

I spotted my target—the woman with the half shaved head. She was rather thin, and her neck was long. She was like an attractive tree. And I liked trees.

Lysander wasn't going to come to mess hall for a while. He had a scheduled shift on the bridge. Which gave me plenty of time to speak to the Lady-Tree.

I sauntered over to her location—a small aluminum bench table. She sat by herself, which was convenient, but also a warning. She probably didn't want company, so I'd have to get to the point.

"How's it going?" I asked as I took a seat opposite her. "Before you send me away, just let me say that I'm here for business only."

Her black hair mixed well with her tawny skin. Her eyebrows were meticulously trimmed into perfect angles. When she lifted one, she reminded me of the superhumans, with her precision and perfect features.

"Business?" she asked, her voice silky. "I'm intrigued."

I smiled. "Good. I'm glad I have your attention." I sat my rum pouch on the table and leaned forward. "First, I have a serious question."

"Oh?"

"What's the difference between a *minister* and an *administer*? I've met Minister Ontwenty, and now I've met Administer Twoine, and I'm not sure what the difference in their station is."

I didn't know the difference, but that wasn't why I had asked. I needed to know more about this woman before I made my pitch, which meant I needed to have at least one pleasant conversation with her.

"Ministers make policies and create budgets," the woman said as she touched her lean neck with some of her slender fingers. "They're in charge of the big picture projects. Administers handle the implementation. They spend the budgets, if that makes sense."

"I see. Makes sense."

The woman set her elbows on the table and locked her gaze to mine. "Was that your *serious business*? Or do you need me to explain why the sky is blue and why we can see stars from such a far-off distance?"

Sawyer sent me a message on my PAD that read: *she got you there.*

I held back a laugh and said, "I have one more question. What's the difference between *your* position and the administer's?"

The woman tensed, her expression subtly shifting from amused to neutral. But she recovered quickly. With a tight smile, she said, "I'm the administer's financial advisor. I keep him appraised of fees, costs, and potential avenues for generating more income. If the administer likes my suggestions, he approves them."

"So, you help him with a tiny sliver of his job," I said. "And how often would you say he takes your advice?"

"Is this going somewhere?" the woman asked, curt. "I don't even know you, yet you have the arrogant audacity to question the administer and his advisors."

I took a sip of my rum pouch and then tipped it in her direction. "I'm Clevon Demarco. I don't think I got your name."

"Olivia Ollester," she said, her eyebrow lifting back into her suspicious position. "Isn't the name of this ship's captain *Clevon Demarco*? If I remember correctly, he was vice-captain to the infamous *Endellion Voight*, the first human planet governor since the formation of the Federation."

I tipped my pouch a second time. "Got me. That's me. Famous by association."

"Why is the captain here?" Olivia motioned to the mess hall with a sarcastically grand sweep of her arm. "Surely, you should be entertaining the administer."

"I'm not a fan of arrogant pricks," I stated.

Olivia's expression didn't change much. "Is that so? I fear you might get your ship in trouble if you say that too loud."

"Don't worry about it." I leaned forward on the table before she could press me further. "But now that we've gotten introductions out of the way, I want to discuss that business I mentioned."

Olivia said nothing.

Sawyer sent another text. *What a smooth transition. And you wonder why you're not swimming in the ladies.*

I covered the screen of my PAD with my free hand. "Ever since Endellion went on to become a planet governor, the *Star Marque* has been missing a few officer positions. We currently don't have anyone to handle our finances."

Olivia half-smiled, but she managed to keep it under control. "Captain Demarco—are you trying to hire me away from Administer Twoine? He would be most insulted to hear about this."

"I'll pay you more than he is," I said, ignoring her statement.

"You don't even know what he pays me."

"Yes, I do."

Sawyer had ways of getting information, and the moment I had asked her about it, she had given me the numbers. Twoine's advisor's weren't paid much, but they were given other perks. They were allowed to rent planetside property—not *own*, just rent—and they stayed with the administer whenever he traveled to other planets. It was a nice set of benefits for most humans, but it meant that Olivia was never far from Twoine.

If I were in her position, I would've killed myself a week in.

"You'll pay me more?" Olivia asked. "And what else?"

"I'll treat you with respect."

That got her genuinely smiling. "And what can I expect, working for a man who is so casual?"

I motioned to myself. "Me? Well, I'm not properly trained in finances. I'll take your advice all the time. I'd love to, as a matter of fact."

Olivia placed a delicate hand near her chin. "The financial officer on an enforcer starship isn't the launching platform for a political career. It's where careers go to die."

I smirked. "Tell that to Endellion."

That one statement silenced Olivia completely.

Then I added, "My medical officer wants to own his own research lab on a planet, and we're going to get him that. If Endellion can do it, so can we."

Olivia reached a hand up to the braided half of her head. Her fingers grazed her hair as she absently stared at the aluminum table. I took a moment to sip my rum.

"And you… know how she got her influence?" Olivia asked.

"You know how she maneuvered her way into power? All from the seat of a starship?"

I nodded once. "Hell, I'm still in contact with her." I was getting close to outright lying, but I kept myself from crossing the line.

"Planet Governor Voight is an inspiration. A visionary." Olivia shook her head. "Ever since I heard about her success, I've been trying to find my own way into a seat of power. I still can't believe she did it. Pure genius."

I held back a slew of curse words, and all my hatred. "Join me, Olivia, and you won't have to work in the superhuman's shadow. When the opportunity arises, we can put you in a position to gain recognition. If you want a political career, we'll help you—as soon as your five-year term on the *Star Marque* is over."

I was leaning heavily on Endellion's successes to build my own, but I didn't care. I would make good on my promises. If every single person on my crew wanted to sling themselves into the stars, I'd find a way to make it happen.

Olivia leaned forward on the table, her tree-like quality high-lighted when she practically brought her face to mine. "You're rather straightforward, Captain Demarco. I like that. Most politicians have a song and dance they go through before they get down to business. And even then, it's a game to them."

"I want success," I stated. "And I have a good feeling about you."

Olivia glanced at her fellow co-workers. When none of them returned her glance, she turned to me with a smile. "I've been looking to leave this trash fire for a while. Once we reach Vectin-10, I'll inform the administer that I'll be leaving his employ." Then she pointed at me. "But if I see anything on this trip that would make me question your promises or leadership, consider the deal off."

"Fair."

She held out a hand.

That was when I smirked. "I need one more favor. I need you to have this conversation a second time."

Olivia stared into my eyes, her gaze searching mine. "Excuse me?"

"My vice-captain is going to come speak with you, and I need to win a bet."

For a long moment, Olivia said nothing. Then half-laughed. "A bet?"

"He bet me you wouldn't be interested in joining the *Star Marque*, and I need to make sure I win this. So, when he comes to speak with you, can you just accept his offer immediately, and tell him you were hoping to get an offer of employment?"

She opened her mouth, like she would say no, but I cut her off.

"I'll give you more than 5% higher on your pay if you do me this favor."

Olivia snorted and leaned away, her smile wide. "Oh, is that how things work around here? Very well. I'll play along. But if you want me to keep this secret forever, it should be 10%."

"Deal."

TWENTY-NINE

Being Hunted

Twenty days until we returned to Vectin-10.

I stood on the bridge, my mind on Sawyer. We had spent a few more nights together. Still hadn't gotten her clothes off, but it had gotten interesting more than once. She had used her mouth. I found myself fantasizing about it more and more.

It was probably interfering with my position as captain.

"Have you heard a thing I've said?" Lysander asked, pulling me back to reality.

Definitely interfering.

"No," I flat said as I turned to him. "What's wrong?"

"Nothing is *wrong*. I was just trying to tell you about Twoine's financial advisor." Lysander sat in the vice-captain's chair, near the display screen for the *Star Marque's* torpedoes and laser charges.

"What about his advisor?" I asked. I stood next to him, my eyes set on the main readout screen, but I didn't see a damn thing.

"I've spoken to her twice now, but I haven't brought up the topic of becoming an officer for the *Star Marque*." He ran a hand through his blond hair. "I'm waiting for an opportunity to broach the subject. Her name is Olivia, by the way. Beautiful, really."

"Just do it already," I drawled. "She seems like she prefers men who get to the point."

"I doubt she'll be open to a desperate grab for her attention." Lysander sighed and turned his attention to the computer. "I need to be professional and feel out the situation."

I glanced over, my arms crossed. "Afraid I'll win our bet? Or are you just afraid of intimacy? Because I'm starting to think it's both."

Something on the main screen blinked red. I stared at the information, but I wasn't sure what was going on. More information flashed in list format, including coordinates and speeds. Our ship, and a second ship.

"What's this?" I asked aloud.

One of the navigators spun his seat around. "I've been sending you updates on this starship that I think has been following us. I, uh, messaged you about it twice yesterday. The starship has been following our course."

"I told you to change our course," Lysander said as he stood from his chair.

"I did. But the other starship changed course as well."

"The *Star Marque* is a vanguard-class starship, right?" I glanced around. The other three navigators nodded at me. "We're one of the fastest ships in space. Let's just pick up the pace, accelerate a little bit, and outrun these guys."

"Accelerating eats fuel," the navigator replied. He was young—maybe twenty—and he spoke with a weak wobble. "We'll probably run out, but it, uh, the costs have increased over the past few years."

"I'd rather have a high fuel bill than a random dogfight."

"Well, there's another problem."

"What?"

The navigator cringed. "The starship following us is also vanguard-class."

I turned to face the man, tense and holding back my anger. "Why didn't you start with that, *flip-stick*? Why haven't I known about this problem until now?"

"I told you about this. For, uh, *days*, sir."

Goddammit.

I should've been paying more attention.

Lysander stepped close, his jaw clenched and his gaze so intense, it was drilling a hole in the floor of the bridge. "I apologize, Demarco. I should've brought this to your attention sooner."

Oh, he was blaming himself. Suited me just fine.

"You should have," I said. Then I quickly patted him on the shoulder. "It's okay. We all make mistakes. Now all I want is options. What're we going to do about this?"

The sheepish navigator held up a hand.

I pointed to him. "Out with it, asshole. Just give me options."

"We could keep accelerating and hope the other ship doesn't have a huge reserve of fuel."

"And what if the other ship matches us?"

"We could start by hailing them," Lysander said. "Perhaps there's a logical reason for their pursuit."

I snapped my fingers. The navigators did whatever they needed to do to open a channel between our starships. I watched the main screen, waiting to see the face of the other captain. I waited, but nothing happened.

"They've ignored our request for communication," the navigator said.

I inhaled, and then tensed, knowing this was serious.

"They're accelerating."

Adrenaline flooded my veins. I didn't know who was chasing us, but I already knew this was a fight.

"Where are we?" I asked. I didn't know how to read star maps.

"We're passing through the orbital trail of Vectin-11," the navigator said.

"Are we close to communication relay? Can we get a message to someone about the situation?"

"Any communications we send won't reach a station or a planet for at least a day."

Goddammit. Whatever we sent now wouldn't matter later. We were going to engage in combat within a couple of hours at this rate. Sending a message now wouldn't do anything to save us—it'd just inform someone we were being chased.

"Send the message," Lysander ordered. "And accelerate."

"Aye, Vice-Captain."

When starfighters accelerated, the G-force increased to the point where it put pressure on the pilot. Technically, starships had gravity dampeners and internal systems that kept us upright, even when out in the darkness of space. Those dampeners couldn't negate the worst of G-forces, however. If we accelerated too quickly, everyone on the *Star Marque* would be squished against the wall, so we sped up at a steady rate that the dampeners could handle.

But we could push it.

"Go faster," I said. Then I snapped my fingers. "Hard jump forward. Send a warning throughout the ship."

A siren went off over the ship's comms, letting everyone know we'd hard jump in thirty seconds. I took a seat in the captain's chair and strapped myself in. With my free hand, I tapped at my PAD and made sure Sawyer was safe in her room. When she replied, she told me she had gone to the captain's quarters, and that was fine by me.

The ship quaked. I held the armrests of my seat.

The *Star Marque* quaked again. Then an intense feeling of increased G-forces crashed upon me. The pressure slammed me back in the chair, to the point where my shoulder blades hurt. Unlike in the starfighter simulation, the pressure didn't last long. Within ten seconds, the ship eased into its new speed, allowing everyone to breathe easy.

Lysander clawed his way out of his chair, his breaths shallow. He tapped the comms on his ship's computer station. "Noah? Are you okay?"

"I'm fine," his brother replied through the comms. "What's going on?"

"Tell the starfighters to get to their stations."

"O-Oh. Yes. I will."

The comms ended. I turned my attention to the main screen, waiting to see readouts on the other ship. I didn't have to wait long. There they were—the other ship was matching our hard jump and picking up pace.

They were coming for us.

"I'm going down to the starfighters," I said.

Lysander slowly nodded. "I think I know what's going on."

I stopped dead in my tracks. "What?"

"It has to be another enforcer ship."

With my eyes narrowed, I turned to Lysander. Another enforcer ship? Why would other enforcers be after us? None of us were wanted criminals. But before I could ask, I answered my own damn question.

They hated us.

The other enforcers.

I had made enemies. I had shut down *The Scorpio*, sold the starship for my own benefit, and then denied Endellion's invitation to "help humanity." I had called her out in a public space, damaging her career. No one knew her heinous crimes. All they saw was a "visionary human leader" and the "out of control starship captain" harming her.

The other enforcers in this star system wanted me out of the picture.

"We're going to have to fight," I said.

Lysander exhaled. "Be careful."

I SLID into the cockpit of the starfighter.

Just like the simulation pod, the cockpit didn't have a speck of light. I allowed the seat to suction me in place, enjoying the sensation of security. Then I grabbed the side-sticks, ready for a fight. The readouts flared to life, and the screen gave me a list of all the fighters currently on-line.

SF-1 [Captain]: Clevon Demarco
SF-2 [Subcommander/Starboard Leader]: Victtra Barten
SF-3 [Starboard Fighter]: Noah Jevons
SF-4 [Starboard Fighter]: Adachi Mara

SF-5 [Port Leader]: Melba Bennett

SF-6 [Port Fighter]: Hattie Andler

SF-7 [Port Fighter]: Haruto Asahi

SF-8 [Support]: Unlisted

SF-9 [Open]: Unlisted

SF-10 [Open]: Unlisted

A SINGLE RED dot appeared on my screen as the enemy starship closed in on the *Star Marque*.

The comms clicked on. Lysander's voice rang through, loud and clear. "Attention, starfighters. The approaching starship has refused to communicate with the *Star Marque*. Our scans have indicated that the vanguard-class starship is armed with a full complement of torpedoes and is carrying ten starfighters."

"Your captain here," I said over the comms. "We're not going to wait for the enemy to strike us first. We'll be disembarking from the ship, and protecting the *Star Marque* the moment the enemy approaches."

"Heard," Melba said.

"Understood," Hattie, Asahi, Noah, and Mara replied in unison.

Only Victtra answered me with, "Do we have your permission to destroy all enemy fighters? Or are we hoping to take hostages to question them afterward?"

"Lysander," I said. "Continually send communications to the enemy starship. Tell them they can surrender at any point. If they *do* surrender, let us know immediately."

"I'll make sure it happens, Captain Demarco."

Satisfied that we had everything in order, I watched the enemy starfighter draw closer and closer. The red dot suddenly flared to life, ten tinier dots appearing on the screen as the enemy starfighters broke away from their ship.

I tapped the screen, ready for this.

"*Disengaging*," the computer intoned.

My starfighter detached from the *Star Marque*. Nothing felt more freeing than grabbing the side-sticks and jetting away from the ship. I could go anywhere—as fast as I could handle—speeding through the darkness of space.

I kept my eyes on the ally dots—Mara, Hattie, Melba, Asahi, Victtra, and Noah—we had seven starfighters to their ten, but *I* was genetically modified, and Victtra was a superhuman. If I was a betting man, I'd say we had this.

The real question: would I lose someone? The *Star Marque* couldn't afford to lose any crew.

I accelerated toward the enemies.

To my surprise, two of the enemy starfighters shot past us and went straight for the *Star Marque*. They launched torpedoes, three striking Deck Five of my starship. The destruction to the hull was slight—and the lower decks were typically filled with more supplies than people, but still.

Enraged, I turned and went for the two bold enemies, speeding up as fast as the starfighter would allow.

6Gs.

7Gs.

"You need to be careful," Sawyer said over the fighter's comms. "The enemy is spreading out. Don't spend too much time on these two fighters."

8Gs.

The extreme G-force pressure prevented me from giving her a reply, but I heard. I just pushed my ship to the extreme. The *second* I reached the enemy, I fired off two torpedoes. My speed was unrivaled by these chumps—they didn't even have time to dodge.

Two dead.

Their red dots disappeared from my screen.

I didn't slow. Every small rock or piece of debris blinked on my screen, letting me know that if I ran into anything, I'd kill myself due to my continually-increasing speed. With twitch-speed, I tilted and turned around the obstacles as I looped back around to fight more of our enemy.

"I'm engaging the main starship," Melba said over the comms.

Her ability to speak meant she wasn't yet at my speeds. She probably never would be—Melba was too old to handle the chest-crushing pressures I felt at 8Gs.

"Following," Asahi said.

"Playing backup," Hattie said.

Both of them sounded strained. I didn't question their strategy. They fired their torpedoes at the main ship, forcing the enemy to engage in evasive maneuvers.

"Noah, Mara, follow me," Victtra said, her voice clear. "We'll keep the enemy fighters at bay."

When I checked my screen, I noticed Victtra was traveling at speeds close to mine. Why wasn't she suffering from the effects of the G-forces? I cursed to myself, already aware of the answer.

Superhumans were designed to handle extreme pressures. She could probably accelerate to well beyond 9Gs and still speak, despite the toll it would take on everyone else.

Sure enough, Victtra's ship shot at the enemy like she was going to punish them for existing. She unleashed three torpedoes, destroying two starfighters. Her third torpedo sailed off into the void of space, narrowly missing its target.

Noah and Mara followed and managed to finish off the third.

Satisfied they would handle the situation, I went to help Melba. The vanguard-class ship would require more than a single torpedo to defeat.

I increased my speed again.

9Gs.

Warnings flashed throughout my cockpit. Normal humans would've passed out long before now. My vision tunneled as the pressure mounted.

9.1Gs. 9.3Gs.

I forced myself to take breaths. I had to stay focused.

I shot close to the starship, well aware I needed to avoid their point-defense system. The numbers blinked on my screen—how close I was, how far I needed to go—and I took it all in at amazing speeds. Everything moved in slow motion for me, and as soon as I was close, I shot one of my hyperweapons, unleashing a glaring flash of brilliant light.

The shot destroyed a chunk of the starship's starboard side, ripping a hole straight into the hull of the ship and exposing its innards to the icy blackness of space.

9.4Gs.

I whipped around, my starfighter quaking. I wanted to ask Lysander if the starship was ready to surrender, but I couldn't find the words.

When I paid attention to the dots of my team, I noticed they flew with coordination. Our training had paid off. Our enemy didn't have teams—they acted individually.

Three of them were after Victtra. She dodged and circled around, but in doing so, she got close to the main ship and almost slammed against the point-defense systems. Was she flustered? I watched as she shifted her course several times over a few short seconds. Hesitation?

"*Demarco*," Sawyer said over the comms.

Torpedoes shot out of the vanguard-class starship *and* the three starfighters, all aimed at Victtra, like they knew they had her on the ropes. I didn't have time to question why. I slightly twitched my side-sticks and angled my ship toward Victtra.

9.5Gs.

It was getting difficult to see.

"*Demarco.* Careful."

I ignored Sawyer and fired my hyperweapon. While torpedoes took time to shoot through space, lasers, hyperweapons, and plasma weapons were much faster.

The bright light of my attack flashed throughout the area. I destroyed two of the torpedoes heading for Victtra before they reached her. Much to my delight, she looped around the other torpedo and shot her own, destroying two more starfighters.

Noah and Melba destroyed another two.

The enemy morale was cracked. They shot away from us, flying in all different directions.

And then Hattie fired her hyperweapon at the starship. Her aim was true, and she destroyed the bridge. In one brilliant blaze of destruction, the vanguard-class ship—worth a lot of credits, dammit—was now just a floating graveyard in the middle of nowhere space.

I decelerated until I could breathe again.

"Demarco," Lysander said over my comms. "The other four starfighters have surrendered. They're the only survivors."

THIRTY

Meeting With An Administer

I docked onto the *Star Marque*, my starfighter shuddering as it attached to the ship.

Sweat dappled my whole body, but I relaxed in my seat, even as the starfighter released me from its hold. The readouts on the screen told me my blood pressure was high, but I didn't care.

"That was a clean fight," Sawyer said over my ship's comms. "Deck Five was damaged, but we suffered no casualties. Two ground enforcers were injured, and they've gone to the infirmary, but they're expected to make a full recovery."

"Excellent."

"You had a few close calls, though."

I smiled. "Right? Every time I almost die, it takes two years off my life expectancy."

"Are you okay?"

I waved away the comment. "I'm fine. Those are the worst years of everyone's life anyway, right?" Then I sat forward and examined the cockpit of my tiny ship. "Hey, you watch the cameras on the ship all the time, don't you?"

"What an odd non-sequitur," Sawyer sarcastically said. "I have a feeling this is going somewhere hilarious."

"Has anyone ever christened these?" I smiled, my excitement at an all-time high. "I'd love to be in a dogfight, and then remember all the carnal escapades I had in the same cockpit."

"You're impossible sometimes."

"Demarco," Lysander said through my PAD's comms, completely interrupting my train of thought. "Administer Twoine wants to see you and the other starfighters. He's demanding to sit with you all in the conference room."

I had known Lysander for a long time. Something about the tone of his voice… the strain and careful word choice… led me to believe this hadn't been his idea. He didn't want to do it, but the administer was probably standing over his shoulder, listening for my response.

"Right now?" I asked. "We have disengagement procedures."

We didn't. But that superhuman asshole didn't know that.

"My team has completed all procedures," Victtra chimed in.

I glanced at the comms channel and saw *all* the other starfighters were in on the conversation.

Melba also added, "We're ready, Captain."

Dammit.

"Seems we're ready, Vice-Captain Jevons. We'll meet in the conference room in less than five minutes."

BEFORE HEADING to the conference room, I went to the captain's quarters and changed. My cargo pants and tank-tops were too casual for mingling with superhuman politicians. I slipped into my enviro-suit and secured it snugly against my body.

I didn't put the helmet up, though.

"Sawyer," I said, knowing she was somehow listening. "Why were these guys in the same area? Why attack us now? Was it just a coincidence, or were they actually after the administer?"

The comms clicked and then Sawyer's whispered voice filled the room. "We weren't on Breakaway Station long. I suspect someone sent a message while we were there. Someone on the station, waiting to see us, or perhaps someone in our crew."

I didn't want to suspect anyone on the ship.

"Could it have been someone from the administer's crew?"

"It could have, but I agree with Lysander. This is likely on us. It's probably angry enforcers who want to play dirty. But until we question the starfighters, we won't really know."

Confident I was presentable, I exited my room and almost ran into someone standing in the corridor.

Victtra.

She stood on the other side of my door, like she had been about to enter. With my breath held, I stared into her eyes. I had forgotten how tall she was for a young superhuman. They all had impressive height.

"Captain," she said in a formal tone.

I waved her away. "Shouldn't you be in the conference room?"

"I wanted to thank you." Victtra straightened her posture. "In private."

I waited, thinking she would follow that statement up with her thanks, but nothing ever happened. Did she want something more private than the officer corridor? I lifted an eyebrow, half-tempted to say something sarcastic.

"What're you thanking me for?" I asked.

"Helping me during the fight."

I snorted and then shrugged. "Forget it. We're members of the same starship, remember? This is what a team does."

"I..." Victtra threw her silvery hair back. "I think this was different. I accelerated beyond what I had practiced with in the simulation pod, and the speed got the better of me. I faltered. I wouldn't have been put in a position that compromised the team if I had stuck to standard speeds."

She was upset about *that?*

I placed a hand on her shoulder. Victtra turned her gaze down to my hand, like she was confused by my touch.

"Don't ever slow down," I said, serious in every regard. "You're a goddamn member of Homo superior. Those simulations are meant to protect weaker Homo sapiens, and to give *a taste* of the intensity one faces in a fight. You hesitated because you're young and inexperienced, not because you can't handle the pressure. Next time, we'll practice in our ships, not the pods."

Victtra glanced at my eyes, her gaze searching mine.

"You don't need to apologize. You just need to keep getting better. And faster." I let go of her shoulder. "Unless you think you can't handle it."

Her eyes flashed with a bit of angry defiance. "I can handle it."

"Then don't ever slow down." I patted her upper arm and then stepped around her. "Now c'mon. We have to see the administer. I'm sure he wants to thank us as well."

"I suspect Feron merely wants to question us about the attack." Victtra strode to my side, keeping my pace with her long strides.

"Who is *Feron*?"

"Feron Twoine," she said. "Feron is Administer Twoine's first name. I thought that was in his file in the ship's archive."

It probably was. But I hadn't committed the man's name to memory. Especially when it was so odd. Victtra had spent so much time with the man that, apparently, she was on a first-name basis.

"The whole reason we picked up *Feron* was because he's paranoid of attacks," I said, realizing the irony. "What're the chances he complains to General Lone about us?"

"High," Victtra said.

And why wouldn't he complain? We were attacked—most likely—because the ship had been after *me*.

Perfect. Just what I had always wanted. Complications in my plans.

We walked together through the emotionless-gray corridor of Deck One. Our footfalls echoed off the duralumin steel, and when I glanced over to Victtra, I saw he distant and unfocused gaze was on her feet.

We reached the conference room without incident. The door opened with a soft whoosh. I motioned Victtra in, and then I followed after.

All my starfighters were gathered, along with Lysander and

Sawyer. No Cai. No Dr. Clay. They sat at the back of the conference table, gathered close together. Five others were in the room. Administer Twoine and four of his advisors. One of the advisors was Olivia. She offered me a slight smile the moment I entered the room.

The chairs around my conference table weren't built for Twoine's impressive stature. He shifted awkwardly in the tiny space until I entered. Then he stood, the little holes on the side of his neck flaring.

"Captain Demarco," he said, his words slow.

I walked over to the head of the table. Victtra strode in and took a seat close to the administer, never even glancing back at me. I thought it odd, but I wouldn't bring it up.

Without answering the administer, I turned to Lysander. "What about the four enemy starfighters?" I asked. "You said they surrendered. Who's in charge of taking them into custody?"

"Cai Qi is handling it, Captain." Lysander motioned to the administer. "But I believe Twoine has a few questions."

The superhuman glared at me, his whole body stiff. He stood straight, and his three meters was enough to get close to the conference room ceiling.

"General Lone recommended the *Star Marque* because of its speed and safety," Twoine stated.

I was prepared to give an answer—to tell him that this was all my fault—but Victtra shot me a glower. I stopped myself from commenting.

Victtra turned her seat to face the administer. "I told you, Feron. Some of the fanatics are dedicated. Not even the *Star Marque* could get us from one safe location to the next."

"Fanatics?" he asked. "You think these were rebellion thugs?"

"Of course. Didn't you hear what happened to Emissary Barten not too long ago? He was murdered while on a diplomatic mission. The rebellion has no honor or moral code. They probably found out you were on this ship and decided to hunt us down."

That was a fine story, but once we picked up the enemy starfighters, I was certain they would sing another tune.

Then again…

I could speak to them first. Perhaps—if they corroborated Victtra's made-up tale—this would work in my favor.

"I apologize for the scare, administer," I said, trying to mimic Lysander's authoritative tone. "But we handled the attackers. Their starship was destroyed, and most of their starfighters were disintegrated."

"The *Star Marque* suffered no casualties," Lysander chimed in. "As I stated in my report to you, I suspect our pursuers noticed we were understaffed, and then they made assumptions. They were probably ill prepared for a superhuman starfighter."

I waited for him to mention my performance—since I was the goddamn MVP—but he never did. Part of me wanted to mention it myself, but I held back. Lysander was probably right to keep it hidden. Twoine likely wanted to hear about how talented superhumans were, not about me or the rest of the crew.

Administer Twoine relaxed, his shoulders dropping as he smoothed his expensive enviro-suit. "I see. Then I was correct. Those rebellion dogs have been getting bolder lately." He motioned to one of his advisors. "Send a message through the relays about our attack. I'll have everyone know of this brazen attempt on my life."

"We haven't questioned the enemy starfighters yet," I said.

Twoine flicked his wrist with such curt dismissal, it felt as though he would order me out of an airlock. "I want the entire system to know of this. The ministers will hear of the details, and I'll be lobbying for more military support to suppress these human dogs."

None of this sounded pleasant.

And I realized why Endellion was so hesitant to get involved with superhumans. They always twisted the events in their favor. This one attack—if Twoine spun it as a rebellion assassination attempt—might help him give more power to military figures. It could even be the foundation for further laws restricting humans.

I *had* been prepared to make the starfighters confess to rebellion crimes, but now I wanted the opposite.

But I wouldn't tell Twoine that.

"As long as you're safe, we're going to resume our trek to Vectin-10," I said. "And if any further incident happens, rest assured my crew and I will handle it."

Twoine nodded. "I would expect nothing less, Captain Demarco."

"We should have a meal together," Victtra said, interjecting into the conversation. "You said you wanted to speak with the captain about current affairs, didn't you? Now is the perfect time to ask about the starfighters and the battles."

I didn't know why Victtra was proposing this, but I nodded along with her suggestion. It was likely related to her father's murder—maybe she thought we could get information if we were friendlier.

Twoine gripped his hands together and then nodded once. "Yes. I would like to discuss things with you, Captain Demarco. Perhaps a meal in my quarters would do us both good."

I SHOULD'VE DENIED this request. I knew nothing about *fancy dinners* or *etiquette*.

The lounge area in the guest quarters was smaller than the captain's quarters, but not by much. It was cramped, and the table in the middle of the room—secured to the floor so that it wouldn't move—didn't give us much space to pull out chairs. The superhumans had a rougher time, since they were so much taller.

Victtra sat at one side of the table, I sat at another, and Olivia sat on the fourth side.

Had Olivia included herself because I was here? I liked to think so.

We didn't have food, just drink pouches. Apparently, one of Twoine's aides knew how to cook, and had taken it upon himself to hurry to the mess hall in order to prepare us something. How long would it take? I had no idea. When I had cooked, it hadn't taken long, but mine was a bland mush of heated vegetables.

Twoine constantly combed at his golden hair, the metallic sheen beautiful, even in the artificial lighting. When he calmed down, he motioned to our surroundings. "These vanguard-class ships weren't built for comfort, I see."

"The *Star Marque* has been upgraded in a few places," Victtra said. "Mostly to accommodate the crew in apprehending criminals."

"That is a noble cause." Twoine sipped from his pouch, his careful movements interesting. He refused to drink from any pouch if it had been opened previously.

The silence that filled the small space irritated me. I took long drags of my pouch, trying to think of something to say. Victtra turned her hard gaze to me, as if *wanting* me to steer the conversation. But to what? Perhaps she didn't want to reveal her motives to Twoine, so she needed me to start the conversations necessary to figure out his loyalties.

"We mostly hunt down rebellion criminals," I said.

The gray walls, steel grated floor, and harsh corners definitely created a militaristic atmosphere. It felt natural to talk about hunting down scum.

Twoine turned to me, his eyes bright with curiosity. "Tell me, Captain Demarco, how many rebellion ships have you shot down?"

"Several," I said, shifting in my seat. "Both as a captain and as a vice-captain."

"Yes. Just as I suspected. I'll want you to make a note of that in all the transmissions that we send. I want first-hand accounts of the infestation."

"Infestation?"

"The rebellion is a plague in this quadrant. Every last one of them should burn in the flare of the Vectin star."

Olivia sipped her drink, her gaze on the aluminum pouch, even when the administer glanced in her direction. She was the only "standard human" in the room. Was she hiding her opinion of the matter, fearing she would upset the superhumans?

"Have you heard that several ministers have argued to cure all rebellion defects?" Victtra asked, smiling brightly. "I heard they want to save the rebellion scum from themselves. They say the humans are only acting out because they're sick and have no access to medication."

Twoine waved away the comment. "Everyone wants to make excuses. The fact of the matter is simple—they're jealous of our talents. Of our power. Of all our accomplishments. The Cygnus Sector wouldn't be as evolved as it is now without superhuman intervention. Those lessor-evolved rebellion thugs can't accept the truth, and *that's* why they lash out."

"I agree."

Victtra's voice sounded unnatural. I doubted Twoine noticed. He sucked his drink down without giving her a second glance. Victtra's father had been one of the individuals who thought healing the rebellion would literally mend relations.

It must've bothered her to hear Twoine speak in such a negative manner.

The man was too arrogant to see how it was affecting her, though.

"I'll happily write whatever you need me to in your reports," I said. "But I should tell you, some ministers and emissaries have approached the *Star Marque* in the past looking to settle things in a peaceful manner. I'm just a human—I feel like I can't tell them no."

"You mean like Emissary Barten?" Twoine asked with a sneer.

Was I being too forward?

I nodded once. "Like him, yeah."

Olivia glanced over, her eyes narrowed, and her lip curled in a frown. She must've seen through my subterfuge—I wasn't making the best lies of my life—but Twoine never called me on it.

"You shouldn't fret." Twoine waved away the comment. "Men like Barten will always disappear. They don't realize the kinds of enemies they're making when they take stances like that."

"So, I shouldn't worry if some other minister approaches the *Star Marque* and asks me to deliver a peaceful message to the rebellion?" I rubbed at my neck, trying to feign my duress.

Twoine shook his head. "Like I said, you needn't worry. Whoever requests such a nonsense tactic will quickly be removed from station. We have other goals—bigger plans. Minister Ontwenty and General Lone have proposed so many new changes, that the only way forward is to wipe the sector clean."

I didn't need to say anything more. Twoine had unwittingly confirmed my suspicions. And when Victtra turned to glance at me, I knew that she understood as well. Ontwenty and General Lone *were* running the show.

Ontwenty had been the one to order Barten's death.

I hoped Victtra would see that and stop searching for the one who plunged the knife. Because I didn't want to have to kill her, too.

Olivia lifted an eyebrow. The half of her head that was shaved was rather striking. I offered her a smile, and she returned my gesture with a quizzical stare. "Does your opinion on this matter have anything to do with Planet Governor Voight's? She recently hired enforcer ships to scour the quadrant looking for rebellion thugs."

"Everything I am, I learned from her," I said, though it killed my soul a bit.

"Fascinating."

Twoine didn't comment. None of the superhumans appreciated Endellion, even when she was on their side.

I lifted my rum pouch and toasted Olivia. She must've known I was bluffing at some level, because her sarcastic return gesture was more humorous than insulting.

When the doors to the room opened, I sat back and divorced myself of most conversation. I had the info I needed, and now I would enjoy the chef's meal. The trek couldn't end fast enough, as far as I was concerned.

I STOOD in the rarely used Central Data Room. It housed the computer we used to display the star maps, and it held archival computer terminals for deep storage information.

It was colder and quieter in the Central Data Room. Everything about the place reminded me of a food storage freezer. Or cannery. Either way, the place had the welcoming warmth of a grave.

Lysander and Cai stood with me in the cool room. The black walls, and the dim light from the computer screens, kept the place dark.

"You managed to get the four starfighters onboard?" I asked as I strolled around the room.

Cai sat in one of the swivel chairs mounted to the floor. "Yeah. They all surrendered, no fight."

"What were they doing?"

"Apparently, someone on Breakaway Station said we were understaffed and carrying valuable material. The captain of the *Gray Gunner* thought he could take the *Star Marque* and sell it through a fence."

I stopped walking and turned to him. "Who would tell another enforcer about our inner workings?"

Cai shrugged. "Someone on your crew. Someone spying on us. Someone who knew most of our details and sent them to the station through relay satellites before we got there. There are tons of explanations. Unfortunately, none of the starfighters knew."

My first instinct, even though it was ridiculous, was to assume it had been Endellion. Who else would do something so roundabout —yet direct—to fuck with me? My second thought was of Victtra. Not for any logical reason, but simply because she was superhuman, and not one of us. Who else was there? No other explanation made sense to me.

But perhaps I didn't have all the information.

"Keep them in the brig until we reach Vectin-10," I said. "Then we'll hand them over to the authorities."

Cai gave me a sarcastic salute. "The best course of action, in my humble opinion."

"We could try to recruit them," Lysander offered.

I shook my head. "They weren't impressive enough to catch my eye. And to be honest, our current team has been excelling. We don't need to alter the dynamic just yet."

"Very well."

"Sawyer," I said.

The comms clicked on. "Yes?"

"What is Victtra doing?"

"She's still speaking with Administer Twoine."

"Why? She has the information she wanted."

"It seems Twoine is deep in the pocket of Ontwenty, and Victtra wants more information. Twoine has interest in her Stellar Engine project, and Emissary Barten was a political rival that threatened everything."

"Anything else?" I asked.

"Apparently, Twoine's part of a team of administrators who are crafting education laws around burying information regarding the Federation Formation War and United-Earth. Victtra keeps pressuring him for information."

Those statements bounced around in my skull.

"Why?" I finally asked.

The comms clicked over, and Sawyer played an audio clip straight from Twoine himself. *"I think it's for the betterment of society. We shouldn't allow such outrageous ideas to reach the Homo sapiens. They shouldn't be taught things that threaten the safety and happiness of the Federation. Telling them they used to be a dominant species, they used to be great, only makes them think they can seize power again. It breeds insurrection. And knowing that information doesn't help them."*

I crossed my arms, my fingers digging into my biceps. While I hated to admit that Endellion was right about *anything*, her loathing of the superhumans was quickly becoming more and more understandable.

"Okay, so is Victtra ready to get off our ship yet?" I asked.

Sawyer returned to the comms to reply, "I don't know. She hasn't said anything to me about the matter, and she hasn't said anything like that to Administer Twoine."

"Having a superhuman aboard isn't so awful," Cai said, leaning back in his chair. "It's definitely making you look more like a badass, that's for sure."

"What do you mean?"

"I keep in touch with bounty hunters around the Vectin Quadrant, and all of them have been talking about the *Star Marque*. I told them about our superhuman starfighter, and that got around the water coolers, if you catch my drift. You're making a name for your-self. Soon, we can charge some pretty steep prices for our services, let me tell you. Especially from human clients. They'll want the honor of ordering a superhuman around, even if it's indirectly."

Cai spoke every word like he was a sleazy salesman ready to offload a lemon.

But his information intrigued me. Endellion had wanted fame and notoriety as well. She hadn't leveraged it for money. She had leveraged it for political favors. That was how she had become a planet governor.

Perhaps… I could do the same. Perhaps I could influence the state of affairs.

To do what?

I cursed under my breath. Lysander and Cai spoke to each other, but I didn't even hear them. I was too busy contemplating my own future. Endellion had had a grand plan. She had always been thirty steps ahead of me, plotting her rise to power, and now she was scheming to gain more.

For what? I didn't know, exactly.

According to Endellion's sycophants, she was doing it to raise up all of humanity. But that was bullshit. She wouldn't have destroyed all of Capital Station if she was concerned about *humanity*. No. She just wanted power. That was it.

Power.

And now that I was getting power, I had to ask myself—what was I going to use it for?

It scared me to think I didn't have a purpose other than revenge. Once Endellion suffered for what she had done, what else was I going to do?

I didn't know.

THIRTY-ONE

Return To Vectin-10

Ten days until we reached Vectin-10.

Sawyer and I curled up together on my bed. The lights were off—just as she liked it—and I only had one arm around her, so she never felt trapped. Her fish, Blub, floated around the room. Although I couldn't see him, I could hear his helium sacs every time he ascended and descended.

The koi fish *toot, toot, tooted* around the ceiling.

I didn't care about that, though. Tonight was special. Sawyer had taken off her jumpsuit.

Not the rest of her clothes, mind you. She still had her shirt, her underwear, and even a pair of fingerless gloves, but at least I got to feel her bare legs.

They were scarred from her thighs down to her ankles, all thanks to General Lone. I could feel every gnarled bump.

When I thought back to Helia, I wondered why Lone had let her sit in the healing vat. Those vats healed someone before scarring could set in. Perhaps he had wanted Sawyer scarred, to hurt emotionally, rather than only physically.

What a fucked up thing to do.

And whenever I thought about it too long, I got myself worked up and ready to kill him *right then*, so I took a deep breath and pushed it from my mind.

"Lysander finally spoke with Olivia about joining the crew of the *Star Marque*," Sawyer whispered. She ran her hand over my chest. "It was a painfully awkward conversation, but Olivia is rather charismatic. She accepted without much complication."

I snorted and laughed. "It only took him thirty-something days. Women like when men take their time, right?"

"Olivia also asked to have drinks with him tonight."

"Damn. She's a woman after my own heart. Goes straight for what she wants."

Sawyer rested her cheek against my side and smiled. "Do you think he'll get together with Olivia?"

"If he doesn't, I'm going to hit him so hard, he'll stop existing in other people's minds."

"He doesn't want to father any genetically defective children."

"No one said anything about *fathering children*," I said, stressing the awkward way she had worded that. "Sanders and Olivia can have a good time without any of that. We do. Let 'em relax."

"Do you want children, Demarco?"

I held my breath, caught off guard by the question. I hadn't even seen her naked yet, and already she wanted to discuss children? "We can have as many floating fish children as you want," I said with a huff. "But human children? I'm not interested. Besides, you don't want to carry them around, right?"

"There are uterine-replicators in most planetside hospitals," Sawyer said, no emotion in her voice. "Once the embryo is detected, doctors can remove it, and allow it to grow within the safety of a lab. No harm to the woman. No one would even know, really."

"Yeah, but they're not going to raise them in the damn lab," I said. "They give those lice-magnets to you the moment they start becoming difficult."

"That's true."

"This is all moot anyway. I don't want any. At least, not right now. If it's important, we can discuss it later—maybe after we've handled Endellion. But until then, I'm not so sure what the future looks like."

Blub moved around the room, his soft *tooting* an awkward song for the evening.

"I want to have children," Sawyer stated.

"Why?" I probably should've have been so icy, but sometimes it was difficult to keep it together.

"I wasn't really *born*." Sawyer laughed once. "And I liked to imagine, with you, life could evolve. Nothing speaks more to change, and hope, *and the future*, more than children. It's probably irrational of me, I know. But I like imagining it."

"Kids?"

"Having a legacy that goes beyond myself. Building something together. With you."

She seemed more emotional in that moment than many other times in our relationship. This was *that* important to her?

Apparently, we needed to have this discussion. "Well, unless we make the kids in the damn uterine-replicators, it's not going to happen. We haven't done anything that'd even slightly result in kids."

Sawyer shifted around my side. "How about we make a deal?"

"A deal?"

"Well, after you… *get inside me*… We'll start trying to have children."

I huffed and snorted. "Sure. Fine. Deal."

Sawyer laughed and then smacked me on the stomach. "Ha! You didn't even take your own advice. You let me set the terms of our agreement and now I've won."

"*What?*" I barked, half sitting up. "What're you talking about?"

Sawyer honestly laughed. Even though it was too dark to see her facial features, I could hear her genuine amusement in her voice.

"I said, *once you've been inside me*, and technically, my mouth is an orifice, so now you've got to hold up your end of the bargain."

For a long moment, I debated on whether to be angry, or amused. Goddammit. She *had* beaten me at my own game. Sawyer was the only one who ever did that to me.

Well, her and Endellion.

But I didn't want to think about Endellion.

With an amused sigh, I rested back on the bed. "Fine. You got me. We can have kids, but I don't want them created in a lab. We have to do it the fun way. No getting around that."

Sawyer's laughter waned. She rolled up to my side and huffed. "That seems fair. Whenever I feel like I can handle the next step of our relationship, I'll let you know."

I closed my eyes, still enjoying the sound of Blub's toots.

"Perfect," I muttered, holding her close.

"Oh, there was one other thing I wanted to speak to you about."

"Hm?" Sleep clawed at my mind.

"It's Victtra. She's been messing around with the administer."

"*Messing around?* What're we? Twelve?" I chuckled, all while growing tense. "How far are we talking here?"

"Nothing I'd have to censor. I just thought you should know."

The information settled on me like a rock dropped in water. I opened my eyes again, suddenly discontent. "Is she old enough for that? I don't know what the fuck the rules are for superhuman consent. Knowing them, *infants* are probably *cognitively capable* of signing a starship loan, but I have no idea."

"Technically, there aren't many laws against it, so long as it's consensual. I think she's doing it to get information, however. I was worried about her."

"Really? Why?"

Sawyer held my side a little tighter. "She reminds me of Endellion. Just a little bit. She seems obsessed. I hear it in her voice sometimes."

I nodded once. "I'll speak to her then."

"Thank you, Demarco. I think it would do her some good."

EIGHT DAYS until we reached Vectin-10.

I waited in the captain's room, biding my time with some simple games on the desk computer. Part of me wondered if Endellion ever played stress-relieving games. I doubted it. She was a woman possessed by demons. She never had any time for anything other than her power plays.

The door opened, and I closed the colorful game.

Victtra strode in. One and Two waited in the corridor. Once the door closed, Victtra took a seat in front of my desk, her posture stiff.

"You summoned me?" she asked.

I swiveled my chair around and leaned forward. Fatigue wore on me a bit, but I pushed it aside for the conversation. "I know what you're doing with Administer Twoine."

The statement was blunt and forward, but I didn't have time to dick around.

Apparently, my brazen attitude didn't surprise or faze Victtra. She swept back her silver hair, her expression unchanging. "I'm not doing anything wrong."

"Yeah, but you don't have to sell yourself out like that. Twoine isn't worth it."

"*My father* is worth it," Victtra snapped, dropping her earlier composure. Once again, the holes on the side of her neck flared along with her nose. "I'm going to find his killer no matter what. And sometimes that requires a price be paid. I'm willing to pay it. Why are you interjecting yourself into my affairs? Does this starship have no privacy?"

I smirked as I leaned back in my chair. "Let me ask you this— would *your father* have thought it's worth it? What would he say if he saw you now?"

She gritted her teeth, her neck holes unable to flare any wider than they already were. "How dare you."

"What? Bring up your father? You're the one always mentioning him. I figured I should remind you."

Victtra stood from her chair and glared down at me. After she took a deep breath, she said, calm and slow, "Captain Demarco, my father was a weak man. Not physically. He was weak of heart. He cared about people. Even humans. Even *defective* humans."

I listened, never moving, never saying anything.

"He *died* on a diplomatic mission trying to secure them free medicine. Look what that got him. Either the humans killed him, because of their barbaric remnants of a time long past its prime, or his fellow members of Homo superior killed him, because his bleeding heart interfered with their plans. Either way, I'm not going to end up like him. Do you understand?"

"So, you're just going to destroy yourself looking for this killer?" I asked, knowing deep in my soul this conversation would send me to hell.

"I'm going to do whatever it takes to make sure my father is avenged." She clenched her fists. "I thought you would understand."

"Why's that?"

"Your medical officer, Dr. Clay, mentioned you had a vendetta of your own. Something between you and Planet Governor Voight. And the way you mentioned her the other night at dinner… I could tell. Your voice is laced with venom."

I tensed, and I knew that Victtra could sense my anxiety. There was no point in hiding it, though. Everyone on the ship basically knew.

"Yeah, I understand," I said as I also stood from my seat. "Endellion almost killed me and the entire crew of the *Star Marque*. I'd give my left nut to see her brought to justice."

Victtra nodded once. "Then you agree with my methods."

"I didn't say that." I motioned to the ship around us. "See this? I'm building this. I'm making a life for myself. Yeah, I want Endellion dead, but the best revenge among pigs is eating well."

Victtra's eyebrows shot to her hairline. Then she hardened herself. "You mean, you're showing her up by being successful?"

"That's right." I walked around the desk until I was standing next to Victtra. Damn, she was tall. I kept forgetting until we were face to face. "Ask yourself this—would your father have rather had you continue his work, making the quadrant a better place? Or would he have rather you kill yourself in the pursuit of his assassin? And which do you think would make your enemies angrier? A little girl dogging their steps? Or having all their efforts to stop your father be for nothing, because you were right there to pick up all of his pieces?"

That struck a chord.

Her expression softened as she mulled over my words.

I knew I was right. Her father wouldn't have wanted her doing this. Of course, it was also to my benefit that she stop.

"Think about it," I said as I pointed to the door. "Now get out of here. I have other things to do on the ship today, and I'd rather not be rushing around."

Victtra turned on her heel and headed out. Before she reached the door, however, she turned back and stared at me. "Thank you, Captain Demarco. You're one of the first people—superhuman or otherwise—who has taken an interest in my safety since I embarked on this quest."

"You're part of the crew now. And crewmates stick together."

She half-smiled, and then turned and left the room.

WE APPROACHED TRINITY STATION, the space port connected to Vectin-10 via a space elevator. Once the *Star Marque* started its docking procedures, Administer Twoine and his entourage gathered near the lifts, anxious to leave.

I wanted them gone, too. Not because Twoine had done anything to us, but because he clearly didn't want to be here. He hadn't interacted with me more than three times since our dinner, and those had been basically to complain. Once about the attacks, once about his meals, and another time due to the lack of entertainment.

We were an enforcer ship, not a luxury yacht. Superhumans were supposed to be intelligent, yet I swear Administer Twoine's IQ was sitting somewhere around room temperature.

Good riddance.

Once our starship docked, I went to the lifts to officially bid them farewell. Dr. Clay was also there to see them off. He bowed to the administer and shook hands with a few of his aides.

Once they were all gone, Dr. Clay turned to me with a sneer. "What a blowhard."

I snorted back a laugh. "What? You didn't enjoy suckin' his dick?"

"Watch your vulgarity." Dr. Clay rubbed at his narrow chin. "Apparently, my station on this ship wasn't high enough to warrant my presence. Despite my attempts to speak to the man, Twoine rejected me at every turn."

"Yeah, he was a pleasant man," I said with a chuckle. "Good thing I hired one of his aides for our ship. I saved her from a life of rolling her eyes."

"Which one?"

"Olivia Ollester."

Dr. Clay sighed and then walked away. "Feh. A financial advisor can't help with my work. I don't care." He didn't even stay and wait for me to respond. He just… left.

What a jack wagon.

It didn't matter. I didn't want to speak with the man anyway. I had other things to accomplish. And the first thing I was going to do was head down to the planet, speak with General Lone, and check in with Helia.

THIRTY-TWO

Genetic Twin

I rode the space elevator down to the planetside. Administer Twoine was here, just in another section of the massive elevator. Apparently, there was a nicer seating arrangement for members of the Vectin Government. Of course there was. Decadent shit like that always irritated me.

Cai was with me. So was Two. Not because I had requested Two join us, but because he had asked to accompany us to the planet's surface. He wore casual clothes, which made us almost twins. He was tall, fit, and his skin a mix of darker colors. He kept his hair shaved short, just like I did.

He didn't have my swagger, though.

The three of us stood at the massive windows overlooking the planet. I felt like I had seen the view of the desert a hundred times, but I still couldn't get enough of it. The golden dunes swirled across the planet's surface like the curves of a woman.

Beautiful. Almost untouchable.

"What're we doing here again?" Cai asked, his gaze narrowed on a distant city. "When I worked as a bounty hunter, I tried to avoid as much unnecessary public transportation as possible. These pieces of shit are slow."

Two glanced down at the golden desert, no indication he wanted to participate in the conversation.

"They won't allow smaller ships to the surface," I said. "Something about the sandstorms."

Cai scoffed. "Why do we have to go down, anyway? We're just here to report to our superhuman masters, right? Send them a message. Then we can be on our way to our next bounty."

"We can't send messages to Lone while he's in his villa. It's a dead zone."

"We can leave him one."

"I'm also here to speak to Helia. The woman in Lone's villa. I want to make sure she's doing okay."

"She your lover?" Cai asked with a smile.

"No." I turned to him, my eyes narrowed. "Doesn't mean I can't be concerned about her safety."

Cai smirked. "Ya know, when I first heard about the *Star Marque* —and I mean, through the media relays, and through reports of other enforcers ships—I thought *Captain Demarco* was a cold killer. I mean, you were vice-captain to Endellion Voight, one of the most controversial people in the Vectin Quadrant. And once you got your hands on her ship, you immediately started making noise."

"And?"

"And…" Cai chuckled. "It's just amusing to see you like *this*. We're taking a multi-hour elevator ride so you can check up on some superhuman's pet. I mean, some men have soft hearts, but this… This is takin' it to a whole new level."

Two glanced over, betraying the fact that he was paying attention.

I shrugged and turned away from Cai. "I never do anything half-ass."

"Even when you pine after a lady, apparently."

I cracked my knuckles, wondering what Sawyer thought. She was listening to the conversation—she was always listening—but when she remained silent, it got my imagination going.

"I have a list of bounties we could go after," Cai said, pointing to the new PAD on his left arm. "I have a few recommendations."

"We have a new financial officer." With a smirk, I added, "She's getting comfortable aboard the *Star Marque*. When we get back, bring it up with her."

I SLEPT most of the ride on the private shuttle.

Cai was awake, searching lists and lists of potential targets. Apparently, evaluating bounties got the man excited. He poked around his PAD, talking nonstop about how easy it was to catch certain types of targets. Deformed humans were some of the easiest and hardest. They were easy, because they had distinct physical features that most camera facial recognition systems could identify, but they were also the worst because they tended to hide among the dregs of humanity.

Fun.

He was probably the reason I had fallen asleep.

When I woke, though, Two was sitting next to me. I hadn't seen before, and I jerked into an upright sitting position. When he said nothing, I stretched and yawned.

"What do you want, Two?" I asked.

"My name is Dellin." Then he pressed his back hard against his seat and frowned. "Listen, I saw you recruitin' for the *Star Marque*. Even Victtra Barten seems excited to work under you."

"Yeah?"

"Maybe *I* want to be part of the *Star Marque*."

I almost laughed. After another yawn, I lodged back. "Why is that? From what I can tell, you're a bodyguard. You've always been a bodyguard, and you were basically designed for that sole function."

Two nodded. Er, rather, *Dellin*. Whatever his real name was. *He* nodded.

"You're a human, though, right?" Dellin asked. "Just like me." He scooted closer, and then kept his voice lower. "To be honest, I didn't think people like us could ever get out of the shadow of superhumans, ya know? They clone and make us. We work for them. That's... all I've ever seen."

I half-smiled. "Okay."

"And then I heard about Endellion."

I held my tongue, almost jumping into a tirade.

Dellin continued, "And then I watched you in action. I don't how to say this, but... I want to be part of the humans who are callin' their own shots."

"Yeah?"

"That's right. I wanna be part of this." He motioned to the shuttle. "Part of your crew. Being *in charge* of superhumans."

"Listen," I said. "My goal isn't to be in charge of superhumans. My goals are—"

But then I cut myself short. I still hadn't really solidified my plans. I thought about it—about how my power wasn't really *for* anything—but I hadn't come to a conclusion. What would I do once Endellion was brought to justice?

Would I fight the superhumans? Or gain political power, like Endellion had?

"I don't know what I'm doing," I earnestly said to the man. "I'm just working on something personal at the moment. When that clears up... I haven't yet decided."

Dellin scoffed and then leaned away from me. "You mean you're doin' all this, and you don't have any plans? Don't bullshit me. You have to have something."

"I do. It's just personal, asshole. I have people I need to make suffer."

Dellin sighed. "Okay, well, I still want to be part of it. I still want to be part of a crew that doesn't answer to anyone."

"Victtra know about this?"

He nodded. "I asked to leave her service before I came on this trip."

Damn. The man definitely had plans. This worked out, actually. Since Dellin was genetically modified, he could pilot starfighters better than an average person, just like me and Victtra. We could have a whole *team* of advanced fighters. Better than even Endellion's fighting squad…

"All right," I said as I patted him on the shoulder. "But I'm still going to call you *Two* every now and then. I mean, you might as well be my twin."

Dellin smirked. "True. I got the better looks, though."

Ha! Maybe he did have my swagger.

I liked the man already.

"You'll be one of my starfighters," I said.

"Deal."

When the shuttle jerked to a stop, I stood and smiled to myself. The *Star Marque* was getting stronger every day. Maybe we would need a second ship, after all. Wouldn't that be grand?

We had reached Lone's underground villa, in the heart of the dead zone. I stepped out and headed for the entrance of the villa. Dellin and Cai flanked me on either side, and I was confident with our combined strength.

The front doors were opened for us, and we were led through the luxurious and pristine rooms of Lone's villa. The screen windows displayed landscapes of flowers and winding roads. The artificial light almost felt real, but I ignored it as we traveled deeper into the building.

Cai gave Dellin an odd glance. "You ever been to one of these places before?"

"Many times," he replied.

"Superhumans do freaky shit here, don't they? I keep hoping I'll catch something, but I haven't been lucky."

Dellin frowned. "If you *haven't* seen anything, then you're definitely among the lucky ones."

The villa was larger than I had remembered. Or perhaps I was anxious and hated every second underground, I wasn't sure. I pressed down my dread and continued forward, not sure of what to say to the others.

When we rounded a corner, a guard at the door lifted his head. He wore an enviro-suit with his visor up, but he motioned to the tall entryway, and I took his suggestion. When I entered, I was surprised to see the gigantic theater room.

I had seen some planetside before, in houses that I had visited, but none had been this grand or spacious. I could probably pilot a starfighter through the room, if I were careful.

The lights were dim, allowing the massive screen at the back of the room to dominate everyone's attention. At least five other people were here—all of them superhumans, except for one human child. It was too dark to see their identities.

Lone stood in front of the four-meter-tall screen. Numbers, schematics, and diagrams covered the entire gigantic surface, organized in a way to display the surface of a massive machine built around a star. I recognized it.

The Stellar Engine.

"Construction has already begun," Lone said to the room. His guests stood around in the shadows, their attention glued to the numbers. "We'll be designing every section to fulfill the needs of the ministers and officials. From our new seat of power, governing the Cygnus Sector will never be the same. No longer will we need to travel far distances. Power and fuel will be a concern of the past."

I stepped into the theater room. Cai and Dellin came in with me. We hovered around the door, never saying anything, our attention on the screen as well.

One of the superhumans in the small "crowd" stepped forward. Her long hair was tied in an elaborate bun on the back of her head, the gold-metallic quality shimmering from the light of the screen.

"We've had trouble with massive projects like this in the past," the woman said. "Especially so close to the stars. Homo sapiens develop cancer at a hideous rate, limiting our work force. And a project like this requires a *massive* work force."

Lone held up a hand. "*Normal* Homo sapiens. Genetically engineered humans last much longer, some never developing cancer."

"Those humans are rarer. Most humans can't afford the genetic modifications. We'll never get the workers required if we only employ the genetically modified."

I listened with rapt fascination. Superhumans discussed the

construction of projects and the cost in human lives with a cold, icy abstractness.

"Minister Ontwenty has already submitted new legislation to be voted on," Lone said, smiling. "The military has access to cloning vats. We've perfected the schematics for engineers and workers who will find happiness and fulfillment designing our project. These humans can be made by the hundreds, so long as the laws limiting production are lifted. That's where everyone here comes in. We need the votes."

Lone wore a thin shirt and loose pants. I normally wouldn't care, but I was suddenly painfully aware of the man's muscle and the sophisticated way he held himself.

The man knew combat like most people knew their shadows.

And those holes on the side of their necks—and along their collarbones—weren't for decoration. They were airways. Superhumans couldn't be *choked out* like humans could be. Superhumans didn't kill themselves by getting something caught in their windpipe. The little airholes basically gave them more oxygen, which heightened their energy and kept them from dying an embarrassing death on chicken wings.

It meant they were harder to kill. More resilient.

If I was going to kill this man, how was I going to do it? Even Emissary Barten—a "weakling" when compared to other superhumans—had been a struggle. General Lone would be different, I could already tell.

"What are the temperaments of these designed workers?" one of the other guests asked. "I've seen schematics for soldiers. They always turn out needlessly aggressive, and the other ministers are afraid of birthing a workforce prone to violence and insurrection."

There had to be other ministers, likely at the same rank as Ontwenty.

Lone held out an arm. "Come here, Fey."

The little human girl stepped forward. I caught my breath when I got a better look at her.

It was Sawyer.

No. Not really. It just *looked* like Sawyer.

Red hair, big, blue eyes. Freckles across her face. How old was she? Six? Seven? Her puffy cheeks and small hands were all indicators of her youth. I wasn't really *familiar* with children. I had never been around them much, and hadn't ever given them much thought. There wasn't time for that on Capital Station.

She wore a white pair of pants and a long shirt. She held her hands together in front of her, a forced smile on her face.

"This is Fey, the latest round of our development made real." Lone patted her head like a dog, stroking Fey's short, red hair. "Her IQ is near superhuman average, and her concentration and focus are beyond compare. We've designed her so that minimal amounts of nutrition are required for full growth, and her temperament is docile. She'll seek to please her superiors, no matter the treatment."

The other superhumans in the room murmured thoughts and comments, but my attention remained on the little girl. She just smiled, her blue eyes glancing between the freakish tall people all around her. *I* felt like a child when standing next to one of the superhumans. The girl must've felt like a mouse surrounded by giants.

They spoke about her as if she weren't even there. One of them even walked forward and patted her head, cooing soft, gentle statements of appreciation.

"She's so cute," one of the superhumans muttered.

"Very pleasing to the eye," another said. "But I don't like her skin color. Perhaps we can modify humans to look a little more like us? The gradient effect isn't natural in humans, but I think we could design something that would work."

I gritted my teeth, unwilling to listen any longer.

"General Lone," I said from the back of the room, clear and distinct.

Lone glanced up, his gaze hardened, and his lips turned down in a slight frown. "Ah. Captain Demarco. I wasn't expecting you today."

I stepped forward, to the edge of the screen's dim lighting.

"I apologize," I said. "But after we returned with Administer Twoine, I figured I should come see you."

"Why's that?" Lone asked, the anger in his voice only increasing with each word. "I'm in the middle of a meeting."

"We were attacked on the way back, and I wanted to tell you that I think it's Endellion."

I had no proof, but Lone would assume it was something Endellion would do. Endellion was vicious, after all. Everyone knew she was willing to do whatever it took to maintain power.

The truth didn't matter, though. What I wanted was Lone's trust and interest. If he thought Endellion was risking herself by going after me, Lone would try to use that to his advantage.

The other superhumans glanced between me and Fey, but ultimately settled on paying me more of their attention. The mere mention of Endellion seemed to agitate the group. They didn't like her—I could tell by the twisted sneers on their disgusting faces.

"Captain Demarco is one of my Homo sapiens subordinates," Lone explained to his guests. When he glanced back at me, he smirked. "We'll meet to discuss this in three days' time. Come to my office in the Naval Affairs Building in the capital. Until then, leave me to my meeting."

"I want to hear about the efforts of Planet Governor Voight," one of Lone's guests said.

I could practically hear the anger in all of Lone's exhales. But he recovered quickly. He held up a hand, and then forced a smile. "You needn't fret. I'll be discussing Voight's rule over Vectin-10 at our next gathering. She can't possibly keep up with the multitude of problems coming her way, and I assure you, she won't be a problem for our plans."

"I heard she opposes the use of cloning vats."

Another superhuman said, with a chuckle in his voice, "I heard she has the ears of Minister Felseven *and* Minister Threen. If they vote against Minister Ontwenty legislation, your Stellar Engine will never have their workers."

"No *human* has that much influence," Lone said, cool and confident.

"I think she does," I stated, my voice an upset in the room.

Everyone went quiet. Deadened, almost. They didn't like that. They didn't like my commentary.

And while I hated invoking Endellion's name and influence, it made me happy to get under their skin. They didn't like that a *human* was disrupting their plans.

"We'll discuss this in three days," Lone drawled. With a glare, he waved his hand. "Now *begone*. I have much to accomplish today."

He was angrier this time. More than the other times. His icy gaze was a challenge, like he almost *wanted* me to stay, just so he could escalate this encounter to the next level without looking too crazed.

This really was a waste of time if I couldn't speak to Lone about future steps. I turned away, not willing to risk his wrath. I glanced over my shoulder once to catch sight of the little Sawyer-looking girl.

Fey.

She had to be another of Sawyer's genetic twins. There was no other explanation.

I didn't know Lone took them to his villa when they were this young. It... enraged me... more than most things. Almost more than my hatred for Endellion.

Almost.

Cai, Dellin, and I returned to the gigantic hallway. The guard with his enviro-suit stood at attention. My breathing was shallow as I thought back to my last time with Helia. She had been in the healing vat, and she had seemed concerned when I had mentioned "her sister."

At the time, I had meant Sawyer, but the two of them had never met. Helia must've been concerned about Fey. That was the only explanation.

"What was that?" Cai asked. He rubbed at his tattooed arms, his body stiff. "Something's bothering you. Why the fuck would you barge in on a meeting and interject like that? Do you *want* to get on Lone's bad side? I think you do."

"I'm opiniated," I sarcastically said. "It comes out."

"No kidding. I feel like you need someone to filter you."

Uninterested with Cai's commentary, I glanced over at the guard. "Where's Helia?"

The man shook his head.

"Just tell me she's okay," I said. "I won't try to visit her this time."

The guard hesitated a long moment. Then he tapped the side of his enviro-suit helmet to activate his verbal comms. "She's not here."

"Where'd she go?"

"No. You don't get it. *She's not here*. No longer with us. She passed last week. Healing vats couldn't even save her."

THIRTY-THREE

A Tense Meeting

My hearing didn't work for a few seconds. I didn't even breathe. It was like a static noise was ringing in my ears, drowning out all other sounds, even my own thoughts.

I didn't need to ask any more questions. I already knew what had happened.

General Lone had killed her.

That fucking son of a bitch had hurt her so much, she couldn't go on living.

Helia hadn't deserved that. No one did. All Helia had known had been this prison underground. A lavish prison, but still a box buried in the desert of a far-off planet, away from anyone and anything that would care.

And apparently, she was just another rung in the ladder to creating the perfect *worker* for this massive Stellar Engine project. One more iteration of an engineer design they were working on.

Although the villa was always kept a pleasant temperature, I felt cold. Ice ran through my veins, and I stepped away from the guard and continued down the hall, still unable to hear anything about me.

I wanted to kill Lone. Right now. No delays.

And I almost turned around, went into his theater room, and started a fight right there. But I didn't have my weapons. I didn't have the element of surprise. And his guards were everywhere. If I attacked him *right now*, I would be swarmed by his security, gunned down in an instant. And then Lone would go to one of his healing vats, and any damage I had done would be *undone* in a matter of hours.

It wouldn't change anything.

But…

"Demarco?" Cai said as he grabbed my arm.

We were already standing at the front door of the villa.

"What?" I asked, my tone so icy, I didn't even recognize my own voice.

"You're not yourself."

Dellin turned to me, his eyes searching my gaze. "You're a man possessed."

"I need to get to the surface," I said as I jerked away from Cai. "My plans have changed. Both of you return to the *Star Marque*. Tell them I'll be there soon."

Cai hesitated a long moment, like he didn't know if I were serious or not. But then he huffed and opened the door. "I understand," he finally muttered. "I'm not sure what got you this way, but men only have that look when something in their life has to change."

I replied with a curt nod. "I'll see you soon."

MY TRAVEL to the city was almost unregistered in my mind. I was so buried in my thoughts, I couldn't see beyond them to my literal surroundings. By the time I left the shuttle, I was shocked how much time had gone by. Then I buried myself in my thoughts again, trying to mull over every possible outcome to the problem.

Before I had realized it, I stood on the planet's surface, glaring at the sky, practically challenging the sun to blind me. The glorious blue of the sky didn't calm me like I had hoped.

How much more time had gone by? The rage in my blood never waned.

"What's wrong?" Sawyer asked over the PAD, bringing me back to reality, at least for a few hard moments.

"He killed her." I said it with all the emotion of a brick.

Silence.

I waited.

Finally, Sawyer replied with, "There's no need to be this upset. You didn't even know her."

That wasn't true. We both knew it. Helia had lived a life just like Sawyer had. But unlike Sawyer, who had managed to get away, she hadn't.

Helia hadn't had the power to change her fate. Or perhaps she hadn't had the will, I wasn't sure. Either way, it frustrated me. All these questions about my future made me think of her, and how she hadn't been able to decide.

"Lone has another little girl," I muttered.

I stood on the edge of a metropolis, far from a walkway or road. Planets were so large once I was standing on them. They seemed so tiny from space, yet here… I felt I could get lost if I weren't careful.

I had to pay more attention to my surroundings.

"He'll always have *another* girl," Sawyer stated. "He grows them."

"You're not upset?"

"I told you before, Demarco. I can barely feel anything."

"Well, I can feel enough for the both of us."

"What're you going to do about it?"

Her question felt like a challenge. Did she think I would fail? Did she think I couldn't rid the universe of Lone? I could. And I would. It didn't matter the cost.

"I'm going to contact Endellion," I muttered, hating every word I spoke.

My PAD was silent. The sun beat down on me relentlessly. The desert wasn't a comforting place, but it helped keep the ice in my veins from freezing over my body. I just wanted to maintain my thoughts and my focus.

"I'm going to send Lysander to join you," Sawyer eventually said.

"Why?"

"Sanders will keep you level. He'll know if something is going too far."

Although I wanted to argue the point, I knew Sawyer was right. Lysander would be there for me. He hadn't ducked out on me yet. And he was more reasonable. Always calm and collected. Always thinking of the future.

"Okay," I said. "Send him."

"You think Endellion will meet with you in-person?"

"She met me in prison."

"That was when you were restrained—and no one could see."

I exhaled, and then crossed my arms. "Can *you* send her a message? Send it through a channel that can't be traced to us. I don't want anyone knowing the *Star Marque* was communicating with Endellion."

"I can do that."

"Set up a time and place to meet. Someplace alone." I turned my attention to the space elevator in the far distance. "Maybe up on Trinity Station."

"She won't go anywhere she doesn't feel safe. I think if you want to speak to Endellion, you're going to have to meet her at a place of her choosing. Can you do that, Demarco? Can you speak to her without breaking down and flying into a rage?"

If I did, everything I had been working toward would be destroyed. *Maybe* I could kill Endellion if I got the drop on her. But then I'd never get Lone—and I needed her help for that.

And I needed to make sure he suffered. Not just for Helia, but for Sawyer, too.

"Okay," I said with a sigh. "Send Endellion a message so that only she would understand I want to meet with her. If she sends a message back with a location and time, great. Let me know."

"I will."

Her voice had a hint of deeper emotion. More than *none at all*, which was a step up.

The wind picked up, and sand whipped across the bare skin of my arms. It stung. I rubbed at my biceps, amused by the sensations. I loved planets. They were nothing like space stations.

Sawyer still hadn't added anything to her statement.

"Are you okay?" I asked.

"I am." Then Sawyer added, her voice soft, "Thank you for this, Demarco."

The heartfelt statement of appreciation got to me. I half-smiled and nodded once. "Don't mention it. I'm not going to let anyone get away with hurting you, Sawyer. Everyone who ever wrongs us is going to get what's coming to them. That's a promise."

I HAD STAYED the night at a local hotel for captains and military personnel—apparently, this was the location where Endellion would meet me. She went in and out of here fairly frequently, so no one wouldn't think it odd when she came again.

I purchased myself one of those cheap-ass, white enviro-suits made of thin material and poke-you-in-the-rib plastics. With the visor up, no one would see me as *Captain Demarco*. They'd probably think I was some low-level punk working on Trinity Station, down on the planet for a vacation.

Now I just had to wait for Lysander.

I had sipped drinks in my room all night, but when I went to the balcony, I took note of people who frequented this place. Starship captains. Superhuman officers. I couldn't speak with them—I didn't want anyone to know I was here, ready to meet with the planet governor.

I had even gone out of my way to avoid having my ID chip scanned. Couldn't leave any traces. I was just a stranger in the night.

If Endellion had been here, she would've worked all the angles, though. She would've used her bad reputation with the other starship captains as a way to gain an "in" with some other group. Then she would've rubbed elbows with every influential superhuman here. She would've made promises. Done all the wheeling and dealing.

But this was a different circumstance.

I had slept fine, but my dreams had been troubled. I woke up without remembering much. All I could picture was the darkness of space. Or maybe the darkness of Capital Station. I wasn't sure.

In the morning, when the sky was the most colorful, I made my way down to the eatery. Lysander was there, sitting at a table, wearing the same type of cheap enviro-suit. To my surprise, Victtra also sat at the same table. She wasn't someone I wanted to speak with, and her presence genuinely irritated me.

She fit in, though. Superhumans loved this place… Whatever it was called, I couldn't remember. My level of giving a damn was at an all-time low. I didn't care if this place was popular. It had likely served Lone at some point, so I already hated everything about it.

Lysander kept his helmet hood down, exposing his face, but I felt that was less of an issue. He kept his head down, and with the terrible suit, most people weren't paying attention. He might show up on cameras, and that would be suspicious, but only to people who knew what they were looking for.

Lysander looked all military, his expression nothing but business. Victtra, on the other hand, wore casual clothing meant for a lady of politics. A sleek black dress and pinned up hair. Her neck, with its two-toned skin and little holes, really marked her as *different* and *superhuman*.

I approached the table, my gait stiff. Lysander immediately stood, but Victtra kept her seat.

"Demarco," Lysander said, his voice low. He gave me the once over, and even though I was fully suited, he frowned. "You look terrible."

"I need a drink," I said, my voice altered a bit.

Lysander grabbed a glass on his table and handed it over. I stared it, and the visor of my suit told me it was just water. No alcohol whatsoever.

He must've realized my irritation, because Lysander said, "I don't drink."

"That's so cute," I quipped. "But I need some warmth."

I took a seat, and so did Lysander. The clink of plates and glass rang throughout the eatery. Soft music played on speakers, a constant and pleasant reminder that I was still grounded and not drowning in my own revenge fantasies.

"Sawyer told me that Endellion has agreed to meet us," Lysander said, his voice so soft, I almost couldn't hear him. "We should go up to the third story of the hotel in about ten minutes."

"Thank you for joining me," I said. It was all I could say.

Lysander nodded once. "Of course."

But Victtra… She just sat there, sipping on her drink, her posture prim and proper. I ignored her. I didn't know why she had joined us, especially since Endellion was one of her ultimate targets, even if Victtra didn't realize it yet.

Minutes passed in utter silence, more awkward than I would've wanted. I probably smelled like anger. No matter what I did, I couldn't shake it.

"What happened?" Lysander asked. "Sawyer and Cai filled me in one some of the details, including the hiring of Dellin. I'd prefer if we spoke about that ahead of time, by the way. I need to know the personal details of our crew."

"General Lone is creating humans and killing them off, all for his personal goals and pleasures," I said, ignoring most of Lysander's commentary.

He took a moment to absorb my words. He was always the type to weigh things—not feel emotions so hot and passion-filled.

"I see," Lysander drawled. "Do you have evidence? Should we go to the Vectin Government?"

"I don't trust the Vectin Government. They're basically allowing Lone to do this already. The military has the authority to create humans and use them for whatever benefit."

Lysander laced his fingers together, his eyes dark with thoughts. Then he turned to me. "The last time I saw you this angry was after the destruction of Capital Station."

"This feels like the same anger," I intoned, unable to voice my true hatred.

When I didn't elaborate, Lysander remained quiet. Victtra glanced between us, her intelligent gaze searching us for answers. She didn't know the truth about the station, and I'd probably never tell her, but I wanted to.

I wanted to tell everyone.

But I couldn't.

"What're we going to do about Lone?" Lysander asked. "Or is this why you're seeing Endellion?"

"I'm going to make sure Lone pays for his crimes."

Victtra snapped her gaze to mine, a slight smile on her face. If there was anyone who felt what I did, it was her. Part of me wanted to tell her everything about her father's death, to admit my crime and take my punishment, but I had too much to accomplish first.

Perhaps, when this was over—everything was over—I'd give Victtra a plasma rifle and tell her everything.

Lysander glanced at his PAD and then motioned to the lift. "We should go. I was hoping we could discuss our tactics when dealing with Endellion, but you're a man who rides by the seat of his pants, I suppose. I'll be there to keep you focused, but you need to be careful. Endellion will have guards and contingencies if you lose yourself and attack."

"I'm not going to attack her."

I wasn't carrying any weapons. I had left them all in my room, even my knife. If Endellion attacked me, I had confidence enough in my abilities to blow out of a hotel room and make it to security or safety.

That was probably foolish of me. Endellion didn't do anything half-ass. If she wanted me dead, this whole building would be nuked to oblivion. But I already knew she wanted my help with Lone, so my fear of her attacking was low.

Lysander and I stood from the table. Again, Victtra said and did nothing. She was here—perhaps as decoration—and I wasn't sure why.

The lift doors opened when Lysander and I approached. We

stepped inside, the marble tile and mirror-finish steel walls glittering with pristine perfection. My appearance… I almost didn't recognize myself. I stood stiff and flexed, my hands curled into tight balls. Angry. Maybe even feral.

I half-smiled to myself. At least I looked how I felt.

A feminine computer voice sounded from the ceiling. "Greetings. Welcome to the Grand Dune Hotel. You've selected the third floor, for conference rooms, social venues, and banquets."

The lift headed up, silent and subtle, but I felt the pressure shift as we moved. It reminded me of the starfighters, even if much less.

"I'm not going to like this, am I?" Lysander asked.

I hadn't told him about my plan to kill Lone. This meeting would likely rock him. A part of me wondered if Sawyer had demanded he attend just so he was in the loop.

"You once told me that methods matter more than the outcome," I muttered.

Lysander nodded once. "I did."

"Well, our enemies don't care about their methods, and they're killing people. I can't stand by and watch it. I'm going to use some of their tactics—I'm going to play their game—and if you don't want to join me for that, you need to leave right now, Sanders."

Lysander held his breath for the short ride of the lift.

Then the lift stopped. The feminine computer voice sounded off again. "Thank you for trusting the Grand Dune Hotel for all your needs. Remember that the Vectin Quadrant Ministers appreciate your support and cooperation."

Lysander and I stepped out into the hall, and we headed to a specific door. During our walk, Lysander fitted his helmet over his head. It hardened into place, creating a mirror-like visor.

He said nothing about my declarations. When I turned to him, he glanced over, my reflection staring back at me.

"I don't have the answers to every situation," he muttered through the helmet's audio. "But I know what you've done for this crew. And what you've done for me and Noah." He stopped and grabbed my upper arm.

I stopped and stared, fearing he was about to leave.

"I trust you, Demarco," Lysander said, earnest in every regard. "You've done so much for us. *All of us*. And I know how you feel about Endellion. If we're here, it's obviously because something terrible is happening."

I nodded once.

"Trust me more, Demarco. I know you're afraid to tell me about your extracurricular activities, but that's exactly why Endellion and I didn't mesh well on the *Star Marque*. She kept everything a secret and played too many games. Don't play games with your crew, Demarco, and we'll follow you into a black hole and back."

His speech made me smile—I couldn't even hold it back. I *had* been afraid to tell Lysander anything substantial about my plans. But I needed to stop that.

If I really was going to be different than Endellion, I needed to trust my crew. And I had a damn good crew, too. The best fucking cyber engineer, a hyper-competent doctor, a goddamn legendary bounty hunter, a military academy vice-captain, a government savvy financial officer, and talented superhuman starfighter.

Was there any other enforcer starship in the whole quadrant better than mine?

Fuck no.

"Thanks, Sanders," I said, patting his arm. "I do trust you. More than you know."

We both exchanged another round of nods and then continued on.

The room we arrived at was labeled as *Conference Hall South*. I pushed open the door, growing tense all over again.

The blue carpets, the white walls, and the crystal-covered ceiling were beautiful, more so than any starship or space station I had ever been in, but I barely saw them. There were eleven people in here— all wearing enviro-suits with their helmets on—but I still recognized Endellion first.

There she was. At the other end of the glass conference table. Her enviro-suit scaled and expensive, her visor reflective, showing me the luxurious scene around us. I recognized the way she sat in seats. It was powerful, confident. A little irritated, probably because I had asked her here on a mere moment's notice.

"Hello, Clevon," Endellion said, her voice filtered by her enviro-suit. "You're looking… tired. Don't tell me you're already fraying from the pressures of being a starship captain? What a shame. I expected more of you."

Helplessness

I removed the helmet of my cheap enviro-suit and then stared at Endellion from across the conference hall with unfiltered vision.

Her ten stooges—all carrying plasma rifles—regarded me with cold seriousness. They already knew who I was, so what did it matter if they got an eyeful of me now? I took a seat on the opposite end of the glass table, trying to signify that this wasn't going to get physical.

"Your guards need to wait outside," I said. "And we need to make sure we're in a place where I can speak to you."

With her helmet up, I had no idea how Endellion felt about my statements. She remained quiet for a long time, never moving. Finally, she said, "This room is secure. I've seen to that. No one will be recording this meeting."

She gestured with a hand and the ten look-a-likes nodded once, practically in sync, and then headed for the door, their rifles still at the ready. That left me, Lysander, and Endellion. Alone. In a room with seats and a glass table, and a window that overlooked the metal and glass cityscape below.

I didn't want to chat, or have pleasantries, or even rehash anything.

"General Lone needs to go," I stated.

Although I couldn't see her face, I could practically hear Endellion's lifted eyebrow and sardonic amusement. "I'm well aware."

"You don't understand. I want it to happen sooner rather than later." I didn't want Lone to hurt the little girl. Helia had died because *I had waited.* I wasn't going to do that anymore.

"You sound angry."

"Wow, what a coincidence. I *am* angry." That was the best I could do without yelling—fucking sarcasm. "Cut the shit, Endellion. Let's make this happen. I know you want it. Help me do this."

Lysander placed a hand on the glass table, reminding me he was still here, and that I should keep my rage contained. He was right.

"What has Lone done that's garnered your ire?" Endellion asked, still amused. "If you're willing to deal with me to see him dead, it must have been significant."

I felt like I had told several people already, and none of them had reacted with any sort of shock or disgust. Endellion already knew what he was doing. She had rescued Sawyer in the first place. Yet she sat here, no rage for his actions.

Then again, this was the woman who had killed millions on Capital Station because they had been in her way. I shouldn't have been fucking surprised.

"You know what he's doing with those cloning vats," I said. "And now he's planning on making more people to create Ontwenty's *Stellar Engine.*" I leaned onto the glass table, my teeth gritted so hard, I thought I might break something. "He'll just do whatever he wants—no one is going to stop him. He'll make a million Sawyers, throw them into a grinder, use the blood as lubricant for his machines, *and not a single person will ever give a damn.*"

"Feeling helpless, Clevon?"

Her question stilled my thoughts.

That was the exact word. Helpless. Like watching myself grow old in the mirror, because it was inevitable. That was how I felt—and I knew it shouldn't have been this way. I should have been able to do *something.*

"I want to make him pay," I admitted, no subterfuge to my

plans, no hidden agenda. "For what he did to Sawyer. And Helia. And everyone else I don't even know about."

Lysander glanced over, but I didn't return his gaze.

Endellion sat forward, her visor reflecting the glass, and its subtle reflections of the room. She never removed her helmet—likely to hide her facial scarring—but I truly wondered what kind of expression she wore under it all.

"I know the feeling," Endellion said.

"Do you?" I scoffed and gritted my teeth. "Are you sure you're not the one always making others feel this way?"

"That feeling of helplessness… It fills my nightmares and haunts my waking thoughts. I know it well, Clevon."

"Bullshit."

Lysander placed his hand on my upper arm.

I tensed, and then remained quiet.

Endellion exhaled, her helmet audio giving her voice a robotic feel. "I grew up in a small mining community. That was where this nightmare started."

I held my breath, thinking back to what I remembered of Endellion. Her parents were dead. She disliked her mother. I didn't think I had heard much other than that.

"You won't get my sympathy," I said.

Endellion darkly chuckled. "Just listen, Clevon. While I still have the patience to tell you." She placed her hand on the table and stared at it. "I was born with defective eyes. Almost blind."

I had already known she was a defect, but she had never really explained how that had affected her throughout her life. I held my breath, waiting for the punchline to this sad tale.

"It was a problem with my optic nerve and choroid. They said I'd never be able to see without cybernetic implants. But my family couldn't afford that—and the butchers who called themselves doctors would never give me *full* eyesight."

Lysander held his hands together, listening intently.

"Everyone told me I'd amount to nothing," Endellion said, no emotion in her voice. "My schoolmates. My teachers. My father. My own mother. They said—with a weakness like mine—I'd be relegated to a quiet life on a space station, unable to travel far. And since I was a defect, I'd never enter a career of any influence."

I could understand why people would think that. Blindness was difficult in the harsh and cold worlds of the space stations. And defects were never given land planetside.

Endellion laughed once, but it was forced and short. "So, when a Homo superior came to my community—a doctor of some fame —I was excited to speak with him. But his assistant wouldn't let me. Not to be dissuaded, I begged the assistant to fix my eyes. He was a Homo sapiens, I thought he would be sympathetic. I told him I'd do anything to see—anything he asked me."

The story…

A part of me already knew where it was heading.

"To my delight, the assistant agreed. I visited him in a lab, and was then put to sleep. When I awoke, I found my eyesight was just as bad. The assistant hadn't helped me. He had taken bodily samples—pieces of organs, blood, marrow—and likely more, given the way I hurt as I stumbled home. But no one cared." Again, Endellion chuckled. "I had told everyone who would listen. But they didn't care. No one was going to fight against the doctor and his assistants. No one was going to side with a little girl who couldn't see."

I cracked my knuckles, wondering what had happened to the assistant.

If any of this was even truthful. She sounded sincere, but knowing Endellion, anything could've happened.

"I remember feeling helpless then," Endellion said, her voice distant. "I remember thinking, *this is my life.* And then I remember letting go of the things I cared about. Like someone had cut the strings holding me in place. Or perhaps a better analogy—I had freed myself from my chains."

"Are you suggesting that's what I need to do now?" I asked. "Are you trying to say your situation is similar to mine?"

Endellion replied with a single nod. "Feeling helpless drove me forward. I never wanted to feel like that again. I never wanted *other people* to have control over my destiny. I think about my childhood a lot—about the days of my life I had lived in darkness. I never want that feeling again. And with the power I wield now, I never will. If you're feeling that way, Clevon, I understand. And I want to help you."

"What did you do about your eyes?" Lysander asked, obviously invested in the tale.

"I went back to the assistant," Endellion said matter-of-factly. "I told him I was tired of living. I told him he could have any part of my body he wanted, so long as he paid my family for the genetic material he was harvesting. And then, when he was about to put me under a second time, I killed him."

I half-smiled. That sounded like Endellion.

"That's it?" I asked. "You're not going to give us the details? How was a sick little girl, who was blind, and missing some of her marrow, able to kill a full-grown man?"

Endellion leaned back in her chair, her arms on both armrests. "You wouldn't appreciate the details, and it's not important regardless. What I'm trying to say is—I'll help you. Although killing Lone *soon* hinders my ultimate plans, I can work around this to make sure he's brought to justice within the week."

"Just like that? No strings attached? There're no *deals* to make or *schemes* you want to plot in return?"

"I told you about my childhood because I wanted you to know why." Endellion touched the side of her helmet and tapped something. A moment later, she lowered her hands. "And just in case you're wondering, the Homo superior—the doctor—found me in the blood of his assistant. After I told him what had happened, he gave me a new pair of eyes. And after that, I left my little mining community. The rest is history."

"I don't believe a word of it," I said straight away.

Lysander turned to me, his visor still up, and my own reflection staring back at me. "Demarco. Please. Just take Endellion's gift and let's not provoke her."

"I don't care if you believe me," Endellion stated. "It's in the past. And that will never change. All I can do now is offer assistance to someone feeling like I once had."

"That's not why you're helping me." I stood from my chair, the heat and anger dying in my veins and becoming an icy chill that threatened to dominate my thoughts. "You're helping me because Lone is going to stop at nothing to ruin your governorship. He's already fucking with you, and you want him gone just as quickly as I do. Whatever story you told me—whatever truth might be in those lies—you only said it to make me feel better about our alliance. Nothing more."

"So cynical," Endellion said as she remained seated. "I'm still human, Clevon. I keep trying to tell you. Sometimes I feel things, too."

"I'm just letting you know that I don't care how many times you were tricked, beaten, robbed, or violated. You can weave whatever sad sack tale you want, and my opinion of you will never shift. You want Lone dead? Good. Let's work together to do that, but don't think I'm ever going to think of you as *human*. You're a demon—and I'll never see you as anything else."

Endellion stood from her chair, calculated and tense. She looked athletic and capable, especially in her fancy enviro-suit. I remembered our fight on Capital Station. But this time would be different.

"General Lone has several ministers coming to Vectin-10 for various meetings and political talks," Endellion said, ignoring my statements. "I'm fairly certain I could ask him to one of the underground military facilities. I can have the power cut, and the surveillance systems neutralized, just like I did in the jail. For a brief period of time, whoever killed Lone would have the possibility of getting away with it."

"That's not enough," I said. "*I* could attack Lone in his dead zone of a villa. My problem is that his security would attack me after. That'll happen in whatever military facility I see him in."

"It won't be a problem." Endellion brushed herself off, her stance more relaxed. "Trust me. I can get Lone to see me without any of his subordinates."

"But fighting him will be—"

"Much easier, once I send an electric pulse throughout the facility." Endellion stepped around the glass table and walked closer to me, though she stopped at least two meters away. "You see, certain electric pulses bother superhumans. The ampullae of Lorenzini—the organ they use to sense electricity—can be disturbed, which causes them to lose balance, much like someone with an inner ear problem. Let's just call it a *defect of their design.*"

She almost laughed when she said it.

I had to admit, the irony was thick.

But then again, it would be difficult to pull off. Most enviro-suits protected against EMP attacks. Which meant Endellion was confident that she could get Lone away from his men *and* unprotected by an enviro-suit.

Ballsy.

This was Endellion, though. Perhaps she could do it.

Lysander stood and placed a hand on my shoulder. In a quiet voice, he said, "Be careful. Whatever you agree to, there's always the possibility that Endellion double crosses you. Remember Capital Station. Please."

He was right. And I had thought about it.

Endellion *would* fuck me, and not in the good way. It was just a matter of time.

But General Lone's death meant more to me than anything else at the moment. Sawyer wanted it. And although I barely knew Helia, I wanted to make sure she was avenged. And I wanted to make sure Fey would live, unharmed and unscarred at the hands of a sadist superhuman.

I probably shouldn't allow Endellion to set the terms of the agreement, but I didn't have much other choice... if I was going to get her help.

"Make it happen," I said. "And I'll be the weapon you wield against this sick fuck of a superhuman."

Endellion nodded again. "Then I'll make arrangements. Tell Sawyer to keep in touch with me, and be ready to move at a moment's notice. Once I have Lone in place, you'll only have a short period of time in which to rid the universe of his stink."

THIRTY-FIVE

Planning

Lysander and I entered the eatery side-by-side. Victtra spotted us the instant we arrived. She stood from her chair and walked over, her long superhuman stride elegant in its own way. When compared to the nearby superhumans, however, she really was still young. She was shorter, and not as bulky—a kitten next to a tom cat.

"Are you finished with your dealings?" Victtra asked.

I nodded and we headed for the main door.

Victtra kept my pace, her gaze on the floor. "I'm curious."

"What?" I asked, curt.

"You said you had a grudge against Governor Voight."

I said nothing. Now wasn't the time to be discussing it.

Victtra continued with, "Have you let your anger go? Your lust for revenge is dead?"

"Never," I hissed as I shot her glare. Her icy blue eyes locked onto my mine, but I didn't flinch away. "Look, this isn't any of your business. Let's just say she'll get what's coming to her once this other business is settled."

"You said she almost destroyed the *Star Marque*."

"Yeah, well, she also used me like a tool, and I'll never forgive that. Sometimes personal grudges aren't worth sacrificing large goals for, do you understand? Some matters affect more than yourself, and they take precedence."

Lysander hurried his step to match mine and Victtra's. "That's one of the wisest things you've said in a while, Demarco."

"Thanks, Sanders," I quipped. "Do I get a gold star? Or are you going to draw a smiley face on my next rum pouch?"

Lysander pinched the bridge of his nose. "Why do I even try to be serious with you?"

The rest of the trek back to the *Star Marque* was in relative silence. Victtra remained quiet and contemplative. I wondered if she was mulling over my statement. I had meant it. My grudge against Endellion could wait while I helped Sawyer. My hatred for *Planet Governor Voight* wouldn't die off while we worked together.

I just had to wait.

TRINITY STATION HAD a wonderful view of Vectin-10. There was a clear aluminum floor on the station where individuals went to stare at the golden dune of the mostly desert planet. I waited, standing on the clear floor, for word from Endellion.

Planets really were wonderful places.

General Lone expected to see me in three days—to meet with him in the Naval Affairs Office—but my PAD lit up with a message from Sawyer, dispelling that thought. Endellion wanted to get this deed done before that. In two days. Apparently, she wanted us to gather in a dead zone a little north of the space elevator. It was underground, just like Lone's villa, and wouldn't have any sort of recording devices nearby.

According to Endellion's message, she would be there. She had said she was the lure—that Lone had agreed to visit because she had asked to have a private discussion.

"You understand what Endellion wants, right?" Sawyer asked over my PAD.

I stared at the planet's surface, never really seeing the details. "I get it. She wants us to help—"

"Don't say anything incriminating. The station has audio-recording security if you say certain words."

"I wasn't." Then I chuckled. "C'mon. I'm better than that."

"Just making sure."

After a long exhale, I said, "She wants us to handle everything. The mess. The cleanup. The fallout. That's the price for asking for her help. She can't get her hands dirty during this."

I had been in this business long enough to get the details. We had to be in the dead zone long before Endellion or Lone arrived. Then Lone had to die—and it couldn't be blamed on Endellion, which meant we'd probably have to come up with a plan to deal with that. When I had killed Barten, Endellion had me pretend to be part of the rebellion. This time, I would need something similar…

And then I'd have to vanish, because if I was found there—or anyone from the *Star Marque*—we'd be ruined. Finished. Maybe even Endellion as well.

"It looks like Endellion delivered on her end of the bargain," Sawyer said over the PAD. "I'm getting word from the capital city that Lone will be making a trip up north."

Endellion always came through. Even now, on a moment's notice, she could somehow get the most hated superhuman into place for me to murder him. Perhaps that was just who she was. Someone who made things happen, no matter the odds against her.

"Sawyer," I whispered. "Do you know anything about Endellion's history? Is all the stuff she told me about her childhood… Is any of that true?"

"I've looked into her history several times." I heard the tapping of her PAD, even through the speakers. "She was born with a defect in her eyes. Mostly blind. And she was born on the prison planet, Ucova. Her parents were miners, and the small community she lived in was far from the supermax facilities. But the gravity was still intense."

I held my breath, slowly nodding with her words.

"She had surgery on her eyes, but I don't know how she paid for it. When she told me she had to kill someone, I looked into the criminal records of the mining communities on Ucova. Everything lines up. A murder was reported, but no one was ever charged. A superhuman doctor later said it was an accident."

Everything had been true?

But still.

I shook my head, dispelling the terrible thoughts. I didn't care if it was true. I didn't care how much she suffered in her childhood, or how many terrible things happened to her. Endellion had tried to kill us all for her ambition.

Could I ever forgive that?

Never.

I SAT in the captain's room, my attention on the computer screen. Cai stood on the other side of my desk, a slight smirk on his face. He had a deep-seated confidence about his abilities, and even though this plan made me nervous, his swagger made it seem possible.

"And you have all this?" I asked.

Cai nodded once. "That's right. I've made lots of contacts throughout my years as bounty hunter. I mean, there isn't a space station in this quadrant I haven't visited."

"How quickly can you get it all together?"

"Rebellion codes, suits, and alibis? I'll have to check with the starships here. If we're lucky, a few hours. If we're unlucky… Maybe a week."

"We don't have a week."

We had a couple days, at best, to put this all together. Cai had access to rebellion tools and codes, which would allow us to impersonate them. It was an adequate cover, but not the best. Why would the rebellion be deep within the dead zone on Vectin-10? There weren't many logical explanations.

Except for one.

The death of Endellion.

Which meant we'd have to plan this operation as though we were targeting the planet governor, and not the general. Obviously, Lone would die, but we wanted the investigators to conclude that he was an accidental casualty, and not the target.

Lysander would know what to do. He had studied at the Ares Military Academy and had successfully hidden his defect status from the HNS Corps for years. He knew military procedures inside out. We could use that information to lead the investigators to the conclusion we wanted.

"I'll see what I can do about acquiring everything sooner," Cai said, rubbing at his smooth chin. "But if I can, it'll definitely work. I've technically impersonated some rebellion communications before in order to snoop some campers out of their hiding holes."

I glanced over at him and narrowed my eyes. "You ever do anything other than work?"

Cai opened his mouth, and then closed it. When he glanced over, he crossed his arms. "What's that supposed to mean?"

"I mean—I never hear much else from you besides work. Even when you talk about your mother, you always just talk about her job first, never really anything else."

"And?"

I shrugged. "And you ever hook up with someone after eighteen hours of solid drinking?"

"I think if I drank for *eighteen hours*, I wouldn't remember half of my childhood." He snorted and glared at me. "We're all not genetically modified, like you. I can drink for a few hours, tops."

"You're dodging the question."

"Fine." Cai paced around the captain's room. It wasn't large, so he turned every couple steps, like a paranoid lunatic. "I've had drinks in the past, but work takes priority. I'm not going to make credits sitting on my ass. I've gotta hustle."

Goddammit.

I ran a hand down my face. "You and Lysander... You're so damn similar."

Cai stopped dead in his tracks. "You take that back."

"Heh. I'm just saying."

I didn't elaborate. Instead, I went back to examining our plan. Sawyer had written up a schedule, including how long we should be in the dead zone before Endellion or General Lone arrived. We'd have to leave soon—and to make it seem like the *Star Marque* wasn't involved, my ship would leave the planet, stranding whoever stayed behind on the planet.

Who would I take with me?

A small team. As small as possible.

Myself, obviously.

But who else?

Perhaps it would be best if were just me. Just like with Emissary Barten. Just me. Murdering a superhuman.

My other officers couldn't handle it. Sawyer was too small and frail. Lysander was military trained, but he suffered from a terrible defect that affected him physically. It was the same with Noah. They could be incapacitated through pain if put through too much stress.

Dr. Clay was laughably incompetent at anything physical. I wouldn't trust him to have my back in a fight. Hell, I wouldn't trust him to deliver a fucking nutra-paste pizza.

What about Cai?

I gave him the once over. He was physically impressive, and I was sure he could hold his own in fight, but could he hold off a superhuman? Probably not. Then again, Endellion said she had a secret weapon to handle Lone—some sort of EMP device—so perhaps I was overthinking this.

Or maybe I just didn't want anyone else to get involved.

If I went alone, and handled this by myself, there was no chance anyone else would get hurt. And if I were caught, perhaps I could convince the courts I acted by myself, and that my crew had no knowledge of the situation.

The door to the captain's room opened with a soft whoosh. Victtra stood on the other side, with her lone bodyguard, now that Two had joined me.

Wait, Two…

He was a man like me. And I remembered his real name was

Dellin, but I didn't care for it. Two was better. It reminded me of the superhumans. Them and their last names—based around which batch of test tubes they originated from.

Victtra stepped into the room and cleared her throat, dragging me from my thoughts.

"Captain Demarco," she said. "I wish to speak with you. In private, if you don't mind."

Before I could say anything, Cai threw his hands up in the air and headed out. "I have things to do anyway. Lots of people to call." He sidestepped around Victtra and One, and then headed down the corridor without another word. I suspected he was agitated, but he'd get over it.

One also stepped out into the corridor. Once the door shut, Victtra walked over to the nearest chair and took a seat. She kept her posture straight and her eyes focused on me.

She practically looked like a statue. So stiff and formal.

"What is it?" I asked.

"I've been poking around the ship's archives."

I caught my breath and waited. Sawyer had said that Victtra was poking around, but according to her, Victtra had found nothing. She couldn't have found anything incriminating, could she have?

"I was trying to find information about the rebellion, and also my father." Victtra threw back her hair, still stiff, but unwavering. "I looked through several of your secure files."

"You want to go to brig?" I asked. "Why tell me any of this?"

"Because after some investigating, I discovered the coding on the *Star Marque* has been tampered with. Expertly tampered with, but still—it violates the Federation's mandates."

I said nothing.

"I'm also telling you this because, when I couldn't find what I was looking for, I decided to record conversations on the *Star Marque*."

That statement caught me off guard. I waited, tenser than I had been in a long time. "And?" I growled.

If she were about to accuse me of murder, right before the eve of my revenge, I didn't know what I would do. Kill her? Run off?

No. If Victtra had evidence, she had probably sent it to the authorities by now.

"And I know about your plot to undo Governor Voight."

That was it? Again, I waited, hoping this went no further.

"I also know about your feud with General Lone. And I suspect, given our change of plans, and the way you're shifting around the work orders of the *Star Marque*, that you're staying behind on the planet to either do something for him… Or do something to him."

"What makes you think that?" I asked, slow and calm, likely betraying my building rage.

Victtra half-smiled. "Considering your feelings for your cyber operations officer, and the way you spoke about Lone's cloned assistant, I can conclude that your anger runs deep. And, since some of your conversations have been on the traitorous side, I can also assume you're the type of man who doesn't mind doing the unthinkable."

I stood from my chair, feeling a fight coming on. Adrenaline flooded my veins.

"How, exactly, did you record conversations around the ship?"

Victtra stared up at me, but she didn't get out of her chair. "Well, given the level of sophistication used to alter the ship's coding, I decided a *low-tech* route would be safer. I used several handheld recording devices, each powered by internal battery, with their own internal memory chip so that no one would detect any broadcasting signals."

I wasn't the most tech savvy, but even I understand what she meant. They were localized—simple devices used by children to maybe record audio within a few feet, usually at terrible quality.

Sawyer couldn't detect those? I suspected not. Without a broadcast signal, how would she even detect them? The *Star Marque* was an older ship, before the time of Federation Formation War.

"Shit like that doesn't usually fly in the courts," I said. And I meant it. On Capital Station, I got real accustomed to what could and couldn't be used as evidence against me. "It's too easy to fake. Too easy to manipulate."

Victtra huffed a single laugh. "I don't think you understand the purpose of my surveillance, Captain Demarco. I'm well aware it wouldn't have flown in a court of law. What I wanted was to know what you were *really* doing here on the *Star Marque*. I suspected it was dubious, given Endellion Voight's reputation—I just didn't know the specifics. Now I do."

Part of me tried to remember every conversation I ever had on the *Star Marque*. She couldn't have put recording devices in my room. They had to been elsewhere.

But where?

Victtra didn't know everything, or else she would've known the plan to kill Lone.

She only knew half of the story—but it was enough to make her feel confidence enough to step forward.

"You aren't the only one who I recorded," Victtra said as she also stood from her chair. This time her hands were gripped tightly —so much that a bead of blood slipped across her left fingers. "When I went to Lone villa, I decided to leave one of my small devices there, in the care of someone I paid. I only recently received the device back… And what I found has rocked me to my core."

Now she had my attention. I relaxed a bit, curious beyond the normal. "What was it?"

"He…" Victtra rubbed her face with the back of her arm. She quickly calmed herself, but for a short moment, she was flushed and neck-holes flaring. "I can't ever forgive him. And if you're planning on doing something soon, I need want to know the details. I want to help."

I gritted my teeth, on the verge of accepting her help. But should I? It was such a risk keeping her close. And she was still a child. As much as I feared she would find out my past deeds, I had also grown slightly fond of her.

Slightly.

If she died on this outing, it would be to my benefit. Especially if she were ultimately accused of Lone's murder. Nothing would be a better alibi than Victtra. If she killed Lone because she blamed him for her father's death, no one would come investigating the *Star Marque*. It'd be a closed case.

"You might not like what you see," I said, my voice low.

"I've seen my father killed right in front of my eyes."

Damn. She was right.

"You might not come back." I stepped around the desk. "It's dangerous."

"I know. But so was getting into the starfighter and helping you defeat that vanguard-class ship."

Victtra really wanted this. I didn't even know what she found on the recording, but whatever it was, that was enough to fuel her own vendetta.

"Fine," I eventually whispered. "You can stay with me on Vectin-10. But if you do, you have to give Sawyer everything you've collected on us. All audio files. *Anything else you might have.*"

Her lip twitched, but then she regained control and nodded once. "Very well. I will. I don't have much, just enough to put the pieces together."

"Sawyer will bring you up to speed on what we're doing. The *Star Marque* will be leaving to run a transport delivery assignment, and we'll stay here."

THIRTY-SIX

The Dead Dead Zone

A day later, Cai had gotten me everything I'd need to impersonate the rebellion.

The plan was simple: head down to the planet, get into the dead zone, change into our outfits, send our fake messages, and kill Lone. If everything went well, we'd be destroying the dead zone afterward, so that no unnecessary evidence was left behind.

Endellion would ultimately live with our plan, and she would report everything to the official authorities about how rebellion humans came for her life. And how Lone died during the conflict, heroically doing what no others would.

I left my starship with Victtra in tow. The plan running through my thoughts several times. No one else joined me because Victtra, which was for the best. Not even Sawyer. I couldn't take her—she had to watch the ship, along with Lysander, to make sure everything went correctly.

Victtra wasn't human, but because she was young, she was still the height of a human adult. With her enviro-suit on, no one would suspect she was anything other than an average adult human.

I checked my PAD as I headed to the dead zone. I had ten messages from the crew, but nothing was marked urgent. I sat inside a luxury car on a mag-lev train, traveling at increasable speeds for a planet. The cool temperature control kept me comfortable, even as we zipped through the desert.

I clicked through my messages.

They thought I was still on the ship, just confined to quarters to recover from an injury.

Melba had sent me a report regarding the other starfighters. She hadn't done that before. She had just done her own thing, ignoring me completely, but now she had numbers, statistic, and hours recorded for training. She had worked with Noah on his accuracy, and worked with Asahi and Hattie on their assertiveness.

I read through the report with a slight smile.

She also brought up Victtra, and how she missed the superhuman's presence in training. That was new, and unexpected. Melba and her small crew integrating with everyone—even getting along with the superhuman?—it was practically unthinkable.

The next message was from Noah. It wasn't anything relevant, it was just a casual note about his time on the ship, and wishing me well. He mentioned Mara in every other sentence, even going so far as referring them as "we" when talking about certain events.

I wished I could've spent more time with him on the ship before heading out.

Just as he was getting better…

Olivia had sent me a message. Yup. My newest officer—*the* financial bigshot. Even her notes to me were more numbers than words. It was an itemized list of suggested repairs to the *Star Marque* along with some potential cutbacks to save credits.

I'd have to let her know I was planning on increasing the size of the crew, not scale it down.

My next message was from Dr. Clay. At first, I almost didn't open it. Did I really want to read a report from him?

Eventually—because I had several hours to kill—I gave it a quick read.

It was a medical report. As I read the details, I smiled to myself. Dr. Clay had focused his efforts on genetic defects, and with all the medical supplies we had purchased, he was able to synthesize treatments that would help both Lysander and Noah.

He even wrote a long paragraph at the end about how the medication would be used on anyone with weak membranes in their body. It meant we'd probably be able to bring on more defects in the future, even if they weren't typically allowed as crewmembers aboard enforcer ships.

He even wrote, "I hope your trip goes well," at the end of the message.

I was legitimately shocked.

"Are you okay, Demarco?" Sawyer asked over my PAD.

I glanced around the train car. Victtra sat at the other end, her gaze on the windows. She barely moved, and she didn't glance over in my direction, not even when I cleared my throat.

"Yeah," I muttered, my voice low. "Why?"

"You've been quiet for a while, I was just curious."

I brought my PAD up close to my mouth. "Miss me already?"

"Of course. Blub misses you, too." I heard her poking away at something in the background. "Lysander is worried about you. He's constantly asking me for a status update. I think he might be more worried than me."

"That's adorable. Tell Sanders I'll be back to cuddle him to sleep shortly."

Although Sawyer didn't laugh, I heard the smile in her voice as she said, "I'll send him that audio clip, for sure."

If I had my way, I would've spoken to Sawyer like that forever.

But I didn't have the luxury.

"Have you heard from Endellion?" I asked.

"No. She's limited all communication. The plan, from my understanding, is that you'll have the weapons and devices to hurt superhumans once you reach the dead zone. Then you'll need to wait for her and Lone to show."

"I understand."

"And Demarco… Please be careful. This is Endellion we're talking about. She might do something unexpected."

"Don't worry about me," I said. "I'll be back on the *Star Marque* before you know it."

But she was right. I was worried. Endellion was capable of anything—even killing millions of innocent lives to get what she wanted. I couldn't get comfortable. I couldn't let me guard down.

And as soon as I see him, I have to attack.

"Good luck, Demarco."

"I'm a badass. I don't need luck."

"It's a shame we can't weaponize your hubris. No superhuman would stand a chance then."

I snorted back a laugh. Then I leaned against my seat. "You're hilarious. But you don't have to worry. I got this."

"If I hadn't been there at Capital Station, I fear you might've died," Sawyer whispered into the speaker.

I gritted my teeth, knowing she was right. But I had to be confident. Not for my ego, but so that no one else worried.

"This time I'm not doing this for myself, or even for Endellion. I'm doing it for *you*, Sawyer. I'll make sure everything goes as planned."

For a long time, she said nothing. I almost worried she hadn't heard me, or that my statement had upset her, for some reason.

"Thank you, Demarco," she eventually said, her voice strained. "You're… special to me."

I smiled, knowing that she must've really meant it if she voiced all those words. In that moment, I thought back to what Sawyer had done for me just as Capital Station was crashing. She had been there for me. Saved me.

And now I wanted to return the favor.

VICTTRA and I arrived at the new dead zone a day before Endellion and the general.

This wasn't a villa, like Lone's little hidey-hole in the ground. This was a warehouse. A massive storage facility used to hide goods and arms. Victtra and I didn't take a shuttle down to our location, we took a mineshaft elevator, the uncomfortable kind, but at least it was spacious. It was just a large grate platform that descended into the darkness of the planet.

It amused me how similar a planet was to space. The moment we got deep, there was no light, no comfort, no safety outside of technology. The atmosphere wouldn't really support us, and some-times the pressures or gases could be dangerous—just like space.

And I hated space.

At least Lone's villa had been filled with windows that tricked me into thinking I was still on the surface. This warehouse hit me with reality harder than a punch to the face. The steel walls, the sweltering rooms, the old-style tech, latch doors with hinges, small personal trains and trams, and hot steam being pumping into vents toward the surface all reminded me that this was deep in the ground, away from all comforts and safeties.

Some gases could be dangerous when trapped underground. It was fantastic this grimy place had a ventilation system.

Steel crates—giant cubes of metal, basically—were stacked in the underground space at least three high. Machines were built into the walls that could lift and lower tons of weight. Some of them looked sadist, with sharp points meant for hooking onto the crates. What a horror show of a facility.

I carried with me the bare essentials. I couldn't carry plasma weapons of any kind, because of the securities measures above ground. Most scanners were attuned to the ionized gas that plasma rifles and blades had contained within.

So I had a pair of steel knives and a laser pistol. They didn't have the stopping power of plasma, but they'd do the trick. Steel knives—the eighteen-centimeter kind—could cut through an enviro-suit. And lasers would eventually do the trick. If I managed to catch Lone without any protection, the laser would become a more viable weapon.

When the lift reached the bottom, the grate door opened on its own, slow and powered through a personal battery, rather than through the warehouse's electricity.

"I don't like the grime of this place," Victtra stated as she rubbed her nose.

I understood. The place stank of sweat and anger.

Only twenty-one people worked the massive 15,000 square meter warehouse. I suspected only one of them was designated "cleaning staff" which resulted in the terrible odors.

"You're a little too prissy," I said as I stepped off the lift and into the ghost town of a warehouse. "If you're going to be an enforcer, you have to be used to getting your hands dirty."

"Getting dirty isn't actually necessary." Victtra followed me with confident steps. "If I'm good enough, I can do things organized, efficient, and cleanly. That's the mark of a true expert, you know. Precision."

"Spoken like a true non-combatant." I snorted and laughed when her nose holes flared. "Look, when a master painter creates a painting, he does so in solitude, and with paints and a canvas that don't fight back. Sure, he can use precision. But when you fight someone—real combat—people will try to stop you with everything they have. And if you respect the dangers of the job, you'll know that their desperation is likely going to make the whole ordeal difficult."

She threw back her silvery hair, irritation in her blue eyes. "Not everything needs to be so dramatic. My father worked with politicians."

"Don't repeat the mistakes of your father," I muttered, my voice dark and low. "You already know the punchline to his story."

Victtra held her breath for a long moment as she mulled over my words. I thought she would be upset, but it was opposite. She turned to me, her expression calmer than before. "I see what you mean, Captain Demarco. Thank you. For opening my eyes to new ways of thinking. I fear my schooling with other superhumans may have led to… Overconfidence."

"Overconfidence can be a killer. But never let go of regular confidence, kid. You'll need that to fuel yourself. To keep moving forward, even when others tell you it's insane."

"Like how I'm continuing to try to find my father's killer."

Now it was my turn to be silent.

I wanted her to find Ontwenty, but part of me hoped she never found out anything related to me. Although… Perhaps I would just tell her one day. I kept going back and forth on it, whether I would say anything or not.

Currently, I opted to remain quiet.

Victtra and I entered the warehouse and went straight for the one of the locker rooms. Endellion had provided us codes and access to all the security measures. Now all we had to do was set up, avoid the workers, and wait for General Lone.

VICTTRA and I waited for the time to pass. We didn't have access to any communications in the dead zone. I couldn't call Sawyer, or talk to Lysander, or ask how Noah was doing with Mara. I just had to wait. Fortunately, I had a few articles on my PAD I wanted to read, like how murder investigations were handled on Vectin-10.

Apparently, there was different rules for investigating the murder of superhumans. Anyone with the designation of Homo superior had to have their murder investigated by another member of Homo superior, and someone trained in forensic science.

Lucky me.

When I had murdered Victtra's father, Minister Ontwenty had hidden most of the details. She hadn't wanted anyone to figure out what was going on, and with her superhuman status, she made sure we weren't caught.

What would Endellion be able to do? She didn't have the status of superhuman. And all of them wanted to see her fail.

I clicked through my PAD, sifting through some of the articles I had downloaded about her. Endellion had opened the mines back up, increasing jobs to humans. She had hired enforcer ships—specifically ones run by all human crews—and even submitted several petitions to open government positions back up to Homo sapiens.

Her short time in office—almost a year and half at this point—had been filled with one drastic change after another. She had no sign of stopping.

No wonder the superhumans hated her.

Endellion…

Even I was starting to think that maybe her plan to change things all along.

Then I shook my head, hating myself for doubting. That was Endellion's special power. She always manipulated things in her favor. She just manipulating people. She needed *someone's* support, and since the superhumans weren't going to help her, she was basically reaching out to the only group left—humanity.

If she could convince the majority of Homo sapiens that she was on *their* side, perhaps she could get real change made. Maybe a superhuman or two would eventually come to her for help, and then they'd create their own power bloc.

I closed my eyes and laughed to myself, my voice echoing in the cold, dark room of the warehouse.

"You really are a master manipulator," I said to no one.

I was probably going insane.

Here I was, doing actually what I had done when I had been working for Endellion.

No. It wasn't the same. I closed my eyes and pictured Sawyer, and the scars on her body, and the way Helia looked at me when she had been in the healing vat.

When I had killed Emissary Barten, it had been cold and passionless. He had been an obstacle to Ontwenty's goals. But General Lone wasn't like that. I wanted him dead because he was a sadist asshole who had it coming. He hated humans. He planned to create them for his own twisted use. And now he needed to go.

If anything, this was the *opposite* of what I had done for Endellion.

She had kept herself uninvested in everything. She never mingled with her crew. She manipulated everyone into helping her achieve her own goals, and she didn't care.

She almost killed us all in order to get what she wanted.

I wouldn't do that.

I was different.

And I was about to prove it. One way or another. I would.

THIRTY-SEVEN

Fate And Destiny

Endellion was the first to arrive at the secret rendezvous.

I stayed out of sight, in one of the worker facilities that had been sealed years prior. Endellion had provided us the access code to get in, and it was the perfect hiding spot. The room was attached to the main storage area and the portable generator room. Plus, Victtra and I could access the onsite computer system.

The computers didn't speak with the outside world, however. I still had no way to communicate with the surface, but it allowed me to keep track of everything happening inside the underground warehouse.

We also had access to one of the portable power generators, thanks to a keycode Endellion had provided us. It only powered half the warehouse—the personnel rooms, all the lights in the ware-house, and the main storage area. Once we turned it off, everything would be chaos.

The generator didn't provide power for the lifts, or the machines used for heavy lifting. Which was fortunate. We would need the lift to escape.

The generator itself was ancient. It was the size of a starfighter, large enough to allow a man to fully climb inside. All the modern portable generators didn't need any of that—they were small storage units of energy that could last for months, sometimes years, if they were exposed to the light of the nearby suns.

I sat in a rusted chair that could no longer swivel, my attention focused on the flickering screen. It gave me a readout of the temperature and the number of containers processed together. It also displayed the camera feed from the only three working cameras.

Endellion's "secret weapon" was already in the sealed room. Someone had placed it there ahead of time, though I wasn't sure who. Most likely one of her minions.

The device was a handheld bomb. Not the explosive kind, but the EMP kind—the type of bomb that emitted an electrical pulse that disrupted electronics in the nearby area. If I used it around Lone, it would supposedly incapacitate him for a short period of time—long enough for me to kill him.

I'd have to make sure I didn't use it around Victtra, however.

Endellion had arrived with limited staff, but I recognized a few of them. The bald man was none other than Commodore Grayson, the military asshole who worked under Lone. Obviously, Endellion had to know that. So why bring him? Was it to make Lone feel more secure with the meeting?

Probably.

Her small group of personnel included a child—more like a babe, but whatever. The kid had to be less than a year old. It was swaddled in temperature-regulating blankets and kept in the care of a single nurse the entire time.

Why bring something like that? Was it to get Lone to drop his guard? Perhaps he wouldn't think we were capable of violence if there was a child nearby.

Endellion had a few laser rifles, though. Nothing plasma. She didn't want to be caught without a means to defend herself, obviously.

Victtra stood with me in the tiny room, her hands constantly rubbing at her nose. "I never want to be underground ever again."

"Agreed," I muttered as I watched the computer display. "It's almost time."

Victtra walked over and stared at the computer screen. "Is that the planet governor?"

"That's right."

"And you hate her? Because she wronged you?"

I nodded once. "Because she used me. Like a tool. And then wanted to throw away everything we had worked on together."

"Used you?"

"That's right. I was just her pawn in some grand scheme." I scoffed and shook my head. "I didn't realize how far she would go until it was too late."

"You're so vague." Victtra crossed her arms. "Why won't you just admit the details? Or are they so horrific that you can't speak them aloud?"

"They're so horrific that I can't speak them aloud," I said, emotionless.

She said nothing after that, her lips pursed. But then she exhaled, her whole body returning to casual posture.

Victtra placed a delicate hand on my shoulder. I tensed at her touch, but quickly relaxed.

"You've helped me so much," Victtra whispered. "If it weren't for you, I wouldn't even be here. If you need help fighting against Governor Voight, you can count on me."

What an innocent offer.

I wanted to take it, I really did. But I couldn't stoop so low.

I pushed her hand off my shoulder. "Victtra… I don't think you understand. My hate runs deep. You should focus on your own. It's best we don't intertwine our hatred."

She took back her hand and balled it into a tight fist. "Clevon, do you believe in things like *fate* and *destiny*?"

I leaned back in the rusted chair. It creaked in agony, but I didn't care. My thoughts dwelled on my first name. No one called me *Clevon*. Except my old gang associates—the dead ones on Capital Station—and Endellion. She always called me Clevon, no matter what anyone else did.

Now Victtra…

"My father dedicated his whole life to advocating for a peaceful future where Homo sapiens and Homo superior could live together, no restrictions or complications between them. He gave several speeches on the matter and wanted to mend the divide between the Federation and the humans of the rebellion. I never understood… I mean, I *understood*, but not really."

I turned to her, though I said nothing.

She continued, "I had never known any Homo sapiens other than the ones who worked for my father. I had never interacted with them or listened to their stories. I thought they were more like pets we needed to care for—nothing like reality. I sometimes think that stepping onto the *Star Marque* is one of the best decisions I've ever made."

With an unsteady hand, I rubbed at my jaw, my stubble rough.

"I never knew what kind of hardships Homo sapiens had to deal with," Victtra muttered. "Or why my father cared so much, when so many Homo superior didn't. I think it's because we're separated— my father was right all along."

"Concepts like *destiny* and *fate* are for the simpleminded," I said with a forced chuckle. "I've never heard a superhuman talk about them like they were real." With a snap of my fingers, I turned back to the computer screen. "Stay focused. Things might get rough."

"I'm ready."

"Once Lone gets here, we'll set off the mini-EMP. He'll collapse, we'll kill him, and then leave on the lift. This needs to be quick and dirty."

"What about witnesses?"

"We want as many as possible," I said. "So they can't blame Endellion for his death." I turned to her, my gaze hardened. "I'm going to attack Endellion during the commotion."

If I actually killed her during the commotion, that would be preferred, but I doubted I would get the chance. Instead, I just wanted to make it appear as though she were the target.

Victtra paced the small room, her intelligent eyes flicking from the rust patches to the dusty floors, to the dilapidated seats. "The day my father was murdered, it was just the two of us."

I gritted my teeth, irritated that she had managed to bring the conversation back to uncomfortable topics no matter what we were doing.

"Oh, yeah?" I managed to say. "I'm sorry to hear that."

Victtra nodded once. "I made sure to always have two guards, to avoid ever being alone with just one other person… And when Dellin told me he was going to transfer to the *Star Marque,* I thought it was more than coincidence."

The more she spoke, the more I thought her naïve. She was still young. I kept forgetting. Part of me wanted to tell her the world was cruel, and fate unkind. It had brought her straight to her father's killer, after all—only to hide that fact from her. Fate was a sadist.

"Let's just stay quiet until it's time," I said as I pulled the hood of my white enviro-suit over my head. The helmet hardened and snapped into place. "Once we've dealt with Lone, we'll be setting fire to the warehouse."

It was a simple technique used by most thugs on Capital Station. Burn everything. It made identifying anything all the harder. And if we were lucky, this whole place would become so damaged, it would start to collapse.

Then they'd find nothing.

IT DIDN'T TAKE General Lone much longer to arrive. A couple of hours, at the most, though I hadn't been paying attention. He arrived in formal military attire—not an enviro-suit—and I wondered if he thought he was slick in his white slacks and crisp, decorated jacket or if he was just arrogant.

Victtra and I were ready the moment I saw Lone enter the central room of the underground warehouse. Like Endellion, he had a small entourage of six individuals, four of which were human. Lone, too, had laser weapons with him—so did the two superhumans who stood by his side. Their rifles were larger, and capable of burning through flesh within a fraction of a second, but still not as dangerous as some of the cheap plasma weapons.

Lone was being cautious. But not *too* cautious. He had also brought along a child. Not as young as Endellion's, but still.

It was Fae, the little Sawyer-clone girl.

Lone was such a disgusting pig. How could he have brought her to something like this? It boiled my blood all over again. But I needed to stick to the plan.

With my heart beating in my ears, I waited at the computer, watching his movements. Victtra sat close, her eyes narrowed. We needed Lone to be in a specific part of the warehouse. We'd cut the power, trap him, and then attack.

Our ancient computer didn't have audio, so when Lone and Endellion met, all I could do was watch their body language. Endellion kept her helmet up, never revealing her face, no matter how long the conversation dragged, or how many other people removed their face coverings. Lone was all smiles and slight touches, his careful movements almost calculated.

Victtra went to the back of the grimy room and placed her slender fingers onto the power generator's control panel. "Whenever you're ready."

I held my breath and nodded.

The members of their entourages were mostly political—small, slender, dressed to impress rather than to protect. They moved from room to room of the disgusting warehouse, some of them obviously searching for accommodations befitting their station. They would find none. All I cared about was their physical locations.

"Now," I said.

Victtra poked at the controls of the power generator. It beeped a warning, and she entered the override Endellion had provided us. The majority of the warehouse was plunged into darkness. The underground was cold and merciless, and the pitch black was impossible to see through.

Superhumans still had the advantage, however. Victtra could sense my movement with her special organ, giving her a sixth sense when it came to fighting in the void. My muscles—and nerves, and brain—all used low levels of electrical currents, which she could sense.

Lone could as well.

So could Endellion, due her cybernetic implant that allowed her to simulate an ampullae of Lorenzini organ. Just like superhumans, Endellion possessed electromagnetism, the ability to sense electrical pulses.

I grabbed the personal EMP device and tapped the side of my enviro-suit helmet. The white suits were cheap, and the visor didn't have any advanced scanning options. It lit up and showed me infrared heat signatures, also allowing me to see in the darkness, but it wasn't detailed data, and I would likely lose it after I set off our trap.

EMPs caused most electrical devices to fail.

Which was why I had brought along a low-tech flashlight, just for this very situation.

The steel casing around the flashlight's batteries would protect it from the low-level pulse of the EMP device. I'd still be able to see, and since the other power generator was out of the EMP's range, I wouldn't run the risk of trapping myself in the underground.

I had thought this out. Endellion would be proud.

"Wait here," I commanded Victtra.

If she were incapacitated by the EMP, I could lose her.

Bathed in darkness, I made my way to the door. Its low-tech hinges meant we could still open it, even without power, and I rushed out of the abandoned room and into the main warehouse. The infrared vision highlighted the heating vents and the people, but I was surprised by the color intensity of a few individuals. Lone, and to a lesser degree, his two superhuman buddies, stuck out like a dead fish in a salad.

And Endellion…

Her cyborg body was mostly machine, and my visor read her heated silhouette much differently than the others'.

"What's happening?" someone asked, their masculine voice echoing in the warehouse.

"*It's a trap,*" a woman shouted. "A coup! The sapiens can't be trusted!"

Violence exploded throughout the dead zone long before I even reached my intended target. The flashes of laser fire caught me momentarily off guard. For some reason, when I had imagined the fight, I hadn't pictured Endellion's and Lone's teams attacking each other.

I was such an idiot for not seeing this.

Lasers shot through the air at rapid speeds, too quick to dodge. Instead, I took cover behind one of the steel crates. Shouts filled the warehouse, and to my surprise, my enviro-suit flashed a warning across the visor.

Gas.

Methane.

Someone had likely damaged one of the warehouse's venting systems. Normally, underground gases were shifted upward, to prevent death and explosions. But now the air was rapidly filling with the dangerous gas.

1%.

My visor continually flashed a warning. Once the methane reached levels above 4%, it was likely to explode. If the levels grew to 9.5%, the gas would erupt with even a slight spark or naked flame.

The lasers were hot enough to ignite the methane.

Fuck me.

This wasn't how I had wanted to start the showdown.

Several of the humans were shot and killed. When I glanced around the crate, my gaze fell immediately on the smallest of heat signatures. Fae and the little child who Endellion had brought.

I was worried about Fae—she covered her head and hurried behind one of the shipping containers. Perhaps she was screaming, I couldn't tell over the sheer commotion. Several warehouse workers shouted, one hit an alarm, and three had gotten shot on their way to the lift. The fire of the rifles, along with the shrieking of betrayal, also added to the music of chaos.

The babe...

I wouldn't have paid attention to it except for the fact that Endellion rushed to the child's side immediately. Lasers flew in multiple directions, lighting up the underground.

The moment I could leave the safety of the crate and get closer to Lone, I did. The EMP had a radius of fifteen meters. I had to be close enough if I wanted to get Lone.

Once my visor said I was within range, I activated the device.

There was no real visual component to the weapon, but I felt a surge of power rush through my body. My visor blinked and went dead for a short moment, since it had been affected by the EMP. My enviro-suit had to take a second to reboot and start back up.

For that short timeframe, I was blind. I couldn't even tell if my EMP had incapacitated Lone or not. The shouting disappeared— the speakers and microphone built into the suit weren't functioning. It was like I had suddenly fallen into a death-like void.

Then my suit rebooted, and all my senses were assaulted at once.

"The lifts! Get to the lifts!"

"*The rifles aren't working!*"

"General Lone!"

4% methane levels.

The infrared scanner in my visor was blinking and flickering everywhere. I couldn't see clearly. The cheap ass enviro-suit had been damaged from the EMP, and the heat signatures of everyone were all over the place.

I tapped the side of my helmet, trying to inform Victtra that she could emerge from the room and not be harmed, but I wasn't sure if the message was transmitted.

Determined to see this through, I pulled out one of my steel knives. Although the infrared wasn't working properly, the superhumans—and Endellion—were still the brightest things in the massive underground room. All the other heat signatures were blurs that seemingly teleported around.

Thankfully, all the superhumans were lying on the floor.

The EMP had done exactly what it was supposed to do. The special organ in the superhumans' heads had been disturbed by Endellion's special EMP, rendering them helpless for a short period of time.

I ran to the first superhuman, my knife held high. When I

reached the body, I stabbed downward, striking into the super-human over and over. I could imagine the man's blood, but I couldn't see or feel it. The enviro-suit kept me sealed away from the problems all around me.

Again and again. The man couldn't move. He simply twitched and writhed, unable to get control of his body.

6% methane gas.

Why were the gas levels rising so quickly? Was there a bigger leak than I had imagined? Were the vents just not working at all?

I stood, my legs shaky. Had I killed Lone? I didn't know. All I knew was that I had stabbed a superhuman.

The laser fire started picking up again. The rifles must've come back online. Which meant the superhumans would likely be able to stand again, no doubt in my mind.

I ran for the next asshole on the floor, but that was when I felt the sear of agony shoot through my side. I grunted as I fell forward, straight onto the face of the superhuman below me. Someone had shot me.

With a shaky hand, I grabbed at my leg. My enviro-suit flashed more warnings. My suit was compromised, and now I was bleeding. Technically, enviro-suits were capable of limiting blood loss. They could constrict slightly around injuries, to help stifle blood flow.

But mine was cheap and could barely hold itself together. It just flashed warning, blocking my already terrible vision with messages that recommended I see a doctor.

Ya think, *suit?* Thank you so much for fucking with me! Very helpful.

With my teeth gritted, I got to my feet. My visor flickered, and a fourth superhuman came into view. At first, I was ready to attack, but then I shook my head to dispel the bloodthirsty thoughts. That was Victtra.

She ran to the machine controls on the far wall.

Power was still flowing to those machines, thanks to the second power generator. And my visor could still detect the electronics in the room, even if it was having a hard time with heat signatures.

Both the superhumans on the floor managed to stand—one

practically leapt to his feet, and I knew that had to be Lone. Through my shitty visor, he just looked like a blob of white and orange.

I had lost my window of opportunity to kill him while he had been incapacitated, though.

But perhaps I could still take him by surprise. I lunged forward, knife ready. Lone moved out of the way, and with my visor flicking, I could barely tell what he was doing. I swung wildly, hoping to strike the man, but no matter how hard I slashed, I couldn't connect.

More laser fire flew through the room.

I stumbled backward, and Lone followed. A powerful fist struck the side of my head. Expensive suits limited kinetic damage by dampening strikes, but not *this* suit. I felt that punch all the way in the roots of my teeth.

I hit the floor, my breathing ragged, and the visor flashed even more warnings.

When Lone's heat signature came lumbering for me, I managed to force myself into a standing position. Before Lone could throw another punch, I dove out of the way. The steel crates were barely visible with my terrible visor, but I managed to duck behind one before more laser fire could tear through my leg.

To my horror, Lone pursued. He grabbed my arm, yanked me out of cover, and then threw me into the middle of the room, his strength so considerable, I felt like a ragdoll. When I hit the floor, my vision went black for a split second.

A terrifying split second.

Everyone was running around and shouting, and besides Lone, I really couldn't distinguish anything. I shoved myself to my feet and held my knife ready.

That was when I saw it.

The machines on the wall—the ones with hooks used to haul the steel crates—moved around. Victtra stood at the controls, no doubt in my mind. A hook moved down toward us, behind Lone. It was large enough, and made of such sturdy metal, that it could easily puncture a man. Did he see it coming? He didn't react to it.

When Lone got close, I swung with my blade. He dodged back-ward. So I did it again.

Victtra kept the machine moving toward him. It wasn't as fast as I would have liked, but it was large enough that—as long as she struck him—it could be lethal.

The second time I swung, Lone grabbed my wrist and twisted. I groaned and dropped the blade, but as he went to retrieve it, I shoved him with all my might. Lone stumbled—never losing his footing—and said something I couldn't hear over the commotion.

And then the hook of the machine caught his arm. Victtra had stabbed his left bicep and was jerking him backward.

Lone struggled with the machine, obviously trying to pull himself free.

The machine began to move upward, and Lone focused all his efforts into unhooking his flesh.

With frantic movements, I knelt and searched the ground for my knife, trying to find my weapon so I could end this monster. My visor was nothing but white, orange, and red, and it made it difficult to find the inanimate object.

I managed to grab my weapon right as another superhuman lunged for me. I stabbed upward, but we both tumbled back to the floor. The superhuman crashed on top of me. Winded, I tried to shove him off, but he punched downward, cracking my visor from the sheer brute force.

Another punch. And another.

Damn. My vision was going again.

I went limp, and the superhuman stopped. In the confusion, and panic, the man leapt off me and ran straight for Lone, obviously not caring whether I lived or died.

Too bad for that sad sack I had been faking.

With all my willpower, I got back to my feet. I figured—with my suit on—the superhuman couldn't see how well I was faring. And since he had probably assumed he had been beating me senseless, the moment I had stopped resisting, he must have just assumed I had been knocked unconscious or had died.

I still had my knife. I gripped the hilt with everything I had.

Then I stalked up behind the second superhuman and stabbed straight into his back. Well, I assumed it was his back. It could've been his stomach. Either way, my blade went so deep, I felt the heat of his blood on my knuckles.

He collapsed to the ground, writhed a bit, and then stopped moving.

With him out of the way, I went straight for Lone.

9.5% methane levels.

My heart skipped a beat.

And then an explosion erupted throughout the warehouse. The floors shook, crates were knocked off their stacks and crashed all around us. They were so big and heavy, that several people were crushed underneath one—their screams cut off mid-cry in one of the most disturbing sounds I had ever heard in my life.

The heat readings from my visor intensified.

We needed to leave. Right now. Before we were all buried in this dead zone.

But I couldn't go without finishing Lone.

With ragged breaths, I turned toward what I thought was Lone's heat signature and stabbed with my knife. I had to use my imagination when I pictured my attack. The blade struck something, but I wasn't sure what. I stabbed again, and again, hoping I was ripping into his body.

Then Lone grabbed me. His large hands wrapped around my head, and then around my neck. At first, I thought he was going to pop my skull straight from my shoulders, but that didn't happen. He closed his grip around my windpipe, crushing my neck, suit and all, until I couldn't breathe.

Hell, I couldn't *think*—his hold on me was so great, I thought he might have been one of the machines mounted to the wall.

"You won't kill *me*, insect," Lone growled, his voice distinct, even when soaked with rage. "I've lived too long, fought too many ingrates, to be stopped by the likes of *you*."

I would've offered something as a retort, if I hadn't been losing blood flow to my brain. My vision tunneled, my suit flashed more warnings about my health, and all I could do was weakly stab at his arms with my knife.

I got him. I could feel it. But he never loosened his grip.

What a sadistic bastard. With each half second, he squeezed tighter and tighter.

Was this how he had hurt Sawyer?

That one thought… It filled me with a rage so intense, I managed to thrust at where his head was. I probably got his face, because he screamed and suddenly released me.

I hit the floor and gulped down air.

Then my visor showed the heat of the wall machine crane down and strike Lone again. I didn't know what *exactly* happened, because I still couldn't see details, but it seemed that the machine knocked the man out. He crumpled to the floor, unmoving.

I couldn't take a chance. With anger fueling my actions, I lunged for him. After a few stabs to his neck, shoulders, and chest, I was satisfied. Nothing could've lived through that. I hit the floor on my knees, still breathing deep.

Fires caused my visor to give me all new readouts. The methane was still a problem, and another explosion rocked the warehouse. I almost couldn't stand due to all the shaking.

More crates fell, creating a disturbing echo throughout the warehouse.

Someone came to help me. They grabbed my arm and yanked me up.

"We have to go, Clevon," Victtra's voice said.

I stumbled and then fell again, my one leg weak. That laser blast had taken its toll, and after all the fighting, I was a little too weak to force myself to walk.

"Get to the lift," I commanded.

"I'm not leaving you."

The roar of fire and the creaking of strained metal was enough to send shivers down my spine.

It reminded me of Capital Station. The heat, the intensity. For some reason, whenever I was around Endellion, the worst came to pass.

I would die here.

"Victtra," I said. "*Leave.* Go. To the lift."

She grabbed my arm and pulled me to my feet. She was strong —obviously, she was a superhuman—and she practically dragged me toward the exit.

"We have to go," she said.

"You'll die along with me, fool. *Get out of here.*"

"We're a team, aren't we?" she said, mimicking my own words right back at me. "We help each other. I'll carry you, if I have to."

What kind of cruel mistress was fate? The daughter of Emissary Barten was risking her life to save mine? It was too much. In that moment—with my head spinning, and the dangers rapidly closing in all around me—I had to tell her.

I didn't want to die knowing I had treated her like Endellion had treated me.

"Leave me," I commanded. "We're not a team." I took in a deep breath, my lungs and throat burning. "*It was me*, Victtra. *Me.* I killed your father. I was the man who assassinated Barten."

THIRTY-EIGHT

The Lift

Victtra held me close.

My head spun. The world wasn't right. My leg burned from the laser blast, and my neck felt like a crushed piece of fruit. Would I even make it up the lift? Part of me doubted it. I wished I could've spoken to Sawyer one last time. But I didn't have that option.

"It couldn't have been you," Victtra said, the symphony of destruction all around us.

I couldn't see. My visor flickered out, leaving me with nothing but blackness.

Unwilling to die blind, I yanked at the enviro-suit helmet and unlocked the base. It fell from my head, returning to its hood form.

The warehouse was bright with fire and mayhem.

Victtra released me, and I hit the floor on one knee. The smoke and debris made it difficult to breathe.

"It was me," I finally coughed out. "Endellion was… asked to kill the emissary…"

It was difficult to speak.

I had wanted to explain to her before, but I couldn't find the words. Now if felt easy.

"You killed my father?" Victtra's voice sounded so distant. "Because…"

"Ontwenty… Endellion… I was their tool."

I never wanted to be used like that again. But now wasn't the time for those thoughts.

What did Victtra think? What did she want? I half expected her to stab me with my own knife, and then run to the lift and exit this hellhole.

But that never happened.

Instead, she grabbed my arm again, and helped me back to my feet. Without a word, she dragged me through the smoky heat and flickering fires, personally taking me to the lifts on the other side of the massive warehouse.

Coughing and wheezing the entire time, I simply allowed Victtra to take me where she pleased. With my knife in hand, I thought of many options. I could stab her and flee on my own. I could stab myself and end it now.

I could even search out all of Lone's associates and kill them, too.

Wait.

Fae.

I jerked my arm free of Victtra's grasp.

"*Fae!*" I shouted. "*Fae!* Where are you?"

Victtra said nothing as she stood next to me. She, too, coughed, but at less of a rate. Superhumans had natural filters in their body that allowed them to breathe smoke and debris without much difficulty. I would pass out and die long before she was inconvenienced.

"Fae! Please! Follow the sound of my voice!"

Was she even still alive? I couldn't leave her here. I just couldn't.

"Help!" a small voice came from somewhere in the warehouse. "Please!"

With one good leg, and one shaky leg, I stumbled toward the sound of her voice. Victtra stayed close, never leaving me. The smoke, fires, and rumbling grew worse. I couldn't hear any shouting anymore, and I suspected the vast majority of the fools were either dead or up the lifts already.

I hurried through the heat and smoke, giving very little damn about my own life. I was still waiting for Victtra to end me at any moment. It would happen. I was sure of it.

"Help!" Fae shouted.

I reached her at the speed of a hobble, and once I got close, she ran to my side. With a grunt, I lifted her into my arms. She wasn't heavy, but I was drained from the fighting. My white enviro-suit was coated with so much blood, I thought I was wearing a red suit for a moment.

Fae wrapped her arms around my sore neck, and I grimaced as I turned around and continued for the lifts. It wasn't far. We were almost there. We'd escape. Surely, we would.

Victtra, Fae, and I went all way to the industrial lifts. There were three remaining, but the closest one was in the midst of departure. I stumbled forward, ready to throw my knife at the bastard trying to leave without us, when I caught my breath.

Endellion.

She stood in the lift, bathed in the single light that still had power, holding a small babe in her arms.

"Clevon," she said. "Find another lift."

The warehouse rumbled again, and the light flickered.

"Are you serious?" I rasped. "Let us up."

"I'm sorry. I can't risk anything happening to our child."

Endellion held up a laser pistol with her other hand.

Our child?

Victtra grabbed my arm and squeezed tightly. Fae softly sobbed into my collarbone, her whole body trembling in my grasp.

There were other lifts. We could leave. We didn't need to go with Endellion. But why was she calling the child *ours?* We had never had any kids. Sure, we had messed around, but—

"I'm sorry I never told you, Clevon," Endellion said as the grate doors started their closing process. "I used a uterine replica so I wouldn't have to carry the boy. I had hoped to show you, but obviously, that won't be happening."

The door shut with no more words between us.

My child? I couldn't believe what she had done. Even after all of this—even now—she had somehow managed to surprise me. I couldn't wrap my head around the concept. So I didn't even bother. I pushed it from my thoughts, my pulse already quick.

The lift left without us, and although Victtra had said nothing so far, she quickly helped me to the next lift and dragged me inside. She operated the lift on her own, tapping away at the controls and shutting the door in record time.

I leaned my back against the grating of the lift wall and then slid down into a sitting position, Fae still tightly wrapped around my neck. It was difficult to get enough air, but I didn't care. I closed my eyes, my heart slamming against my ribs.

A single light shone overhead, casting harsh shadows over Victtra's face.

"You killed him?" she whispered as we went upward, her voice barely audible between the clicking of the lift's motors. "You killed my father?"

"That's right," I said as I let Fae go. "It was me."

I pushed Fae away from me, knowing this was going to turn into my final conflict. We were trapped in a perfectly square lift with nowhere to go. Victtra would surely kill me. No doubt in my mind.

But when Victtra turned to me, her eyes were glassy, and her fists clenched. "Why did you let me live?"

I stared at her for a prolonged moment, trying to wrap my mind around her question.

"Why?" Victtra demanded. "You killed my father in cold blood, but then you didn't kill me? *Even though I had witnessed your assassination?* Why? Tell me. *Tell me, Clevon.*"

She rubbed at her face, calming her hysterics.

Still a child. Even now.

I relaxed against the wall of the lift, my body so sore, I almost couldn't hear my own thoughts.

"I just couldn't," I muttered. "Kill a kid? I just… I didn't have it in me. Even when… Even when Endellion said I couldn't leave anyone alive. I just couldn't." I darkly chuckled and leaned my head on the grating. "I guess destiny really does exist, right?"

Victtra stomped over, took my second knife from the belt of my ruined enviro-suit, and then loomed over me.

Poor little Fae. She stood in the corner of the lift, watching this exchange with giant blue eyes, her red hair matted, her face so flushed, I could barely see her freckles. If she wasn't traumatized by the end of this, it would be a miracle.

"You lied to me," Victtra said.

"I told you Ontwenty was responsible." With a forced smirk, I added, "I just never told you the full truth."

She held my knife tightly in her hand. But the longer we stared at each other, the more I could sense her fire dying. It was sad, in a way. Like she didn't want it to go. I didn't know what to say.

"You let me live," Victtra whispered. "More than once."

"What do you mean?"

"I mean—thinking back to my time on the *Star Marque*… You saved me in that dog fight. You helped me become a starfighter. Why? Why do all that when you knew who I was? Why let me live, even when it had no purpose?"

"At that point… you were my crew."

Silence settled between us.

Then Victtra stepped away from me. "You told me all of this now because you wanted me to escape, didn't you? So I would leave you."

And to that, I said nothing. Even now, it still felt like I might die.

"A life for a life," she said. "I… I never wanted any of this to happen, but now that I'm on this path, I know this isn't what my father would've wanted. You were right. He would have wanted me to continue his work. He would have wanted me to… to move on. And thrive. And forgive."

"You're going to let me live?" I asked, shock and disbelief thick in my voice.

"I just… can't bring myself to kill you." Victtra dropped the knife to the lift floor, her gaze deadened. "I guess I didn't have what it took, after all."

After a deep inhale, I sighed. My leg still bled, my throat had been crushed, and now I felt like the all-consuming dread of death had left me weak and apathic.

At least I had done what I had set out to accomplish.

General Lone was dead.

And once we reached the surface, the *Star Marque* would be returning to Trinity Station, just in time to pick us up. As long as we weren't caught, we'd be able to leave Vectin-10 without anyone knowing of our terrible deed.

Except for Endellion and our child.

THIRTY-NINE

Debts Settled

I stood at the head of the *Star Marque's* conference table. My officers sat around the table, each one more dour than the last. Cai, Dr. Clay, Sawyer, Olivia, Victtra, Lysander, and Noah didn't speak. They continued to read the reports scrolling across their computer screens.

Occasionally, Sawyer smirked to herself. She was the only one in the room who delighted in some of the morbid reports. I understood her amusement. The man she had hated—General Lone—was now dead, and in dramatic fashion.

The fallout of General Lone's death had been swift and severe, however. More than I had imagined. More than any of us had imagined.

Vectin-10 was now surrounded by military starships, including a dreadnaught-class carrier, the *Relentless Nova.* It was a behemoth of metal alloys shaped like a diamond, now orbiting the planet. Smaller ships buzzed around the *Relentless Nova,* all prepared to scour the quadrant for any and all suspects.

The *Star Marque* was on the list of suspects. So was Endellion. I thought that meant we were done for—if Endellion didn't have the power to control this, what did we have?—but it seemed as though she still had plenty of power.

Both Minister Felseven and Threen had announced their intention to travel to Vectin-10 in order to help Endellion through the legal proceedings. Apparently, they weren't fans of General Lone or Minster Ontwenty, and now the superhuman power blocs were preparing for war.

"Do you realize what this means?" Dr. Clay asked, his narrow face pale. "This won't go away anytime soon. Things may never be the same."

Cai shook his head. He leaned back in his chair and then kicked his boots onto the table. "Listen, I've been in some tight situations before. If we lie low, it'll blow over."

With her posture stiff, and her gaze drilling a hole in the table, Victtra said, "General Lone comes from the first line of superhumans. Some among my kind will want the murderer caught simply because of what Lone represented."

"No. You don't understand. Whenever superhumans get riled like this, they start lighting everything on fire, especially each other." Cai huffed and crossed his arms. "If we hide, they'll sort this all out. They'll drag someone out to publicly punish, they'll raze Vectin-10, and then they'll hang Endellion for allowing this to happen on her watch."

Lysander stood from his chair. He sighed as he paced around the table. "I could contact some people in the Ares Military Base. They might tell me what's going on. We could use it to stay ahead of the fires, as you so lovingly called them."

Cai shrugged. "We should leave this area as soon as they'll let us. Trust me."

"We could offer to find the killer for them," Olivia asked. She touched her slender neck with her delicate fingers, her attention locked onto her PAD. "The reward for providing any information that leads to the killer's identity is already well over half a million credits."

Obviously, Olivia didn't know what was going on. I regretted recruiting her so close to this entire ordeal, but now that we were here, I'd have to roll with it.

Sawyer sat at the opposite end of the table, tapping away at her PAD, rarely blinking. When the conversation quieted down, she glanced up, met my gaze, and then sighed. "What should we do about Lone's little clone? We can turn her own to the authorities, or—"

"Fae will stay on the *Star Marque*," I said, no hesitation.

I wasn't about to turn her over to a bunch of bloodthirsty superhumans.

"She might know something," Olivia said.

I shook my head. "Fae was already questioned."

"Then why keep her? This isn't a place for a child."

"I… I knew her mother." It wasn't the best lie, but it wasn't the worst one, either.

Then I turned to Sawyer. She had said she wanted children. Now we had one. Just not related to me. And only Sawyer really understood why we needed to protect Fae. The little girl didn't have any family or friends, and we were the only ones between her and other superhumans like Lone.

"I'll take her," Sawyer said to the room. "We're genetically related, after all. And I can handle the responsibility."

"You do have a fish," Dr. Clay quipped. "Which is basically the same."

"Are you questioning my ability to care for Fae?"

"Yes." Dr. Clay sighed. Then he laced his fingers together in front of him. "I'll help care for the child. I'm the only one here with a medical degree, and an understanding of clone development. Their psychology is much different than normal children."

Normal children.

I grimaced when he said it. Sawyer gave no reaction, but I could feel her cringe from across the room. Dr. Clay had no social tact. Unfortunately, we didn't have many on the starship who understood people.

"It's settled," I said. "We're going to keep Fae aboard the ship."

"What about the military?" Noah asked, his voice unsteady. He nervously glanced at the giant windows on the far side of the room. The clear duralumin walls gave us a wonderful sight of all the other starships. "They might start investigating everything."

There wasn't much I could do about that, and all the discussions around kids had gotten my thoughts returning to Endellion. She had brought a child to the underground warehouse to show me? What kind of sick woman was she? Why would she do that?

She was trying to hurt me. I knew it in my gut.

And I couldn't let her. If Endellion knew how much the existence of a child upset me, she'd use it to control me.

A beeping over the ship's comms drew my attention. I tapped on my PAD to send the message through.

"Yes?" I asked.

"Captain Demarco, this is the bridge. We're being contacted by the Vectin-10 authorities. The planet governor is demanding your presence on the surface. The summons says that failure to comply will result in the military seizing the *Star Marque* and all of your assets."

The others in the room turned to me with wide eyes.

Endellion.

Somehow, she was going to come out of this on top, even if she had to throw us all into the flames of the nearest star. If I was going to beat her at her own game, I would have to play better.

Starting right now.

THANK YOU SO MUCH FOR READING!

Please consider leaving a review—any and all feedback is much appreciated!

Will Demarco and Endellion settle their
debts?

To find out more about Shami Stovall and the Star Marque Trilogy, take a look at her website:

https://sastovallauthor.com/newsletter/

To help Shami Stovall (and see advanced chapters ahead of time) take a look at her Patreon:

https://www.patreon.com/shamistovall